SOUL SNATCHER

JACKIE EGAN

For every woman who was pushed to her limit, and found out exactly what she was made of. Don't ever let anyone else tell you what you're capable of.

PLAYLIST

The Weeknd- Call out my name

The Weeknd- Acquainted

Travis Scott- Wake up

Morgan Wallen- Thinkin' 'bout me

Austin Giorgio- Dangerous Hands

Dove Cameron- Breakfast

Three Days Grace- Hate everything about you

Tommee Profitt- Bullet with butterfly wings

Austin Giorgio- Put a spell on you

1

BELLATRIX

They call me Soul Snatcher because of my pussy. Or rather, because of what it can do. Anyone else might be horrified at the moniker, but there's no denying the truth. I am the Soul Snatcher of my land; a land I have recently taken over due to my father, the king's illness. Or at least, I will be taking over.

While I won't deny how beautiful our land is, I cannot say it was something I ever wanted to rule over. Not really. But I knew it was inevitable. Being an only child means I am, by default, next in line for the throne. There is just one problem; it also needs a king.

Tenuma is the land our kingdom sits on. The snowy realm surrounded by beautiful, lush forests and towering snow-capped mountains has always taken my breath away. It is not what I was shown to appreciate about our posh life growing up, but I've learned to appreciate the small things that others take for granted.

I cannot get enough of the fresh, crisp air that surrounds the castle, or the thick mysterious forests that go on as far as the eye can see. Tenuma gives our people everything it needs—food fresh water, and safety from other lands. And from those that might come to harm our people.

The mountains and hundreds of caves that inhabit the area create both; the perfect vantage point from any possible threat, and the quintessential hiding place for our people, if there is ever another war thrust upon our land. The lands have had peace for thousands of years, and we hope to keep it that way.

While my father might not share my ideals of protecting our people as a priority, or making our land a better place for everyone, not just royalty; it will be my mission when I eventually take over. It also might be the only upside to becoming queen. Getting there is another story.

In order to become queen and gain control of Tenuma, my father has ordered that I find a king to rule alongside and lead our people with me. Old ideals die hard, and as much as I would prefer to hold power on my own, it is simply not permitted. Tenuma exhibits *"more power"* having a male ruler, as father puts it.

It would seem simple enough–find a man *worthy* enough to rule with me–because it seems incredibly unlikely to find a man that I will truly love. Even more unlikely that any man will survive an encounter with me to become king.

My mother was handpicked by my father's father, but they were not in love in the traditional sense, not at first. Love has never been a priority in our family line. If it were not for my mother's love for me, I am not sure I'd even believe love existed.

For myself, it is not as simple as just choosing a mate. As I said, my mother's love for me knows no bounds. For that I have always been grateful, having seen the converse option from my father. While my father and I have never been close, my mother and I have always been a team. That was before things changed between us. When I was just entering womanhood, she took me in the middle of the night, to an enchantress where a deal was created for my protection, she told me.

My mother has ruled with strength, grace, and bravery. I look up to her in every way, especially in the way she has always fought to put me first and do everything to protect me. But this was different. The deal may have intended to protect me, but it has taken more than it has given.

The deal my mother made that unforgettable night with the enchantress changed the entire course of my future and the life I live. The choice was never mine to make, and it was not explained to me until just a few years ago, exactly how the spell would work. I can safely say that I would not have chosen any part of this life for me, if I had known the cost.

Protection.

From all unworthy men. I am protected from all men who only seek to take over the kingdom for the riches of my family. In order to become king, they must pass a foolproof test.

Me.

Before we wed, we are to have sex, and if their intentions are pure, they will live. If their intentions are malicious in any way, they will immediately die. I wish I could say that nobody has succumbed to that fate, but that would be a lie. Leave it up to a man to have the audacity to think they can outsmart an enchantress curse. I guess it is easy to throw your life away for a pretty face, and the promise of land and riches.

This is how I am known now: the princess who kills men with her pussy. Bad for me, and worse for our entire family who already is not favored among our people. But can I really be blamed for men willing to come to me and offer their bodies up for the chance at being king? On one hand, I cannot exactly blame them; I know my father has created a hard life for our people, but on the other hand, why would one willingly give up their life for a slim chance at becoming king? A life that I can attest to firsthand not being as wonderful as it may seem from the outside.

This life is not really my own, and the choices I make

are an illusion. I do not have the freedom to make my choices, it only appears that way. All my decisions have always been predetermined for me. From where I am allowed to go, to who I spend my time with, how I spend my time, and yes—who I even have sex with.

My experience with sex has been more of a business deal rather than anything contributing to love, lust, or desire. Sure, sometimes I enjoy it if I am attracted to the male, but then when the inevitable hits, I am left naked and rarely satisfied, having caused another death. It does not do much to entice me to voluntarily continue the ritual. As if I have a choice in the matter. So, I do what I must, so I can get through it each time. I am to be queen and I must show strength at all times.

In the back of my mind, I have plans to change many things once I take the title of queen, but I grit my teeth thinking about how I am ever going to get there. Sex with new men will continue until I come across the one who is not just after our riches. If I could, I would undo the curse. I would allow myself a normal sex life, because I have urges and desires just like anybody else. And it would be nice if my pussy didn't make the male parish afterwards.

I stand at my floor length mirror in my bedchamber as I brush out my silky black hair that reaches beyond my buttocks. Normally, Quirina, my handmaiden, would help me but I rather enjoy doing things on my own. Having so much power and wealth seems like it would come with freedoms, but I have so few. Having so little say over one's life makes doing even the little things in your life that much more coveted.

Quirina is not only my handmaiden, but she is also my

best friend. It is also the main reason I don't like asking her to do many things for me. While it's in my blood, I was not born with the role of ruler etched into my skin like the rest of my family. I find it difficult delegating every aspect of my life when I bear knowing, as the ruler, I should be doing so much more. Quirina gets that, and she gets me. She is the only one who truly understands how unhappy I am with this curse on me, and the freedom I long for.

She has been there for me after every encounter with a male, to comfort me and remind me that it is not my fault. Even though I try to portray my best "evil bitch" persona outside these walls to deter men from coming into my chambers, they continue to show up. Although envious of their freedom to choose, I still cannot help but feel pity for the families at their loss.

These men come to me seeking a better life, on just a fraction of a chance that they will be the one to beat the curse, but instead meet their demise. I am left here feeling like the toxic queen I suppose I am.

Quirina enters my chambers and sees me brushing my hair, giving me an annoyed glance.

"Lady Bellatrix, why didn't you call for me to do that for you?" she asks.

I sigh heavily. "You know I don't like asking you for such trivial things," I reply.

"Yes, My Lady, but this is what I am here to do," Quirina reminds me. As a member of staff for my parents, she is not wrong.

"No, you are here because you are my best friend. It is your "job" to keep me sane," I joke, setting down my brush on my vanity with the large gold oval-shaped mirror.

"Trix, you know I'm here for that, too. But you have to let me do things for you otherwise the king or queen might catch wind and realize they have no need for me."

"Yes. You're right. I have your back, Rina. You know I always will," I tell her.

She nods and continues with her purpose in my room. "The queen. She's sent for you. She has requested your presence in the dining hall," she says hesitantly.

I sit on the edge of my bed, my green eyes on the floor. We both know what a request from my mother means.

"Darling!" my mother says with a breath it seems she's been holding.

I walk into the grand dining hall where my mother sits at the head of a twenty-person granite table, surrounded by high-back red suede chairs, each placement set up to perfection, as usual. The room is surrounded by floor to ceiling windows that allow the glistening snow to be a backdrop for each meal. The impressive chandelier above the table, adorned with enough crystal worth enough to feed the entire land, sits brightly–almost too brightly, like a reminder of what we have that others do not–allowing me to see the strained look on my mother's face.

"Hello, Mother," I say softly, coming to stand next to where she sits finishing her coffee and breakfast.

"Your father and I have set up another meeting for you this evening," she says matter of factly, picking at the fruit on her plate. There's no use fighting it, since we both know I don't have a choice in the matter. I am to be queen, and this is the only way.

I scoff. "A meeting," I repeat. "I suppose it's better than calling it what it actually is, right?" I say with an edge to my voice.

My mother gives me a provoking stare. "And what exactly

would that be?" She challenges me.

"An offering. A sacrifice. Take your pick," I say, each word clipped.

Her eyes narrow at me. "Do not start. This is nothing new, Bellatrix. You know it is your royal duty to find an appropriate suitor to rule the Kingdom with you. This is what must be done," she snaps at me, and then gently grabs my hand. "I have only ever wanted to protect you, my dear. The men out there only take what they want. You have much to offer, and they view you as a prize. This ensures that you will find a man that will care for you and have your best interests in mind. Do not feel sorry for the ones that do not make the cut."

"You say it so casually, as if they are simply dismissed, and taken out of the running to be my king. This is anything but that," I say back, my voice pleading.

"Bellatrix, these men come to you on their own accord. Nobody is forcing them to be here. Nobody forces them into your bed. Nobody forces them to have sex with you. They all want what you have, and if their intentions are pure, they shall have it. I don't know why you would feel guilty for the ones that don't survive it. They had malintentions. They deserve what they get," she says harshly.

I nod in agreement, because there's no use arguing, and walk away from the table. "Unless their families are forcing them to, like mine is," I whisper to myself.

Tonight, I shall have sex with another man, who will, more than likely, parish before the evening is over. I still won't have a king, and I will have to do this all over again, and again until I find the man that by some miracle can survive the curse.

Me.

2

KOEN

Alarm forces my eyes to open as I hear my little sister Mellani coughing and struggling to breathe. She's had this cold for two weeks now, and doesn't seem to be getting any better. I've done my best to keep her fed, warm, and hydrated. It doesn't help that our cabin is ice cold and drafty. It's nearly impossible to stay warm, even when you're fully clothed and under blankets. It doesn't bother me much, but for a young sick child, it can be the difference between life and death.

I stretch my limbs as I become more awake and alert. I rise to grab the last of our logs and I throw them in our small fireplace to reignite the dying fire. She needs as much warmth as she can get. Once it's steadily going, I gently lift Mellani up and lay her on some soft blankets in front of the fire so she can warm up. As soon as I set her down, her eyes flutter open and she glances up at me.

She smiles affectionately at me, her soft brown curls falling in her face. "Are you leaving?" she asks softly.

I'm usually gone before she wakes up, hunting, gathering wood, or doing work around town so we can survive another day.

Our father left us shortly after she was born, but I can't say he was really around before that anyway. Unless you count showing up drunk to yell at my mother–or getting her pregnant–while staying out most of the day, and sleeping with other women every chance he got. Truth is, we are better off without him. He was just another mouth to feed.

I've been the man of the house, and sole provider for our family for many years now, even before he left. We could never count on him to come home, and we knew better than to expect he would bring food home. I don't mind taking care of my mother and little sister though, it gives me pride and purpose. I love knowing that they're taken care of.

I gently move the curls out of her golden-brown eyes. "I have a big important job today. I will be back later tonight."

She looks at me through heavy eyes. "Promise?"

The way she always asks me this when I leave breaks my heart. Our father left one day and never came back, so now she thinks whenever somebody else leaves she will never see them again.

I kiss her forehead, and reply in the same reassuring way I always do. "With my life."

She smiles back, and then rolls back over on her side facing the warm fire, closing her eyes.

I grab my bow and arrow, knife, boots and jacket, heading for the door when my mother stops me with a hand on my arm. I turn around and see her glancing at Mellani, making sure she's asleep.

She sticks a hand-woven black bracelet with an onyx bead in the center at me. "Wear this," she whispers.

"One of your bracelets?" I ask, skeptically.

"It will protect you. Just wear it, and do not argue with me, boy," she says sternly but sweetly. It makes me smile when she calls me boy, as I'm about a foot and a half taller than her. She's short and stocky with dark brown hair that's starting to show traces of gray—from stress or age, I can't be sure.

"Of course, Mother. But you do know I go hunting every day. This isn't any more dangerous than those days," I tell her quietly, half laughing. I love that she feels protective. It makes me laugh, because as a six-foot-one professional hunter that also practices self-defense and has been trained to use numerous weapons since age nine, I can defend our family from just about anything.

She looks at me shaking her head. "No. Today you are going to the castle. I have a bad feeling about it. You won't listen when I have repeatedly begged you not to go, and since you still insist on going, you will wear this." Her voice is almost a whisper, but firm. She glances back at Mellani who is now quietly snoring in front of the fire.

I laugh. "Mother, you know I have to go. I am doing work *at* the castle. I'm not going to 'service' the princess. I'm not that kind of man. That's not something you need to worry about. I like to think I have more wits about me than that."

She grabs my arm tightly. "Listen to me, something doesn't feel right. Just please be careful, my boy. She needs you," she says, gesturing to Mellani.

I follow my mother's gaze to where Mellani is sleeping sweetly. "What about you, mom? Do you need me too?" I ask playfully, but it's nice to hear you're needed.

"Always, my son." She reaches up as I bend down so she can kiss my cheek, and I turn to leave, slowly closing the cabin door behind me.

As often as my mother tells me that she has a 'bad feeling' about things, I can't help but shudder as I put on the black woven bracelet. I secure it tightly, as I think to myself, *there's no harm in playing along.*

My mother earns a few dollars here and there selling her *protection bracelets* in town. Ever since word got out about the princess and her deadly escapades, more people have been seeking her out to make their sons one. My mother used to have powers when she was younger, I've been told. Mostly of protection, and a sort of telepathy. It would explain how she always knows when I'm lying–not that I make a habit of it. When I was younger, I used to tell little white lies, but as I've gotten older I realize the immaturity and danger of making lying one of my personality traits.

If that magic is hereditary, I wouldn't know. Neither myself, nor Mellani have shown any evidence of having any sort of power. People on our lands possess powers, but it's seldomly seen.

As my mother has gotten older, her powers have gotten weaker, and she doesn't seem to bring them up in conversation like she used to. I don't know much about them, or how much of it I really believe in. But being her only son, and as the man of the house, it's my job to humor her, not make her feel stupid.

The kingdom has requested I come to the castle today after I put in word for some work. As often as I hunt, it's rare that I hunt down anything to feed us for more than a day or two. The snow keeps most big game far from our town, or they're in hibernation. This has been an especially rough winter, so food has been slim. I know I need to scrape up more money to purchase goods from the local merchants in town. Fruits and fresh vegetables are a luxury that we don't often indulge in. The king has added tax after tax onto our people to the point of poverty for about ninety percent of the people on this land. My best friend, Nikandros owns the busiest tavern in town, and even he struggles.

My family is amongst that ninety percent.

I didn't tell my mother that I volunteered to help at the castle, because I knew she would not have approved, so I told her they requested my skills. One cannot deny a summons from the castle. If they ask for your presence, you show up. I knew that would be my only way to get my mother off my back, and even that didn't stop her pleading. I don't like to argue or fight with her, but we need the money.

It was not my first choice, but after I saw they needed somebody to help out with a project for the next couple of weeks and seeing what they paid, it was a no-brainer. That kind of money can afford us the food and medicine we need for Mellani.

As much as I know it's the right thing to do, I'm not happy about it. Knowing I will be in the same building as that wretched princess makes me feel queasy. I don't exactly know how it works, but from what the people in the village know, once someone sleeps with the princess, they end up dead. She's never held accountable for the killings—presumably because she's the only daughter of the king, who makes the rules—and I don't want to be within ten feet of her, personally. As far as I can tell, she's a murderer and a whore. Knowing I'll be in her vicinity for a few weeks is enough to make my blood boil, and my stomach queasy.

It is a mystery why so many men keep falling to her feet, knowing what fate lies ahead. I don't care how badly we need the money they offer; I would rather do anything else than give myself over to her. She's not even pleasant to be around from what I've been told. Plump lips wasted on a face that never smiles, and a personality that is rude to every man that comes her way.

I guess you could say that's just how bad things are around here. The lengths people will go to for the security she offers. But not me, not ever. Even if one thought they could actually fall in love with her, how stupid does one need to be to throw their life away for a woman. A beautiful face isn't worth my life, especially when her soul is as ugly as Princess Bellatrix's.

My heavy boots make giant prints on the snow-covered ground as I make my way over to the castle. I have my gear with me today, as I am hoping to make my way to the forest after I'm done at the castle, to see if I can catch us anything to eat. When I heard the castle needed someone skilled in window repair and insulation, I knew I was one of few that knew how to do this in our area. It's a great skill to have in a place like this. The extreme cold can kill a person in just a few short hours if left out in the elements.

Today, while the ground is covered in fresh sparkling snow from last night's fall, the sky is clear, and the sun is shining down making the day surprisingly warm, as the white powder starts to melt beneath my feet. The warmth won't last long, but it's nice to see the sun while it's out. I spend so much time outside as it is, but I genuinely enjoy being outdoors. We have such a beautiful land, it's a shame that it's in the hands of such an evil family.

The castle comes into view, and I can't help but stop and gawk at it. I always forget how grand and astonishing it truly is. The size of our land would impress anybody and half of it could fit inside the castle comfortably. It sits snugly against the base of one of our beautiful mountains, as if it were built right into it. It juts up into the sky alongside all the other mountain tops, standing tall like an imposter trying to fit in with the crowd. It's covered in ground to ceiling windows on every side, glittering in the sunlight, appearing as if their wealth is pouring out through the windows.

My jaw tenses, as I think of all the people suffering in our town while the king continues to raise the taxes on Tenuma's people higher and higher. He has been a greedy ruler as long as he's been in power. It seems cruel to make others suffer for your own benefit. Much like his daughter is. The apple doesn't fall far from the tree.

I take a long breath and then let it out, making my final steps toward the front gate of the castle. I need to hide my contempt for this family as long as I'm here or not only will I be fired, but I could suffer a much worse fate. I would be gone, and my family would suffer in my absence, so I need to shove every bad feeling I have down, and do the job they hired me to do. I will keep my mouth shut and get through this, showing them nothing but gratitude.

"Stop." The guard at the front gate with a clipboard, and a stone face expression says to me without looking up. When I don't say anything, he continues. "Name," he demands.

"Archer. Koen Archer. I'm here for a job. I've been hired to work on the windows," I respond quickly in a deep confident voice. The royal family summoned me to insulate, glaze and tint the windows to keep the cold out, and heat in, along with installing new blinds for every window.

The guard scans his list, and then glances over his shoulder at another guard with another checklist. "I have a Koen Archer here. He's reporting for work inside the castle today." We stand there and wait while the second guard scans his list for my name.

A minute later a man responds, his voice gruff. "Yes, the king approved of him. Send him in."

"You will leave your weapons here," he demands. He notes my hesitation and then continues. "Weapons are not permitted beyond the gates. You may pick them up at the end of the day when your work is complete." His request is more of a demand, and I'm not in any position to be questioning the king's armed forces.

I nod in agreement and surrender my weapons. To them they're weapons, to me it's my family's means of survival. The only lifeline my family has, and I just handed them over to a stranger, who I'm hoping keeps more of an eye on them than he's glanced at me so far.

The guard waves me past the gate, and then looks back out in front of the castle as if he's expecting an enemy to turn up at any minute. I walk past him, and follow the long stone pathway that is lined with a handful of guards on both sides. I note the trees surrounding the castle, like it's trying to camouflage itself. It's beautiful, and yet it feels like a prison. The entire building is made of rough, gray stone. The edges are jagged and off-putting, reminding me of the way a rose has thorns to prevent it from being plucked from its environment. It feels completely closed off from the rest of the land, like the people inside are trapped animals. I'm about to become one of them.

My home is past town in the opposite direction of the castle, so it took me most of the morning to arrive. The long walk has made me start to sweat under all my clothing, so I stop to wipe my brow on my sleeve, and tie back my long, dark hair. As I do, my eyes drift up to one of the windows and that's when I see her.

My initial reaction is disgust and hatred. The whole town knows what the princess is capable of. She's not a person I would purposely spend any time around. I plan to come and do my job, avoid being in her presence as much as possible, and then get the hell out of here. I can't pull my eyes off of her, though and as I look closer, I see something unexpected.

The princess is gazing out of a window, blankly. Clothed in a tight sparkly cream-colored corset dress that flows down past her feet with a lace train, and a low-cut neckline to accentuate her perky breasts. I can't help but notice how beautiful she looks, even when she's not smiling. There's a softness to her face. She seems sad, almost like she's trying to see beyond the castle. Beyond her life. It's not the face I expected to see on the Ice Queen-in-training. Her reputation has been nothing less than intimidating and terrifying. She doesn't notice me looking at her, so she doesn't know that I see her wipe away a stray tear. Just one, and then she walks away from the window.

I didn't expect to find her beauty so breathtaking. Of course, I've seen her before, but always from a far-off distance in a crowd, surrounded by others. There's only one reason a commoner would be in close proximity to the princess, and that's not something I would ever volunteer for. I feel like I've just seen a behind-the-scenes face of the princess. One she doesn't show to anybody else. It feels like something I wasn't supposed to see.

Making my way through the front entrance, I step onto the white marbled floors in the grand castle. A man hurriedly strides towards me in the typical royal uniform. Dark pants, combat boots, and a tan long-sleeve shirt with the kingdom's black and gold crest upon it. A crown sits at the top of the crest, symbolizing the royals as the ultimate ruler. A pair of swords cross near the bottom for protection, and represent the strong armies our land has. The center of the crest has the triple moon sign—this represents the magic that has existed within our lands for centuries.

Not every person is born with magic, or ever has any abilities. I've never seen what true magic our people possess, so it's difficult to say whether it is still around or not. In my twenty-five years of life, I have yet to experience any powers myself. My mother swears to have powers—or at least she used to, and I know there are enchantresses who claim to make things happen. Mostly, whatever magic exists seems to be contained within the royal family. Most of it is kept secret, as the commoners know very little of it.

The uniformed man walks towards me with a scowl on his face, glancing down at my dirty boots making a mess on the marble floors. He looks annoyed that I'm even in his presence. I'm clearly "the help," and will be treated as such. If this is the way the staff treats outsiders, I don't even want to know how the royals will treat me while I'm in their home.

Keep your head down, and your mouth shut, I remind myself.

"Koen Archer?" he asks me, even though he already knows I am. There's not a single person that moves about this castle that isn't approved of and watched very closely.

"Yes, sir. I'm ready to work," I reply as eagerly as possible. The sooner I can get this work done, the sooner I can get paid and get the hell out of here.

He raises an eyebrow at me, as if he's not impressed by my act. It's fine, the feeling is mutual. He doesn't want me here, and I don't want to be here.

"Yes," he starts with a clipped tone. "First, you will start upstairs in the bedrooms. The king needs the family's private quarters to be first priority," he states as he points up the grand staircase. The wide stairs lead up to a second floor that opens out into a large space overlooking the ground floor, and hallways leading in both directions.

"Understood." I am trying to say as little as possible, so he doesn't misread my tone as anything less than respectful. I have heard stories of help being thrown out of an upstairs window simply because they were disliked. If you actually commit a crime or offend the family, is another story. You would be tortured and then disposed of. Neither of which I am eager to succumb to.

"Follow me," he demands and then we both head up the long staircase to the second level of the castle.

Once on the landing, the floor opens up on the left and the right to numerous rooms and hallways. Above us at the top of the staircase is an incredible round skylight that unveils the bright blue sky above. The man directs us down the left hallway, where I can see several doors on the left and right side, all closed. The doors are magnificent and are about twelve feet tall. The wooden doors are thick, and have delicate ornate designs on them. They look heavy and impenetrable. Once we get to the end of the hall, he stops at a giant door on the left side that is slightly cracked open. He knocks twice on it before calling out for the princess.

"Lady Bellatrix," he calls out loudly, in a booming, authoritative voice.

A moment later the door swings open, and I glance up to see the princess standing right in front of us, a completely different look upon her face than I had seen a few minutes ago.

Her pale face is stern, and she looks bored and annoyed. This is the face of the princess that we all know.

"What is it, now?" she snaps, impatiently tapping her foot on the marble flooring.

"My apologies, My Lady. The king has hired help to come work on the windows, and we require access to your quarters for the day," he responds, and the sweetness drips off his words like honey. Clearly, commoners aren't the only ones afraid of this horrid family. The change in his tone would have made me chuckle if not for the Ice Princess standing eight feet in front of me.

She glances in my direction, sporting a scowl even worse than the man in front of me greeted me with. Her eyes are trailing me up and down, as if assessing my worthiness of entering her quarters. Finally settling her eyes back on my face, her gaze sends a shiver down my spine. Her expression gives nothing away. Without a word she shoves her door open, and steps to the side to let us in.

Gee, thanks for the approval, Princess, I think.

The uniformed man steps quickly inside, heading over to the larger window I had seen the princess through a few minutes prior. I hesitantly step into her room, as if simply crossing the threshold to her room will immediately put me in danger. Just being in her presence feels like enough of a risk, and I'm not enthusiastic about having to be in her bed chambers for the next few days.

My wrist starts to tingle where the bracelet sits, as if in response to the room itself. As if it can sense something unwelcome in its wake. My other hand tugs at the bracelet, spinning it once around my wrist, trying to ease the unwelcome feeling.

You're imagining it. It's not real, I try to convince myself. My mother would disagree, and right now, I might find myself siding with her.

As I slowly make my way inside, I bow my head slightly to the princess, and pull my eyes away, worried I won't be able to hide my disgust for her plastered on my face. For one second, I think I catch her lips twitching upwards into a smirk. As if she lives to make others quiver in her presence. But the look is gone before I can be sure. I keep my eyes on the uniformed man as he leads me towards the windows and tells me to work quickly.

"Where are all of my supplies?" I ask him, noting there is nothing for me to work with. I glance around, but there's nothing for me to get started with. No supplies and no ladders to reach these twelve-foot-high windows.

"It's all downstairs by the entryway table. Best to get everything you need and get started. The king and queen would like this done as quickly as possible."

Thanks, jackass. That information would have been good to know before we climbed all those stairs, I think, but resist voicing.

I nod my head, and it's almost a bow to show the man some respect. He turns away from me before he sees it, reminding me of my insignificance here. I unceremoniously dismiss myself and head back down the long hallway, and down the stairs to retrieve said materials I will be needing to start working on these colossal windows, including a large ladder.

Once I am back inside the princess's room, I notice she has vacated the room. I set up the ladder and release a heavy sigh in relief that she won't be hovering over me while I'm working.

Now that I'm alone, I take a moment to glance around the giant room. This giant room that only one person inhabits. This room alone is twice the size of the cottage my family and I have lived in our entire lives. Some might call the cottage cozy, but really it's just small.

There's a giant four-post bed made of a deep rich wood that looks like three beds combined. It sits in the left of the room with a giant sheer overhead canopy, covered in red silk sheets and half a dozen pillows. It looks plush, heavenly, and clearly too large for one person.

The thought sends a chill down my spine, as I recall that this bed doesn't just bed one person. It frequently beds a new man. A man that never sees the light of day again after he enters it. Suddenly, the comfort and luxurious feeling it evoked dissolves, making me feel lightheaded instead. Now it looks repellent, more like the trap of a black widow's web.

Next to the giant bed is a small table on both sides; each with a small lamp, a large candle, a book, and a few other trinkets I can't make out from where I'm standing.

Across the bed on the other side of the room, stands a giant fireplace built into the wall, in between two doors. Bathroom to the left of it, closet to the right. I can't help but wonder why they need the windows re-done, as the fireplace standing in this one room would be enough to heat the entire floor. There's no way the castle gets as cold and drafty as my family's little cottage. But I'm grateful for the job, nonetheless. The money they are offering is too good to pass up, regardless of how necessary I deem it.

I'm busy gazing around the room, unaware that the princess is standing in the doorway watching me judge her life.

"Will you be in my chambers for the rest of the day, then?" the princess asks, completely unfazed.

I bristle at her question, not realizing I am being watched.

"I will work quickly, so I can be out of your chambers as fast as possible," I reply.

"I was just curious. You don't have to rush." Her tone is indifferent.

"I won't be any longer than necessary, rest assured. I'm sure you have suitors to tend to." The snotty remark slips out of my mouth before I can stop it. I quickly turn around and clench my teeth, my jaw so tense I think I might crack a tooth.

What were you thinking? Are you crazy? I think.

I can hear the whoosh of the princess's dress as she moves in my direction and stands against the window. I glance over and see she's suddenly next to me, arms crossed, grinning like a cat with a mouse. Her cunning smile makes the hair on my arms stand on end.

"Suitors, huh? What do you know of my suitors?" Her tone is playful, but warning bells are going off deep in my gut. She's the predator and I'm clearly her prey.

You idiot. Look what you've done now.

I busy my hands with the tools at my feet, avoiding her gaze. "I didn't mean anything by it. I'm just sure a princess has plenty of company she needs to tend to. Other priorities to take care of. That's all." I try to recover my foolish remark, unsuccessfully.

"You don't like me," she states. It's not a question. She's not wrong, but I won't be telling her that.

"I don't know you," I reply, keeping my hands and eyes busy with the materials in my hands. It feels like I'm fidgeting but she's been standing completely still this entire time.

"Oh, but you think you do," she replies cooly, it's almost seductive. The way a snake would flick its tongue in and out.

"I know enough," I respond truthfully. I don't know what's made me decide to be honest—with somebody who has the ability to order my death if she doesn't like me—but I can't stop the words as they're coming out. Something about her invokes full transparency. She's already seen right through me, anyway, so there's no point in the charade.

I quickly sneak a side glance of her, and she still has that smirk on her face, but it's anything but friendly. She leans against the window, with her arms crossed loosely over her chest.

She looks at me intently, contemplating her response. Surprise lingers under that smirk, as I'm sure most people don't speak to her this way. She opens her mouth to say something, then closes it, clearly deciding against it. A moment later, her expression hardens.

"Please be finished before sundown, I will have male company," she hurls back. She says it knowing we both know exactly the kind of company she will be having later.

Pushing off the wall as she goes to leave, she pauses glancing down at the bracelet on my wrist for just a moment, raising an eyebrow and then hurrying off so fast I think I imagined her pausing at all.

A few hours later, I am still working on the upper part of the window in her room. I underestimated the sheer size and time it would take me to finish it. This room has two more windows the same size. At the bottom of the ladder, I slump my shoulders realizing that I will need to be inside the princess's room for a few more days, at least. I work all day until just before the sun starts going down, and then begin to gather my things to head downstairs. Just as I'm almost out the door, the princess stands in front of me glaring at the windows behind me.

"These don't look done," she retorts.

I refrain from scoffing. "Unfortunately, these are much bigger than I was informed, and it will take me most of the week to get all three windows finished," I tell her.

She scoffs, and pushes past me. "Well, I guess this isn't your specialty then," she responds with a click of her tongue.

Ice Queen. I groan internally.

She thinks because she has money and power that she can talk down to everybody else. That somehow, it makes her better than us. She happened to be born into a rich family. Lucky. I happened to be born into a family with a bastard father, and a hopeless romantic for a mother who let him walk all over her. Very not-lucky.

"I know you're used to everything being done for you, Princess, so let me explain it for you. Things like this *take time.* If you want it done right, it will take me more than half of a day, since you know… you live in a mansion with windows taller than every home in town." I realize my voice is getting louder, and I am now much closer to her than I was a minute ago. I don't know when I moved towards her, but it was anything but intentional.

The look on her face is of many emotions. I see shock, anger, and something else I can't put my finger on.

She takes a few steps back, and responds calmly. "You should leave and not come back here."

"That's not an option for me. I was hired to do a job," I reply with frustration.

"Well, you need to quit. Find another one. We will replace you. I don't want you here. I don't want you in my chambers any longer," she says, still calm and collected.

What is her problem with me? I wonder.

"No. I can't. Not all of us have riches at our fingertips, and the power to make others do whatever they want. So unless you're firing me, I will be finishing the job I was assigned," I spit back. The nerve of this princess to assume I have the freedom to leave jobs whenever I want, just because I don't like it. If that were the case, I never would have come here to begin with. The princess has all the freedom in the world and just assumes that's the way of the world.

She considers this for a moment, sitting on the edge of her bed, leaning back on her arms, her legs stretched out in front of her, long black hair cascading behind her.

"Then you need to stay out of my way, while you're here," she says while staring at me with her cat-like stare. Her green eyes bore into me, and the intensity of her gaze could slice right through me.

"That won't be an issue for me. I hope you will be able to reciprocate." I stare right back at her. As we hold each other's gaze, it turns into a contest. Who will flinch first, look away first, speak first? It's a clear power struggle. Both of us seeing who can outlast the other.

The longer we stare, the more intense it gets. Suddenly, I can feel my cheeks heat up, and my chest starts rising and falling deeper as my breathing gets heavier. I notice her breathing has also sped up. Her cheeks turn a shade of pink that's noticeable against her pale porcelain skin. The entire room is silent except for both of us breathing, and the air feels thick with tension.

Suddenly, and quickly she snaps her gaze from me and stands. She flicks a wrist, dismissing me. I walk out the door, closing it quickly behind me, to shut out both the princess and whatever just happened in there.

What the fuck was that? I think leaning up against the door behind me.

The bracelet on my wrist tingled the entire time the princess was in the room with me, and it was hard not to take note of that.

3

BELLATRIX

My legs are spread wide open, as I'm bent over the giant bed in my quarters. A glass of whiskey sits on my bedside table, condensation dripping all the way down the glass soaking where it sits, similar to my wetness dripping down my legs right now. The black lace nightgown I have on is hiked up over my ass, so my pussy is on display for tonight's suitor.

Usually, it takes me many drinks and a lot of swaying from the men to get me even mildly into "the mood." Tonight is different. Having only had a few sips of my whiskey, I'm slick and eager to fuck. After today's encounter with the handyman in my quarters, I found myself eager to get into bed with a man. Any man. The aching at my core didn't go away all day.

I need to be fucked. Hard.

I have never met anyone who dared speak to me that way. I knew there wasn't a chance in all of Tenuma that this man would ever be after anything I had to offer. The hatred he had in those steel gray eyes for me was all too evident. He tried to hide it, but I saw it. I could *feel* it.

And that hatred only made me want him more. As we

stood in front of each other, all I could picture was straddling his rugged face. I wanted to know what that lush beard felt like between my legs. I wanted to know what it would feel like to be pinned down by his big, powerful arms. I wanted to know how his muscular body felt on top of mine.

I feel a slap on my ass, as my suitor does as I command. A pink handprint lightly begins to surface on my skin. I love seeing handprints on my ass.

"Again. Harder," I demand. I'm aching, needing more.

He slaps my ass cheek again, and this time it's going to leave a welt. So, I ask him to do it once more. He pulls his hand back and slaps my ass once, twice, three more times. My skin immediately swells, as welted handprints rise on my ass.

My pussy is aching, and dripping for... him. Not the man behind me, ready to fuck my brains out. No. The man from this morning–the handyman. I'm picturing him behind me; his strong hands slapping my ass. *That* is who my pussy is dripping for. The one I can't have.

My sexual encounters with these suitors are never this... extreme. They always stay on the side of tender, and sweet. Ironic, since I never have any emotional attachment to these men. They all think the sweeter they are, the closer to *love making* they make it, the better their odds will be of beating the curse. Wrong.

There is no cheat code for this curse, believe me. I've tried. Killing men on a nightly basis isn't my idea of a good time. Yet here I am. Bound to the curse, forever fucking to find a worthy king.

The suitor behind me–staring at my ass, rubbing his hands all over me, shoving his fingers inside of me–won't make it to daylight. But what a way to go. I know these are his last moments, his last act before he meets his fate. I figure I should show him a good time.

"This isn't what I thought having sex with you would be

like," he says half chuckling to himself.

"What did you expect it to be?" I reply breathily. He pushes two fingers in and out my pussy as I'm still bent over for him, my hands sunk deeply into the mattress.

He leans down and presses his lips close to my ear. "I thought you'd want to make love. I figured a princess would want sweet, slow sex," he says softly.

I snarl, whipping my head back towards him. "You thought wrong. There's nothing sweet about me. If you thought you wouldn't have to work for this, you were wrong."

I stand up, turn around grabbing him by the shoulders and shoving him on the bed. I climb on top of him, and push him down flat, while I climb and straddle his face.

"Eat," I demand.

He grabs my hips and presses his face into my pussy, kissing, licking, and biting my tender parts. It drives me wild. Each bite makes me ravenous. I grind my hips harder into his face, demanding more and more. I press harder into him, as I picture the man that I won't ever have.

The suitor sucks and licks up all of my wetness while slipping two fingers inside me with one of his hands, as the other grips my hip with his fingernails digging into my skin. I moan loudly as he enters me. He pumps his fingers in and out of me slowly. A torturing pace, as I try to grind on him faster, harder. But then I pull back and climb off his face.

The longer I prolong this, the better for both of us.

I crawl backwards down to straddle his legs. He's still trying to catch his breath when I put my mouth on his dick. I immediately take it as far as I can take it until it hits the back of my throat. I pull my mouth off, and do it again. My mouth is overflowing with saliva, my body still pulsing with need. The need for that euphoric high.

I start sucking harder, with my hand gripping his shaft, stroking him up and down. His quiet moans are getting louder and needier, and I can feel his hips thrusting further and faster into my mouth. He's close.

I pull back.

Why am I prolonging this? I think to myself. *This is not the handyman, and his fate will come, regardless of how long this takes.*

I'm still straddling him, on my knees looking at him, but trying to avoid his eyes. He's staring at me with desire, and fear. He wants this to happen, and yet I can tell the fear is setting in.

"You don't have to do this. You can leave if you've changed your mind," I tell him softly.

He shakes his head. "No. My family needs this," he responds.

There it is. These foolish men don't even realize they confess their greedy intentions right to my face. With one sentence, he's revealed he's only after my riches and power that come with my bloodline.

I smile at him, knowing two things; one, I will get my climax regardless. And two, I won't feel bad about it, because that's what happens when you try to use a female for personal gain in Tenuma.

"Okay then, princesses first," I say coyly, as I start to climb my way back up to his face.

"I love the way you taste," he tells me as I sit on his face. I think to myself, *I don't care whether he does or not.* Whether he's telling the truth, or just trying to outsmart the curse by saying sweet things. It won't change what happens after we both hit that high.

"Good. Finish your meal then," I tell him, grinding my hips on his mouth.

He starts licking and sucking all over again, and then starts pumping his tongue in and out of my pussy. It feels so good, and yet I still have to force my thoughts to re-route.

Stop thinking of death. You have no control here. Let go.

The only thought that lets me past that mental barrier is to think of the handyman again. I start picturing that rough beard, and those rough hands. His face is the only thing I can see. Those intense gray eyes that bore into my soul right before he left my quarters for the day. I swear he saw right through me. I can still feel the tension of our stare-off, the heat and the intensity between us.

I scream, slamming my hands onto the wall behind us. I stay on his lips, quivering, as his tongue laps up all of my juices dripping onto his face. I climb off his face, and pull him off the bed. I resume my bent over position at the edge of the bed. I bend over and lay my hands, palms flat on the bed, spreading my legs. He gently rubs my pussy from behind, and then I feel his dick guiding its way towards my entry.

He doesn't hesitate like the others do. I thought I saw fear on his face earlier, but whatever I saw is gone. He doesn't care that he's about to throw his life away by fucking me. Once he comes, he will go. He doesn't hesitate. Once his dick gets close, his hand grips my long black hair and wraps it around his hand as he thrusts inside me.

"Ahhh," I involuntarily yelp as he thrusts inside me, stretching me out.

"Yeah, you like that, Princess?" he asks confidently.

"Yes. Fuck me harder," I beg. But I'm not begging him, I'm not even picturing him.

"Harder? You're no princess at all, are you? You want to be fucked like a little whore, don't you," he says, but it's not really a question.

The whole land thinks I'm a whore anyway, may as well get fucked like one. I don't love these men and they don't love me. They're using me and since I'm not permitted to refuse a suitor, here we are. I guess, technically–I am a whore.

"Yes," I pant. "Fuck me like I'm your little whore. Fuck me hard," I beg, feeling myself climaxing again.

It only takes a few more thrusts before we are both lying flat on the bed, out of breath and coming down from our high. I've never climaxed like this with any of the other suitors, and that almost gives me hope that this one won't parish. It almost feels like he might overcome the curse's cruel fate. But then I remember his comment, and I know he doesn't stand a chance.

I grab my panties off the floor, pull down my black lace nightgown, and crawl into bed.

I see the man getting dressed, and I tell him, "You can see yourself out."

The quicker he leaves, the better. The time it takes for these men to fall to their fate varies, but it's usually pretty quick.

The man leaves without another word, and I know we will never see each other again.

Hours later, I'm still lying awake in bed trying to get myself to sleep. Usually after spending an evening with a suitor, I'm extremely intoxicated and exhausted so it doesn't take me too long. But tonight, I feel wide awake.

He will never be yours. He loathes you, I remind myself.

I can't figure out why this man is stuck in my mind. He was cruel to me, he clearly has no interest in me. Usually, men take one look at me, see my beautiful face and they immediately ask my mother for a meeting with me.

But not this man. He didn't care about my face. In fact, I think he hated me because of it. It takes me most of the night to try and figure out why I can't stop thinking about him. Maybe it's because he has been the only one to stand up to me my whole life. Maybe it's because he's godly handsome, and so strong that I want to explore every rugged part of his body. But mostly, I think it's because of the way he despises me. He despises me so much that I know he will never try to pursue me for a single thing I have to offer, including my appearance. He might be the only man in all of Tenuma that isn't trying to use me.

The only thing I'm sure of is that I need him to stay as far away from me as possible, because I don't know how much longer I can continue being a complete wretch to him and I can't risk him changing his opinion of me. That would be fatal for him. For some reason, this is one man I don't think I could stomach doing this to.

4

KOEN

Having spent most of the day at the castle, I was unable to hunt for the day. As the main provider for our family, it makes me feel like a failure. We still had a little bit of bread, fruit and rabbit meat leftover from yesterday's kill. My mother doesn't eat much, and my little sister hasn't been eating much because she's been so ill. I decide to make vegetable soup for her to soothe her cough when I get home.

"Mmm, that smells wonderful, son." My mother comes into the kitchen behind me, inhaling the smell that steams out of the pot.

"Hi, ma. I thought it might help relieve Mellani's cough. How's she doing?" I ask, stirring the soup on the stove.

"She seems a little bit better. You know her, she's always in good spirits," she says admiringly.

I laugh. "Yeah, I love that about her. I hope she never changes." What I really hope is that she never experiences the unforgiving, cruel world the way I have.

She sees the worry etched on my face, and rubs my arm. "What's wrong, my son?"

"This work is a lot more extensive than I thought. It's going to take me a lot longer than I expected." I sigh thinking of the amount of time I'll be spending at the castle.

"But the pay is good, yes?" she asks, knowing it's the only good thing about me having this job.

"Yes. It's good. But I'm just going to have so little time to hunt as it is. I thought this would take maybe a week, but it will take me a week just to get finished with the princess's room." I confess, rubbing my forehead in frustration.

My mother's breath catches. "What? You're working *in* the princess's room? For an entire week?"

My mouth forms a thin line as I realize I should have kept this information to myself. "It would appear so. I don't have much choice, we are almost out of food. We can't afford for me to not do it," I tell her.

She shakes her head. "I will go to town tomorrow and sell all the bracelets that I have. I made another fifty today. That should be enough to get us food for the next few days," she says, decidedly.

I wrap one arm around her pulling her into me, and kiss her on top of her head. "It will all work out, mom. Don't worry."

She chuckles. "I should be telling *you* that."

I smile, pulling her back in for another hug. My family means the world to me. I would do anything for them, including work for that wretched princess for another week. Knowing it's going to bring in money that will help feed us and heat our home makes it all worth it. The irony of insulating those ridiculous windows in that massive mansion, is that I come home to a dwelling that is typically colder than outdoors and actually needs the work. Maybe if there's any leftover material, I will be allowed to take it with me and I can use it for a few of our windows. Not for me, but for my mom and sister. I tend to run warmer than most, but my priority is to make sure my family is comfortable and warm.

Mellani comes to our small table to eat after I've called her for dinner. She sits in the chair next to me, and puts her hand on mine on top of the table as she spoons some of the vegetable soup into her mouth.

I put the remainder of the rabbit we had into the soup, and gave Mellani and my mom the last of our bread. I will be hungry, but I'd rather they go to bed with full bellies over me.

I give Mellani's hand a squeeze. "How are you feeling, sweet girl?"

She smiles up at me, looking much better than this morning. The color is back in her face, and she seems to have more energy. "Good. But I missed you. I'm glad you're back," she says softly.

"She watched out the window all day, waiting for you. I had to tell her repeatedly to get back in bed and rest," my mother chimes in, giving Mellani a disapproving glance.

"Is that true, Mel?" I ask her.

She gives me her best pouty face. "I-I just wanted to see when you were walking back. I just missed you, that's all."

Her sweet voice kills me. She has to be the most innocent six-year-old I've ever known. It won't ever stop breaking my heart the way she watches and waits for me to come home. There's only one person I can think of to blame for that. Our father. The fact that he never came back hasn't slipped her mind for a second.

I cup her chin with my hand. "Sweet girl. I will *always* come back. I tell you that every day. You don't need to worry about it. Ever. Okay?" I tell her firmly, looking right into her big, beautiful honey-brown eyes.

"Tell me just one more time?" she asks sweetly, her eyes giving puppy-dog vibes.

"I will *always* come back for you, baby girl," I say and then plant a quick kiss on top of her head.

I may be her older brother, but the role I've taken in our family the last few years have made her feel more like my child, than my sister. I feel this overwhelming protection for her. I have taken care of her more than our father-figure ever has.

I remember him coming home late–drunk–meanwhile, I would have spent half the day hunting, then go home and take care of Mellani. I would be in charge of feedings when my mother was too tired or depressed to keep going. I like to think I held us together when she couldn't. She did her best, but having a deadbeat for a partner who did nothing but cheat on her and make her feel worthless took its toll on her.

Most would think I have resentment for my mother at having to step into the father role. But I don't. I feel pride. I feel proud that I was able to find the strength to take over for a grown ass man who had no interest in taking care of his own family. I feel proud that I have been able to keep my family fed, warm, and alive. I will never feel anything but happiness at the fact that, despite our worthless father running out on us, we have survived and stuck together. I will never give up on us the way he did. If anything, it's what drives me to work harder.

Lying in bed that night, sleep proves to be difficult. My mind keeps drifting back to my encounter with the princess. Was she threatening me today? I didn't hide my distaste for her very well, in fact I all but outright said it. She didn't seem to approve of me being there, and now I'm fearful of my life going back tomorrow. She seemed to accept that I needed the money, but she clearly didn't want to see my face again. Part of me feels like she would be happy to see me dead.

Then what was the deal with the strange tension that hung between us before I left? It felt almost like anger, but different. Not quite anger, not quite lust. Something in between.

Was it coming from her, or me? I squash the thought before it can transform into anything further. I don't have the time to be thinking of any female in that capacity. Even if I did, it certainly wouldn't be that evil princess. There are plenty of women in Tenuma who make their interest in me known. I could have my pick of any if I wanted, not that I do. I would have to be the dumbest man alive to think of putting myself in her path. To think that I stand a chance to beat her deadly curse.

No. I won't entertain it. I think, shaking my head.

I roll over on the thin cot on the floor. It's thin, and miserable. But it's what we've got. My mother and sister share the only bed in the only bedroom we have. They always try to trade off with me, or make me sleep in it with them for warmth. But it doesn't seem right with how small the bed is. I don't mind too much. After a hard day of work, it isn't the most comfortable, but I sleep better knowing they're comfortable and warm. Half of the time, Mellani ends up on the floor with me anyway, huddled up against me. She says I keep her warm.

Maybe it's my own form of self-preservation, this abnormal warmth I have about myself. Our land is primarily snow and cold, yet I am always comfortably warm no matter what I'm wearing. Hunting is a lot easier for someone like me. You could spend hours and hours out in the woods trying to find your dinner with no luck. A man could freeze in that time, but because of my internal warmth, I'm able to stay out much longer than most are able to.

Just as I'm rolling onto my back again, I hear the pitter patter of small feet on the tile. Glancing over, I see Mellani tip-toeing over to me with her little blanket in her hands. I can't help but smile. Knowing I'm her source of comfort makes me a happy man.

I lift the thin blanket I'm covered in. "Get in," I say quietly.

She eagerly lays down next to me, curling up as close to me as she can. I throw an arm around her, so she feels warm and protected. I try to get some sleep, because I know tomorrow will be another long day of trying to avoid the princess and trying not to get fired or killed.

5

BELLATRIX

There aren't many things I do just for me. I don't have the luxury of doing anything I want at any given time. My days are packed with nauseating royal meetings regarding taxes, safety concerns, military updates, potential threats, etc. Basically, anything that I might need to know once I do become queen.

I've also been taking etiquette classes since I was a little girl, which basically means learning manners, 'lady-like' behaviors, social etiquette, and so on. Boring crap decided by men hundreds of years ago. Things that I plan on eliminating once I'm in power. Being queen isn't something I've aspired to be, but it's what my family needs from me. At least I will be able to do some good once I sit on the throne.

Every once in a while, there's nothing on my schedule for the day. Which means I have a block of time where I can go do the one thing that actually brings me pleasure in this life. It doesn't happen often, but when it does it, I take full advantage.

While it's near impossible to leave the castle without being tracked, this is something I do in secret. The only person who knows is my best friend, Quirina. She helps me sneak out of the castle. You'd think I was doing something immoral, having to sneak out of my chambers in secret. Nope. The immoral activities are held at the castle under my family's watch.

"Trix, be safe. You know what could happen if anybody finds out it's you under this disguise?" Quirina warns.

I nod. "I know. I will be alert," I say and give her a kiss on each cheek before sneaking out the back door. It's reserved mainly for the service staff, but it creates the perfect escape route for me.

I move quickly, disappearing into the thick trees that surround the castle. I'm heading towards town with pockets full of coins. My black hair is pinned back into a tight bun at the bottom of my neck and hidden beneath a dark gray hooded shawl. I have a black scarf around my neck so I can hide my face, if necessary. Luckily, it's freezing outside, so my outfit won't draw any attention. Everybody moving through town will be covered in layers as well.

I'm well aware that my father's politics have landed so many of our people into poverty. Thinking about all the families struggling for survival doesn't sit well with me. It's one of the policies I plan to change once I'm in charge, but for now this is my way of giving back.

I go to town with as much money as I can stuff into my pockets and hand it out to the children in town. I know every little bit makes a difference, and I want to do something good. The majority of my existence has been spent looking for a mate, in the evilest way. I don't have any say in the amount of men I've killed. If I could stop it, I would.

I have tried. So many times.

Maybe this is a way to make up for all the evil things I do at night. All of the pain I bring to all of the families. Maybe this is how I try to make things right on my own terms.

The center of town is quaint and beautiful. If I didn't know how badly the people here struggle, I'd call it beautiful. But I know the suffering that goes on here. The streets are lined with lanterns, each topped with sparkling snow from the last snowfall. On each side of the cobblestone street are all kinds of different shops for the owners that can still afford to hold permanent spots. Down the center of the street are merchant pop-ups for all of the local families that cannot afford a shop. They sell all things from soaps, homemade jams, jewelry, blankets, and even trinkets to ward off evil spirits and protect against magic.

Maybe that's something I should get and see if it cures my curse. I laugh to myself as I pass a local jewelry shop that claims to reverse magic spells. If it were that easy, I would have done so years ago. While magic doesn't play a huge role in most people's lives anymore, it still exists. Many hide their *gifts* in order to protect themselves from being enslaved and used as weapons, or tools by the royal army.

I'm greeted with bright smiles, and warm welcomes from each seller as they wave their hands attempting to gain a sale. Their genuine welcomes are part of the reason I love coming to town. Despite their shortcomings, these people never seem to waver in their positivity. Their kindness is never lacking.

"Miss! Would you like one of my homemade bracelets? They can ward off any danger, and protect against magic," the lady shouts at me as I'm making my way down the street.

I move slowly, and speak as little as possible so as not to draw attention to myself. The last thing I need is to be recognized and have word get back to my parents that I'm gallivanting all over town without permission.

I keep my head mostly down, as I glance her way, flashing her a smile. I shake my head no. Before I can move past her to the next seller, she reaches out and grabs my elbow pulling me back towards her.

She gasps and immediately pulls her hand back up to her mouth as if I've burned her.

"Ohhh. Oh my. Here," she says, handing me a red woven bracelet with a rose quarts gem in the center of it.

I shake my head no at her. "No, thank you." I kindly reject her offer.

"Please. Miss, you have…" She stops, searching for the right words. "There's something truly dark within you. Take this. For protection. You must. Take it," she says urgently, shoving the bracelet into my hand, folding my hand around it.

I hesitantly look up to see if she's recognized me, but her expression gives nothing away. It seems that she doesn't know who I am. But her face looks vaguely familiar, although I'm not sure from when or where I'd know her.

"How much?" I ask, because at this point, I don't think I am getting away from this woman until I take a bracelet. I've dealt with pushy merchants before, desperate for a sale–not that I can blame them–but this is on another level. This feels like more than the need to make a sale.

As I start reaching into my pocket for coins when she stops me. "No. Not necessary, miss. Please. You must take it," she says firmly, and steps back away from me as if I'm made of fire and she doesn't want to get burned again.

She tries to look busy, rearranging some of the jewelry on her small table, as I stand there. I can't leave without paying her. I quietly drop some coins on her table and from what the sign says, it's three times what she's asking.

"Thank you," I quietly mutter, and walk away.

That was a strange interaction, I think to myself.

I've been coming here for the last year, and I've never had an experience like that before. A nagging voice inside keeps telling me that she recognized me. I have to shove the feeling down because I'm here for a reason, and I need to see it through.

I slip the bracelet on my wrist as I put distance between me and the merchant. I glance back quickly, seeing that nobody is following me or even paying me any attention, so I feel like I'm still in the clear. Up ahead is a group of kids that usually hang out around the tall fountain waterfall while their mothers sell their products. There are about fifteen kids running around, playing cards together on the ground, and splashing in the freezing water with their hands. Even though there's snow on the ground, the kids seem to enjoy the water.

I find myself envious of the freedom to be a kid. While I may have been born with riches and security, I've never truly known what it meant to be a kid. The innocence they possess is something I'm forever jealous of. Making it another one of the main reasons I love coming here. I love watching them play around and just be kids.

My eyes scan their tattered wardrobes, from the holes in their thin shoes, to the cloth that barely covers their arms and legs. Most of it looks to be second and third-hand worn, ill-fitting clothing. Thinking of my own profligate wardrobe, my heart lurches in my chest.

Their families struggle most of the time, nevertheless they're able to play and joke, not letting it consume them with dread. It's why I love coming here and giving money to the kids. Seeing their smiles makes me happier than anything else does. It gives me the sort of temporary happiness and hope that makes me believe life won't always be like this. Maybe one day, I won't be a slave to my sex life, and a murderer for my family's benefit.

"You came!" a little girl with curly brown hair and big brown eyes shouts at me, running towards me and gives me a tight hug.

I smile brightly down at her. "I told you I'd be back," I say, hugging her back.

"I know," she says shyly. She always seems so surprised to see me, even when I tell her I'm going to come back. It makes me think that she must not have many adults in her life that she can count on. The thought makes my heart squeeze. I can't imagine doing anything to put disappointment on her sweet face.

"How are you feeling? You have your voice back," I say excitedly. She sounded pretty sick last week, so I had given her money for food and medicine but it's not up to me how their family spends it, so I never really know how it's used.

"Yeah, I feel better. I…" she starts, and then looks down at her feet.

"What is it, honey?" I ask softly, lifting her chin.

"I didn't get to buy any medicine," she admits.

"Oh. Why not?" I ask curiously. She would have benefited from it, but it's not my decision how the money is spent.

"Well. My… dad… couldn't get us enough food for a few days, so I gave it to my mom so we could eat," she says like she's ashamed.

I shake my head. "Hey. That's for you to use however you need it. If you needed the food, then you did the right thing," I reassure her, so she stops looking so sad. "You didn't tell your mom where you got the money, did you?" I ask her worriedly.

Usually, I'm not in the habit of making kids keep secrets from their parents, but this is an exception. In secrecy is the only way I can help these kids without both myself and them being in danger. If my father knew I was spending his money on the children in town, I'm not sure what he would do. He has no issue taking over every part of my life, including my sex life so I don't put it past him to harm me in other ways for doing this behind his back. He might be bed-ridden but he still wields his power like he's still sitting at the throne.

"No. I told her I found it around the shops while she was working a few days ago." She smiles mischievously. I can tell she's proud of her made-up excuse.

I smile at her. For such a young girl, she's already so clever and smart beyond her years. She doesn't know who I really am, but she seems to understand the importance of the secret. I've always felt this pull towards her. She has this genuine heart of gold, and you can see that she just wants to be loved. I can relate to that in so many ways.

Living the way I have, has completely altered how I view love and relationships. Love doesn't seem to be a possibility for me. No man gets close enough to me in order to fall in love with me. The men that are stupid enough to jump into bed with me, end up dead. They all want power, and all I really want is someone to genuinely give a shit about *me*, not what I have to offer. I'm just the trophy that sits on the shelf as proof of the title won.

"That's really good. Thank you for your trust. I brought you more today. I still wish you had medicine for your cough, though. I don't have any with me, but I will bring you some in the next day or two. How about that? I don't know if I will make it back tomorrow, but I will try to be back the day after that, okay? For now, take this for whatever else your family needs." I reach into my pocket and hand her a fistful of coins. She never asks me for anything and she's never greedy about it. The gratitude is clear from the affection she shows me. It's nice to be needed for something good.

Her eyes bulge out. "That's a lot! I don't know if mama will believe I found all of this," she says apprehensively.

"It's okay, just don't give it to her all at once. But please take it. I want you to have it. Take it home and hide it. I don't want you to have to worry about food," I tell her. The way my heart has grown for this little girl over the last few months is wild to me. I don't get close to anyone, but sometimes I see myself in her. I don't want to return to the castle tonight and wonder if she's had dinner tonight.

"Okay…" she replies hesitantly and opens her hands tentatively for the coins.

I smile at her, happy that I won't have to worry about her tonight. I'm not sure what her father does for work, but she tells me often that they don't have very much to eat. Maybe she's got a large family. Men don't usually have many issues finding work around here, it's usually the women who aren't taken as seriously in Tenuma. They are seen primarily as homemakers. Another image I plan to shatter once I'm queen.

As I drop the coins in her little hands, she looks at my arm and makes an excited noise. "Ooooh. Pretty!" she says excitedly.

I move my eyes to see what she's looking at.

I let out a low laugh. "Oh, my tattoo." I run my fingers over the tattoo on my forearm. It's a sword tattoo piercing through a giant red rose, and the triple moons behind the handle of the sword. The handle has an intricate shape and design. I wanted something to represent the ruler I plan to be. I want to rule with love and feminine power. While others may see women as weak–or unable to rule as well as men–I know women are strong and powerful beyond imagination. I also know that I don't have to rule the same way my father does. Fear and greed are not feelings I wish to be associated with when I am queen.

I bend down and whisper, "It's my power tattoo. It represents how strong and powerful women are. Just like you will be one day," I say and wink at her. Even as I say the words to her, I know I'm saying them for my own benefit as well. My life doesn't make me feel powerful. I'm supposed to exude power and grace, and yet I am a tool for finding the next king. I know I'm meant for more than this, I just wish I had the strength to find it.

She gives me a beaming, wonderous smile and then giggles. She may be the cutest thing I've ever seen.

"I have to get back, okay? But I will see you soon. I'm going to bring you that medicine, sweet girl. Keep yourself warm," I say ruffling her curls, making a mental note to bring her a thicker sweater next time I come. I make my way over to the children playing and *accidentally* drop the rest of the coins I brought with me, as I walk by.

I keep going, walking back behind the buildings towards the castle so I don't catch any attention on the way back. Glancing back, I see the children scrambling and shrieking in joy as they all rush to pick up the coins. It's not much and I wish I could do more, but the joy this brings me is unparalleled. I love knowing that I am able to help in any small way, even if it may get me killed.

6

KOEN

The princess isn't around the second or third day I'm working at the castle, which I'm grateful for. I wasn't looking forward to faking any sort of goodwill towards her. The amount of families that have lost a good man—a contributing, working man—because they were foolish enough to get into bed with that witch makes me sick. Sure, they go there on their own free will. But look at what she's offering them—a golden ticket to a better life. Meanwhile, her father made sure the entire land suffers and starves, so there's not a lot of choice in the matter, if you ask me. Any chance at a better life is worth the risk in these men's eyes. It's not free will, it's desperation.

Whatever interactions I had with the princess that first day seemed to have had some sort of negative effect on her because I haven't seen her since. Which is fine by me, since my mother asks me fifty questions each night when I return home. She worries too much. I'm not desperate like those other men. She knows me well enough to know that I'd never be tempted by her anyway, so I'm not sure where her anxiety stems from. I'd like to think she knows that I will just work harder and keep fighting to keep us afloat. There's nothing about that witch or her lifestyle that entices me. I'd rather live in our drafty cottage with a clear conscience, than in her castle with all the riches, doing what she does. It's sickening.

Passing through the gates and seeing the princess standing in her window again, it appears my luck has run out. She's reappeared and in her chambers where I plan on working today. Looks like I won't be able to avoid her icy presence today.

She stands in the window, staring off the same way she was the first day I saw her. That same longing expression on her face. Her long black hair hangs down on both of her shoulders in loose curls. She's wearing a deep blue velvet long sleeve corset dress that pushes her breasts up to her neck.

Not that I noticed.

The look on her face disturbs me as much as it did the first time I saw it. It doesn't make sense with what I know of the princess. The cruel persona and the lavish lifestyle. What could she possibly long for? She has a new man in her bed each night, with more men throwing themselves at her. Watching her intensifies my hatred for her. That woman has all the power in the world, and has the nerve to look as if she wants for *anything* in this life?!

There's one window left of three in the princess's room. I should be able to finish in the next couple of days. I have been left to work in silence the entire day, which has been exactly what I had hoped for. Running hot like I always do, I can freely strip my shirt off and not worry that there are any prying eyes on me. The thought of having to spend another day with the princess hanging around waiting for me to mess up, makes my skin crawl. Just as I'm getting into a work groove and letting my guard down, I hear footsteps behind me.

Whipping my head around to see who's entered the room, I see the princess striding in with her head hung low, and her wiping at her eyes.

Is she crying? I wonder.

It's strange to see her cry; it's like seeing a snake have emotions. Even visibly upset, she carries a strength and an aura of peril. The sight of her makes me unbalanced and I have to shift on the ladder, so I don't fall off. I swear the skin underneath my bracelet tingles. Warning me or tempting me, I can't be sure.

The ladder makes a loud squeaking noise when I shift to grab my shirt at the bottom of the ladder, causing her head to jerk up as she comes further into the large room heading towards the bathroom, it seems. Her eyes catch mine, and for just a moment I can see just how sad she looks.

Why does it make my heart squeeze? The thought is here and gone before I can comprehend where it came from.

"Umm, I can give you a moment alone if you need," I volunteer, already climbing down off the ladder. Sitting in the same room with a crying princess is not the sort of situation I want to find myself in the middle of.

Her head juts back down, her black hair fanning over her face as she continues towards her restroom. "No, I will be out in just a moment. You may continue what you're doing," she answers back emotionlessly.

How one looks like she does right now and is able to sound so empty, is yet another reason I need to stay away from this woman. The princess is clearly one of many faces, and who knows which one is authentic.

As she hurries off to the bathroom, closing the large heavy black door behind her, I turn back and continue working on the top of the window frame. I have tinted and glazed the windows, now I'm installing the large shades. My arms feel sore and heavy after working another long day here. Today is unseasonably warm, and since I already run hot, I'm finding the work to be unbearable today. Suddenly aware of my half naked state, I wonder if I should dress now that she's back in her chambers. It's not exactly professional, and I don't want there to be *any* hint of enticement coming from me. If she mistakes anything I do for flirting, I'll wind up in her death bed. And that is the last place I ever want to be.

The door to the bathroom opens, and the princess emerges as she typically appears–cold and emotionless. Her tears have been wiped away, and her face looks as though they were never there. I find myself staring at her longer than I intend to, and try to look away before she catches me.

"Is there something I can help you with, beast?" she barks at me.

"Wow," I mutter, mostly to myself while shaking my head. The shock of her comment makes the word escape my mouth before I can control it. I face the window again, not allowing myself to gaze into those soul sucking eyes. How so many men can stand to be around her is astonishing to me.

"What was that now?" she demands.

"Nothing, *Princess.*" The word princess comes out forced and harsh, dripping with sarcasm, as she conducts herself as anything but a princess.

"If you wish to say something, by all means say it," she says, placing both of her hands on her hips facing me directly. Looking back at her, I force my eyes not to go lower than her neckline.

"I don't wish to say anything," I force through clenched teeth, realizing I may have gone too far.

She flips back one side of her hair, rolling her eyes. She

turns around and saunters back to the door as I turn back to my work. As if she flipped an emotional switch from crying to churlish.

Now that she's leaving, I decide it's okay to leave my shirt off. I drop the shirt back on one of the ladder rungs. The cool air is very much needed after the sudden heatwave that was brought in with the princess.

Why am I so scared to let her see my skin?

Because I don't want that snake of a woman to picture me naked in her bed, I remind myself.

I'm not a conceited man by any means, but I know that a man of my physique can draw attention from most females—not that I'm trying to. From my days of hunting and laboring, my back is bulging with firm muscles, and my powerful arms bulge against the sleeves of my clothing. I consider myself strong and protective, but those aren't traits I'm wanting to flaunt around the castle; lest her father order me to enter her bed.

As I begin climbing back up the ladder, I hear a commotion behind me and before I realize what's happening my feet are on the ground rushing over to catch the princess just before she hits the ground.

My hand is wrapped behind her cradling her head, and my other arm is draped across her, hand firmly pressed into her back, keeping her upright. Both of her hands are gripping onto me as tight as she can, her fingers sinking into the flesh of my arms as if I'm her lifeline. The thought of saving her makes my chest unwelcomingly warm. She's essentially laying in my arms and I'm holding her while half-naked. This won't look good if anybody walks in.

Burning skin replaces my once cool flesh, and the world around us stops. I swear I felt a breeze just before this, but if it was there, it's now still. It feels like I'm having an out of body experience, looking down at the princess in my arms and I don't hate the way it looks. Even though I'll never admit it, it looks right. It feels like she's always been there. As my heart begins to race, I find that the usual loathing I feel for her, replaced with desire.

What the hell is happening? I think to myself.

She's staring up at me with a look I haven't seen before, I can't quite place it, but it sends a shiver up my arms. It feels dangerous, yet alluring. The coldness and anger I usually see is replaced with warmth, gratitude, and yearning.

Stop staring into those beautiful green eyes, I demand, trying to pull myself out of this trance-like state.

Our faces are so close that I can feel her warm breath on my arm and every sense I have is standing on edge. The feel of her porcelain skin is soft and smooth, her green eyes are piercing, and I can see every freckle that covers her nose and cheeks. The room is silent and still, as if the world just stopped. I'm holding my breath, scared to disturb the moment we're in.

As her eyes continue to bore into mine, the intensity generates a sense of panic to rise in my chest, snapping me out of the moment as I pull her upright. Realization of how long we've been suspended in this position hits and I come back to reality. I release her from my grip, taking a step back. I notice her sleeve has bunched up on her forearm, revealing a sword and rose tattoo on her wrist. I pull my eyes away from it before my greedy eyes examine it further.

Awkwardly standing in front of me, she cocks her head sideways at me. "Th-thank you. That would have been a nasty fall," the princess manages to sound grateful, and I almost believe it to be sincere.

"Not bad for a beast," I reply with a scoff, and a smirk.

The corners of her mouth pull up slightly before she forces them back down, stifling a smile. Her eyes wander over my shirtless body, taking in my large muscular frame. I watch her lips part and eyes go heavy for a split second like she's picturing something else entirely. The look is gone before I can even react to it.

"You should have let me fall," she responds harshly before fleeing the room once again, leaving me standing there feeling confused and flustered and much too warm.

The room feels hotter than it did a few minutes ago. I want to slap myself for the thoughts that have been slipping through the cracks. I need to get the hell out of here.

7
BELLATRIX

I need to get the hell out of here, I think to myself, as I rush from my bedroom. I find my entire body flushed after just a moment in that man's strong arms.

Strong, firm arms, I think. No. Stop. I cannot have these thoughts about him, and if anybody were to have seen what just occurred, he could very well be headed for doom. If anyone has the slightest indication that I might be attracted to him, a meeting would be set up before I had time to object to it or even laugh at the suggestion.

Even if I wanted to risk a night with that brooding, tall, muscular man, there's no way he would ever come willingly. He might be the one man on our entire land that wouldn't want to risk his life for a life of riches and power. Good. It's refreshing, and probably why I find myself so drawn to him. But it feels like more. The attraction feels so strong. Too strong. I'll have to be more vigilant at staying away from him. Even my bracelet seemed to be having an unexplained tingling effect in his presence.

I feel embarrassed having tripped over my own dress in front of him. He loathes me, and on top of it, he must think I'm an emotional empty-headed fool. If I hadn't been rushing to my bathroom upset from another chat with the king and queen regarding another meeting this evening, I would have remembered that that man was still working in my bedroom. The last thing I need him to see is me being vulnerable and upset. I told myself I'd keep my distance from him, and today I wound up in his arms.

Enjoying the feeling of his embrace far too much, I flee the room. I rush outside to catch some much needed fresh air and find a bench in the garden to sit on. The ground is still covered in snow from the storm last week, but the day is somewhat warm and the bench is dry. And the best part is it's private.

The flower garden sits to the left of the castle entrance and resides inside a modest, but tall, hedge maze. The garden is in the center and is full of my favorite flowers–peonies, calla lilies, and what flower garden would be complete without roses? It's completely secluded to anybody walking by, which is exactly what I need right now.

My entire body is still ignited from the quick, but intimate interaction with that man upstairs. The cool air isn't enough to cool me down, and I'm realizing now that there's only one thing that's going to relieve the heat coursing through my body.

I glance around my surroundings just to make sure there's nobody else in here, even though it was empty when I walked in. As a princess, I usually have somebody trailing me.

Once I'm satisfied that I'm in fact alone in the flower garden, I smile to myself.

The coast is clear.

I lean back against the bench, and begin lifting my dress. As the dress inches higher, I spread my legs wider so I can reach my center. Once I have the dress high enough, I place one foot on the bench, giving me better access, and begin rubbing my clit over my blue lacy panties. My pussy is wet before I begin rubbing myself. I am already pulsing and swollen, aching to find release. I continue to rub the swollen bud until I feel the pressure building, needing to be filled.

I slide a finger into my soaked entrance and immediately needing more, I add another finger and begin pumping them in and out. My head falls back, as the pressure builds faster now.

I'm pumping them faster and faster as I picture the man's strong arms around me, holding me tightly and gazing into my eyes. While his eyes mostly exhibit hatred, for just a moment, I saw something more. I've spent enough time with men to know that the look in his eyes was passion. For a brief second, he let his guard down and I saw a moment of weakness, a moment of weakness from both of us that cannot happen again.

Realizing I will never have his hands on me again makes the need build faster and faster, until I hear myself moaning out loud. I'm unable to stifle the noises coming from me as I ascend my way to climax. I add another finger, pumping them in and out while my other hand rubs my clit. I'm working both hands together until I come crashing down in ecstasy letting out a loud moan of satisfaction. Breathing heavy, eyes rolled back, and a smile at my lips I start to come down.

My dress is still pushed up over my knees and I start to pull my hands away from my pussy before anybody happens to come looking for me, when my gaze happens to travel upwards towards my bedroom windows. The windows I didn't realize were right in front of where my pussy is completely on display.

Just as my eyes make out my windows, I see a shadow move across one of the windows for a split second.

No. Please tell me he didn't see me, I say to myself, as I rush to pull my dress back down and cover my face with my hands.

I decide to spend a few more minutes here in the garden, because the thought of accidentally running into him now is insufferable.

Just as I'm convincing myself he didn't see anything, I hear heavy feet going by in a rush just as I hear the handyman loudly tell the guard out front that he is done for the day and will be back in a few days.

There's only one reason he would be rushing out of the castle like this right now. There's not a chance he didn't see what I was doing down here just after he held me in his arms.

FUCK.

8

KOEN

Fuck. Are my eyes really seeing this right now? I'm still reeling from the electricity the princess left behind after such a stupid, accidentally intimate moment with her, and this is the last thing I need to be looking at.

The princess has her dress pulled up over her knees and legs spread wide open as she fingers herself in the middle of the castle garden.

Does she know that I can see her? No. There's no way. Her remark before she left, tells me she would have rather fallen than have my hands on her. This act can't be for *my* benefit. She doesn't want me touching her. Not that I want to be touching her either. Nothing has changed, I still despise the woman. I'm not a man that can be swayed by an easy pussy.

Then why can't you stop looking? My subconscious taunts.

Just as I'm about to turn away a voice startles me. "What are you staring at so intently?"

I jump and rush away from the window to gather my supplies before I even realize who's spoken. When I glance up, my blood drains. I have to do a double-take. For a split second I think it's the princess. I can see black hair, and *blue* eyes. Nope, not her. It could be worse, but this is still going to be bad.

Quirina, the princess's handmaid, stands before me with a tray of tea for the princess, and a smirk on her face.

"I was, uh…just looking at the beautiful view here. So many trees, there's not a view like this in town. I'm finished for the day, so I will see you next time, Lady Quirina," I sputter, hoping to leave before this conversation goes further. My only hope is that Quirina and the princess aren't close enough to talk about such things. Me.

"You know," she says, setting the tray of tea on the vanity sitting against the wall. "You don't have to call me lady. I'm not a royal. From what I know about you, you don't even call the princess, *Lady*." She crosses her arms, her suspicion evident as she moves slowly over to me while I gather my supplies and tools.

Fuck. There goes that theory. I can't help but wonder what's been said to Quirina about me. Was it a conversation out of boredom or is she debating whether I should be punished?

"I don't mean to be disrespectful," I say quickly, panicking.

"Yes, you do," Quirina responds, still smirking at me. I'm glad she's finding the humor in this. Even though her remarks are said in jest, it still fills me with dread.

She starts to move towards the window, and my panic rises.

"Until next time, Quirina. Lovely to see you, as always." I rush from the room, stealing a glance back to see Quirina looking out the same window I just saw the princess pleasuring herself. All I can think is that after she talks with Quirina, there's no way the princess won't know what I've just witnessed.

I rush down the hallway, down the stairs and out the front door as quickly as I can without raising suspicion. When I reach the front gate, I tell the guy with the clipboard that I won't be back tomorrow, but the day after and try to get the hell away from this castle as fast as possible.

I make it home just as the sun is starting to lower beneath the mountains. My back and arms are aching with all the work I've been doing at the castle, and my temples are pulsing with a headache I've given myself with all the overthinking I've done walking home.

There are so many things rushing through my mind that I can't seem to push from my forethoughts.

Why was the princess cruel to me, calling me 'beast'?

What was the weird electricity between us when she came back into the room?

How did she end up in my arms?

Why didn't I hate it?

Why did she seem to enjoy it before being rude and running from the room?

Why was she masturbating minutes after our interaction in plain view of the window she knew I was working on?

When I make it back to the cottage, I drop all of my tools and gear at the front door and scrub a hand down my face, trying to shake off the weird day I just had, before I go inside. This strange energy is not what I want to bring home.

Pushing the door open, I see my mother scrubbing at my little sister's arm with a wet rag.

"You're home!!" my sister shrieks.

"What's happening here?" I ask curiously.

My mother looks up from her scrubbing of Mellani's arm.

"Your little sister decided to give herself her first tattoo." She rolls her eyes at me, and then goes back to scrubbing it off.

"Ah. A tattoo. Aren't we a little young for that, my sweet girl?" I ask playfully.

Mellani looks at me with her big brown eyes that she knows I can never stay mad at. "But it looked so cool! I want a real one when I get big," she says excitedly.

"Where on earth did you even get the idea for a tattoo?" I ask her.

Her eyes bounce around the room, and she hesitantly answers. "Just from a girl I saw in town."

I glance at my mom. "You guys went to town today?" I ask her. She knows I don't like when they go without me there to protect them. Since the king has upped the taxes again, he's made life even harder for our people, which in turn makes them desperate. Desperate people do desperate things in the name of survival.

My mother waves off my question. "It was fine, my son. You must stop worrying so much," she says to me.

I hold my arm up bearing the bracelet. "Says the woman who makes me wear *this* just to leave the house," I comment on the irony.

"Yes, but I'm your mother. I'm supposed to worry," she says firmly.

I chuckle, and walk past them, making my way to the bathroom to shower and wash off this strange day. I'm hoping a cold shower can clear my mind of the day's activities as well as the annoying thoughts that keep creeping in.

As I close the door behind me, I hear my mom and sister's muffled talking.

"Sweetie, why a sword and a rose? Is that what you saw on your friend?" my mom asks Mellani.

"Yes! It was beautiful, just like her. I can't wait to get a real one someday," my sister responds back to my mom.

Where have I seen that tattoo? I think to myself. The thought melts away as I step into the shower. I lather shampoo in my hair, rubbing my scalp and suddenly I'm picturing the princess's hands in my hair. The goosebumps up my arms halt the lathering.

I rinse my hair and start lathering up a bar of soap until it's nice and sudsy. Rubbing it up and down my arms, over my shoulders, back and stomach until I'm covered in bubbles. I finally feel like I've left the day behind me until I start lathering up my dick.

The response is immediate, and my dick is throbbing at the same time I see the princess's long black hair and huge perky tits in my mind. I mindlessly fist my cock, and start stroking it.

She wanted to be in your arms.

The look in her eyes was pure lust.

She was fucking her own pussy thinking about you.

The devil on my shoulder whispers everything I would never admit to myself. I can't help but wonder where the angel went.

No. Stop. There's the angel.

I force myself to stop despite how good it feels, and regardless of how good the release would feel. I know I can't allow my thoughts to go down this road. Even though part of me feels like there may be more to her than what I know or what I've seen. The strange mixed signals she gives me make me wonder what else she's hiding. There's no way to misinterpret the look she gave me as I saved her from plummeting to the ground, and there's no way to ignore the way she felt in my arms.

She seemed softer and kinder. It's like I got to see behind the curtain and saw who she really is for just a split second. Maybe there's more to what's been said about her. Was I wrong to completely write her off?

Maybe I've been wrong about her.

As I towel dry myself after a longer-than-necessary shower, thanks to the confusing thoughts in my head tonight, I hear a knock at the front door. A few seconds later I hear my mom chatting friendly with whoever has come knocking and she calls for me.

"Koen. You have company," she calls from the living space.

Walking out to where my mother stands, I see my friend Landric standing there.

"Hey man, what brings you by?" I ask, giving him a quick handshake/hug/smack on the back.

"Not much, I was in the area and wanted to run something by you really quick. Can we talk outside?" he asks.

Landric has been a close friend of mine for many years now. We met at a job we were both working together after his father's business went under.

I step outside with Landric onto the stone path in front of our cottage, waiting for him to tell me why he's stopped by at such an unusual hour. We typically get together on the weekends; if we don't go hunting together, we are at the local bar–Nik's–that my best friend owns. His name is Nikandros, and he's really the only mildly thriving business on our land. While I don't drink all that much, some of the guys get together to play poker there on the weekends for small bets. Money isn't something any of us have in excess, but for as hard as we all work, it's nice to let loose a little bit with each other.

Landric is stalling, kicking around stones with his feet and I already know I'm not going to like what he's about to say.

"So, what's goin' on?" I finally ask him.

"It's been hard, man. You know we've been struggling. My family, we…we are barely staying afloat."

"I know. It's been tough all around. If I had anything extra, I would help you guys…" I start but he cuts me off, putting one hand up.

Landric shakes his head. "No, man. That's not why I'm here. You have your mom and little sister to take care of, I could never take anything from you."

"I'm not sure what you're trying to tell me then." My eyebrows pinch together as he draws this conversation out.

He stops kicking the little stones with his feet, and stands taller, summoning the courage to speak. "I have a meeting with the princess," he states tightly.

My entire body goes cold at what this means. I will never see him again.

"I don't think I heard you right. It sounds like you just said something insane," I tell him.

"I don't have any other options at this point. We are struggling. I need a way to protect my family. This way, I can give back to you and Nik, and–" he starts but I cut him off, not willing to listen to his excuses.

"That's bullshit, man. You have options. Keep looking for work. Maybe it's time to go to another land. But you won't be able to give *anything* back when you're dead!" I shout, pointing my finger in his chest.

"There's a chance. I might be able to beat the curse," he says unconvincingly.

"No, you won't. Nobody has so far. How many men have there been? What you are doing is stupid. You will die, and you will leave your family for dead. You understand that, don't you?" I say, pleading for him to change his mind.

He sighs heavily running a hand through his thick brown hair.

"Look, man. I don't know what else to do and it's done. If this works, I can help my family out and yours. It's worth the risk. I can beat it," he states stubbornly.

"I don't want your help. Landric. Please listen to me. I don't think that's the way this thing works. I'm not sure there's a man on this entire land that can survive it. You'd have to possess some sort of magic." I refuse to believe he's thought this through thoroughly. "Have you even told your family yet? Please reconsider. That woman is a monster, and you won't get what you want out of that *meeting*. She is going to fuck you and you will die," I retort.

"I left them a note. It's going to be okay. You'll see. I came by, just in case. I just wanted to thank you for being a great friend," he says softer.

"You don't even realize that you're already saying your good-byes. Deep down, you know this is a terrible idea. You are walking straight towards your death. Come on, man. You've gotta be smarter than this," I tell him.

"Koen. I have to go, but I'll see you soon." He looks suddenly forlorn and throws himself into my arms hugging me tightly.

He holds on longer than is typical for a manly embrace, and then turns and walks quickly away.

How could he be so stupid? I think as I watch him disappear into the distance.

I throw my fist into a nearby tree, shaking the snow from the branches overhead to come sprinkling down on me. I walk back to the cottage and step inside. I make it over to a chair and barely sit down before my mother, who's cooking in the kitchen, starts prying for information.

"What was that about, honey? Everything okay? He seemed off tonight," she says. My mom can usually get a good read off of people by a simple touch.

"No. Not really. He has a…" I start to say, trying to word it carefully since Mellani is in the room, and I don't want to say too much. "He has a *meeting* at the castle."

"Oh, he's going to be working with you then?" she asks unaware.

"No. He has a meeting with the princess," I say with my face buried in my arms on our table.

I hear a clang, and look up to see that my mother has dropped the knife she was using to cut a loaf of bread. "No. Tell me this is a joke," she begs.

I shake my head.

"What is he thinking?" she asks.

"The same thing every other man is. They want to protect their family. They all think they can beat whatever kind of curse this is, and be the one to rule Tenuma. They're all crazy. I'm not even sure why commoners are trying. If it's even possible, it will probably be someone from another royal family," I state plainly.

I say this all so confidently, wishing my friend could see Princess Bellatrix the way I see her. I wish they all had the same hatred for her that I do. It would make the choice simple. Actually, it would eliminate the issue altogether.

Although, for a brief moment today, I found myself thinking there might be something more to her than this spell. I thought maybe she could be a decent person. But what kind of person keeps this charade up for so long? She should have put a stop to this knowing how many lives she's taken. Whatever I briefly felt this afternoon is long gone. The confusion is no longer there. The feeling is replaced with the same hatred I've had for her all along and then some. Tonight, she will take the life of one of my closest friends, and then I'm supposed to continue working at the castle with her. Impossible.

Not wanting to talk about this further, I opt to change the subject. "Mother, it smells amazing in here. What are you cooking? I thought we didn't have much food left. I was going to go hunting in the morning so we could have food for the rest of the week and through the weekend."

This castle job is very well paying, but I don't get paid until I finish. And because I'm there all day long, it leaves me without any time to go hunting for my family.

"I bought some bread, cheese, and I made a meatloaf that has just finished. I also have a bottle of wine if you'd like some," she pridefully tells me.

"Mother. Where in the world did you get money for all of that? Did you sell your entire jewelry collection?" I ask her. I can't remember the last time we had a hearty meal like this *and* wine.

"Oh heavens, no. Our sweet little Mel was lucky enough to find coins that somebody had dropped in town," she states excitedly. "I know, I know, their misfortune. But we didn't steal it, we happened upon it. So, it's okay to keep." She knows that I try to lead my life with integrity, which is a trait that's hard to come by on our land.

I try not to be judgmental either, I understand the misfortunes of so many of us around here, but I also wish most had more common sense. Especially my friend Landric.

I shake the thought of him from my mind, as I help my mother plate dinner and we sit down to eat.

"This is incredible," I say to my mother, and then turn to Mellani. "You really just found a bunch of money laying on the ground again?" I ask her as she stuffs a forkful of meatloaf into her mouth.

She nods her head yes, trying to smile with her mouth full, making her look like a chipmunk. Mel isn't a very mischievous little girl by any means, but something in her smile makes me think there's more to the story than she's leading on. Every once in a while, small amounts of money show up and she claims to have just found it. Folks around don't have much of it to begin with, so I find it hard to believe that so many of them keep misplacing the little they do have. Nonetheless, I'm grateful that my family has dinner on the table tonight because of it.

I'm laying on the thin cot mattress on the floor trying to sleep but my mind won't shut off. I keep replaying everything that happened during the day. It feels like it's all connected somehow. It's just too many strange things happening in one day.

I feel sick to my stomach that right now, Landric is probably taking his last breath. That foolish man thinks having sex with that woman is going to be the answer to all of his problems. Does he really believe that or is he being led with his dick drawn to a pretty face?

I felt that for a split-second today—which is exactly how a predator lures in their prey. A beautiful face can make any man forget what he's going to be giving up.

I don't know what I'm going to do, but I need to stop her. It was bad enough when it was happening around town to people I didn't personally know, but now it's become personal and I can't continue seeing her without saying anything, or doing something.

This needs to stop.

9

BELLATRIX

This needs to stop.

I begged my parents earlier today to stop sending suitors to me, but they refused *again.* They don't care that they're forcing me to have sex with strangers.

"Why do I have to have sex with them? Can't we just marry?" I asked them.

"You must produce an heir, whether it be male or female. You must produce offspring from our bloodline to rule the throne after you're gone," my father commanded from his bed. Even though I'm his daughter, he is more concerned with 'the rules.' The throne comes before everything else, in his eyes. I should feel sad that his death is creeping closer but truthfully, all I feel is relief that he will soon be gone.

I voiced to both of them that I was done and I wasn't going to do this anymore. That resulted in my father calmly telling me that I would forfeit the throne and be evicted from the castle, having to fend for myself like the rest of the land. He was *kind enough* to remind me of my lack of life skills.

It's not my fault I wasn't taught valuable life skills from my parents.

But hey, I can throw a hell of a tea party and schmooze a room full of royals, if need be.

Why am I about to be handed the throne to rule over our entire land then? I couldn't help thinking to myself. I can rule over a land but in his eyes, I'm not capable of learning a trade skill. Hell, I'm not even trusted to find my own mate. I'm starting to wonder how capable *he* was to rule over our land, considering he's an obvious misogynist.

I tried talking with my mother privately again because I think she genuinely means well. But I have had enough. This has gone on long enough, I'm starting to think this curse is just meant to kill. I asked her for any way out of this, any loophole. I just need another way to find a mate without having to sleep with any more men. But the conversation didn't go well. She barely looked remorseful and I know she's seen what this has done to me. What *she's* done to me. Somewhere along the way, she went from being my mother and protector to someone who puts power over her family.

A decision initially made out of fear for her daughter has led to more pain and misery than it has actually protected. I'd rather have my heart shattered a million times over than have one more death on my hands… or pussy.

She stands firm in her decision, stating it's what's best for me. What she really means is, it's what's best for the kingdom.

After a conversation leading nowhere, I went rushing into my room crying, where I ran into the man working on my windows. My mind was in such a panic that I completely forgot he was in there. My surprise and embarrassment had me rushing into the bathroom for some privacy while I pulled myself together.

Seeing him in there made me completely flustered. I'm not used to being flustered and self-conscious in front of men. That's usually where I'm calm and confident, mostly because I have nothing to lose. But for some reason, around this muscular giant, I find myself out of my element. He's somebody I know I can never, and will never have.

He feels forbidden, like the poisonous flower that you can't help but be drawn to. Except I'm the poison.

But he also looks at me like he might be the only person to realize there's more to me than this damn curse.

The more I try to pull away from him, the closer to him I end up. His demeanor towards me says he hates me, but then why did he rush to me when I slipped on my dress? How could he look at me the way he did if he hates me? The look in his eyes, and the heat between us isn't something anybody could fake.

As I'm thinking of the possibilities that he might not despise me, I have to squash the thought because I *need* him to hate me. Today was too close of a call. I can't ever be that close to him again. I don't know what it is about him, but I find myself drawn to him, and that's exactly why I have to stay away. He feels different, his heart feels different. The way he guards himself and pushes me away, makes me think he's the only one with any morals left. He's the only man not chasing me for financial gain.

I find myself feeling protective of him. In order to keep him safe, I need him to keep hating me. This shouldn't be hard to do, most people hate me anyway. Families hate me for taking their sons and brothers away, and women hate me for taking away their crushes, friends or family members. I'm an easy person to hate.

All I need is my best friend, Quirina. She understands me, and she knows who I truly am. She knew me before I was damned with this curse. Rina knows my heart, and that this isn't who I truly am.

When I get back to my room after being caught masturbating in the garden, Quirina is waiting in my room with a tray full of tea and pastries.

"Tea. Got anything stronger Rina?" I say, chuckling as I walk over to mix some sugar into the tea.

She eyes me suspiciously, her lips curled upwards into a sly grin.

I look up at her confused. "What?" I ask her.

"What were you doing down in the garden just now?" Her question makes my heart race.

Oh God. Maybe she caught me. Which is still better than that man watching what I was doing.

"How did you know I was just in the garden?" I ask her.

She laughs, making her short black curls bounce. "Well, our favorite handyman was watching you from the window. He looked deeply invested in whatever he saw," she says.

I throw myself onto my bed face down in embarrassment and scream into a pillow.

Quirina just keeps laughing at me, as she comes to sit down on the bed next to me. "Trix, what on earth were you doing that held his attention like that? I mean, he didn't even hear me come into the room. Did something happen with you two?" she asks, her interest piqued.

"Of course not!" I shout, half out of shock and half out of embarrassment from this whole situation. "You know nothing can actually happen with me and any man and him live to tell the tale," I remind her.

"Well, I know that. But you can do other things. I mean if you actually liked each other. You wouldn't have to have sex. You could do… other things. Right?" she asks, and truthfully the thought has never really occurred to me.

Suddenly an image of his face between my legs pops in my head, making me squeeze my legs together.

I shake my head. "No, nothing happened between us. Nothing is going to happen. I am looking for a king to rule with, not a fuck boy toy," I tell her, trying to convince us both that there's nothing I want with him.

She looks entirely too amused. "Oookay. Well, his name is Koen. And that doesn't answer my question. What were you doing in the garden?" she asks for the second time.

I just tried to convince her that I don't want anything to do with *Koen,* so now how am I supposed to tell her I had to go masturbate in the garden after he held me in his arms for .05 seconds? Yeah, I don't want anything to do with him *at all.*

Liar.

Liar.

Liar.

When I don't answer, her eyes widen. "Something *did* happen." She gets up to close my bedroom door, and comes back to sit next to me. "Spill. All of it," she demands.

"Rina," I protest. "It's nothing. Not really."

"Not really? Oh, something happened." Her blue eyes light up so bright they're basically glowing, waiting for my response.

"I just tripped and he caught me. Out of nowhere, he caught me. I was heading right to the floor, and he wasn't anywhere near me and then he appeared and next thing I know I'm in his arms," I say with a smile.

"Did he kiss you?!" she almost shouts.

"Shhh! And no, he despises me. He absolutely did not kiss me, nor did I kiss him," I inform her.

"That man does not hate you," she replies confidently.

"What makes you say that, how would you know?" I question her.

"Well for starters, I saw the way he was watching you, for way too long. He looked very intrigued." She laughs. "And secondly, I told him you had mentioned that he refuses to call you Lady and the look on his face completely shifted," she explains.

I shrug. "Yeah, it was probably a look of fear. Why did you tell him I told you that? Now he's going to think the Princess of Tenuma sits around and talks about him." I facepalm myself.

"But we do," she counters, stifling a laugh.

"Yes, but he didn't need to know that. And you know exactly why," I scold.

She's playing with the silk fabric on my bed, biting her lip while she contemplates whatever it is she wants to say.

"Say it, Rina," I demand.

She sighs heavily. "Don't you think that he might be exactly what you need?" she suggests.

My eyebrows pinch together confused. "What makes you ask that?" I counter.

"Think about it. You claim he can't stand you–yet, you guys have this weird...*heat* between you," she claims.

I gesture a hand, urging her to continue talking.

"You seriously don't get it?" she says exasperated, rolling her eyes. "If all you guys have between you is this *heat*, then maybe a good angry fuck would solve all your problems. For starters, you'd at least get it out of both of your systems."

I cut in. "Rina, my faithful friend, you're forgetting one thing. Every man I have sex with *dies*," I say with a bite to my words.

"Except he doesn't even want what you have to offer. Maybe he's exactly what the curse is after. What if he's the one who survives it?" she speculates.

The question stuns me as I sit back on the bed. I hadn't considered the possibility, mostly because at this point, I'm convinced there won't be a man who will survive it. But also, I'm in shock that others can detect the strange chemistry between me and Koen. I barely recognized it myself.

Liar.

Okay, I definitely noticed it. Felt it. Feel it still. Whatever is going on, I need to reel it in and get it under control. This can only lead to one place.

When I don't respond, she continues. "Look, I'm not trying to push you into doing anything. It just seems different. You seem different. Hell, you avoided your chambers for two entire days while he was here. You spent it downstairs with the king and queen. Don't tell me that was because you were looking for more quality time with them. We both know you can't stand them, and what they've done to you," she reminds me. Quirina is the one person who truly knows the hell I've gone through because of my parents.

I roll my eyes playfully, trying to avoid what we both know to be true. "I was gaining knowledge of the kingdom that I will soon be ruling over," I tell her, unconvincingly.

She rolls her eyes at me, putting her hands on her hips dramatically. We both break out in laughter.

"I'm more interested in talking about how things are going with you and Edwin." I know if there's one way to shift the conversation, it's discussing her love interest. I have yet to meet the guy she can't stop gushing about, but as long as he makes her happy, I'm happy.

Rina's eyes brighten at the mention of his name, and she dramatically sighs. "He is so incredible, Trix. We are meeting up later tonight," she tells me.

Edwin works somewhere in the castle as well, and their romance has been under the radar. It's forbidden for any fraternization to occur within the castle walls between employees, so they've been keeping it between them. Rina tells me everything and I tell her everything, so I've known of their romance since it sprouted about three months ago. They don't get to see each other often, so I know that every chance they get together means a lot to Quirina.

"That's amazing. What are you guys going to do? You know, aside from mauling each other's faces off," I joke.

She laughs giddily. "He said he wanted to take the horses out of town so we could look at the stars. And have privacy, of course." Her eyes look as if she's already picturing her night.

"That sounds so romantic," I say with a bit of despair in my voice.

Quirina grabs my hand. "It will happen for you too. I know it will," she assures me.

I laugh sarcastically. "How? I'm obligated to sleep with every damn man in this town until one of those bastards is strong enough to survive a night with me. It's never going to happen. The evenings barely start with romance. Killing a man nightly isn't exactly what I'd call romance or even dating," I say deadpan.

Quirina bites the corners of her mouth, unsure of how to respond. She has seen firsthand the way I've suffered all these years. She's been there beforehand to help me get through it, and she's always there for me afterwards to pick me back up.

Sure, every once in a while, I enjoy the sex part of it. Maybe that's part of the curse, being addicted to sex. It's a short-lived high. I always know shortly after the man leaves that he will die, and *I'm* the reason why.

Quirina is the one who's always there to pick me back up out of my depression and guilt when it's really bad. By now, I've mostly accepted this life, so I rebound much quicker. But do you ever really learn to accept this sort of life? I think mostly, I've become numb to it.

My best friend deserves to find love and a mate she can share her life with. I guess I just can't help but feel sorry for myself knowing that will never be me.

I shake my head, as if shaking off the lingering sadness. "No, it's okay. This is just how things are right now, and maybe one day, things will be different," I say, forcing an unconvincing smile.

She squeezes my hand. "They will. I just know it," she says smiling back.

The meeting with each suitor usually begins with a dinner at our large dining table with some extravagant meal, and red wine. This way, it gives the illusion of a date and the king and queen can feel less guilty for what they put me through.

Before me, there's a wide variety of meats, cheeses, bread, the creamiest butter from our land, fruits, greens, and wine. The wine is really what I'm focused on. This array of food isn't new to me, but it's always interesting to see the look on each suitor's face when they see the spread. It's clear that seeing this much food out at once isn't something they're used to, and is enough reason for them to make this evening go well. As if they have any control over which way the curse will go.

"Are you enjoying dinner?" I ask the man.

He drops his fork, and it clanks against the plate as I speak. This man seems more nervous than the rest do. Usually the men are quite arrogant, as if they are courting queens in their everyday routines. But not this one. He might not want to be here at all.

"Apologies, Princess. Yes, I am enjoying it greatly. It's all wonderful," he replies, sounding genuine.

Taking a greedy sip from my wine I look him over. He's a very attractive man, which will make the rest of this *date* much more pleasant to get through.

I smile mischievously. I'm already picturing him pinning me down beneath his strong body, and spreading me open. "Good, I'm glad you're enjoying yourself." I take another sip of my wine.

The night usually starts with wine, and then I will switch to whiskey once we move to my chambers. A good buzz is enough to dull whatever angry voice may be lingering beneath the surface. Anger towards my parents, who don't give me a voice and force me to continue these meetings. I could and would happily rule the kingdom on my own. The idea of it was laughable to the king, though. And I've never had the courage to bring it up again.

Once we've finished dinner and we are a bottle and half into the evening, we head upstairs to my chambers.

Now the fun can begin.

I close the door behind us as we enter. "Pour us a couple of whiskeys, I will be right back," I tell the man, and head to my bathroom to change.

I slip out of my tight blue dress, and as it slips down my body and for just a moment, I remember being in the garden and looking up to see Koen watching me. The thought sends a shiver down my body. I can't seem to keep my thoughts off of him for long, and it's becoming a habit.

I put on black lacy panties, and throw on my silk robe overtop. There's really no point in dressing up, but I do still like to feel sexy. I like to believe that the more confident I feel, that maybe it will be enough for me to feel comfortable and secure while I'm having sex with these men and maybe the curse will spare them. *Maybe.*

As I exit the bathroom, I see the room is now only lit by candlelight, and the man sits at the edge of my bed holding two glasses of whiskey, one arm outstretched to hand me one as I head towards him.

"Thank you." I take the glass, and just as I'm lifting it to my lips, his words stop me.

"Should we make a *cheers* to something?" he asks more confidently than he seemed at dinner. Maybe it's the bottle of wine we went through or maybe it's because there aren't a handful of serving staff and guards nearby listening to our conversation.

It makes me pause, as I lower the glass. "Sure…" I reply.

"Here's to the future, whatever it may hold," the man states confidently.

My eyebrows pinch together just for a moment, as I think what a strange toast for him to make.

I'm fairly certain I know what your future holds, I think.

We drain our glasses and pour another when he finally makes his move. I never like to be the one to initiate, in case the man wants to change his mind, I don't want to feel like I forced anyone into this situation—much like I have been.

I wonder if anybody knows I'm being forced to do this.

Do they believe I enjoy sex so much that I happily do this, regardless of it killing men?

He starts by running his fingers up my leg, slipping his hand up under the lace hem of my robe. It opens slightly, opening up to reveal my bare stomach and black lacy underwear.

He sucks in a breath and then sets his glass on the ground beside the bed. He tries to take mine, but I finish it off and then hand it to him. He sets mine on the ground next to his, and then moves until his body is over mine. He unties the string, and slowly pulls both sides of the robe open revealing the hard peaks of my breasts.

The whiskey is coursing through my blood, making it warm and fuzzy. It feels so good, and it's making me crave something even more.

I pull the man on top of me, as my hands start roaming his

chest and back. I pull him closer to me, but I don't see his face.

I see the rugged, sharp-tongued man who despises me, but also watched me masturbate from the very windows in here. I see Koen. I picture him, and I can almost smell his soapy, woodsy scent. It pulls a soft moan of yearning from me.

The man takes it as a cue to move forward and he cups my breast in one hand as his mouth moves over my hard nipple. His tongue flicks my nipple, and he sucks softly, earning another moan from me. Lifting his mouth, he moves up towards my face and tries to kiss me on the mouth, but I quickly turn my face away and he goes for my neck instead.

It may seem laughable, but I don't kiss any of these men. It feels too intimate. I may not have any choice in who I have sex with, but this is something I have control over. I can choose not to kiss any of these men. There has never been a man who made me want to. It's my small act of rebellion, and I want to save my kisses for the man I will love and marry. The one who will become my mate, and my king. I want to save that passion for him.

As the man kisses and sucks on my neck, my back starts to arch slightly, pulling me closer to his body. I push him off of me and as I sit on the edge of the bed with him standing in front of me breathing heavily, his eyes heavy, I start to undo his belt. I un-buckle it, and slide his dress pants down, along with his trousers.

Underneath, I find his dick hard and eager to play. He quickly steps out of his clothing, and I wrap my mouth around his cock. I take as much of it as I can in my mouth. It touches the back of my throat, and then I pull it back out again and do it over and over until I'm gagging and covered in saliva.

We are both moaning when he grabs the back of my head and starts fucking my mouth as I'm on my knees in front of him and I feel myself getting wetter and wetter.

Finally, he pulls out of my mouth. I rise from my knees, and he gently pushes me backwards onto the bed. He slips my panties down my legs, and tosses them on the ground. His hands each grab a knee and he slowly pushes my legs apart, as he savors spreading me open. He positions himself between my legs, his hand gently caressing my pussy.

His eyes go wide, as he finds how wet I am. "You like doing that?" he asks quietly.

"Yes," I say confidently. There may not be a lot of things I'm allowed to do in my life, but this is one and I enjoy it. I try to enjoy it anyway.

He likes my answer and as he removes his hand from my pussy, he places his dick at my entrance. He tries to go in for another kiss, which I deny a second time, turning my head and exposing my neck. This earns a confused grin, but he proceeds. He gives me a soft peck, and then a bite as he thrusts inside me.

"Ahhh," I gasp, as he pushes inside my pussy, stretching me, making me feel full.

He thrusts in and out, slow at first and then faster as my nails dig into his back.

Koen. I think.

His face fills my head as my eyes are closed, and I can't escape it. His gray eyes are haunting me, and it's both terrifying and intoxicating. I both fear and crave him. I can't stop picturing him when I'm having sex. I can't stop picturing him when I want to have sex. He is always on my mind.

As the man continues to fuck me, going harder and getting closer and closer to his orgasm, I start rubbing circles on my clit, climbing with him. We are both chasing that high, and as I'm about to come, I picture Koen's strong arms around me. I can almost feel him against me, and that's my undoing.

The man pulls out as he reaches climax, and explodes all over my stomach and breasts, and then falls on his back next to me, breathing heavily.

We both lay there for a moment, coming down from our highs, ecstasy coursing through our veins.

Koen.

"Koen was wrong. There's no way something can feel that good and be bad," he mumbles as he lays next to me, breathing heavily.

My head jerks up at Koen's name. I sit up on my elbows and look over at him.

"What did you say?" I ask firmly.

His head turns towards me. "My friend Koen tried to talk me out of coming here. Told me you were the devil or something. But there's no way it can feel like this with everyone. This was… wow," he says, putting one hand to his forehead.

I am in complete shock right now, that this man knows Koen and is bringing him up right now. "You're friends with Koen?" I repeat back.

"Yeah. He told me I would never survive it. But–" he starts, but I cut him off.

I stand quickly and cover myself up immediately. "Why did you come here? You need to leave right now!" I shout at him.

He's sitting up on the bed confused now. "What? Why?"

I throw his clothes at him. "I didn't realize you were friends with him. You need to leave right now," I beg.

"What does he have to do with this? Look, it's fine. He was clearly wrong. I didn't mean to upset you." He comes towards me as if he can comfort me, or fix what's about to happen.

I put both hands up in front of me to stop him from coming closer. "You didn't upset me. Look, I just didn't realize you two were friends, I wouldn't have…" I pause looking for how to explain this and then realize it doesn't matter because he won't be alive long enough to make sense of it anyway. "You need to go. Your friend was absolutely right. You shouldn't have come here," I state.

"I don't understand," he tells me.

I sigh. "I know, and that's why you shouldn't have come here tonight."

He finishes getting dressed and I all but shove him out of my bedroom, slamming the door shut and locking it behind me.

I fucked up, I think. That man thinks I'm the devil as it is and now, I've just killed his friend. Who knows how many other friends of his I've killed? No wonder he hates me. I wanted him to continue disliking me, but this isn't what I had in mind. I don't exactly know why it bothers me, as I barely know him. All I know is, it makes me feel sick.

I run to the bathroom and immediately throw up.

10

KOEN

Reluctantly, I force myself to get up the next morning after very little sleep. All I could think of all night was my poor, stupid friend Landric. He seemed so confident, so sure that this would work and yet, he came to say his goodbyes. I won't ever understand it. There are plenty of girls with beautiful faces he could have made a life with. But for him, it wasn't about the girl. It was about what she had to offer. It was the lifestyle and the comfort of security it would provide.

The sun is just starting to rise, but I want to make sure I make some breakfast for my mother and Mellani before I go hunting for the day. I never know how long I will be gone, just as I never know if I'll be returning with anything.

I cut up a few potatoes and mix in some onion and the remainder of a bell pepper we have. I fry this up on the stove and scramble a few eggs for both my mom and sister. I cut a few pieces of bread, and lay it out with the butter and some jam. I'm just finishing up when I hear Mellani's small feet coming up behind me.

I turn just as I see her tripping over my cot. She lands on

her hands and knees and whatever she was holding goes crashing on the floor. I put down the plate I was holding and go over to help her up, realizing that what she dropped is more money than I've seen all year.

I kneel down beside her as she frantically picks up the coins. "Where did you get all of this?" I demand her to tell me.

Her eyes go wide with worry. "I fo–"

She starts to tell me she found all of this on the street in town again, but I shake my head and cut her off. "No. There's not a chance in hell that somebody happened to misplace *this much* money. Now, tell me the truth. Did you steal this, Mel?" I ask her softer than my previous tone.

She stares at the floor, looking hesitant to tell me.

I lift her chin with my fingers. "Hey, I'm not mad. I just don't like when you lie. You can tell me anything, sweet girl. You know that, right?" I ask her softly, now feeling remorseful at the harsh tone I took with her.

She slowly lifts her head, nodding yes. She goes to hand me all the coins she has in her hands but there are still many strewn about the floor.

"Where did this come from?" I ask again.

"She told me not to tell anyone," Mellani says so softly it's almost a whisper.

"*Who* told you not to tell?" I ask her.

She shrugs. "The lady with the money," she states as if it's somebody I should know based on that description.

I look at her confused, still crouched down to the floor. "What lady with the money? Who is she? Has she given you money before?" I ask her.

She nods.

"What do you have to do in order to get the money?" I ask, my stomach slowly turning to acid at the thought of any adult taking advantage of my baby sister. Nobody in all of Tenuma is that selfless—or blessed with enough money—to give away this kind of money.

Her head shakes hurriedly. "Nothing. She just comes sometimes and gives me money. Me and the other kids."

I eye her suspiciously, not sure what to make of the story.

Who would have that kind of money?

And who would come and give it away to a bunch of kids in the middle of town?

"Thank you for telling me the truth. I'm going to hold onto all of this for now. I think there's been a misunderstanding. I want to make sure whoever gave this to you doesn't need it back, okay?" I tell her softly, bracing myself for a fit.

"Okay!" she says chipper, and hops up and over to the table to eat her breakfast.

I shake my head at the way she bounces back so quickly. Even when she's being a pain in the ass, she makes me smile.

My mother and I join Mellani at the table and we eat our breakfast as we listen to the birds starting to wake outside. The fire crackles in the room, keeping it slightly warmer than it would be otherwise. All I can think about is this mysterious *lady with money* who seems to know my baby sister.

"Hey, mom. Did you see anybody talking with Mellani when you went into town the other day?" I ask once Mellani has left to get washed up.

"No, why do you ask?" she responds to me, finishing up the last bite of her breakfast.

"She keeps coming home with money. You didn't wonder where it came from?" I ask her.

"She said she found it." As if it explains why we have more than four times what we see in a year just laying on our countertop.

I need to find a safe spot for this before we get robbed, I think.

"Mother, did you see how much she had?" I get up and scoop up all the coins from the counter holding them out for my mother to see. "There's no way somebody misplaced this much money. She told me that some lady gave it to her," I say sitting back down next to her, on one of the creaky wooden chairs.

Her eyes go wide at the amount of money I just placed in front of her. "Did she say who?" she asks me.

"No. She doesn't seem to know. Just some 'money lady.' It seems weird, right?" I ask her.

Mother waves me off. "Oh honey, you think everybody's up to something. All the time."

I give my mom a cynical expression. "Well, they usually are. My mistrust for people has kept us safe, hasn't it? I have to be on guard all the time because people are not trustworthy." We might be talking about this mysterious woman, but my mother doesn't miss the reference to my father. It's not hard to see that my mistrust stems from the fact that we couldn't trust our own family member.

Her hand comes up to caress my cheek. "Yes. I suppose you're right, my son. But it's also kept people out. There are still good people out there. They're not all bad," she tells me sweetly.

I roll my eyes at her. "Yeah? Like dad?"

She flinches, pulling her hand back, not saying anything. I've upset her, which isn't my intention at all. I'm trying to make a point as to why I don't trust many people. Plus, maybe I'm a little on edge today because of the visit from Landric last night.

"Look, I'm sorry. I love you. I'm going to be out hunting today. The forest has been pretty scarce, but I want to make sure we are set for at least a few days, so I'll probably be gone for the day. Please don't spend any of that money until we figure out who it's from. The last thing we need is to be indebted to some sick monster," I say to her.

She nods, forcing a smile. "Okay. Be safe." Her hand caresses my face once more and then she gets up to check on Mellani.

I'm gathering my hunting equipment and getting my boots on when Mellani comes out and sees me.

"You're leaving? Are you going to the castle?" Her inquisitive mind never slows down. I love that about her.

"Not today, sweetheart. I'm going hunting. I will be back, but it will be pretty late," I tell her so she knows not to wait up for me.

"When do you go back to the castle? Will you see the princess? Is she as beautiful as they say?" She fires off question after question.

More beautiful, I think, but never dare to say aloud. Because as beautiful as she might be, she's a murdering monster.

"Sweet girl, *you* are beautiful. You're more beautiful than any princess ever could be," I tell her.

She giggles. "I want to be a princess someday," she says.

I want to roll my eyes, because in Tenuma, being a princess isn't as glamorous as it appeals to little girls. In Tenuma, it creates selfish monsters.

"You, my sweet girl, will be better than any princess that has ever lived." I ruffle her brown curls and kiss the top of her head. "I will see you later," I assure her.

"You promise?" she asks because she always asks.

"With my life," I promise her.

I'm making my way through the forest, knowing that the

deeper I go, the better my odds are of finding any wild game. The day is overcast and cold with a storm brewing nearby. It could be here tomorrow, but I should be okay for the day. I take in the crispness of the air, the softness of the untouched snow underneath my feet. The soft snow mutes my footsteps, increasing my odds of finding a kill.

As hard as life can be in Tenuma, it's hard to think of anywhere else as home. It's such a beautiful place, and when I am away from the forest for too long, I forget. I forget how wonderful it is here, and I become resentful. I resent being here, where kings and queens squeeze families for every dime they have, to add to their pile of wealth. Where there's a princess who slaughters men in her free time and tosses them from the castle. It's easy to forget how wonderful it is, especially when I've been trapped inside that castle with her.

I've always been pulled to the forest. I can't explain it, but something in me has always craved being surrounded by the beautiful endless trees. It feels safe and it feels familiar. When I come back to the forest, I feel at peace. I can let go of what happened with my father, with Landric, and the princess. I can leave it all on the edge of the forest, and come here and finally breathe.

Typically, I leave here with a rabbit, maybe two if I get really lucky. But on a really good day, I'll cross paths with a deer. A deer can feed us for more than two weeks, if I store it right. We can make stews from it, chilis, jerky, and meat patties with potatoes–if we have them. There's so much more we can do with deer meat, and we prefer the taste over rabbit, but it's been a few months since I have seen one so I'm hoping after the long week I've had at the castle, that luck will be in my favor today.

I have the best odds of finding a deer earlier in the day. Once afternoon hits, I will have to wait until close to sunset before I'm likely to come across one. I'd rather not be out when the mountain lions come out to hunt for themselves. Usually they don't bother us, but with food being so slim, it's not just the humans that suffer. We are all just trying to survive.

My bow and arrow is strapped to my back, and I have several knives that I might need. In my backpack, I have several bottles of water and a few snacks as I don't know how long I will be away. I can't take myself all the way back home just because I get hungry or thirsty. Although with how cold it is out here, the water might freeze before I can get to it. I'm dressed in several layers, despite the cold not affecting me as much as others. I like to be prepared for anything. If you're not smart, it's easy to get lost out here and wind up wandering the forest for days before you're either found or you can find your way back. Having spent so much time in these woods all my life, I know them like I know the back of my hand, but survival is not something I take my chances with.

As I slowly creep further into the woods, I stop to listen. Hoping to hear the crunch or crackle of any branches or bushes. I listen for any type of footsteps or any animal calls.

It's silent. Not even the wind blows. The snow mutes all sounds, and the silence is almost deafening. The dark clouds are moving in overhead, though it's harder to see now through the density of the lush trees. I've always thought it's incredible that even through the harshest of winters, our trees stay green and full. Despite the elements beating them down and trying to force them to change, the trees manage to hold onto their beauty.

A few hours later, as I'm observing my surroundings, sitting as still as I can next to a tree that had a bare spot under it, I hear the first noise. I instinctively go for the bow and arrow on my back, preparing to load my arrow should a deer reveal itself.

Out of the corner of my eye, I see movement but by the time I shift my eyes to the direction it came from, it's gone. I strain my ears to listen for more movement, not daring to move just yet. Sometimes I sit out here for so long that I start to imagine seeing movement in the forest. But I know I saw something. Something large. It looked much larger than a deer would be.

And faster.

I am about to put my arrow away thinking I imagined it, when suddenly, there's a flurry of commotion and noise. It's all happening so fast. I see a large, dark figure moving in the distance ahead of me–so large that I can't figure out what it is. Before I have time to figure it out, it takes off through the trees.

It's chasing something much smaller than itself. I hear shrieking, growling, stomping of feet or paws maybe. I don't know what it's chasing, but all I know is something that large is way too close to the edge of the forest and I don't want it coming closer to terrorize the town.

Before I have time to wonder what it might be, I'm raising both arms cradling my bow and arrow firm and precise. I start running towards the large animal, the trees getting denser, and the light becoming less and less.

I pull my arm back, and just as I release the bow, I watch it float through the air and I hear a woman's scream. And then I hear something heavy hit the ground.

11

BELLATRIX

I'm screaming into a pillow on my oversized bed when I hear a knock at the door. The sun is barely up, and I already need to get out of here. Last night did not go how I thought it would. It should have just been another fuck-capade with some poor schmuck who doesn't know how to keep his dick in his pants.

But it wasn't just some random guy though, it was Koen's guy. One of his friends. And as much as I need him to despise me, I'm now scared he might try and kill me. The rest of the land is either too terrified of my family and I or they blindly admire me. But not Koen. He's the only man who's ever challenged me in any way, and the only man I'm a little scared of. He doesn't fear me, he hates me. I definitely didn't need to add any gasoline to that fire.

As much as I want to ignore the knocking, I'd know that knock anywhere. I sit upright, pulling the satin sheets and heavy blanket up to my waist, and tucking my long black hair behind my ears.

"Come in," I say loudly.

The heavy door creaks open slowly and Quirina peeks inside.

"Are you okay?" she asks tenderly. She's always here to check on me the day after I meet with a suitor.

I shrug, pulling my bottom lip into my mouth to keep from crying. "I don't know," I reply simply.

"What happened? I came by late last night to check on you and I could hear you crying. I wanted to give you some space but…what happened?" she asks, rubbing my leg delicately over the blanket.

My eyes well up, thinking about the man whose life I took last night. It's not like it's something new that occurred, it's the fact that it got personal. I never know who these men are. I don't know anything about their lives. I don't have to think about them having friends or a family who might miss them, who might need them. This was different. Koen was his friend.

My thoughts tortured me all night.

What did they do for fun?

Did their families know each other?

Were they close?

Did he know how much Koen despises me?

What will Koen say or do when he realizes what I've done?

Wiping the tears away from under my eyes, I shake my head in frustration. "I can't do this anymore, Rina. Why won't they let me stop? This can't be the only way, it doesn't make sense. I can't keep doing this to people." I'm sobbing now.

"I know. I am so sorry. You know if I had any say, I'd do what I could. But nobody would ever listen to a handmaiden. What was it about last night that changed things?" she asks tenderly.

"It was his friend," I say, but clarify when she looks at me with a confused expression. "Koen. He was friends with Koen," I say, wiping away the tears running down my face.

"Oh," Quirina responds softly.

"I don't even know why it bothers me so much. He hates me, and now he'll probably just kill me. Which would be best for everybody. I won't be able to keep taking men's lives."

"Don't say that!" She scolds me. "You're my best friend, and you're a good person. *This–*" She gestures around the room where these atrocities occur. "Is not your doing. It's not who you really are. You don't have any say over this. You didn't ask for this curse and you have tried to make it stop," she reminds me.

She's right, but it doesn't eliminate the guilt, or the way I feel about myself. I squeeze her hand. "Thank you. It just feels like this is never going to end."

"Well, what happens if your father dies and you still don't have a mate? You'd be ruling without a mate anyway, right? Why can't they just let you do that now?" Quirina inquires.

"No. I won't get the throne. It will go to the male heir from another land," I say bitterly.

"No, that cannot happen," she exclaims.

"I know, but there's not much I can do about it. This curse prevents me from just choosing a mate on my own. I can't just pick one and move on. But the quicker I try to find my mate, the more men that die. I don't know what to do anymore," I reply, defeated.

Quirina quietly takes in all the information I've just given her. She knew the gist of my curse, but she didn't know I had the possibility of losing the throne. Especially to some of the cruelest known rulers. Our land would more than likely end up in the hands of the King of Sperantia. This would be bad for everybody in Tenuma. While my father isn't known for being a sympathetic and just ruler, he is a saint compared to their king.

The kingdom staff would most likely all be killed and replaced with people from their own land–which is what they did when they took over their most recent land–and the poverty would only get worse. As much as my father is strict and greedy, it's nothing compared to what other lands implement. He's kind by comparison.

"Putting that aside," Quirina slowly starts. "The fact that you sort of knew this one man from last night, do you think it's worth continuing?" she asks.

"I don't have a choice," I reply harshly, getting up and walking towards the bathroom.

"Where are you going?" she asks.

I turn around facing her, leaning against the doorway with one hand raking through my hair. "I have to get out of here. I need to clear my head. I'm going to head into town. You got me?" I ask.

"I've got your back, girl. Always," she replies with a forced smile.

I give a half smile back, and turn around to jump in the shower. I think going to town would provide some valuable perspective. Plus, I still owe that little girl the medicine I promised her. I'm going to focus on what I can control. I can help the people of our land this way, so this is what I will do.

Quirina aids me in sneaking out of the castle again, along with helping me get my hands on the medicine for that sweet little girl. I placed it in one of my glass vials that I usually use for new perfumes, but I had a few unused ones so I figured it would be the perfect way to get it out, in case I was caught. It wouldn't look good if I was sneaking off and was found with medicine in my pockets. I'm not supposed to be going off to town by myself anyway, my parents claim that it could be dangerous.

Which, I'm sure it might be but mostly, I think it's just another way for them to control me.

My long black hair is pulled into one side braid, and I have on my oversized black cloak over a long sleeve skin-tight black bodysuit, and black water-resistant boots. It's not exactly incognito but it won't draw attention once I'm in town. I pocket the vial of medicine and a bunch of coins I plan to hand out to the kids as I usually do, and then I'm off.

There's a storm brewing overhead and will most likely hit later this evening so the day is much colder than it has been earlier in the week. It makes me wish I had thrown on an extra layer of clothing before leaving. I usually run very cold, but I'm still sorting through all of my emotions from last night and this morning, so the brisk air isn't bothering me too much.

The little girl sees me before I see her and comes running up to me like she usually does with her bright enthusiasm.

"Hi!" she says loudly as she buries her face into my side as she hugs me. She pulls back, covering her face as she has a mini coughing fit. It hurts my heart. I don't know why she's taken such a liking to me, and me to her, but I feel connected to her. I feel protective over her.

"Hi, sweet girl! I'm so glad you're here, I brought you something," I tell her eagerly.

"Oh. I can't take money anymore," she says embarrassed.

I'm about to pull the vial out of my pocket when her comment stops me. "Wait. What do you mean? Why not?" I ask her.

"My, umm… dad took the money you gave to me and said that we can't use it. He seemed angry. He doesn't want me taking money from other people," she tells me sadly.

As much as I want to be annoyed that I'm risking my own life to help her and her family, just for them to reject it…I understand. I can only imagine what her father is thinking. He probably thinks I'm some pervert who makes her do things for money in return. The thought makes my skin crawl. All I wanted was to do something good. Be a part of making someone's life easier.

"That's okay. You didn't tell him where you got it, did you?" I ask worriedly.

Her foot kicks around in the dirt underneath our feet, sniffling. "Sort of," she replies.

"What do you mean, sweetie?" I ask softly. I don't want her to think she's in trouble, but I am getting a little worried at this point.

"I told him it was the money lady with the tattoo," she says smiling, pointing to my wrist.

I can't help but chuckle, because I don't know why I was so worried. She doesn't know who I am, and I must be one of a thousand women here who have an arm tattoo. I let out a breath in relief. "Okay, sweetie. That's fine, but I still want you to have this," I tell her, pulling out the vial of medicine.

She coughs into the crook of her elbow, her eyes watering, and then reaches out for the vial I'm handing her. "What is it?" she asks inquisitively.

"The medicine I promised you, silly. I want you to feel better. I hate seeing you sick, it makes me so sad," I tell her, crouching down to her level. "See, you will take this much of this," I say pointing to the lines I made on the bottle to indicate how much to take at a time. "Each night until it's gone. You should feel so much better in a few days."

She looks up at me with those big, beautiful eyes. "Thank you. We never have medicine. Will it taste bad?" she asks, worried.

I laugh at her innocence. I love that her biggest worry is whether medicine will taste bad or not. "No, sweetie. I made sure to get the one that tastes good. It should taste like fruit." I try to assure her she has nothing to worry about.

"Yum!" she says and then coughs into her sleeve again.

"Are you sure you don't want to take just a little of the money just in case your dad changes his mind or you might need it?" I ask her. I want so badly for her to take the money. Knowing that she's been sick for a few weeks, and she's yet to have taken any medicine makes my heart ache. I hate thinking that the families here suffer like this.

"Um, I don't know. I don't want to get in trouble," she says anxiously.

"Okay, okay. I don't want you to get into trouble either, sweetie. I just want you to know that I only ever want to help. I would never ask anything of you. You know that, right?" I question her, my eyes welling up. I can't help but think that if her family did realize it was the princess helping that they'd have even more concern.

"Yeah…" she replies shyly.

"Hey, I mean it. I just want to make sure you have enough food in your belly," I say playfully poking at her little tummy. "And medicine so you're healthy. Take this home and make sure you don't forget to drink this to the line before bed," I tell her.

I worry that her family will find it and throw it away before she gets the chance to. Even though I don't like making her hide things from her parents, this is something I can feel good about. If she has to tell a few white lies to have medicine and money for food for her family, so be it. Sometimes, it's not the act that determines whether something is good or bad, but the intention behind it.

She giggles when I poke her tummy, and then nods in understanding. "Okay, I'll remember," she tells me.

I give her a tight hug and say goodbye so I have time to give money to the other kids in town. Just as I'm turning away from her, I see the lady with the bracelets gazing at me intensely from her table alongside the other merchants. She's giving me a strange, mysterious look and I don't know if she's here with the little girl I adore or if she recognizes me. Either way, I don't think it's in my best interests to stick around and find out.

I duck my head, and quickly head in the other direction, heading for the rest of the children playing by the fountain. I do a quick circle around the fountain, discreetly placing all of the coins down on the ledge of the fountain and on the ground in front of it for them to find. I walk away to the sound of squeals and cheers as the children start to find the coins. I smile as I make my way out of town.

As I get further from the busy downtown streets, I can't help but feel like I'm still being watched. The eerie feeling makes me pick up my pace, so I can make it back to the castle quickly. Where I'm safe and protected.

This is why you must continue. You wouldn't last a day out here. I can't help but think, my father's words flooding my head.

Maybe he's right. Maybe I've been too sheltered, and I wouldn't survive outside of the castle without food and security being handed to me. Some days I can convince myself I don't need the comfort of the castle. If other people can do it, so can I. But moments like right now—when I feel like I'm being watched and followed—make me feel like I have no fucking clue what I'm talking about.

The quicker I move my feet, the more scared I get. I hear footsteps behind me, so I start going down different streets in an attempt to lose whoever is trailing me. I don't want to lead them straight back to the castle and remove all doubt that I'm the princess. I start making every turn that I can, just trying to lose them. It backfires and I end up confusing myself.

Getting myself lost and still feeling the eyes of someone boring into my back, I start to panic. I'm fleeing town and getting lost in the process. I have to get back to the castle, but I also cannot lead a stalker there. I see the forest up ahead and start to run towards the trees.

Just as I'm picking up speed, I feel a breeze blow past and see an arrow shoot into the tree ahead of me to my left. Someone's trying to kill me.

I let out an involuntary scream and run even faster. As soon as I enter the trees, I quickly sneak a glance behind me and see a man dressed not unlike myself, still aiming his bow and arrow at me, but not coming any closer. The man has piercing gray eyes, so light they're almost silver. They look like snake eyes, and it makes my skin crawl. He isn't somebody I recognize, so why is he trying to kill me? I let out another shriek, and head further into the trees to hide.

It's freezing in the forest, as the trees provide such a dense covering from the sun and the sky. It has to be at least twenty degrees colder here. I'm running, my cheeks and lips getting wind-chapped when finally, I'm out of breath and need to stop. I'm panicked, and freezing so my teeth are chattering and all I can think is that the noise from my teeth will be the cause of my death. I find the largest nearby tree and squat down behind it, my eyes glued to the entrance of the forest from which I just came.

I strain my ears to listen for any sound. I listen for breathing, walking, crunching, or the subtle sound of a bow being placed and pulled back. I don't hear anything. I'm terrified to look up and see those cold gray eyes staring in my direction.

Still struggling to quiet my teeth chattering, I slowly rise using the tree for cover, doing a full rotation to take in my full surroundings before I move. That's when I hear it.

Why do I hear growling?

Why does it sound so close?

I look up to see something dark and giant with wings and sharp teeth gazing down at me from the trees. I can't make out what the creature is, but every fiber in my body knows it will bring harm to me. Before I can even tell myself to run, my feet are moving. I take off even further into the forest and I feel the ground violently shake. As I glance back, I can see that whatever creature was in the tree is now on the ground chasing me at full speed, and is much, much bigger than I originally thought.

What the hell is that? I think.

My legs are burning from trudging through the thick snow on the ground, my lungs are on fire from my panicked breathing, and these could be my last thoughts. I'm living a life I'm not in control of, only to be killed by some creature in the forest. I've never even really lived.

I don't know how far I've run, and I'm too scared to look back. I can still hear the creature behind me and coming in fast. Just as I feel my legs are about to give out, I hear the whoosh of an arrow and hear the creature groan and squeal in pain which only makes me react equally terrified.

I scream a blood curdling scream before I trip over a branch hidden by snow and faceplant in the snow. I bury my face in my arms, bracing to be eaten. Whatever creature was chasing me has slammed into the ground not far behind me causing the ground to shake once more. Whatever is behind me is bigger than anything I've ever seen.

Don't look, don't look. Get up and run, Bellatrix, I tell myself. But I can't move, I'm frozen with fear. Maybe if I pretend to be dead, it will leave me be. I can't be much of a meal to a monster that size. But I know I need to get up and run, because something out here will make a meal of me, even if this thing doesn't.

I hear the running of feet and it only makes me press my face harder into my arms attempting to hide. Though, I'm wearing all black in a sea of white snow, so I'm not blending into a damn thing.

Just as I convince myself I'm going to die out here, I hear the last thing I expect to hear.

"Princess?" Koen says out of breath.

My head jerks up at Koen's voice, he looks confused and panicked.

"W-what are you doing? How are you here right now?" I ask flustered, relieved, scared, grateful.

"Uh, Princess. We need to go. Now," he states calmly, but firmly.

I twist my head around to where I heard the creature chasing me. It's not a creature at all. It's a monster from my nightmares and it's right in front of us.

"Is that…?" I ask as he pulls me up by my arm and drags me away running.

"Yep. It's a dragon. Run, Princess," he answers expressionlessly.

The dragon is on its side, but not dead. It's struggling to yank out or break the arrow that's in its chest with one of its wings. It looks angry and it sees exactly where we are standing. Once it gets back up, we won't get another chance to escape. There's no way we will outrun a dragon.

I run as quickly as my legs will allow, following Koen through the forest. He looks like he's heading further into the thick of it, towards the mountains.

I yell over the loud scuffing of our feet. "We need to head back to town!"

Without looking back at me he replies. "Sure, Princess, you can go back and let that thing eat you."

I roll my eyes at his sarcasm. Even in a life and death situation, he can't even pretend he doesn't hate me. Although, he could have left me there to die, so why did he come over to pick me up and drag me away?

"Koen!" I yell once I hear the dragon get to its feet and start racing towards us.

"Keep running!" he shouts.

Suddenly, we hear a roaring that doesn't come from either of our shrieks, and it doesn't come from the dragon chasing us. All of us stop, for just a second, to listen to where the growing noise is coming from. That's when we see it, an avalanche of snow coming down the mountain in front of us at a speed quicker than we can outrun. Realization hits that I've managed to escape a dragon, just to be pummeled to death by an avalanche of snow.

Koen glances back at me, and grabs my hand before yanking me off my feet into his arms and pressed against his chest. The bracelet on my wrist feels like it's pulsing along with my heartbeat, causing goosebumps to form up my arm. For just a second, I forget we're about to die. But I snap out of it, when Koen takes off running with me in his arms.

12

 KOEN

The bracelet on my wrist tingles as I cradle the princess in my arms, running from not one, but two elements attempting to kill us both. I don't know what it is about being in the presence of Princess Bellatrix, but every time I am near her, the bracelet my mother forced me to wear seems to tingle like a beacon. Or a warning.

Regardless of my personal issues with the princess, I'm not a man who can sit back and watch her be killed. Which is exactly what would have happened. She can't run very fast apparently, so it's a miracle that the dragon didn't kill her when it had the chance. The avalanche coming our way would have swallowed her whole.

I take off towards the bottom of the mountain, as I know of several caves nearby. I spend plenty of time in these woods and I know various spots to hide out if need be. I like to be prepared, unlike my current travel companion. I don't know how she'd survive a single day out here on her own. She almost didn't.

What is she doing out here alone in the woods? I think.

We make it to the cave entrance, and I set the princess

down. I rush inside, only to look back and see her still standing at the entrance.

"What are you doing?" I ask her like I'm scolding a toddler.

"I can't go in there. I'm not even supposed to be out of the castle," she replies panicked.

"That won't matter when you're dead. Get inside. That snow will cover this entire area in about fifteen seconds," I shout, stunned that she's even questioning coming inside where she will be safe.

Maybe it's me she's afraid of. I think, but then immediately shoo the thought away, because if anyone should be afraid, it's me. I'll be stuck inside this damn cave, snowed in with the Soul Snatcher.

As the rumbling gets louder, she runs inside and towards the back of the cave just before the entire entrance is covered entirely with snow, making it pitch black.

Even though I can't see her face, I can't resist the jab. "Still wish you'd stayed outside with a dragon?" I criticize, as silence once again takes over.

She doesn't respond.

I pull a light globe from the side pocket of my backpack. It's small, but it manages to create enough light that we can both see our surroundings. As it illuminates the cave, I see her sitting on the ground at the back of the cave, clearly defeated. She looks worn out and worried.

Her hair is to the side in a braid that's coming undone, and her porcelain skin is now pink and red as she's cold and flushed from the snow and adrenaline. She starts to shiver, and pulls her knees up to her chest wrapping both arms around them.

Having spent so much time out here, I stash things in a handful of caves in case a situation like this ever arises, but it hasn't. Not this kind, anyway… not until now. I've been chased by mountain lions before though and had to hide out for one very long night. But this time, my provisions will prove to have been a smart move.

Opposite to where the princess sits, I have a large bag underneath a tarp. This cave keeps the elements out, but it's still moist and it's better to try and protect what I can in case a storm comes and makes its way inside. I pull off the tarp that was held down with large rocks, and open the bag.

I have a shovel standing against the wall of the cave, a large canister of water, a few light globes, jerky, nuts, and a small blanket that I'd use as a pillow. My internal temperature stays high at all times, so I rarely have use for a blanket. I can't say the same for the shivering princess across from me.

"Here." I toss the blanket at her.

She takes it without looking up at me. "Thanks," she replies, sounding clipped, as she unfolds it and wraps it around herself.

She watches me pulling the items from the backpack with curiosity. "Why do you have all these things here? Is this where you live?" she asks, her eyes going wide.

I chuckle humorlessly. Of course, a princess would think that anyone who isn't royalty should be living in a cave. "No, this is not where I live. I live at my home in town, with my family," I reply harshly.

"Oh. I just… you have all these things here," she hesitantly responds, understanding that she has insulted me. Usually, she seems so high and mighty. It seems like she's on some sort of pedestal that nobody can ever reach. But right now, in this cave she seems softer, somehow. Vulnerable in a way I never thought she'd portray. Maybe it's because I just saved her life. Maybe it's because she isn't putting on some prissy act for everyone around.

"I like to be prepared." Is the only explanation I give her.

Her eyebrows raise and her lips purse out in a look that says, *"Alright, pal, I was just asking."* I may be stuck here with her, but after what she's done, there's no way I'm going to suddenly be her friend. She's still a snake and a murderer. She killed my friend. Had I known it was her laying in the snow, I may not have been as quick to run over as I had been.

You would have run faster, and you know it. You were never planning on leaving her behind, my inner monologue taunts.

Assuming the dragon is still outside nearby, wanting to kill us both for both revenge and a hearty meal, I know we'll be staying here overnight. If the dragon got away, which its chances were much greater than our own, it might still be out there waiting or looking for us nearby. I don't want to risk escaping, just to be that monster's dinner.

Dragons. There are actual real-life dragons here. All my life, it's been known that dragons used to live amongst our people, but they haven't been seen for thousands of years. After the last great war among all of the lands, where dragons were used as both transportation and weapons, most of them were killed. The rest were unable to breed, and died out. Or so legends say. Apparently, there's still at least one on Tenuma. The princess probably knew. It's probably her pet that got off its leash, maybe that's why she was here.

"Did you know there were dragons here? Does that thing belong to you, Princess?" I interrogate.

Her head snaps up from where it was laying on her knees. "What?" she says softly, maybe I woke her from sleeping.

"I asked if that was your pet dragon, Princess," I repeat.

She sits up straighter now. "You know, you're the only one in all of Tenuma not to speak to me formally. Some might see that as a sign of disrespect," she retorts.

"I just saved you from a dragon and an avalanche, some might call you ungrateful," I snap back.

Her shoulder tense as she contemplates what to say back to me. I pretend to make myself busy, rearranging my supplies so I don't have to sit here and look into her glowing, angry eyes. She always manages to look both intimidating and sultry all at once. I suppose that's the alluring part of the curse.

"*Ungrateful?* I have barely said a word, and you manage to keep throwing jabs at me. I'm sorry you have to be stuck here with me. It's clear you regret saving me. You should have just let me die out there," she professes.

I know I should keep my mouth shut. I know it's anger driving me to keep making comment after comment, but now I'm fuming at the thought that she thinks of *me* as a murderer. That I would be capable of just letting somebody die as I watch. That could never be me.

I stomp over to her, my boots making loud smacks on the ground as I make my way over to her and crouch down to where she is. Instinctively, she scoots back, unsure what I'm about to do.

My voice is low and controlled as I set the record straight. "I *never* said I regret saving you, Princess. I am not the murderer here. *You* are." I point my finger at her and then back away slowly.

With my back to her, I make my way back to the other side of the cave. Before I'm even sitting down, I hear her crying.

"I didn't know he was your friend. I had no idea," she pleads through tears.

Unable to sit still, I fidget with the pocketknife I always carry, opening and closing it. "What difference does it make? You don't know me. You don't owe me anything. You opened your legs and killed my friend. He had a family!" I angrily respond.

She winces as if I just slapped her. "You're right. I don't owe you a damn thing. But don't talk to me like that again. You don't know a thing about me either, so don't pretend you do," she demands.

"Oh, so your pussy doesn't kill men? They all just happen

to drop dead after a night with you? Astonishing!" I scoff.

She shrugs off the blanket, and stomps over to me, her loose braid swinging back and forth and yanks the shovel from beside me.

I roll my eyes, watching as she stomps dramatically towards the front of the cave. "What are you doing?" I ask her annoyed, although slightly relieved she didn't hit me over the head with it.

"I am digging my way out of here, I won't spend another minute in here with somebody who despises me as much as you do," she shouts back.

"Oh, and what will you do when the dragon is waiting right outside for you? Do you plan on having sex with it, so it drops dead?" I laugh humorlessly.

She glares back at me with even less humor on her face. She ignores me and turns back, and starts whacking at the snow with her skinny arms.

I lazily get up and make my way over to her. When she pulls back to swing, I grab the shovel and gently take it from her. "Stop."

She's turned towards me, our faces inches apart. She's breathing heavily, and her eyes are glossy and red, filled with tears. Tears of rage. Her entire face is squished like she's glaring right into the sun and for the first time since I saw her crying in her room, I see a person. The rage is real. She might feel an ounce of the same anger I feel towards her.

She waits for me to do or say something else and part of me feels like she's looking for another excuse to lunge on my face and claw my eyes out. I know I've crossed a line and I know she could have me killed for what I've said. But I couldn't stop it. It needed to be said. Does it even occur to her what she's doing to people?

She takes a deep breath, and responds as if reading my

mind. "I know what I do is wrong. I know all it does is hurt people," she says tensely.

"Then why do you continue to do it?" I ask, throwing the shovel on the ground with a clang.

Her head hangs, and then she looks back up at me, biting the inside of her cheeks before she speaks. "I don't have a choice," she explains and walks back to the backside of the cave.

I follow behind her. "What is that supposed to mean? Everybody has a choice."

Is this her way of exonerating herself from the harm she does? What a cop out.

"No, handyman, YOU have a choice. You can choose to leave Tenuma. You can choose a mate, you can fall in love, and create a family. I cannot," she reveals.

My eyebrows pinch together, hearing the longing in her voice for those things. The way her voice cracked as she said fall in love. All this time, she's been nothing more than a monster to me, but maybe it's more than it seems.

"Well, explain it to me then," I request.

"You wouldn't understand. You don't understand and you've made up your mind about me. Let's just leave it at that. You hate me and that's the way it needs to be," she states.

The princess goes to sit back down and cover herself with the blanket, and I decide to give up the argument and get some rest as well.

"We'll be here overnight. There's no way we will dig our way out and the kingdom will most likely find us tomorrow anyway, since you're missing. They will find our footsteps to the edge of the avalanche, hopefully. Let's just pray your kingdom sends enough men to dig us out or we could be here a few days," I tell her.

"A few days in a dark, cold cave with the man who hates

me more than anything. Great," she says, mostly to herself.

For both of our sakes, I pretend I don't hear it and lay my head against the pack, stretching my legs out in front of me. We may be here a few days, there's no sense in arguing the entire time we're here.

It's hard to tell how much time has passed. The pocket watch I usually have on me must have slipped out of my jacket during the chaos with the dragon and the avalanche. Princess Bellatrix has been quiet for a while, and I don't know if she's asleep or just pretending to be so she doesn't have to listen to me anymore. I can't blame her, I don't think I'm capable of anything other than jabs right now, anyway.

What did she mean I'm supposed to hate her? Somehow, her acceptance of my dislike for her doesn't sit well. There's something she's hiding. There are probably many things that she's hiding, actually. Part of me wants to pry and ask her again what she means, but the other part thinks I've done enough damage and I should leave well enough alone.

It must be getting dark out–if not already–because the temperature has dropped drastically, and the princess is shivering twice as intensely as she was earlier. It looks like she could be having a seizure.

Stop watching her. She will be fine. It's not that cold.

Shit.

As I fight with the angel and the devil on my shoulders, I drag myself over to her and lay next to the curled ball of black hair on the ground. I press myself against her for warmth, but before I get my arm all the way across her, she bolts upright.

She turns to look back at me, her face seared with shock. "What the fuck are you doing?" she practically shouts.

"Relax, I'm trying to keep you warm." I hold my hand up, trying my best to convey innocence. I guess this doesn't look great, but she has to know that at this point there's no way I would ever be interested in her. As beautiful as she may be, there's no way I'd be stupid enough to leave my family for her.

"Look, just because you think I'm the whore of Tenuma, doesn't give you the right to put your hands on me." She starts scooting away from me.

"Okay, you're right," I say, backing up too.

She scoffs. "So, you do think I'm a whore?" she snaps.

"I meant you're right that I shouldn't be putting my hands on you," I correct her. Although I'm not sure she's wrong, there's no reason for me to bring that up right now.

She looks shocked that I've agreed with her. "Yes. Well, good. Besides, you said you have a family at home. I'm not sure your wife would be pleased to find out you have been cuddling with the whore of Tenuma," she says bitterly.

"I never said I was married, and would you stop calling yourself that? It's going to take all the sting out of it, if I say it now," I say, trying to lighten the situation.

The corners of her mouth lift slightly just for a moment, before she squashes the smile refusing to let me see I've affected her. "You said you had a family."

"Yeah," I respond, shrugging. "I have a mother and a little sister at home. There are all kinds of families, Princess," I inform her.

"Well, you still don't need to do that. I'll be fine," she says unconvincingly.

I laugh. "No. You won't," I reply.

"Excuse me?" she asks, crossing her arms over her large breasts.

Not that I noticed them.

"You're in a thin bodysuit and a sweater with a hood. You have no business being in the woods dressed like this. What were you even thinking? You will freeze to death. Just let me keep you warm," I tell her.

"Why? Why do you even care?" she asks interrogatively.

I could tell her that I don't know why I suddenly care. I could tell her that I can't explain that as much as I despise her, I also feel drawn to her. At this moment, I also feel protective over her. I can't explain it, and I don't want to feel it. Not for anyone, but especially not for her. I could tell her that I hate seeing her shivering like a leaf in the wind and that I'm scared she's going to get pneumonia and die.

But I can't tell her any of that, because I can't even tell myself that I care. I can't let myself believe that I care for someone like this. I pride myself on being an honorable man, a good man. If that's true, I cannot possibly care for a monster like her. Even as the word passes through my mind, it feels wrong. Now that I've been in her company, even knowing what I know, it doesn't feel right. There are so many ways I could tell her why I care, but she's right. It's better if I despise her.

"It's not going to look great for me if the king and queen find me in a cave with their daughter who I let freeze to death. Some might call that suicide," I lie. Even though the words are true, it's not the reason why I'm trying to keep her warm.

13

BELLATRIX

Deciding to allow Koen to drape his warm body over me for tonight may not have been the wisest decision, but I suppose it's better than the alternative. Knowing that he thinks I'm incapable of surviving on my own—the same way my father does—makes my stomach churn. I plan to rule as a strong queen and I don't ever want to be perceived as weak or incapable. It's hard to prove you're strong when nobody ever gives you the chance to be.

Right now, in Koen's arms, I find that I want to do anything to prove him wrong. To show that I am capable. I don't want him to see me as a stupid little girl. I want to show everyone that I'm capable of being the strong queen they need.

I'm curled up under the blanket, and he's curled into my backside with his heavy, muscular arm draped over me. He wasn't lying, he really does run warm. If I close my eyes, I could swear that I'm next to a fireplace. The warmth radiating off of him is that strong. I almost wish he was wrong, so I could push him off of me and act like I don't need his help. But unfortunately, he's right—I'd absolutely freeze to death tonight.

I can hear his breathing get deeper and louder as he drifts

off to sleep. His large chest rising and falling against my back is like a lullaby carrying me off to sleep. Despite the unfamiliar surroundings, and anxiety of what awaits–both outside the cave and when I return home–I manage to fall asleep.

The last thing I remember as I fell asleep is how comfortable and safe I felt in Koen's arms. An unexpected way to feel with a man determined to misunderstand and hate you. I drift further into sleep, and my imagination takes off, carrying me into a peculiar dream.

Koen's heavy arm is wrapped around me, but his hand has started to shift downwards. My eyes are still closed, and I like the way it feels so I don't move. I let it happen. Without me stopping him, his hand moves over my pussy, and he softly starts rubbing me over my clothing. My body starts involuntarily arching and leaning into his hand, showing him that I like it.

I feel his dick harden behind me, as he firmly pushes it against my ass, letting me know he's aching for me as much as I'm aching for him. I turn so I'm flat on my back. This way he can touch more of me, but also so I can touch him.

As I grab his dick over his pants, I realize he's much larger than it felt behind me. I swear I feel my mouth salivate. My hand rubs him roughly over his pants, and a soft moan escapes me. He's caressing me more frantically, as if he knows I could wake up any moment. My entire body tingles as I match his eagerness, rubbing him, and arching my hips off the floor to feel him more.

"More." I pant.

"Princess..." he whispers back.

"More, please," I beg.

His rubbing has stopped, and it takes me a minute to realize that this isn't entirely a dream.

I open my eyes and see that I'm flat on my back, and my hand is still grabbing hold of him. I yank my hand back, and quickly turn on my side, my back facing him.

"Princess. W-what just happened?" he asks me softly.

"Nothing. I was dreaming. I- I'm sorry," I blurt out.

"I shouldn't have… I didn't mean to touch you," he pleads.

"Nothing happened, it's fine. We were both just dreaming," I blurt out quickly.

Even with Koen no longer draped over me, I feel overheated. I don't know what the hell just happened, but it can't happen again. What if one of us hadn't woken up and it went further. I don't know what came over me. I've never done anything like this. This is just one more reason why I need to stay the hell away from this man. I just gave him the validation he needed to continue thinking I'm the whore of our land.

Except a thought occurs to me–his hands were on me, too. He felt just as eager, just as desperate for more. I didn't imagine that, I didn't imagine any of it. If I remember right, he touched me first, actually. A fact that I'd be happy to enlighten him with should he ever bring this back up to use against me.

Why is my pussy still pulsing with pleasure, anticipating his touch? Hoping he will put his hands on me again.

No. That will never happen again. I don't know how to explain what just happened, but clearly, he's in as much shock as me, because I can still hear him breathing unevenly behind me perched up on his elbow over me. Neither of us know quite what to make of what just happened. We're both frozen with fear, confusion, and desire? All I want to do is force myself back to sleep, and avoid this entire situation.

I toss and turn for what seems like hours. The concept

of time is what you first lose once you're trapped inside a dark cave. Between the man shooting at me, being chased by an actual dragon, and now being trapped in a cave with the one man that actually might be glad to see me dead, my mind is reeling. I can't slow it down, and I can't make sense of any of this.

How could we not have known all this time there were dragons on our land?

Who was trying to kill me, and why?

Why do Koen and I seem to be drawn to each other despite us both clearly trying to do anything but be close to one other?

Further away, I hear Koen shuffling behind me and I realize he's not sleeping either. He's been moving around for a while. I keep hearing him let out heavy, frustrated puffs of air. Though part of me expects this to be his natural state: annoyed and angry.

The night is managing to grow colder somehow and my shivering quickens. I don't know how I will survive if we have to stay here for more than tonight. I can't help but wonder if Koen is right and that I'm not cut out for this shit. I have been isolated in my protective bubble my whole life, and I have no idea how to survive on my own.

Not that I'd ever admit this to him. Letting Koen believe he's right about any assumptions he makes of me is the last thing I'm going to do. Though, based on the way my body is rattling right now, in all likelihood, he's already aware.

14

KOEN

I cannot watch her petite body shake for another minute. I know she won't allow me to keep her warm after what just happened–not that I can explain it myself–but I can't sit here and watch her freeze to death. Sitting here waiting for her to fall asleep, so I can wrap her in my body heat again, is frustrating me beyond words.

Once I'm certain she's fallen back asleep, I take off my jacket and throw it over the small blanket she's cocooned herself in and gently place it over her body so she doesn't wake. I may not like her very much, but I'm not going to sit here and watch her freeze to death. I can already picture the guards knocking down my door to imprison me for killing their precious princess.

Yeah, that's why you're doing it. Keep telling yourself that. Just as the obnoxious thought races through my mind, I feel my dick tug at my pants.

Why does she have this effect on me??

I watch her body continue to shake for longer than she should after placing my heavy jacket on top of her.

Will she ever stop? I think to myself, annoyed.

Somehow, I know there's only one way she's going to survive this cave tonight and she's not going to be happy about it.

But you are, my subconscious taunts.

I shake my head, as if I can shake the thought away. Quietly scooting back over to where she lays, I press back up against her, but keep my dick a few inches away so she can't feel it hardening and growing up against her body. I place my arm across her, and sure enough, a few minutes later her shaking finally slows and she relaxes.

Finally, I think.

As I lay with the princess, I can't help but worry for my mom and little sister. Mellani worries on days that I do come home and tonight, I won't be. Poor sweet girl is always worried someone else will walk out on her, the way our asshole father did. I don't know who could take one look at her, and decide they won't be coming back home to her. Just thinking about it makes my heart ache for her. He left me too, I suppose. But I knew he was never content with our family. He always wanted more. He didn't want to settle for a life in the cottage in town. He always had his eyes set on the kingdom, the castle. For as long as I remember, he was always looking for ways to get in good with the royals. He temporarily worked there, but because of his terrible temper and drinking problem–that exacerbated the situation–he didn't last there long. Shortly after is when he stopped coming home. Fine by me, we're better off without him.

The princess twitches in her sleep and takes a big breath, making me worry that she might wake up. But her heavy breathing tells me she's in a deep sleep. The bracelet on my wrist pulses. I unintentionally tighten my grip around the princess pulling her closer, as I think of Mellani. It makes me desperately wish that I was home with her, making sure she's safe and warm. Her favorite thing is to cuddle with me at night, and I never realized how much I need it as much as she does until now.

Mel hasn't been able to get rid of this sickness she's had and it makes my heart gnaw thinking she might be cold tonight. Luckily, she has my mother, and while the cottage isn't nearly as warm as I'd like it to be for them, it's certainly a lot better than being in a snow-covered cave. I mentally decide that once I finally snag a few hours of sleep I'm digging us out of here. I need to get home to my family. The princess has an entire staff looking out for her, but I'm all my family has. They rely on me for food and to keep them safe. I can't stand the thought of something happening to them now that I'm not there. Especially since our land just got a brand-new threat.

Dragons.

I have so many lingering questions. How long has it been here, and are there more we need to look out for? It's been thousands of years since anyone has seen one that we don't know what they're capable of, and we don't know how to keep ourselves safe from them. Will they just make their way through town, turning the townspeople into snacks?

Helplessness settles in my chest as the urge to get back to my family grows stronger by the minute. I should have never followed to see what that damn dragon was chasing. I should have run back towards town. I should have run home.

Leaning up on my elbows, I glance down at the princess's serene face. As much as I want to hate her at this moment and as much as I want to blame her for being stuck in here, I can't help the warmth swirling in my chest for her. Her breathing is even, and I watch her chest rise and fall for just a few moments. I see a small smile dance on her lips for just a moment before she lets out a soft, sweet-sounding sigh. The protector in me can't help but feel like I'm part of the reason she feels so safe right now. It's my favorite role in this life. It's a role I usually preserve for those I love, but this doesn't feel so bad either. I lay back down and lay my head down to rest, finding it easier than I expected.

The sound of clanging metal jolts me from my sleep. As I become more cognizant, I remember that I'm trapped in a cave with the princess. My eyes dart open and I see her taking whack after whack at the snowy entrance to our cave, without much success.

"Princess, what are you doing?" I ask her groggily, stretching out my aching limbs.

"Getting us the hell out of here," she says with determination and without even sparing a glance back towards me.

"Hmm. Not like that, you're not," I say with amusement.

Bellatrix finally glances back at me, shooting daggers with her eyes. "Well, handyman, you're welcome to get up and help me anytime you'd like," she snaps.

I raise an eyebrow. "I'm sorry?" I reply, confused at the anger dripping off every word she says.

She looks sweaty and flushed, wearing the jacket I put over her last night. She's drowning in it, but damn it, if she doesn't look incredible in it anyway. She's left it unzipped so I can still see her skintight black bodysuit hugging every curve of her body. She's slender, but has big perky tits, and great hips I can picture holding onto.

No. I shut it down before the thoughts go further. Why is it that the more she fights me, the more these dirty thoughts creep into my mind? I know better. I'm a sensible, responsible man and I won't get wrapped up in whatever is happening silently between us. Not happening.

"We need to get out of here. I'm the princess. I have duties and responsibilities. I can't just wait here and hope somebody finds our footprints by some miracle. I'm done being stuck in here with *you,*" she hisses.

I sit up, leaning against the wall of the cave. "I don't really understand what's going on here. I'm not the one who got us into this mess. I was hunting for food for my family when *you* crossed my path. I would have been more than happy to let that dragon chase you down had I known this was how I'd be repaid for saving your life," I inform her.

She sucks in her cheeks, and her eyes turn to slits, revealing her typical irritated gaze, directed solely at me. Through gritted teeth she hurls back something I didn't expect. "I didn't want to be saved."

I'm so utterly stunned by her abrasive response that I can't hide the look of shock on my face. Did she just not want to be saved by me, personally? Or does she mean she didn't want to be saved at all?

Why is she so stubborn?

I get up slowly, reaching for the shovel in her hands. "Let's sit down and eat something. It's been a long night. Then I will dig us out," I say calmly. There are so many things I can say to her right now, but something inside of me is telling me that it will only make the situation worse.

She hands over the shovel without fight and follows me back to where I have the supplies sitting. I pull out some jerky and dried fruit–that I'm sure she will turn her nose up at, but it's all we have.

I hand her the jerky and fruit, she reaches for it and her sleeve pulls back revealing a tattoo. A tattoo I've seen before, but haven't registered until this moment when I get a flashback of the drawing Mellani had of a sword tattoo with a rose on her own skin.

How is that possible? It can't be her, I think. My eyes are locked on her tattoo.

Bellatrix's hand freezes as she looks to where my eyes have drifted and then back to my horrified face.

Dropping the food into her open hand, I pull back and ask something I already know the answer to. "Princess, you never did tell me what you were doing in town. You said yourself that you weren't supposed to be there. So…?" I ask accusingly.

"I just wanted to get out of the castle. It gets to be…too much," she lies.

My bracelet tingles. "You're lying. You have an entire forest surrounding your castle and a private garden you could visit if you wanted," I say, purposely mentioning the garden to see how she responds.

Her cheeks turn red, and her eyes flutter in panic a few times at the mention of the garden. We both know what happened that day. We both know I saw her masturbating. What shocks me is her embarrassment. For someone who's known as the Soul Snatcher and sleeps with a considerable amount of men, I would have thought she'd be a lot less ashamed of her sexual urges.

I nod my head towards the part of the tattoo showing on her wrist as she pulls her hand back. "It's a very unique tattoo you have there. What's strange is that I came home the other day, and my little sister had drawn a very similar one on own arm. She said the *"money lady"* had one," I say tightly.

She shrugs, popping some of the dried fruit in her mouth. "Weird. Must be a coincidence," she states, blankly.

"Yeah, it could be. But the weird thing is, she says that the same lady has been giving her quite a bit of money each time she sees her. There's only one family I can think of that has that kind of money to spare."

Bellatrix doesn't look up from her hand where she's anxiously moving the fruit around on her hand with her index finger. She doesn't dare meet my eyes.

"Bellatrix. It's you, isn't it?" I ask softly now.

Her gaze slowly meets mine at the use of her name. "You never say my name," she points out.

"Why?" I ask her.

"Because you hate me, I assume," she purposely answers the wrong question.

I shake my head, still serious. "No. Why have you been giving her money?"

Nervously she bites the corner of her cheek trying to find the answer that won't send me into the blind rage she feels coming. "I-I'm not," she squeaks out.

I've never heard the princess so unsure of herself, so vulnerable. Except maybe last night when she had my cock in her hand.

"Tell me," I beg softly.

She looks up, her eyes welling to the brim. She clears her throat, trying to change her expression to something resembling strength. "I did it, in case I need an extra handmaid, I know she will be loyal and willing to do whatever I want," she says, unconvincingly.

"Bellatrix," I start firmly. "Stop lying to me. Tell me," I challenge her.

She gets up, huffing and throws off my jacket she's been wearing. Pacing the length of the cave, she throws her hands up in the air. "It doesn't matter. Why can't you just leave this alone? Just take it. Just let me do this," she pleads, sounding exhausted.

I stand up, moving towards where she's been pacing and gently grab both of her shoulders, forcing her to face me. My breathing is heavy and the air feels thick. She's looking at me with glossy eyes and a soft pouty mouth. A mouth that I'm picturing is incredibly warm and soft. She opens her mouth slightly to say something, then obviously changes her mind and closes it again.

I can feel her sweet breath on me and it takes all of my self control not to lean in. The bracelet on my wrist tingles more than it ever has and as much as I want to let go and walk away, I want to hold on even more. I don't know exactly what the tingly bracelet is supposed to mean, but since it's the princess I'm touching, I'm going to assume it's a warning.

I reluctantly drop my hands, taking one step back giving us both room to breathe. Bellatrix reaches over with one hand and rubs her wrist. A wrist that contains a very similar bracelet to the one I wear.

Is she wearing one of my mother's bracelets?

How am I finding this woman more and more intertwined in my life with each minute that goes by?

What the fuck is going on?

Realizing that she's not going to speak, I break the silence. "Tell me why you've been doing this. Please," I beg.

She takes a deep breath before speaking. "Because I feel drawn to her. She's a sweet kid and thinking of her wanting for anything torments me. And…it's the only way I can live with myself," she confesses.

My eyebrows cinch together in confusion, before I realize what she means. "This is your way to balance the scales, for the other part of your life," I declare.

She nods, and the tears freely fall down her cheeks. I can't help but reach out and wipe them off her porcelain skin. I'm feeling so many raw emotions standing here in front of her. The anger for what she's done to so many families and my friends. Confusion for her contradictory personality and a warm aching for the way she's been unknowingly helping my sister. One minute she's completely cold and cruel and the next, she's like a pot of warm melted caramel, looking delicate and sweet. Even though she can be cruel, I can feel the unhappiness that consumes her. Part of me wants to laugh at the fact that someone like her can feel any misery, but I also want to heal that misery. I don't know how to keep my emotions from riding the rollercoaster when I'm near her.

My fingers go under her chin and lift until our gazes meet again. "Bellatrix. You help because you want to. There's nothing in it for you at all, is there?" I ask, knowing it to be true even before she answers.

Her voice is so soft when she speaks, I have to strain my ears to hear it. "I just want to know I've done something good in my life."

I take in her sorrowful face, peer into her gorgeous green eyes and all I can think about is pulling her face to mine and putting my lips on hers. The pull is so forceful I almost lean forward. I know she feels it too. I can see in her eyes that she's fighting the same battle inside.

Her lips part slightly and I notice her breathing get heavy again. Whatever she wants to say is right on the tip of her tongue, but she stays silent. I can see her mind reeling, sorting through what to say at this moment, but not wanting to disturb the tension that's building between us. The tension that's moved between my legs, causing my dick to throb painfully. I see her shift back and forth on her feet as she places her hands softly on my arms. She bites her bottom lip and I swear my legs almost give out. Part of me wants her to stop having this effect on me, and another larger part is hoping the same effect is happening between her own legs.

If I reach into her panties, will she be wet for me?

I can almost feel her on the tips of my fingers like I did last night. The thoughts pierce through my mind, taking me back to when we laid together, half asleep, and caressing each other desperately, as if we had that one moment to give into our deepest desires.

Not that I feel anything for her other than disgust. No. The rest of this is just pure, male urge. It will pass. It's not something I feel specifically for *her*, I would very likely feel the same way for any beautiful female standing before me all but panting and looking at me with pure lust in her eyes.

Why is she looking at me like that?

I drop my hand from her chin stepping back again, because as much as I'd love to give in just a little bit, I can't let this happen. I have to be smart and level headed. I have a family to think about. I can't allow myself to think with my dick.

Bellatrix steps back until she's leaning against the cave wall for support, but never takes her eyes off of me.

A thought keeps nudging me, urging me to ask. "What do you mean you feel drawn to my sister? How do you even know her?" I question her.

The low sultry voice gone, and is back to normal now, though her face still says *take me, fuck me.* "I go to town a few times a week with as much money as I can get my hands on for the local kids. I met her over by the fountain where all the merchants are set up to sell. I always see her playing by the fountain. I don't know, I just took a liking to her. She's so genuinely sweet, curious and affectionate. I just couldn't stop thinking about her from the minute I met her," she tells me and when I don't respond, she continues. "Aside from that, I don't know her. I don't ask anything of her. Well. Except not to tell anyone where she got it from. I could just be in a lot of trouble for doing that, and I like knowing I'm helping these kids' families. I don't want to stop," she confesses.

The transparency and vulnerability of her words surprise me. I've seen a whole other side to her since we've been trapped here. But I suppose fear and lack of sleep will do that. So will grasping someone's dick.

My heart is pounding so hard at her confession that it might burst out of my chest. I try to stifle the feeling. "Can you please just not ask her to keep any more secrets from her family. I don't like that. She's never lied to me about anything until she told me she found all the money you gave her."

"I'm sorry," she replies sincerely. The way she's looking at me, I know she's not just referring to lies about money. "I really didn't know she was your sister. She never mentioned a brother, only a father who wouldn't let her continue to accept the offered money," she reveals.

The mention of the word *father* makes my heart sink. Knowing that Mellani tells people I'm her father just goes to show how badly she yearns for that connection. It makes my heart both squeeze with affection and ache for her loss. "Our father left us a long time ago. It's just us and our mother," I respond.

Her face shifts from confusion to understanding as she nods her head. "Sometimes we're better off without them. At least she has you and it's obvious how much you two love each other. She's a lucky girl." I can sense the envy in her voice. She doesn't have anybody who loves her, the way I love Mel.

As much as my chest aches for the princess, I have to remind myself that I still don't know her very well and that regardless of how I feel when I'm in her vicinity, she's still dangerous. But damn it, if I don't want to throw caution to the wind, because before I know it, I'm standing inches from her face as she's pressed against the cave wall.

15

BELLATRIX

I can't breathe. I can't breathe when he's this close to me, and if he continues looking into my eyes this way, I'll happily never take another breath. It takes everything in me not to give into the urge to rip my panties off and sit on that scruffy thick beard, and let him feast on me. One arm rests on the wall next to me, high above my head caging me in, and the other grips my hip, his face inches from mine. The way his stormy gray eyes stare into mine makes me feel like he's trying to steal my soul and I have to look away. Before I can find anything else to set my eyes upon, he removes his hand from my hip and lifts my chin back up to meet his gaze. His stare is intense and unwavering. It rocks me to my core, making my body shake slightly. For once, I don't think it's due to the cold. I've never felt this way with any man. I'm always the one who's in charge and has control but when I'm around Koen, he seems to seize all control.

"Look at me, Bellatrix," he says slowly, his voice deep and gravelly.

The shaking of my body increases when he says my name and I can't stop it. My body feels like a rubber band that is stretched out and ready to snap. I'm unraveling all at once. I wish

I knew what was going on in his mind, because I feel like I get whiplash trying to decide whether he hates me or wants to ravish me. I still can't explain how we both woke up with our hands all over each other, and I don't think either of us will be the same after that. Something has shifted between us and I don't know what to make of it.

"Koen, no. I-I'm bad for you. You despise me and that's the way it needs to stay. We need to stay away from each other," I tell him softly, my words begging for him to let me go, but my body begs for him to hold on.

As much as it pains me to say out loud, it's nothing we both don't already know. I'm dangerous to any man, and it's not somewhere I'm willing to go with him. As much as he fights me, he might be the only person who truly sees me. Other than Quirina. The irony of this whole damn tragedy is that Koen might actually be the man I'm supposed to be with, if I wouldn't kill him once we finally had our way. It's not something I'm ever going to be willing to risk. Especially after finding out that the sweet little girl I've been helping is Koen's little sister. How is this even possible?

It feels like some sick cosmic joke that the man I have no self-control around, the man I find painfully sexy—and just so happens to be related to the little girl who I already am obsessed with—is the same man that despises me and can't be with me anyway. Thinking that I'll never be able to be with him makes my chest tighten and my heart pang. It hurts to know that I will never get the chance to explore this further and let him actually see who I am. I will always have to keep him at arm's length, so I never have the chance to hurt him. We can't ever have a close call like that again, because it will kill me if I harm him.

He drops my chin again and steps out of my embrace just as we hear shouting from the other side of the snow-packed entrance.

An authoritative voice booms through the wall of snow.

"Lady Bellatrix! Lady Bellatrix!" the voice shouts over and over.

It takes me a moment to comprehend what's happening as I'm still caught under the spell of Koen's stormy gray eyes, so he responds instead. "Hello! We are in here!" he responds.

I tear my eyes away from him, taking in the situation. "Yes! I'm here! Help us!" I shout.

"Stand back, Lady Bellatrix. We are getting you out of there!" the man shouts back, and we move to the back of the cave in silence, as instructed.

I stand next to Koen, our arms touching ever so slightly, and I want to reach out and intertwine our fingers. But I can't. I can't let him believe there's anything between us or that there ever could be. I'm a deadend. Literally. There is no future with me, and I refuse to be his doom.

As we stand next to each other, I can feel the heat building again, and the bracelet on my wrist starts tingling, warming my wrist and I gaze down at it, noticing as I do that Koen is wearing the same exact bracelet. My eyes shoot up and he's already staring at me intensely.

"What..." I manage to get out before all the snow comes crashing down into the cave letting the bright light of day pour into the cave, temporarily blinding us both. We both reach up to shield our eyes from the brightness of it.

Castle guards and soldiers rush in towards us, immediately assessing me for any injuries.

"I'm fine, I'm fine," I say, using my hand to partially conceal my eyes from the light. Once my eyes finally adjust, I see them throwing handcuffs on Koen.

"What are you doing?" I shout to the guard angrily.

"My Lady, he's under arrest for kidnapping you," he says firmly.

I can't help but let out an irritated laugh. "What are you

talking about? Are you stupid? He saved my life, and then we got trapped in here. Take those handcuffs off of him immediately!" I demand.

The guard glances around to the men in charge at the front and they nod at each other, and he finally releases the cuffs, setting Koen's hands free. I sigh in relief, not realizing just how terrified it made me to see him in danger until they took the cuffs off. My stomach aches with terror, knowing how close he just came to a certain death. The king and queen never would have let him live, believing that he had kidnapped me. This is just more evidence that he should stay as far away from me as possible.

I go to shake his hand, to properly thank him so the guards understand he is not to be harmed and that he is free to go. I stick my hand out. "Thank you for saving my life and keeping me safe. The royal family is indebted to you." All the formality is back in place now that we're heading back to reality.

He gives me an unreadable look—God, what I would give to know what he's thinking right now—and slowly sticks his hand in mine and shakes it. The bracelet once again starts tingling the skin underneath. He gives me a nod and lets go without a word.

I pull my hand back, biting my lip. I'm holding back so many things I want to say, but can't. So many things I feel bubbling out of me, but won't say because it won't do either of us any good. I say the only thing he needs to hear, "Goodbye, Koen." And then I walk out with the guards.

"Where are my parents?" I ask the men, looking around as I sit atop one of our beautiful horses as we prepare to leave.

"They are waiting for your arrival at the castle. They've been quite worried," one of the guards responds back.

I roll my eyes. "Sure they have." I don't know why it bothers me so much that they aren't here with the rescue team. It just seems strange, that a man who hates me can save my life by risking his own, but my parents can't join a rescue team to retrieve me when their lives surely wouldn't be in any danger. My father, being on his deathbed can be forgiven, but what about my mother? I shouldn't be surprised and I guess I'm not. I can't help but feel the sting of another disappointment.

Once everyone has mounted their horse, we start trotting off in the other direction and I can't help but glance back towards the cave. Koen is still inside, and despite knowing that nothing can change, in a way it feels like everything has changed.

"**O**h my gosh! I have been freaking out, I am so happy you're back safe. What the hell happened to you?" Quirina has me in a hug so tight I might actually have rib damage. I wish I had received the same greeting from my parents. All I got from them was a half-hearted gasp of relief and a scolding for leaving the castle unaccompanied by guards.

"Everything. Too much happened," I tell her, exhausted. I'm freshly showered and tucked tightly under my heavy blankets on my plush oversized bed. I have never been so happy to see it. I never realized how comfortable it was before, and yet it still feels like it's missing something.

"I want to hear everything. I was really worried. I helped you sneak out and then you just went missing. It felt like I was to blame. I wouldn't be able to forgive myself if something happened to you," she says with tears in her eyes.

I take her hand between both of mine. "Rina, please don't ever think that. If anything does ever happen to me, that's on me, not you. Okay?" I tell her.

She nods, but I can still see the guilt in her face.

"I was with Koen," I tell her, hoping she takes the gossipy bait.

Her eyes widen and I know I've really got her attention now. "What?! What do you mean you were with him? How did that come about?" she asks, intrigued.

"It's complicated. It's something I need to discuss with the king and queen actually, but he saved my life, Rina. He saved my life by risking his, and then we got trapped under an avalanche in a cave for two days," I tell her dramatically.

"It sounds so romantic," she replies sweetly.

I scoff at her. "It wasn't romantic. I slept on the cold ground surrounded by snow. I almost died, and was trapped in a cave with a man who hates me." I react with as much frustration towards the situation as I can muster.

Quirina glares at me unconvinced. "Oh, Lady Bellatrix, for such a rough few days, you still arrive with a smile upon your face." She circles her index finger in the air around my face.

I lift my hand to my face, letting my fingers graze my mouth as if I can prove she's lying when I know she's right. I did come home with a smile, but it was a tainted one. A smile I wear for someone I can't have. For a possibility that can never come to fruition.

I lean back against my headboard and sigh. I could lie to her, but what's the point? She knows me better than anybody. If there's one person I can count on not to judge me, it's her. "Yes, I suppose I can't hide it."

"What happened inside that cave, Trix?" she pries.

"I think he almost kissed me. Twice," I say wistfully, my mouth turning down.

"That sounds amazing, why the glum face?" she questions.

"There's more." I wince, thinking about the way we woke

up together grabbing at each other.

"What is it?" Quirina asks, eyes wide and eager.

"Keep in mind that the cave was *FREEZING* and you know how cold I get here even," I remind her, hoping it will make me less of a guilty party.

She laughs. "Yes, I know. Continue." She knows exactly what I'm doing and just wants me to get to the juicy part.

"I was trying to sleep in his arms. Only because he runs so hot. Rina, I swear this man feels like his own fireplace!" I sputter out quickly.

"That's not that big of a deal, you were in survival mode. Most would say that's pretty acceptable," she says with the flick of her hand.

I pull at a thread on the blanket. "Maybe, but that's not the part that I can't get out of my head," I confess.

The corners of her mouth twist into a mischievous grin. "What is?"

I chew on my lip anxiously, trying not to smile because as good as it felt then, it's quite the opposite. "The part where I woke up and his hands were in between my legs, and I was holding his cock," I say and then cover my face embarrassed. Sure, I have a lot of sex, but both parties are always awake. I've never had such an intense chemistry with somebody where our bodies couldn't resist while we were unconscious. I can't make sense of it.

Quirina lets out a half laugh, half gasp, as she cups her hands around her mouth to hide her amusement.

I playfully smack her leg. "Rina, stop laughing! It's not funny."

She calms her laughter. "Oh, except that it is," she counters.

My face turns serious. "What if we hadn't woken up?" I ask. "What if things went further, and we... you know."

She smiles mockingly at me. *"You know?* I've never seen you so prudish like this. What has he done to you?" She giggles.

I roll my eyes. "Okay, what if we *fucked?* Happy now?" I ask.

"I'd be happier if you actually had." She jokes, forcing another eyeroll out of me. "I know, I know. I understand that you can't and why you can't. But can't you do other things? I mean, if you actually like this guy, which it seems like you do, what's the harm in… doing everything else?" she asks, genuinely interested.

I can't say that it's ever really occurred to me. Sex for me has always been this dutiful task. Something I have to do to earn the throne and find my mate. I never thought it could feel electric the way I feel when I'm around Koen. Maybe I've been looking at this situation all wrong. Even if we mutually decide to take things to the next level, it will have to be in secret since we can never have sex. Sex would kill him. What kind of relationship is that? How long could we sustain any sort of bond when we can't ever have sex? He's a man and eventually, it's something he's going to want or need, even. We can only do so many things and it can never be a substitution for what he will inevitably really want. He wouldn't get it from me and he would have to find another woman to get it from. Frankly, thinking about him with anyone else at this point makes my stomach twist in knots. I can't imagine what it would feel like if we ever started anything up.

None of this matters because he despises me. There is no relationship to speak of. We had a moment in the cave, because we had a near death experience, but the moment has passed. The lust-fog has lifted and now we'll both realize what a mistake it would have been to let anything happen.

I think it over, realizing that although Rina makes a point, it's still not a solution. I shake my head. "No, I can't do that. We were just caught up in a moment after a near death experience, but I'm thinking clearly again. I have decided to keep my space from him during the remainder of his time here. He won't be here that much longer, and then I won't ever have to see him again. It's fine. I'm looking for a mate, someone to share the throne with me, not love."

Rina gives me an incredulous look. "If you say so, Trix," she says with a shrug.

I want to be angry with her for putting that thought in my head for even a minute, because I need to stay focused, which is the opposite of what I've been doing around Koen. Secretly, it's given me a small sliver of hope that I can have part of him one day. Because as much as he makes me believe that he hates me, there's a part of me that knows he's just as lust-crazed for me as I am for him. The issue is that there's more downside than good that can come from anything we might attempt. Koen is the only one that stands to lose in this situation and it's not something I'll ever ask him to participate in. From here on out, I will be focused on my search for my future king, and mate. Koen is nothing more than a handyman to me.

16

KOEN

I am nothing more than a handyman to her. I have to keep reminding myself of this as I make my way back to the cottage. I can still feel my pulse racing and the way she made the air thick around us. The cave changed things for us, though I don't know if it's for the better.

If somebody told me a week ago that I would be a breath away from kissing Princess Bellatrix, I would have socked them in the face for thinking I'm that stupid. But now, I just might be that stupid because that's exactly what I was about to do. There has been a magnetic pull between us since I started working at the castle, and as much as I've tried to ignore it and continue to despise her—it should be easy enough, there's certainly enough reason to—I can't. I thought the hard part would be working for her and having to be in the same room with her, but now I'm finding the hard part to keep my hands to myself, and my eyes off of her bewitching face.

Yes, stupid is absolutely the correct word for me. Luckily, the royal guards showed up and freed us from the lust-filled cave. One more night in there with her and I don't know what might have happened.

Is this part of her curse? It makes you throw your wits out the window, crazed with lust for her?

The thought flows through me and I feel a flash of anger rise in my chest. I am so stupid to think a woman, a princess like Bellatrix, would actually be interested in a peasant like me. Imagining touching her delicate, soft body with my rough hands is comical when I really think about it. It was the curse and nothing more. I almost lost my way because I was caught underneath the wave of her beauty.

Never again. I will be strong and I will use my head. I can't let a moment of weakness let me forget who she really is.

Murderer.

Liar.

Thief.

Do not forget she killed your friend just a few days ago.

Yeah, but don't forget she's also been secretly giving your family money for survival. The devil and the angel on my shoulders argue back and forth and unfortunately, I can't tell which is which anymore.

None of that matters, I'm redirecting my focus back to my family. Two weeks ago, Bellatrix was just the daughter of the wicked king and queen who made our lives hell, and I won't let the last week change that. I am still just the handyman for them, and she is nothing to me.

I quicken my pace the closer I get to the cottage, eager to see my mom and Mellani. I turn the corner and see a crowd of people gathered in front of my home.

"Koen!" I hear a high-pitched shriek that can only come from one person.

"Mel! My sweet girl!" I shout back as we run towards each other.

I stoop down once I reach her and lift her in my arms.

It feels so good to be back with her, I hadn't realized how much I depend on her affection and how much I'm sure she relies on mine.

Tears well in my eyes as I hold her tightly against me not wanting to let her go. I came close to being killed by something we thought didn't exist anymore, and after surviving that, I almost threw it all away because I can't control myself around the princess. Never again. It would never be worth losing this sweet, tiny little human in my arms. I could never leave her.

"Baby girl, I missed you so much. I am so sorry I was gone so long," I apologize, hoping she didn't think I left like our father did.

The crowd joins us in the street, embracing, and snowballing questions all at once.

"What happened to you?"

"Where have you been?"

"Is it true you saved the princess?"

"Are you okay?"

"Man, we missed you!"

"We were worried sick!"

"We thought you were gone, man. We thought you went to the castle and were never coming back!" That last question came from my best friend, Nikandros. He has no idea how right he almost was.

"I am so sorry. There was an accident and then an avalanche and I had to take cover in a nearby cave. I am okay. I have a lot to explain, I know. But right now, I just need to be with my family," I say, giving a weak smile to those around us. "Thank you all for your worry and for being there for my family in my absence." I thank the crowd, and then with Mel in my arms, I walk with my mother into our cottage.

"What do you mean a dragon was in the woods?" my mother asks, horrified.

We sit around the table, drinking hot tea–whiskey added to mine, courtesy of Nikandros–while Mel is sitting on my lap, not wanting to move since I've returned home. I gently caress the back of her hair and plant a kiss on top of her head.

"Mel, why don't you go draw, and give mom and I some time to talk about grown-up things." She looks up at me hesitantly, as if I will disappear the moment she gets up. "I will be right here at the table with mom. Swear." I tell her, holding out my pinky.

She takes my large finger in her pinky finger looping them together. "Okay, I'll go draw you a picture," she says sweetly. It's one of the many things I love about Mellani, she's an incredible artist.

She hops down and I watch her trot over to the shelf where she keeps all of her paper, notebooks, pencils, and colored pencils. It's hard for me to take my eyes off of her, knowing how worried she was. I hate that as young as she is, within her are these deep-rooted abandonment issues. Each and every one easily traced back to our asshole father, made more aware by the fact that she tells other people I'm her dad. If I ever saw that coward again, it wouldn't be a pretty sight.

I sigh heavily, returning to the conversation with my mother. "It was a dragon. There's no mistaking what we saw."

"WE?" my mother asks, shocked. I may have left out the part where I was trapped inside the cave with Princess Bellatrix.

Another heavy sigh leaves my body. "Mother, I don't want

you to freak out when I tell you this." I pause, trying to gauge how this is about to go. "The dragon I saw was technically chasing Princess Bellatrix when–"

My mother cuts me off before I can finish. "You were in a cave, trapped with Bellatrix?" she repeats shocked, and another emotion, anger maybe. Fear?

I rub my forehead with my hand. "I know, Mother. It wasn't what I had planned for the day either," I tell her.

My mother gives me a skeptical look. "Koen, what was she even doing in the woods with you to begin with? That's not a place the royals typically frequent," she interrogates.

I roll my eyes. "Mother, she wasn't there *with* me. I was trying to hunt, and she was just… there. She said somebody was chasing her, trying to kill her. Not that I can say that was a surprise. Then, she ran into the woods for cover and then there was a dragon. I didn't know it was the princess when I saved her. I would have saved her anyway, but I didn't know it was her," I tell my mother, hoping she will get the distrusting look off of her face. I would think she knows better than anyone that I'm not stupid enough to risk my life for princess pussy. Although the electric connection between us cannot be ignored, that's not something I'm willing to admit to my mother.

"It just doesn't make sense," she says, rubbing her pointer finger under her lip, pondering what I've said.

"What doesn't?" I ask.

"Dragons. They've been gone for… thousands of years. Nobody has seen one or even thought about them in just as long. How could this be? You're sure that's what it was?" she asks, looking for any hint of doubt.

I take a large drink from my whiskey-infused tea, feeling the exhaustion from the last few days starting to weigh heavily, as I try to suppress a yawn. "It was right in front of me. It was a dragon, bigger than anything I've ever seen. I saw its giant sharp teeth, hard amor-skin, long tail, sharp claws. It was a dragon, Mother. No doubt.

My mother shakes her head, incredulously. "This can't be right," she states, more to herself than me.

My eyebrows cinch together. "What is it, Mother?" I ask, unable to quiet the voice telling me there's something she's not telling me.

She glances over to make sure Mellani is focusing on her drawing and not paying attention to our conversation. She lowers her voice to a near whisper anyway. "There's a prophecy of the lands. That when fire-breathing dragons walk with us again, there will be a great war. It's said there will be great loss of life and a shift in power," she recites, grimly staring off beyond the room we're sitting in.

"So, just because a dragon shows itself there's going to be a war? That doesn't make much sense. All it means is that everyone was wrong about them all being destroyed. Clearly," I state, matter of factly.

I see a shudder go through my mother and when she doesn't elaborate further, I decide that I need a shower and some sleep. "Look, Mother, more than likely, it's not what you're thinking. It's been a stressful few days and I really need to get some sleep so I can go get us some food."

At the change of subject, my mother snaps out of her thought trance, and squeezes my hand. "Get some sleep, my son. Don't worry about food, we went to town and gathered some things. I will make you a hot meal when you wake up."

"We didn't have much money before I left. How did you manage?" I ask, and then judging by her guilty face, I realize she used the money Mellani received from the princess. I can't help but shake my head and smile at the irony of it all. "Okay, Mother. I love you," I tell her as I rise from the table, kissing her on top of her head. She's warm and smells like my mother always does: like lavender and worry.

The smell of sizzling garlic and onions flood my senses as I awake from a much needed rest. The aroma is heavenly and comforting. Even without opening my eyes, I know my mother is in the kitchen making one of my favorite dishes. Pan-fried beef with onions and garlic, paired with potatoes and a homemade salsa. As much as I feel like the head of the household, my mother is still my mother. She enjoys protecting me and taking care of me as if I'm still her little boy, like making me my favorite comfort dish.

Slowly and a little groggily, I pull myself upright and rub both eyes with the palms of my hands. I'm not sure how long I've slept, but the sun is down, indicating that I've slept all day.

Inhaling deeply as I go towards the kitchen, I see my mother glance up and smile. "That smells amazing," I say, practically drooling.

Taking a spatula, stirring the food frying in the pan, she smiles brightly at me. "Well, I figured you deserved a comfort meal after the last few days you've had," she tells me.

The comment makes me laugh. "Well, it was probably much harder on the princess than it was on me." I think about the way she couldn't warm up and the fact that she wouldn't eat, and overall, how she seemed so helpless.

My mother's face twists into something I can't quite describe and I can tell she wants to say something but just before she can, Mellani comes bursting out of the bathroom, her eyes going wide when she sees I'm awake.

"You're up!" she squeals excitedly, racing towards me for a hug, her brown curls bouncing up and down.

"I am! Were you in the bath?" I ask, noticing her wet hair and fresh, clean scent.

"Yes, smell me!" she says as she tips her head all the way down so I can smell the top of her head.

"Mmm!" I exaggerate. "You smell like flowers. I love it. And you sound so much better! How are you feeling?" I ask her.

"I feel great! The medicine helped a lot. You sound better too, you were asleep all day," she tells me with the surprise only a little kid could have at that statement. She can't fathom sleeping for so long. Kids resist sleep as if they'll miss something amazing while they slumber.

"Yeah, I guess I did," I reply, grateful that they managed to get not only food with the money from Bellatrix but medicine for Mellani, as well. The stuff they give to the town folk isn't nearly as good or as fast-acting as somebody in the castle would get, so I'm amazed that in a day or two she's improved so much.

"Mama said I had to be quiet and let you sleep all day. It was so boring," she tells me, faking a pout.

"I'm sorry, sweet girl. But I'm awake now and I'm so happy to see you," I tell her.

"I drew you a picture!" she tells me, running off to the other side of the room and picking up a piece of paper from her shelf.

She comes running back towards me excitedly with a white piece of paper filled up with her drawing. "See, this is you stuck in the cave, and that's all the snow out in front covering it. I drew your bracelet on your arm that you always wear, and your bow and arrow! See?" She points out everything as she describes it to me.

"Who's that?" I point to a man on the outside of the cave,

facing the snow covered opening of the cave with his bow and arrow pulled taut.

"That's the bad man. That's dad," she states casually, as if it should be obvious.

My eyebrows pull together, and I can't help glancing up at my mom to see if she heard the same thing I did. Her fearful face tells me that she did.

"What do you mean, sweetie?" I ask her. The comment is strange because she never talks about him, and neither do we. While my hatred for him goes deep, it's not something I'd ever discuss with Mellani.

"Yeah, it's dad. He is crouching behind the trees, so you don't see him. But he's outside the cave with the arrow," she says again, calm and casual.

"Why did you draw that, baby?" my mother asks her gently.

Mellani just shrugs and then scampers off to sit on the couch, already starting another drawing. My mother and I are frozen in place in the kitchen, staring at each other trying to decipher each other's thoughts and figure out what just happened.

"I'm sure she just associates him with bad things because she knows he left and it hurt her," my mother states, cautiously.

"She's not wrong. He's an asshole," I retort.

My mother ignores my comment, instead serving me a plate of food and calls for Mellani to come sit down with us. Even though the last few days have been terrifying, confusing, and downright shocking, this meal with my family brings me back down to earth and reminds me what's important. Them. Always finding my way back to them, no matter what.

If there's a dragon out there now terrorizing our land, we will handle it. If there truly is a prophecy that will bring forth a war, we will face it. I will do what I've always done and protect my family.

17

BELLATRIX

My father lays in bed, his head slightly elevated so he can see myself, my mother, and a few of the royal guards surrounding him.

"We need to hold an emergency meeting. There is a dragon on our land and it means to do harm. After I was chased by a man trying to kill me, the dragon was hiding within the trees," I recount for my parents.

My father reaches for the glass of water on the bedside table, guiding it to his thin, dry lips. I use that moment to take him in. His once dark beard is now thin and gray. His sunken eyes reveal the damage this disease has done to him over the course of the last six months. Yet somehow, he still manages to look regal and powerful. I guess it helps that everyone must answer to him, regardless of his health. Leave it to a man on his deathbed to still be wielding power.

After drinking the water, he clears his throat before speaking. His voice is low but firm and powerful. "Lothar," he states clearly.

I give him a quizzical stare. "The King of Sperantia?

What does a dragon have to do with him?" I ask, confused.

"He is the one who sent men to kill you. Without an acting king, we are weak. We have become a target for his greedy power grab." He stops when he has a coughing fit. My mother rushes to his side, but my father puts his hand up in protest, signaling he's fine. "Lothar plans to get rid of you, send his men to overthrow our army, and his son will take over the throne with whomever he chooses to be his mate."

The revelation hits me right between the eyes. For the first time in my life, I suddenly feel death's icy grip on me. As the king's daughter, I've always felt secure and it's never occurred to me that somebody might be able to come harm me.

"Why would they want to take the throne from us? They have their own land," I reply, sounding alarmed.

"Why does anybody want the throne to begin with? Power. We know Lothar to be one of the cruelest, most greedy and unforgiving kings of all the lands. It only stands to reason that at some point he would crave more power," my father states in a strained voice.

I wring my hands together in front of me, trying to stand tall and hide my fear. "Father, wouldn't this be the perfect time to let me take over the throne—" I start but am interrupted by a burst of anger from the king.

"No! Bellatrix, I have told you, that will never happen. Tenuma will fall to Sperantia if there is not a king ruling alongside you. They will come in and take it from you. Can't you see we are trying to protect you?" he asks angrily.

My mother chimes in. "Not just you, dear, but all of Tenuma," she states softly, interrupting the buzzing of anger stirring in the room. "The fate of Tenuma rests in your hand, and it is essential we find you a mate."

"Which is why..." my father starts, between coughs. "Now that you're back, we have set up your meetings again." He says *meetings* but he means fuck dates. Meet-ups with the men I fuck in hopes of one surviving, so we can rule this land and prevent a war from happening.

My frustration at the situation and the pressure that lays solely on my shoulders boils over and I erupt. "Then take this forsaken curse from me! Reverse it and let me find someone, *anyone* I can rule with. I don't care who! I don't care what they want or if they love me!" I shout at both my parents. At this point, survival trumps a love connection if war truly is imminent.

My father's face doesn't change throughout my outburst, and simply responds. "It's not that simple, Bellatrix."

"What do you mean? There has to be a way to undo it. Magic isn't linear, it's magic! Take it from me," I beg.

My father gives my mother a knowing glance, and she then takes my hand in hers replying softly. "Not this one, sweetie."

I pull back my hand in frustration and disgust. They put me in this ugly position and I have no say in how my life unfolds. I didn't ask for this life. "What is that supposed to mean?" I ask her, on the verge of tears.

My mother pushes her long black braid off of her shoulder, and I see her bite her lip anxiously, mulling over whether she wants to tell me or not. When she doesn't respond, I grow impatient. "Tell me," I demand.

"This particular spell can only be reversed if I'm to be killed or if I die. I'm the one who requested the spell be put on you, so for it to be reversed, I have to give my life," she reveals.

The tears spill over the bottoms of my lashes, and I feel the heat in my chest engulf my lungs threatening to pour out of me. "Why would you do this? How could you do this to me, Mother?" I ask her desperately.

"Bellatrix," she starts, reaching for my hand again but I pull away.

"No. Don't. You did this to me, this was not my choice and now people are going to die either way." I shake my head at her, and then glance at my father, giving him a disappointed stare. I didn't realize that the only people in the world meant to protect you, would also be the ones to destroy you.

I rush from the room and down the long hallway to the other side of the castle, heading for my room. I just need to be alone. Alone to sort my thoughts. In the last two days, I've come to understand that; there's a hit out on me from a king in another land, dragons exist on our lands again and unless I find a king to rule with me, I'll probably be murdered so I have to keep fucking men until one of them survives, and that my mother will have to give her life if I want to reverse the spell put upon me. And the most shocking of all, is that somehow, I have this undeniable chemistry with a man who despises me and I almost took his life in my sleep because I couldn't keep my hands off of him.

It's good to be me, I think sarcastically.

I can't deny that he did save my life. Regardless of how he may feel about me, he chose to save my life by risking his. He said he didn't realize it was me, but even after he did, he had many chances to leave me behind and let the dragon or the warrior from Sperantia kill me. But he chose to pick me up and take me to safety. That's more than I can say for my parents. They've put me in danger far more times than they have seemed to guard me from it.

Throwing myself onto my comfortable bed, just as the sun starts to set, I realize just how coddled I've been here. I barely survived in that cave with Koen, between the cold and the fear. Yet, he hardly seemed phased by it all. His preparedness and re-sourcefulness made me look fragile and weak. It makes me wonder how many days and nights he's spent in the forest, hunting and creating his secret safety cave.

Doubt is weaving its way into my soul, causing me to rethink the world I thought I knew. Maybe I'm not cut out for being queen on my own. This week has shown me that I'm not as strong as I thought I was. Despite projecting a tough exterior for the men that come my way, I feel terrified inside. Terrified and unsure of my future in Tenuma. A future that after today is looking pretty grim.

A gentle knock comes at my door. "Hey, Trix," Quirina softly shouts across the room and rushes towards me. "I know you're exhausted and I won't stay long. I just wanted to come check in on you. What do you need? A fire? Food? Tea?" She begins firing off anything she can bring me.

A heavy sigh leaves my weak body. "All of that sounds wonderful, actually. I didn't have the energy to go down to the dining room today," I say softly with a yawn.

Quirina gets up to start a fire on the other side of the room in the giant stone fireplace. It's large enough that I can comfortably feel the heat through the entire room. I've never felt more grateful for its warmth.

After starting a fire, she heads out and comes back about ten minutes later with a tray full of bread, cheese, meat, fruit, and a mug of mint tea. My favorite. I pick up the steaming mug and carefully bring it to my lips. A satisfied groan escapes my lips as the liquid makes its way down, warming me from the inside out.

"I heard shouting from the king's room. I figured it was you in there with them. Are you okay?" Rina asks, concerned.

I shake my head, my watery eyes threatening to burst. "No. But I don't have much choice. I have to be," I tell her.

The truth is I feel terrified, but I feel like all I do is make her pity me. I don't want to keep giving her my sob story when truthfully, things could be much worse. If I've learned anything this week, it's that. And as much as I don't want to keep spreading my legs for the men of Tenuma, if this is what I have to do to protect the people here, I'll consider it a small price to pay. It's time I start becoming the strong queen I want to be. There's no room for weakness.

Wiping my eyes, refusing to cry anymore, I shoot for a change of subject. "How are things going with your perfect man?" I ask her, eating pieces of the soft delicious cheese, and hearty pieces of meat she brought.

She hesitates, not wanting to throw her happiness in the wake of my misery, but I need something to take my mind off of everything brought to light the last few days. My eyebrows raise and I give her a lopsided smirk urging her to answer.

The way she tries to suppress the giant smile that wants to plaster itself on her face says it all. "You had sex!" I shout at her.

She presses her index finger to her lips, glancing around nervously. "Shh!! No, not yet. But I think it's going to happen soon. I think he could be the one, Trix. I think I'm falling for him," she tells me softly.

My heart aches and my eyes water because while I do feel a little jealousy, mostly I'm happy for her. I love Rina and if there's anybody who deserves to be loved it's her. "Wow. You're falling in love? I'm so happy for you. You really deserve it, you know. I mean it," I say, squeezing her hand.

She smiles at me, squeezing my hand back. "I know you do. Look, whatever is going on, it's all going to work out. You're so strong, Trix. One day you'll be queen and you'll realize all this worry was for nothing," she tells me, but she has no idea the storm that's heading our way if I don't find a mate soon.

I twist the red bracelet around my wrist, pondering all the different ways tragedy can strike if things don't go as planned. Quirina looks down, taking my wrist in her hand. "This is beautiful. I don't think I've seen it before. Definitely not your usual style, Trix," she tells me, eyeing the bracelet.

I give her a soft smile, thinking of the kind woman who gave it to me in town. She probably needed the money for it just as badly as anybody else there and yet she was willing to give it to me for protection–her words. "No, I guess it's not. But I think it's my favorite piece." I pause, wanting to open up to her. Quirina is one of the smartest people I know and one of the few people who can talk me off a ledge. "Can I tell you something strange?" I ask her.

"Stranger than you killing men with your pussy? Sure, fire away, My Lady." Rina playfully flips her hair over her shoulder and leans forward, eagerly listening.

I can't help but let out a small laugh at her absurdness. I can always count on Quirina. "When I wear it, sometimes it… tingles. My skin feels as if it's pulsing or tingling underneath it." I tell her, running an index finger underneath, between my skin and the bracelet.

She eyes me warily. "What do you mean it tingles? All the time? Or when you're having sex?" she asks.

I shake my head. "No. Not during sex at all, actually. It just feels like it's pulsing, but only at certain times," I tell her hesitantly, knowing she's going to make more of it than she should. But I also know I'm doing the same thing in my head.

"Well, what are you doing when it tingles?" she asks me with a curious smile on her face.

"It only does it when I'm close to Koen. Or if we're touching," I tell her quietly, not wanting anybody else walking by to hear. Even though my room is giant, and my door is thick–and closed–I can't be too careful anymore.

Her eyes go wide and her mouth drops open. "Trix! How many more signs do you need? For some reason, you two are drawn to each other and this seems like more than a coincidence," Rina points out.

"A sign for what?" I ask her.

"That you guys might be drawn to each other for a specific reason," she says plainly.

"There's definitely something between us that I can't explain. But even so, it's not something I can explore. We both know that," I explain.

She sighs dramatically. "Maybe. Wouldn't it be weird if he has the same bracelet, though?" she says casually with a laugh. When I don't respond, and I pull my lips inward together, making a face, she gasps. "Was he wearing the same bracelet, Bellatrix?" she asks me.

I nod, which causes Quirina to bury her face in her hands like she cannot believe all the stacking evidence I'm ignoring.

"It's not that big of a deal. I mean, I'm sure half of Tenuma bought the same bracelet from that lady at the market," I tell her.

She rolls her eyes dramatically. "A guy, though? This doesn't look like something a guy typically wears by choice. I've never seen a male in town wearing something like this, have you?" she asks me.

Nope. Just Koen, I think to myself. Even without speaking, she knows what I'm thinking. The smirk she gives me makes me throw a pillow at her face.

"Hey!" she gasps.

"Go have sex with your Prince Charming and let the princess sleep. I'm tired and I don't need you filling my head with fantasies," I tell her and then throw my head back into my pile of fluffy pillows, pulling my blanket up to my neck.

"I love you, Trix," she tells me, picking up the trays of food and tea, heading towards the door.

As she exits the room, I tell her I love her too.

With the room silent once more, I watch the fireplace crackle and dance and my mind can't help but wander to Koen. I wonder what he's thinking and if I'm crossing his mind as he lays in bed the same way it is for me. I scrub my hands down my face and groan in frustration. I need to push all thoughts of him from my mind, because tomorrow, my meetings start again and now it feels like the race is on to find a king. Not only to preserve my blood line in the castle, but to protect all of Tenuma.

18

KOEN

I lay in bed awake for two reasons; one, I slept all day, and two, I remembered I have to resume work at the castle tomorrow and will have to see the princess. After what happened in the cave, I don't know how to act around her. I'm there to do a job, so I shouldn't worry about it, but part of me can't stop thinking about her hands on me and what it would be like to kiss her. Every time she crosses my mind, I have to internally slap myself for allowing my thoughts to go there.

She's off limits.

She's deadly.

She is not for me.

Yet, I know something happened in the cave with her. We both awoke to discover that our hands were on each other. Who initiated it? Was it her or was it me? Why didn't either of us realize what was happening? That's not typical behavior for me. I may not have had sex with a woman in a very long time, but I'm not an animal. I can control myself.

It's hard to ignore the way my body responds to hers. Whenever she's near, it's not only the bracelet that tingles, but my entire body. The way my dick responds to her voice, the way her corset dresses push her perky breasts up even further and the confidence she oozes. It's not just the confidence, but the vulnerable side that she keeps hidden, that I find completely irresistible. My mind knows she's deadly, but I wish my body was also aware.

Mellani is in bed with our mother, despite usually wanting to be cuddled up next to me at night. She got up shortly after we went to bed; I think all my tossing and turning kept disturbing her and she was sick of me knocking into her tiny body. Lying here wide awake only makes it easier for my mind to reluctantly drift back to Bellatrix.

Her hands.

Her lips.

No. You decided to put all thoughts of her out of your mind.

She. Will. Kill. You.

Even though I tell myself this, I still fall asleep and dream I'm back in the cave with the princess and our hands are all over each other. It's the second time I've dreamt of her and each time, I wake just before I get to kiss her.

"Wake up, big brother!" Mellani shouts as she plops her little body on top of mine, crushing my lungs.

I crack an eye open and see her smiling brightly at me. "I'm awake. Why are you crushing me?"

She giggles and hops off. "Sorry! Will you help me with my medicine before me and mommy go to town?" she asks sweetly.

I stretch out my limbs and pull myself up, following Mellani to a shelf against the wall where she keeps all her drawing supplies. On the top shelf sits her vial of medicine. It looks more like a perfume bottle than medicine, so I take the lid off and sniff it before I start measuring it out. The light blue pear-shaped bottle is partially see-through, with gold décor laying around the top part of the bottle that looks like lace and butterflies intertwined. The lid is a stopper with a bright blue butterfly on top. It's beautiful, but looks expensive and I can't help but wonder who would have put this in such an intricate bottle.

I take the bottle off the shelf holding it in front of me. "This is your medicine, Mel?" I ask her, sniffing the contents. It's definitely medicine.

"Mhmm," she mumbles, opening her mouth and pointing to her tongue so I can drop some of the liquid into her mouth. She swallows it without a fight, which she almost never does.

"Wow, good job, Mel. I'm glad this stuff seems to be working. Where did you say you got this?" I ask putting the stopper back in and placing it back on the shelf.

"In town," she says as she skips off towards the front door.

"Where are you going?" I shout after her.

"To play out front," she says over her shoulder, shutting the door behind her.

"Mel…" I protest but she is already out front. I don't like her playing out front, even if it is fenced in, knowing there's a dragon somewhere on our land.

"Good morning, honey," my mother says sweetly, as she comes over to caress my cheek. Her long dark brown, curly hair is braided to the side. It looks soft and smells just like my mother. She smells like lavender, warm and inviting with just a hint of spice.

"Good morning, Mother. Mel is out front, but look, I don't think it's a great idea with a dragon out there somewhere.

She needs to stay inside," I object.

She waves her hand flippantly at me. "If that beast is anywhere nearby it won't matter if she's inside or not. I'm leaving with her right now, anyway," she tells me.

"Are you sure you don't want to wait until I can walk you both into town?" I ask, hoping she will acknowledge the very real threat outside.

"We will be fine," she says confidently. "See, I'm protected." She raises her wrist, showing off her own bracelet. Even though it's ridiculous, it makes me smile. She swears these protect us, but if that were the case, wouldn't everyone in town be protected then?

"Mother, I don't know that it works that way," I say laughing lightly.

"You've been wearing yours since I gave it to you right?" she asks and I nod holding up my wrist so she can see it. "Did any harm come to you that day in the woods, or while in the cave with *her?*" She talks of the princess like she's poison. I guess she's not entirely wrong.

"Are you telling me that you actually possess powers to apply a protection spell on these?" I ask, pointing to my wrist.

She smiles at me and then just shrugs as she walks out the door to grab Mellani and head to town. "Don't you know not to question your mother? I love you, Koen," she says playfully right before she shuts the door behind her.

I sit back down after they leave, mulling over what she said. It would be strange to think my mother actually has any sort of powers. It would be even weirder if that's what protected me that day in the woods with the princess. Looking back, that winged monster could have shot flame from its wretched mouth and incinerated us, but it let us run.

Why did it let us run?

Is that the reason why my wrist always tingles?

Why does it only tingle in the princess's presence?

I don't have the time to sit here and wonder about it all day, because today, I have to resume work at the castle like nothing happened. Afterall, I need to get paid, so I have a job to finish. Since we have food, I don't have to worry about food or hunting and I can focus on the work at the castle.

I gather my toolbelt–even though most of what I need is provided, brush my thick brown hair and secure it back out of my face, smooth out my facial hair, tug on my boots, and grab a jacket. I sigh heavily as I walk out the door, knowing that today is going to be hard. It was so much simpler when my hate for the princess was glaringly clear. Now I'm not sure what I feel.

19

BELLATRIX

Today, Koen is coming back to finish working on the windows in my room. My plan is to be downstairs for the duration of his stay. It's not much of a plan, but I can't put either of us in the same fragile situation that we had in the cave. It's not fair to him. My focus is on my meeting this evening. I had a thought that if I put more effort into these *meetings*, then maybe my suitor will have a chance to genuinely like me. Maybe I can shift their intentions and he will survive.

Enjoying the sex part of it, is not an issue for me. I love sex. I love the way it feels, I love how powerful it makes me feel. The obvious downfall is that it takes men's lives. I've been so focused on the sex part, that maybe if I try to focus more on our interactions beforehand, I can change his fate. Maybe.

I'm sitting at my vanity, staring into my gold filigree-trimmed oval mirror, trying to make myself as beautiful as I can for tonight. I want to look like someone he will want to wake up to every day, not just for tonight. I swipe my cheeks with some pink blush, swipe a light gold shimmer across my eyes and paint on my signature red lipstick. Using my makeup like armor, I try to mentally prepare myself for tonight.

And Koen, I think before I can stop it.

No. I cannot lust after him, even in secret, anymore.

I'm just finishing up my lipstick when I hear my door squeak open and look up to see Koen standing in the entrance as if I summoned him with my thoughts. I gaze all the way up at his tall stature and all I want to do is climb him like a tree. His gray eyes take me in as I stare back, unable to stop myself. Neither one of us says a word. Immediately, that familiar tension and heat has returned, making my chest heavy and my throat tighten. We don't need to talk, simply being in each other's presence is enough to cause a full body tremble.

He clears his throat, snapping me out of my trance. I force my gaze back to my mirror. "I'm just finishing up, I will be out of your way shortly," I say coldly.

I hear his footsteps move into the room and then pass behind me, as he makes his way towards the last window he needs to finish.

"No need to leave on my account, Princess," he says, matching my tone.

"I have a busy day. I can't stay here with the handyman all day," I snap back. He clearly still despises me, which should please me. Instead of relief, I feel disappointment.

He scoffs, crudely slamming down the ladder and tools, causing me to jump in my seat. "Sorry, Princess. The dumb handyman slipped," he responds, mockingly.

He's looking for a fight and I don't know why. This is how things are supposed to be between us, and in all fairness, he treated me poorly when he first met me. I would have been happy to be polite and civil, but he couldn't stand to be in the same room as me.

I roll my eyes and glance back at the mirror. I need to finish my hair and get the hell out of here. I braid my long hair down my back and then twist it into a bun and secure it behind my head. I spritz myself a few times with one of my perfume bottles, and then slam it back down as I exit the room.

With my head down, I start walking down the hall when hearing my name stops me.

"Oh, there you are, Bellatrix." My mother stands before me, proudly wearing her crown, sporting her typical floor length corset dress, not unlike mine. Hers is a deep maroon color, whereas mine is an emerald green. Her neckline doesn't dip as low as my sweetheart neckline goes and her train is longer. I'm grateful for the shorter train, I hate feeling like I'm always stepping on all that extra fabric. She looks as beautiful as she always does, but she's come here to deliver a message I know I'm not excited to hear.

"Hello, Mother," I simply respond.

"You look beautiful!" she comments, taking in my hair and makeup. "Quirina is really wonderful, isn't she? She did a great job!" I force myself to hold back an eye roll. My mother doesn't even think I'm capable of doing my own hair and makeup, yet I'm to be trusted being queen one day. Very soon.

Through gritted teeth, I force a smile. "Thanks."

She takes my hand in hers as we stand in the hall. "I know the last few days have been tough, but I wanted to make sure you were prepared for…tonight." She hesitates on the last word as if I've forgotten. As if, for one second of the day I forgot that my duty is to have sex with men, so I can be worthy of the throne.

"Yes, mother. Eye on the prize, don't worry," I tell her.

"Oh honey, don't be cross. I know this is a lot on your shoulders, but you're built for this. It really is better this way. You can handle it, and you're going to make a fantastic queen," she tells me.

"Well, if you didn't make this stupid deal for a curse to be put upon me, I could already be ruling with a mate of my choosing," I snap back.

Her back stiffens, and she pulls her hand back and clasps her hands in front of herself. "I was trying to protect you."

A manic laugh bursts out of me. "Ha! Protection? Some protection! You've subjected me to having sex with every man on this damn land! How is that protecting me?!" I yell back.

My mother's face has gone dark. "Lower your voice, Bellatrix. You are not to speak to your queen this way." Her eyes soften a little as she continues. "I never thought that, once word got out, that men would continue to sign up for this life. I only wanted you to have a mate who genuinely cares for you. I wanted you to have a better life than I did." I could be wrong, but it looks like her eyes are tearing up. As for how genuine it is, I can't be sure.

"Well, Mother, all you've done is turn me into a murderer. I think I'm better off without any more protection you have to offer," I say calmly, and start to walk past her. "Oh, and don't worry. I know how important it is to find a king, so I will continue to fulfill my duties," I say plainly and make my way down the long staircase.

It's just sex, I can do that. Except it's not just sex anymore. It's not just about a mate anymore. The fate of all of Tenuma rests on my shoulders…er, pussy. No pressure. But maybe, I've been looking at this all wrong. Maybe I am being selfish. Afterall, I enjoy having sex. Maybe this is just a way to make me stronger and more prepared to rule. I'm sure there will be all sorts of awful things I will have to do as queen. Maybe this isn't as bad as I make it seem. It's to protect Tenuma, to save it. I can do this.

I hold my head up higher and straighten my back. I will no longer be ashamed of who I am or what I do. There is a bigger picture here. It will prevent an even bigger atrocity from happening and I can stop it. I can't think of myself right now. I have to think of all the people here. Their survival depends on me finding a mate, so I will find a mate

20

KOEN

My knuckles are turning white as my hand tightly grips the sides of the ladder. I can't believe what I'm hearing right now. It turns out that I don't know the princess like I thought I did. There has been enough talk around town about her, with the men winding up dead, and seeing her cold personality, it's easy to make assumptions.

It *was* easy. Now I have no idea what to believe as I stand here listening to Bellatrix and her mother discuss her evening.

"Well, if you didn't make this stupid deal for a curse to be put upon me, I could already be ruling with a mate of my choosing."

"…all you've done is turn me into a murderer. I think I'm better off without any more protection you have to offer."

"Oh, and don't worry, I know how important it is to find a king, so I will continue to fulfill my duties."

I cannot be hearing this right. Their daughter comes home after almost being murdered by a stranger *and* a dragon and they immediately force her back into having sex with random men. I didn't even realize the princess didn't have a choice in the

My head is spinning at the revelation and my stomach feels queasy. As much as this is none of my business, I can't help but wonder if I should do something.

Keep your mouth shut. Meddling will get you killed. This is not your place.

I'm fighting with the angel and the devil on my shoulders once again, and one of them wins out, forcing me to get back to work. I take a deep breath and remind myself that she's not my princess and this is not my fight. This is the last day I will be working inside the princess's room and I will most likely never see her again.

She made it very clear she didn't want to be anywhere near me, so I'm sure she will seclude herself to her chambers once I've moved onto other parts of the castle.

This job cannot be finished soon enough.

I chug half of the large canteen of water I brought with me once I've finished up on the princess's last window. It definitely feels warmer than when I was here that first day. I stand back to admire my flawless work and I'm pleased with myself.

I gather my things to head home for the day, and when walking through the large room, something blue catches my eye on the princess's vanity. I walk over and pick up the item, noticing there's four identical items sitting on top of the vanity. It's blue, and pear shaped, with a blue butterfly on top of the stopper.

What the hell? This looks exactly like the one Mellani was taking medicine out of earlier.

How does the princess have the same exact ones?

She gave my sister money and medicine? But why?

Why is she going out of her way to take care of somebody else's child?

My heart aches in my chest and I want to scream. It's not her place to take care of Mellani. It's mine, and I'm fully capable of taking care of my family. I don't need her pity and I don't want her dirty money. She could get both of them in trouble for it.

Needing to get out of here before I say something I regret, I quickly make my way out the door and down the long staircase. I inform the man at the front that I will return tomorrow to start in the dining room, and I head for the door. As I make my way outside, something at the entrance of the garden catches my eye. I see the deep green train of Bellatrix's dress disappear beyond the hedges. I don't know what possesses me to do it, but I follow her inside.

Walking through the maze, I can't help but notice the craftsmanship and care taken to such a useless part of the castle. Why do they need this elaborate hedge maze/garden? I follow it around, until I'm finally at the center where it opens up into a beautiful garden. The aroma is heavenly, as the different flower perfumes invade my nostrils at once. But it's not the flowers that catch my eye, it's Bellatrix sitting on the bench, where just a few days ago I watched her pleasure herself.

Her back is facing me, and her head rests on her hand as her elbow is perched on the back portion of the bench. She appears to be consumed with whatever thoughts she's having, be- cause she doesn't hear me approach.

"Back for another round?" I boldly ask her.

She startles at the sound of my deep voice. "W-what?" Her voice cracks.

"I asked if you came back here for another round," I say, glancing up at her windows. Her eyes follow, understanding that I'm referring to the day she fucked herself right here in the garden.

Her eyes find mine again and widen when she realizes that I saw everything she did. "You weren't supposed to see that," she sputters out, still sitting. Her back twisted halfway towards me in an awkward position.

"You opened your legs in plain view of the windows I was working on. Did you think I *wouldn't* see you?" I ask, my voice laced with anger.

She looks at me confused. "Why are you yelling at me?" she asks.

I take a step towards her, lowering my voice. "Why are you going out of your way to take care of my little sister? The medicine you gave her, it's in the same bottle as your precious perfume collection upstairs," I say, glancing around to make sure nobody has heard us. We both could be in serious trouble if caught.

She stands up to walk away from me, clearly not interested in what I have to say. I grab her arm tightly, spinning her back around. The bracelet on my hand tingles immediately.

"What are you doing?" she asks in a panicked voice.

I loosen my grip, but grab her other shoulder so she's facing me just a few inches from my face. I try to concentrate, but I'm entranced by her red stained lips, and the way they immediately part when I'm this close to her.

"Why do you keep trying to take care of my sister?" I repeat softly.

She shakes her head. "We've covered this. So, unless you have any further questions for me, you need to get your hands off me," she demands.

I don't make any efforts to remove my hands, and I continue staring into her bright green eyes. My face softens as my dick grows harder against my better judgment.

"I do have one more question, actually," I say to her. "Are

you going to have sex with another random man tonight?" I ask, dreading the answer.

The shock on her face tells me that she wasn't expecting the question, as well as the fact that there aren't many people here who would talk to her this way. I truthfully don't know why she allows *me* to get away with it and I can't seem to control myself enough to stop.

"My sex life is none of your business, handyman," she fires back.

"Stop pretending like you don't know my name. And please, stop pretending that I didn't see you masturbate after I had my hands on you. You know my name, Princess," I say softly.

She bites her lip, and I feel her shoulders slump in defeat. Whatever defense she had just a moment ago, has completely faded away.

"Say my name, Bellatrix." I need to know that what I feel between us isn't just in my head. I'm aching to know if she feels it too.

"Koen," she starts softly. "I..."

"Don't do it," I plead with her.

Her eyebrows pinch together in confusion. Confusion at my concern for her. She doesn't know where this affection is coming from and frankly, neither do I. Evidently, there's a fine line between anger and attraction.

Unease settles between us as her head falls. When she looks up again, her eyes are filled with tears. "I don't have a choice. Please, I have to go," she says, wiggling out of my grip.

I hold on for just a moment longer. "Bellatrix, you don't have to do this. What they're doing to you... it's not right. I didn't understand before," I tell her.

She shakes her head. "It doesn't matter. I don't have a choice..." She pauses, pulling both lips in together. "It's okay, I want to do it."

She's lying, I know she's lying. I can see it in her fearful eyes. But what I don't know is why. Why won't she just tell me the truth? Granted, she doesn't owe me an explanation, but there's more going on here than a working relationship. There was more in the cave and there's more between us right now.

"Did you think I might see you? That day?" I ask her, referring back to the day I saw her pleasuring herself in the garden.

She takes two steps away from me before she answers. "Yes. I knew you might," she says quietly.

"Why?" I ask breathy.

I can see her chest rising and falling just as heavily. "I wanted you to see me," she says.

I reach for her, but she shakes her head, and backs away. "No. I'm not good for you, and I'm to be somebody else's mate. Go back and take care of Mellani. I have to do this," she says before hurrying back out of the garden, leaving me standing alone.

She wanted me to see her, which means that the hatred she portrays when I'm nearby is nothing but an act. There's more to her. She's been secretly taking care of my little sister, and she definitely feels that electric current running between us. If a simple interaction where I save her from falling on her face has her rushing to a private place just to masturbate, it's safe to assume she feels it too.

I smile to myself before exiting the garden and heading home. Something new just took over my dislike for her. Everything I thought I knew of her, is in flux.

How can I blame her for the lives she's taken when it's never been her choice? How can I hate her when she has such a sweet soul? She refuses to show it to anybody but Mellani. Maybe her handmaiden, Quirina, too–they seem to be fairly close. What I don't understand is why she portrays herself so cold and cruel when she clearly has a conscience and a warm heart that wants to give.

I went to the garden to get answers, but I'm leaving with even more questions. All I know is, the princess can run and hide from me all she wants…but for the first time, I'm starting to see exactly who she is. What's happening here is going to stop.

21

BELLATRIX

I don't ever want this to stop. My thighs grip his face between my legs and my suitor is licking up my juices like his life depends on it, which I suppose it sort of does.

"Don't stop!" I shout at him when he tries to rise and I grab the back of his head and hold it in place as I grind against his face. I wish I could say I'm picturing him, and not Koen between my legs. Not that it would change the outcome if I was.

After the way he grabbed me and confronted me today, it's been painful getting to tonight. All I wanted to do was to grab Koen's face and straddle him right there in the garden. There's no way we can be together, without him suffering the same fate as the rest of these men, and I know my heart would die right alongside his afterwards. Koen is where I draw the line, even if every bone in my body aches for him in a way I didn't know was possible.

Tonight, I get the next best thing: an eager man with a big dick, and a beard similar to Koen's. Okay, so it's not the next best thing, but it's still pretty good. Dinner with him was stimulating enough. He wasn't a complete bore, but he also didn't feel the need to fill the silence with pointless conversation. He drinks whiskey like I do, whereas most of the other men opt for red wine because they think it's what I would drink. Don't get me wrong, I love red wine too, but whiskey is my go-to drink. Just like my signature lip is red, my signature drink is whiskey on the rocks.

Tonight's suitor is sucking and biting me in all the right places, but it's just not going to get me off and deep down, I know why. I'm staring at the wrong face. I know he's not Koen and deep down–but not that deep down–I'm simply not interested in anybody that isn't him, so my body is going to reject them. This should make finding a mate fun.

I try to store away the guilty feeling that comes along with that for another time.

I place my foot on his shoulder and push him away, his face lifting from my pussy. "Stand up, I want to suck your dick," I tell him. Usually, I don't do this with my suitors, but I've been so horny all day since my talk with Koen, acknowledging that he saw me masturbate for him.

I kneel in front of him on the floor and take his large cock in my hand. I close my eyes, picturing Koen's tall, muscular body standing before me. Spitting on my hand, I stroke him a few times before opening my mouth and shoving his large cock in. It's girthier than it is long, so I have a hard time getting it very far into my mouth, but I keep going. I need to get myself off so fucking bad, so maybe shoving his dick down my throat will do the trick.

With my other hand, I bring my fingers to my clit, massaging it as my pussy gets wetter. The wetter my pussy gets, the easier sucking a dick gets. Weird how that happens. I let out a moan with my mouth still wrapped around his dick, moving my fingers down to my opening. I slide one finger in and then two. Two fingers doesn't feel like enough, so I push a third finger inside my pussy and start pumping them in and out. I gag on his big dick while I finger fuck myself, and the release I'm already feeling is making me lightheaded. I want more.

I pull my head back and let his dick fall from my mouth, taking my fingers out of my pussy and smile up at the bearded man. I stand up and crook my finger for him to follow me over to the bed. Enough play time, I need my release.

I lay on my stomach on the bed and arch my ass into the air, inviting him to come closer. On my forearms, I twist my head back, my silky black hair falling over my opposite shoulder, and give him a seductive smile.

"You want it?" I ask in my most bewitching tone.

He nods and inches closer, his eyes taking in the scene before him. The look on his face shifting from lust to worry back to 'fuck-it,' likely realizing that my naked body might be one of the last things he sees.

"Then come over here and fuck me," I demand, arching my ass higher and laying my chest flat on the bed.

Suddenly, he's kneeling on the bed, gripping my hips tightly with both hands and I feel his dick at my entrance, slick with anticipation. "Anything you want, Princess," he says, and then thrusts into me, making me gasp.

He feels even bigger than he looks as he fills my pussy. He thrusts in and out, hitting me just where I need him to in this position. Clenching the sheets with my hands in front of me, my climax is already so close. I can feel my body starting to tingle from my toes, moving upwards. I take one hand and rub my clit, and that sends me over the edge.

My whole body tightens and my pussy grips his cock as I come. As soon as I finish, he pulls out and unloads himself, drizzling it across my ass. Once he's finished, he collapses next to me panting heavily on his back next to me on my stomach.

Turning towards him, I know our time together is over. "Get me a towel," I request.

The naked, bearded man quickly pads across the large room and grabs one of my plush white towels from the rack, returning to clean me up. He might be fucking me to gain power, but at least he has some manners.

We both get dressed in silence, knowing what is likely to come next. It's easier for me to get them out of my room as quickly as possible so I don't have to witness it. I swallow the remainder of whiskey in my glass, and walk him to the door in my long silk red robe.

"Thank you for the opportunity, Princess," he states as if this were a business deal. I guess in his eyes, it was.

I sigh, my lips forming a tight-lipped smile that is neither genuine nor happy. "Goodbye," I say and open the large door for him.

As he's stepping out, I notice my best friend, Rina coming down the hall right on cue, to get me through another one of these ridiculous evenings. Her face is scrunched together like she's not feeling well. I guess I'm not the only one who had a bad night.

Suddenly, the look on her face is no longer a mystery. "Edwin?" she asks the man leaving my room.

The bearded man glances back and forth between us, his face suddenly matching her panic and worry. "Quirina… I-I'm sorry," he says quickly, and then runs down the hall towards the stairs and out of the castle.

Pure panic rises in my chest. My eyes are wide, and my mouth wide open. I just had sex and probably killed my best friend's boyfriend. My hands start to shake as I realize what just transpired.

Rina's eyes have completely filled with tears, standing motionless, her eyes locked on mine with absolute horror as she registers the betrayal. "No. Trix, no." She can't seem to get a full sentence out, so she just keeps saying 'no.'

I pull both lips into my mouth to keep them from trembling. I don't know what to say to her. How could I not have realized this was her boyfriend? He works here, I should have known. So many of the workers have similar builds and beards. He looked like any of those other schmucks. But he wasn't. He was her schmuck. The man she was falling in love with.

I slowly move forward reaching for her with one hand before realizing that I still need a shower. I pull my hand back. "I didn't know. Oh God, Rina. I didn't know. You know I would never—"

She cuts me off before I can finish, holding one hand up defensively. "Stop. I don't need to hear that. I talk to you about him every day. How could you not know?" she asks me. It's a fair question.

I run my hands through my hair frustratingly. "I don't know, Rina! I just didn't. I don't set these stupid things up. You know that. I don't have any choice here! These are not my decisions. This was more *his* decision than it was mine!" I say trying to justify my involvement. But as soon as it leaves my mouth, I know it's the wrong thing to say. I'm in panic mode and all I want is to rewind the night and somehow take this whole encounter back, so my best friend doesn't hate me.

"Oh. So, it's all his fault then? Everything you do is everyone else's fault?" She pauses, raising her index finger to rub her lips clearly getting angrier. "When are you ever going to start taking control of your life, Trix? One day you will have to start taking responsibility for things you do," she says furiously.

My eyes are watering now because of the way she's talking to me. I've never seen her like this. Finding out she felt this way about me all along is almost enough to make me buckle right here in the hall. Quirina is the only person I've been able to confide in all my life. She's been here for me since this all began and I thought she understood what I was up against. Turns out, she has the same mindset as the rest of Tenuma. She thinks I'm a selfish whore.

I take a step back like I've been hit. "I am so sorry, Rina. I don't know what to say. What can I do?" I beg.

She scoffs at me, a scowl plastered on her face. "You can stop sleeping with other women's men. It needs to stop." Her response is like a slap to the face and it makes my cheeks burn.

I don't reply, because there's nothing I can say to her right now. She's understandably hurt and anything I say will only make things worse. I need to let her go. She needs to be angry. It's clear from her words and the way she's looking at me, that she needs to be anywhere but here. After a moment of neither of us saying anything, she turns around and walks back down the hall away from my doorway.

I'm left standing in my doorway staring down after her, wearing a robe, but feeling completely exposed. I've tried my hardest to make the best of these meetings and not think of the horrible thoughts about me that are so easy to do. But tonight, I feel like a whore.

Having sex with these random men was for my parents, for the townspeople, for all of Tenuma. I've never done this for me. I never wanted this, but it still all falls on me. I know in my heart that I didn't know that man was Rina's boyfriend—not that I feel bad in the slightest that he will perish, but what would I have done had I known? Would I have finally put my foot down and stopped it? Would I have found Rina and told her?

In all honesty, that scumbag deserves what he has coming any minute now. He was with one of the sweetest, most beautiful women in all of Tenuma, and he still threw away what they had together for a shot at power. I don't feel bad for what he's about to endure. I do feel bad that my best friend got hurt in the process by both me and him.

Quietly closing the door behind me, I rinse off in the hottest shower I can stand, needing to wash this awful night away, and then I climb into bed where I cry myself to sleep. I don't know what I need to do, but I have to make things right with Rina. She's the only person I have and she didn't deserve this. I don't want to be the kind of woman that causes other women pain and heartache. It needs to stop.

22

KOEN

Taking the sword from the leather belt around my waist, I thank the deer for its sacrifice and put him out of his misery with a quick slice under its throat. My arrow shot through its leg, but I am not one for letting animals suffer, so I quickly got up to end any pain it was feeling.

There are different types of hunters. Most use bow and arrows to wound the animal and then we quickly end its life. These are the men who are just trying to survive. Men providing for their families.

Then, there are the ones who let the suffering prolong. Men who shoot an animal and then torture it before it dies, amused by watching it suffer before choosing to ends its life. These are the ones who enjoy the chase. They aren't just trying to survive, they are looking for power. These men enjoy the minis-cule power they hold over the dying animal and bask in it as long as they can, feeling like a God.

My father was one of those men. He taught me many valuable lessons while he was with us, but one I will never forget is his greed for power. I watched him let a deer suffer for nearly twenty-five minutes while I bawled my eyes out, begging him to make the whining stop. He called me weak and told me I'd never be strong enough to survive in this world. I'll never forget that day. I was eight years old and I knew from that moment that I never wanted anything to do with the power he was trying to harness. I learned that power was evil. Even though I wouldn't admit it until much later, I knew my father was evil. I decided I would never be that kind of hunter. I would suffer myself, before I let another living thing suffer because of me.

The deer I shot today will feed us for many days, and I'm pleased that I can bring this home for my mother and sister.

Nobody has heard or seen the dragon since the princess and I first witnessed it last week and it's starting to feel like I imagined it. Nothing has changed, and it doesn't feel any more dangerous in the woods than it ever did before. If the kingdom is doing anything about its existence, I wouldn't know. There has been no mention around town of any dragon, aside from what I have told my family and a few close friends. I could ask the princess if she knows anything, but when I'm in her presence, mythical creatures are the last thing on my mind.

Grabbing the deer by the legs, I load it onto my sled and pull it home to show my family my prized kill.

Swinging the door open to our cottage, I step inside, leaving the sled with the deer out front.

"Whoa, Koen. Baby, you stink," my mother says in this way only a mother can insult you and yet, still sound sweet.

I laugh, walk up to her and kiss the top of her head.

"That's the smell of being a man, Mother. I had a great day in the woods today," I tell her proudly.

She rolls her eyes. "Oh no. Not another rendezvous with the princess I hope," she pleads.

I throw both of my hands up in the air. "What? Why would you even think that?" I ask her, confused.

She's standing at the kitchen counter making sandwiches for the three of us, alongside some sliced apples. She lifts the knife she's using and points it up at me, talking to make her point. "I see the way your face lights up when you talk about her, even when you're saying something nasty about her," she claims.

I can always count on my mother to call me on my bullshit. I raise an eyebrow at her. I definitely have *nasty thoughts* about her, but it's not the kind she's thinking. Definitely none I'm willing to admit out loud. "Is that so?" I put my index finger on top of the knife slowly lowering it back down, so it's no longer pointed at me. "Well, regardless, let's keep the weapons down on the counter." I chuckle.

My mother rolls her eyes, looks up smiling at me and then resumes cutting the apples. "I'm just saying. I know how men think, and you need to stay away from her." She's told me this many times before, but she acts like it's the first time I've heard it.

"Mother. I understand that and believe me I'm not going anywhere near her. But what is your issue with her? You seem to really despise her," I say, genuinely curious. I understand her fear of not wanting me to sleep with her, but I've made it clear that I'm not going to. So, what else is it?

She flings her hand flippantly at me. "Oh honey, I don't even really know her. You know me, just an overprotective mother. I don't want you losing your head around her. I wouldn't want you to forget what power she holds and make a mistake you can't take back. She's not like other women in town," she says in a light tone, but there's a heaviness to her words.

I sigh. "Okay, Mother, I hear you. I do. Now, can you just let me be excited that I brought us home a deer?" I change the subject, hoping she will stop forcing me to think about Bellatrix. I'm having enough trouble doing that on my own.

Her expression shifts to surprise. "That's great, honey, but we have money now and I don't mind going to town with Mel. We can get food in town and it's easier than having to go hunt and prepare it for us to use," she informs me.

"I know, Mother, but this way you two don't have to walk to town alone. With this dragon situation… I know it sounds dramatic, since it seems like it just vanished, but I worry about you two. I'd rather you two didn't spend as much time outdoors, just for now," I plead.

The corners of my mother's mouth turn up as she slides a plate in front of me. "My boy, you are going to make a wonderful father one day. But you have to stop worrying so much. I am an old woman and I have both experience and wisdom. Taking care of myself and Mel is nothing new." She slides her palm up to my cheek and caresses it for just a moment before calling Mel for lunch.

I make my way to work, taking comfort in the fact that I convinced my mother to stay home for the week with Mellani. Without knowing what's to come regarding dragons possibly being in our world, my sanity needs to make sure they are somewhere safe. Feeling at ease, I push thoughts of my mother and sister to the back of my mind as thoughts of the princess begin to surface.

Like a snowstorm, this woman came blowing into my life suddenly and froze me in my tracks. My hatred for her is dissolving, suddenly replaced with feelings of compassion. I'm unsure why she seems to be drawn to a commoner like me. I have nothing to offer her other than snide comments. Not that I'm offering her anything, anyway.

Get it together man, I reprimand myself.

The princess's room was finished, so I no longer have any reason to be up in her chambers, and I suspect she will be avoiding me at all costs after our last interaction. My work today will take place downstairs in the dining area; I'd call it a room, but it's large enough to fit three of my cottages inside. There are six floor-to-ceiling windows in this room as well, so I will be here for at least another week. I used to cringe at the thought of being here, however, now I find myself eager to come back. I'm determined to get to the bottom of why the princess feels like she can't stop killing these men.

Princess Bellatrix doesn't bat an eye when she sees me walking through the front doors of the castle, as she's making her way downstairs. It appears as though my timing is perfect, because she's heading to join the Queen in the dining area.

I walk around the large table, which is obscenely too large for the two women sitting there currently. The table is covered in more food than I've ever seen at one time, and I laugh internally at the thought of these two women making a dent in all of the food laid-out before them.

Quirina makes her rounds and pours the princess a coffee, dropping a small stack of papers next to it on the table. "Your schedule for the week, My Lady," she says, clipped. Her words are respectful, but her tone is harsher than I've ever seen her talk to the princess.

That's peculiar, I think to myself.

Making my way over to the first window just behind the table, I set my tools down on the ground and greet the women at the table. "Your Majesty," I say, bowing to the queen. "Princess," I address Bellatrix directly. "Should I wait until you both have finished your breakfast to begin? I would hate to disturb your meal."

Bellatrix doesn't even look up at me so I can't read her face. She didn't respond to Quirina either. There's something going on with her this morning. It's the queen who speaks up first.

"No, that won't be necessary. Do what you need to do," she says politely.

I nod, with a kind smile, turning back to my work.

"Why do you look so morose today, sweetie? Don't worry about last night. We will find your mate. We just need to be patient." I overhear the queen tell Bellatrix.

My hands grip the sides of the ladder as I'm working my way up, frozen in my tracks. My knuckles turn white, but I keep my head dipped down only sneaking a quick glance towards the princess. I see her eyes flicker up at me for just a moment. It happens so fast that if I wasn't already looking at her, I would have missed it.

Bellatrix scoffs quietly. "Easy for you to say."

Her mother, clearly not appreciating the response, drops her fork with a clang against her plate. "What is that supposed to mean?" she asks, her voice laced with anger. She sits up straighter, and her hands are flat on the table. She's a snake ready to strike.

A heavy sigh leaves Bellatrix in response. "Can we discuss this at a later time, Mother?" she asks.

"Why? You clearly have a lot to say. So, let's hear it," she hisses.

The princess takes a sip from her coffee, clearly not interested in a back and forth with her mother this morning. "It doesn't matter what I say," she responds calmly, setting her small porcelain cup gently back down.

Between the stand-off with the two women, and me frozen to the ladder, the room is silent. I can see the princess digging her nails into the table, and the queen's rigid posture. The energy is palpable and it feels like things could erupt any moment. Luckily, one of the guards comes in, addressing the queen.

"Your Majesty," he says bowing, his eyes panning over to see me standing at the window, halfway up the ladder. He looks back at the queen, then moves in, whispering something in her ear that clearly, I'm not meant to hear.

The queen dabs her mouth with her napkin and slowly rises from the table. If the message is urgent, she doesn't show it. "We will have to continue this another time, dear," she says, addressing Bellatrix as if they were having a tea party.

The princess flips her hand dismissively, earning a hostile glare from her mother who leaves the room with the gentleman, leaving me alone with the princess. Even though she just sat down, I worry she will get up any moment just to avoid my presence.

"Are you finding your chambers warmer now that my work is completed?" I ask her.

A small smile threatens to dance on her lips, but she forces it down. "Yes, it's been quite lovely. Although, anything is better than the cold of that cave," she adds.

I can't help but chuckle. "I didn't mind it," I tell her, thinking of how cold my cottage can get.

Her eyes go wide. "I don't know how you can stand it," she says dramatically, still mostly paying attention to her finger trailing the lip of her coffee cup.

"It's not much colder than it is at my cottage," I confess.

Her head snaps up at me. "What?" she asks, appearing aghast.

I huff in response. "Not all of us can afford a great big castle to live in, that's already pretty well heated and then hire somebody to come and make it even cozier for them."

She looks at me confused. "Yeah, but you know how to do this, you wouldn't have to hire anybody, you could just do it yourself," she insists.

I shake my head. "Supplies cost money, Princess," I say, clipped.

Her head lowers a bit, realizing how it must sound to me. The expression on her face from earlier is back, and I recognize it now as shame.

"It's fine, Princess. It's how most of us live. We manage," I tell her, trying to suppress whatever mental warfare she's currently battling. I don't want her to pity me or feel guilty for the life she was born into.

I see her twisting a bracelet around her wrist, the one that looks familiar to mine. A hand-woven red bracelet cradling a rose quartz gem in the center of it, laying delicately on her small wrist. The one I wear is a black hand-woven bracelet holding an onyx gem in the center. I know, because my mother made them both.

I feel a rush of cold surge through my body, wondering how and when she got it. Realizing that she must have gotten it when she was in town all those times she gave money to Mellani.

"I'm sorry," she finally voices.

My eyebrows furrow at her, confused at her apology. "For what?" I ask. Both of our voices are still low, as if we don't want to risk breaking the bubble we're in.

"For everything. I know you despise me and you think I'm disgusting. You don't know how I wish things could be different. You look at me and think I have it all. I look at you and think the same thing," she confesses.

I climb down the ladder, feeling unsteady when I talk to

her. The way she clouds my head when we talk, both frightens and excites me. "Things can be different. If you demand that they change," I tell her.

She shakes her head. "No. They can't. I… I'm not good. This is how things are."

The way she talks about herself–and thinks of herself–makes my heart twist in my chest. I know what she's thinking, because these are the same thoughts I had before I met her. "Stop. Just stop having sex with all those men. Refuse to keep going," I beg her.

Another shake of her head. "I can't, I have to find a mate. Our land needs a king," she replies firmly, tucking a strand of her long black hair behind her ear.

Anxiously playing with my beard, I find myself frustrated at the entire situation. "I don't want you having sex with random men anymore, Princess," I confess simply because I can't hold it back any longer.

The shock on her face as her eyes rise to meet mine is devastating. She's shockingly beautiful regardless of what her facial expression shows. "Why do you even care?" she asks.

I run my hands through my hair in frustration at myself, at her, at her parents. Mostly at me, for being a dumb ass and allowing myself to care about this in the slightest. "I don't know," I start. "All I know is you've got it all backwards, Princess. You've convinced yourself that your power is what you have to offer. You need to understand that *you* are the prize being offered." As I'm speaking to her, I close the distance between us and lift her chin with my fingers so I can gaze directly into her eyes. I swear to god, I haven't even slept with this woman but just looking into her gorgeous emerald eyes might steal my soul. My wrist tingles under her chin, the heat threatening to burn a hole right through me.

I watch as her chest begins to rise and fall more rapidly,

and her lips part, and her eyes plead with me. She could easily back away, but I feel her leaning in. A sick part of me can't help but picture her worshiping me on her knees. Those perfect red lips wrapped around me.

She is not your queen. She is not your mate, I have to remind myself.

But I still find myself leaning down towards her face. I'm desperate to feel her lips on mine. We are inches apart, and as easy as it would be to close the distance so I could taste the coffee and sugar on her tongue, I know I can't.

"You deserve more, Princess," I whisper against her lips, hovering for just a moment and then back away from her making my way back to the window.

I hear a loud screech against the flooring and without looking back, I know the sound is her chair legs scraping against the floor as she leaves the table. Resisting turning around, I hear her quickly making her exit.

You fool. What have you done? I scold myself again for not being able to keep my mouth shut around her.

One way or another, this woman is going to be the death of me.

23

BELLATRIX

Do I want to go upstairs and cry or do I want to go upstairs and masturbate? Every time I have a conversation with Koen, my body seems to be incredibly conflicted, but I'd say the overall theme is *horny*. My body screams at me to give in to him, but I know that I can't.

You are the prize being offered.

Why would he say that to me? Is he trying to get in my head? If so, why? Trusting men hasn't come easy for me. Even with my father. He always has expectations of me. If he's being nice to me, it's because he's going to ask me to do something I don't want to do. I just figured this was the male species, in general. This is just men, right?

Koen seems different, somehow. I can feel it. Not only that, he keeps *showing* me.

Once inside my room, I close the door behind me and lean up against it sitting on the floor, needing the cool against my body. Realistically, I know I can't have him, but I still find myself wanting to climb onto my bed and masturbate and pray he walks in on me. I want to give him a better view.

The knocking against the door snaps me from my day-dream causing me to jump, and rise from where I was seated. I swing the door open on the third knock.

"Oh, Princess..." Quirina says flustered. "I just wanted to leave this here with you. Koen mentioned that you didn't get a chance to eat," she states, holding up a tray of pastries, fruit, and a few pieces of sliced ham.

"That's very kind. Thank you. Please, come in." I step back, allowing her to step inside.

She sets the try on my vanity, and then giving me a tight nod, she heads towards the door to leave.

I move myself in her path to stop her. "Rina, wait. Please," I beg.

She stops, but says nothing.

"I don't know what to say to make this right. But I would never intentionally hurt you. What I said last night was stupid. Of course he didn't choose me over you. That's not what I meant at all. I should have known it was him and stopped it. You know this isn't the life I want. You know–" I'm talking as fast as I can because I don't know how long I have until she storms out of the room again, but she cuts me off before I can get out anymore.

"Stop," she says firmly, but quietly. "I know. I know all of this, Trix. Seeing him come out of your room was incredibly hurtful no matter the circumstance. You're my princess, and soon-to-be queen so I can't really stay mad at you, regardless..."

"Yes, you can. You should be mad. Just don't stop loving me. You're all I have, Rina. I can't lose you," I plead.

"I've been doing some thinking," she starts, and I'm terri-fied of where this is heading. "I think it might be time for me to move on. I would like to request a release from duty," she informs me.

My hand goes to my mouth as a weak gasp leaves my

mouth. "What? You want to leave?" I ask her, hoping I heard wrong.

She tucks her short curls behind her ear. "I just think it's for the best. What's going on… it's not right, Trix. We've both known since it began and I don't think I can be involved anymore." Her face looks defeated. What I did to her last night broke her usual bubbly, positive spirit and it makes me hate myself even more. Seeing her like this would be painful enough, but knowing I'm the reason why is unbearable.

My parents keep me forced into this lifestyle under the guise that it's for the good of Tenuma. If that's the case, why does it seem like all it's doing is hurting everyone around me?

My eyes are now welling up, and my throat feels like it's on fire. "Please." I don't even recognize my own voice, it's so frail. "Reconsider. Please don't leave me." My voice cracks around the lump in my throat.

Rina has been my best friend, and the only person who has kept me sane through this whole ordeal. She's been my rock, keeping me steady and picking me back up when I need it the most. I know I can't lose her.

Quirina can't even look at me, as she nods. "I'm sorry. I can't stay here anymore. It's too painful." She pauses, wiping away a tear on her own cheek. "Please let me go. I need to leave. I can't be here," she begs.

Knowing that as hurt as I am, it's nothing to what she's feeling. So I nod. "You're relieved from duty, but… I hope you change your mind. I still need you." My voice cracks on the last two words.

Quirina simply nods and her mouth forms a hard line, as she walks around me and out the door, leaving me quietly sobbing into my hands.

I want to be angry with her and I so badly want to have somebody else to blame, but it all comes down to me. I am the one who hurt her. My actions chased her away. It has felt as if my hands were tied in this situation, but maybe I just haven't fought hard enough for it to change. My parents have taken advantage of the fact that I depend on them, so I've been used as a tool to continue harnessing power over our people. For the first time, I see just how wrong it all is.

Between Koen and Quirina, I don't know how much more of a mental beating I can take, but there's still something I need to take care of.

$\mathcal{B}$ursting through the door to the king's room, I don't bother knocking because I know he'll be in the same spot–in bed–and unable to stop me.

There's a nurse and a guard standing close to his bedside, their eyes going wide as I burst into the room. They're alarmed, until they realize it's just me. My father is slightly elevated, drinking some sort of liquid from a spoon the nurse is feeding him with.

"Father, we need to talk," I command.

In a hoarse voice, he replies. "Is that how you address your king?" he asks.

"You're not the ruling king anymore and whomever I marry will be king. He will be the king I serve from here on out," I state.

His shocked face lets me know that I've finally got his attention, and with a weak flick of his wrist, he shoos out both the nurse and the guard leaving us alone.

"Okay, Bellatrix." His voice sounds weak and hoarse, but

is still so deep and carries so much bass I can feel it in my chest. "Say what you need to say," he commands.

Even though he's bed-ridden and doesn't technically hold the throne any longer, I can still see the powerful king that once ruled. A man that I used to look up to and fear. He still emits a power that sends a chill down my spine. I force myself to stand up straighter, refusing to let him intimidate me any longer.

"I'm done," I say, lacing my hands together in front of me, so they don't shake.

His lips slightly curl in a half smile. "Done with what?" he taunts, knowing exactly what I'm referring to.

"You know damn well what. The meetings. All of them. Stop scheduling them, because I am no longer going to be participating. All it's done is hurt everybody involved and I am no closer to finding a mate. It's not working. I am done," I say confidently, proud that I practiced this in my mirror before heading over here.

My father attempts to sit up higher in the bed. "Young lady, you are done when I say you're done. Otherwise, you can pack your things and get out of my castle," he threatens and I bet he's still counting on the weak girl I've been to continue being frightened and do what he tells me. What he doesn't realize is that I'm finally awake, and I'm done being controlled.

My mouth forms a sinister grin. "I thought you might say that. But here's the thing, you're going to have to go through your queen–my mother, and your new queen–me. Nobody is going to help you evict their future queen. It would be a death wish. So let me repeat it for you: I am done," I say, anger now clearly evident in my voice. I am daring him to contradict me, to challenge me.

He nods his head tightly, letting me know he understands me. Underneath I think I detect something resembling pride. Apparently, this family only responds to threats. I narrow my eyes and give another sinister, approving grin before I turn and walk towards the door. I reach for the handle before a thought stops me in my tracks. I turn around one more time. Having been going along with this for so long, it never occurred to me that I could actually put a stop to it, and I need to make sure he knows how serious I am.

"What you and mother have been forcing me to do is selfish and it's sick. I don't owe my body to anybody," I say with less anger and more conviction. I don't want to exit this room, and leave behind any doubt that I'm officially putting a stop to this.

I slam the door shut as I walk out feeling like a brand-new woman. Standing up to him felt fucking amazing, but the pit in my stomach makes me wonder what price I'm going to have to pay for what I've just done. As I stand on the other side of the door, the adrenaline starts wearing off and I can feel my body start to tremble.

Please don't let this be a mistake, I think to myself.

My mind is a blur the entire way back to my chambers, and it doesn't even occur to me that Koen was standing at the top of the stairs staring at me as I passed by until I'm behind my closed door.

What is he doing up here? I think to myself.

I hear a knock on my door but I don't even have to open it to know that it's him.

The door slowly swings open before I've invited him in. I see his face and partial body emerge from behind the door, with a worried expression. "Are you alright, Princess?" His voice is low and comforting.

Feeling the adrenaline and anger still coursing through my veins, I snap back at him. "I'm fine, handyman. I don't need you worrying about me, and I would like some privacy," I tell him firmly. It's like the last few years of allowing men to dictate everything I've done, every orgasm I have, every move I make, every decision I make has finally caught up with me and seeing a man is the last thing I need right now.

He raises one eyebrow in shock. "That's what you want?" he asks me, but really, he's asking if I want *him* to leave me alone.

"Yes, that's what I really want. I don't want you checking on me and I don't need you filling my head with your crap. I can handle myself," I spit out.

Instead of looking angry, and instead of yelling back at me, his face crumples. His eyes look disappointed, sad even.

He nods once. "Apologies, My Lady, I will conduct myself professionally from here on out," he quietly says, backing out of the room. It's not lost on me the fact that he finally used my proper title, but coming from him, it feels wrong.

I know he didn't deserve my cruelty, but right now, it's not about him. It's not about any man. My focus is less men. The last thing I need is a man clouding my judgment or telling me what I should be doing, especially Koen. I've never had a man impact my mind and my body in this way before. My words may have hurt him just now, but if he keeps trying to rescue me, I don't know how much longer I will be able to stay away from him and the pain he would then suffer would be far worse.

In time, he will see that I did him a favor and if not, then I'm okay still being the villain in his story. I'm used to it, I've been the villain my entire life. Willing to be the bad guy in someone else's story is different than taking lives and ruining the ones you leave behind. And that, I will not continue to do.

The dining room table is set for dinner, with its traditional resplendent spread. Sliced ham, turkey and beef, along with every vegetable known to man. There is also an array of home-made desserts that I can't wait to get my hands on. Looking at the quantity of food in front of me, I can't help but think of Koen and his little sister. I can't imagine living in fear of not knowing where my next meal will come from. The castle has been both shelter, and isolation from the real world. I have no idea what really goes on outside this castle, and that needs to change.

Mother joins me at the table, while father has plates brought up to him in his chambers, though he doesn't eat much anymore. While I'm not looking forward to the conversation that I'm sure is bound to happen with my mother, I'm grateful I won't have to see my father's face tonight.

Something shifted in me today and the longer I think about my life, the angrier I get for the way I've been treated. I've never been known to purposely stir up trouble or go against my parents' wishes. On occasion, I had pleaded with them to make the meetings stop, but never yelled at or demanded anything of them. As much as I don't want Koen in my head, he's a big reason why I felt compelled to stand up to my father in the first place.

Taking my seat next to my mother at the head of the table, I place my napkin in my lap, requesting wine in my glass. Whiskey is for when I'm feeling frisky, but tonight, I just want to sleep and ignore reality for a while.

"Well, dear, I hope you're pleased with yourself," my mother starts the conversation.

I raise my gaze to meet hers, unable to make out her expression. I don't know if I'm heading into the snake pit, or if she's going to accept the terms that I forced my father to.

I nod, giving a weak smile and tip my wine goblet up to my mouth, greedily allowing the red liquid to fill my mouth and coat my tongue before swallowing.

My mother, clearly not impressed with my non-response, clicks her tongue. "Don't you have anything to say for yourself,

Bella?" she says, making me cringe. My mother is the only one that calls me Bella and I used to find it sweet, but now it just makes me feel like a little girl. I hate it.

I shake my head. "No. I said everything I needed to say to father. You both know where I stand," I tell her, finishing my wine and setting my goblet back down and slicing up the meat on my plate.

"You don't know what you're doing. Not having a king will doom us all," she replies grimly.

I ignore her, instead directing my comment to one of the castle's servants walking by. "Excuse me." The man stops in his tracks, and comes over to where I'm sitting.

His head bows. "My Lady, how can I be of service?" he asks kindly.

I nudge my head to the windows where Koen was working today. "Those supplies there," I say gesturing to the remainder of supplies left on the ground. "Do we have any extra?" I ask.

The man looks over to the supplies on the ground and then back at me in confusion. "Pardon me, ma'am, I don't understand. Extra supplies?" he repeats.

"I am wondering if we have any extra supplies for the window project. I'd like some sent over to the handyman's home," I state, earning a strange look from my mother.

"I…I'm not sure," he stutters nervously.

Instead of protesting, my mother chimes in. "Please find his address and make sure the supplies are sent to his home. Please inform him that it was sent directly from Princess Bellatrix," she commands.

The man now facing my mother, bows his head in cooperation. "Yes, Your Majesty, I will make certain it is done," he says, quickly exiting the room, no doubt to find somebody else to follow through with the request.

I fill my goblet back up, staring at my mother, my eyes forming thin slits, but she just smiles back at me. I don't know why she just did what she did and I also don't know if I can trust it. It feels like a trap, somehow. My mother is never this agreeable.

She raises her own wine goblet, urging me to raise mine as well for a toast. I raise an eyebrow. "What are you doing?" I ask without lifting my glass.

"Let's toast, Bella," she says cheerfully.

"To what?" I ask skeptically.

She looks like she's thinking it over, but something tells me she already knows what she wants to say. "To getting what we want in this life," she states.

I roll my eyes. "I'm not going to change my mind, Mother. I'm done being used to wield power," I reiterate.

She laughs humorlessly. "Oh honey, that much is very clear. Now I know why," she taunts.

Fear rises in my gut, and my skin flushes, because I realize I just revealed a very important tell in front of my mother. One she can use against me whenever she wants to. "What are you talking about?" I ask, trying to play dumb.

"The *handyman?* I've never seen you do something like that before. I've noticed you two chatting quite a bit. You seem to be drawn to him," she confesses.

"What are you talking about? That man saved my life, Mother. I think the least we can do is let him utilize the leftover material for his own home. Heaven knows they need it more than we do," I say defensively. "Look around, I think we can afford it."

My mother swirls the wine around in her goblet, and I can see the wheels turning in her head. "You know," she starts with a sly grin. "You never did tell your father and I what you were doing outside the castle ground to end up in the woods to begin with. Maybe you were visiting a male friend. Maybe the handyman?" She accuses me.

The wine induced euphoric feeling I had moments ago fades as panic shoots through me, fearing what's to come next. I just had to open my big mouth in front of my mother. Wanting to sew my mouth shut for being so stupid, I pull my bottom lip into my mouth, nervously biting it, trying to figure out the best way to navigate this conversation.

I fake a bored sigh. "Mother, we both know that if I was seeing the handyman, he would be long dead. Why are you even accusing me of such a thing? He's a commoner, he's dirty and he works for us. That's not exactly the kind of man I want ruling next to me." I lie. It tastes bitter on my tongue. He's not here to listen to the awful things I'm saying, yet I still feel sick.

"It would explain why you were out of the castle grounds and why you're suddenly no longer interested in all the men throwing themselves at your feet, allowing you to find the perfect specimen to rule with. You don't know how good you have it, Bella," she shoots back, firmly.

I arch my eyebrow at her. "You sound jealous, Mother. I'd be happy to let you take my place and you can go fuck any of those men you like," I suggest, coolly.

Her hand smacks the table in anger, causing wine to spill over her glass. "Don't get smart with me, girl," she snaps. "Whatever you thought you decided earlier, forget it. You will continue looking for your mate as long as I'm around. I'm your mother and your queen. You will obey me," she commands.

My throat tightens and aches as I realize the last ally I thought I had, is gone. All of them are. I knew my mother wouldn't be happy about it, but part of me thought she might have my back. Afterall, it was her idea to put this curse on me for *protection*.

Anger and confusion swirling in my gut, I find myself wanting to throw up the few pieces of ham I managed to eat during this conversation. Feeling weak and defeated, my voice lowers to almost a whisper. "It's never been about protecting me, has it?" I ask, my voice shaky, scared to hear the response.

She ignores my question. "Hear me, Bella. You will continue searching for a mate, otherwise your new handyman friend will be answering to me for interfering in your life. He's not about to come in here and screw it all up now. Not when we're this close," she says, stabbing her fork into a piece of meat on her plate.

My eyes begin to well as I see the fury in her eyes, eyes that look so much like mine, but right now, terrify me. "So close to what?" I ask.

As if snapping out of a trance, she gently sets her fork down and her facial expression softens, her voice finding its sweetness again. "Enough business. Let us finish our dinner and get some rest. You have a few meetings tomorrow," she reveals.

My eyes go wide. "A few?" I ask, horrified. I've never been forced to meet with multiple men in one day before.

"Well, it seems like there are a lot of men with bad intentions out there, so we need to speed this thing up if we're going to filter through them to find the one man that can survive my strong queen-in-training," she says with the sort of cheer and sweetness that sends chills down my spine. I think I've had this all wrong. This isn't about protection at all. Whatever's going on, my mother is heavily involved. I need to figure out what she's hiding.

24

KOEN

A knock at the door in the evening never brings good news. The last time, it was Landric telling me he was going to meet with the princess and I never saw him again. I walk towards our front door hesitantly, anticipating what bad news is heading our way.

I swing the door open to see a man wearing the royal crest standing before me. "Koen Archer?" he asks.

"Yes…?" I respond cautiously. I glance around him to see two more men wearing the same royal crest on their lapels, standing next to stunning stallions, carrying what looks like the supplies I've been using on the windows at the castle.

Did I just get fired? I wonder.

"This is for you," the man states. He snaps his fingers and the other two men start unloading the supplies off the horses.

I put my hand up in protest. "Wait, these aren't mine. I don't understand," I tell them. These don't belong to me, and I definitely don't want to be accused of stealing from the king and queen.

The men bring forth all the items, laying them in front of

me on the front path. "This is a gift from Princess Bellatrix," the man states in an official manner.

My eyebrows furrow together and then I quickly turn my mouth up into a thoughtful smile when the man looks up at me. I might be confused as fuck right now, but I'm not dumb enough to send away a gift like this from the castle.

I take a handful of things one of the men hand me. "Please express my gratitude for the gift," I tell him.

My mom and sister are standing in the doorway behind me, watching the whole scene with curiosity, but staying quiet. Seeing three armed men from the castle in your front yard can have that effect on a person.

Once they get back on their horses and turn around, Mellani pounces out of the house eagerly to assess the situation. "What is all this?" she asks excitedly.

I look back to see my mother giving me an accusatory glare. "From the princess?" she asks, but it's not the question she wants to ask.

I shrug. "Apparently so." I pick up the mountain of supplies, thinking that *clearly* the princess has no clue how commoners live, because I could do the windows of four houses with what she sent over. The gesture was thoughtful, nonetheless.

Mellani helps me with some of the smaller items at first, but quickly gets bored and goes back to her drawings. As I make my last trip inside, my mother still has the same look on her face.

I glance up to see her arms crossed, staring at me. "What?" I ask her.

"What's going on with you and the princess?"

Scraping my fingers through the hair on my chin feeling agitated, I glare back at her. "Not this again, Mother."

"This." She waves her hand around at the new piles in our living space. "Is not a gift that the kingdom is known to send out of the goodness of their hearts. So, I'll ask you again, what is going on with you and Princess Bellatrix?" she demands to know.

I may be a grown man, and stand two and a half feet taller than her, but this woman still terrifies me to my core. I soften my glance at her when I see how serious she is. "Mother, there is nothing going on with the princess and I. Even saying that out loud is comical." I force out a harsh laugh.

She narrows her eyes at me, holding up my wrist in search of my bracelet. "Mmhmm. I'm just glad you've kept this on," she says to me, letting my hand drop.

Putting my fingers back through my beard, I recall seeing a similar bracelet on the princess's wrist. "Since we're on the subject of the princess, I've been meaning to ask you. Did you make a bracelet for her? Because I saw an eerily similar looking bracelet on her wrist recently," I accuse.

She puts both of her hands up, palms facing me that may as well be a white flag. "I don't know what you're talking about, son," she says, walking away from me to sit down next to Mellani on the couch where she's coloring.

I walk over and stand next to her. "Mother, now, you wouldn't lie to me, would you? Because it seems like you were very hesitant to have me working in close quarters with her and somehow, we both end up with your protection bracelets. That's quite the coincidence," I say facetiously.

She's mindlessly playing with Mellani's short brown curls—who is coloring on the table in front of the couch—and avoiding eye contact with me. She thought she was going to catch me in a lie and instead I may have caught her up to no good.

"Mother..." I push.

"Have I ever told you about all the magic I used to possess?" she asks.

I chuckle. "Yes, Mother. You used to possess the magic of protection, you can read *energies*–" I start but she cuts me off.

"Empath, baby. I am an empath. I can deeply feel other people's emotions. I know what they hold inside and what they hide from others. And don't forget–regeneration," she points out.

"Ah yes, the ability to heal quickly. Too bad you can't still harness that, because poor Mel gets sick so often." I chuckle.

"You laugh, but it's all true. I was once a very powerful woman," she tells me.

I sit down next to her, humoring her. "Well, what happened? Why don't you still possess these great powers?" I ask her.

Her eyes grow dark. "Because sometimes, magic backfires. Everything we do has repercussions. I am being punished for the magic I cast." She is still stroking Mel's hair, but gazing off into the room at nothing in particular.

The look on her face becomes completely serious and I've never seen her look so distraught when talking about the power she used to have. She's always used it as a way to make us eat the vegetables on our plate or clean up after ourselves. It's always been used in a humorous way. I've never seen this dark, distressed look she's currently portraying, like she's reliving an entire scene from the past in her mind.

I grab her forearm. "Mother…" I say quietly and her head snaps in my direction immediately snapping out of her daze. "Are you okay?" I ask, concerned.

She pats my hand on her arm. "Yes, I'm fine. Just got lost in memories for a moment. I'm going to get washed up for bed."

"Hey, would you mind if I went to Nik's for a bit tonight? It would be nice to catch up."

"Baby, you are a grown man, you don't need to ask my permission. As long as you promise me you'll be safe." She smiles at me.

"Always," I tell her.

"You're leaving?" Mel asks me with her best pouty lip,

looking up at me from the table where she's coloring another one of her many masterpieces.

"Just for a little while, sweet girl. So, you should cuddle up with mama tonight so you're nice and warm," I say to her.

She frowns at me.

"Don't worry, I'll be here in the morning to make breakfast," I reassure her.

"You promise?" she asks.

"With my life." I smile and kiss the top of her head.

"Koen!" Nik shouts as I walk through his bar doors.

The smile that forms on my lips is impossible to stop. Nik has such great energy. He's as tall as I am, thinner, and clean cut–which I always found endearing for a bar owner–with a chiseled jaw, chestnut brown wavy hair that's always combed and slicked back and brown eyes that look more like gold.

"Hey man!" I return the greeting and take a seat at the nearest stool at the bar.

Nik reaches out and grabs my hand in a firm shake. "I'm glad you came in. I've been wanting to catch up. Usual?" he asks.

I nod. "Yeah, when you get a chance." I glance around the bar and see that it's packed right now. I notice a bead of sweat over Nik's eyebrow when he moves about the bar.

"No problem. Give me a few minutes, I've been wanting to talk to you," he says, grabbing three beers between his hands and delivering them to the other side of the bar for a group of guys.

Nik's bar isn't the biggest or fanciest bar in town, but it's where most of the town likes to come. You get quality, affordable drinks, and everybody loves Nik. He's easily one of the most likable guys in all of Tenuma. He's always looking at the positive side of things, and is always there when you need a friend.

He comes back a few minutes later, brushing the hair out of his eyes with his hands. "Sorry, man. It's crazy in here, tonight," he says, dropping a drink in front of me.

I've been coming here as long as he's owned the place, so he knows my usual drink is whiskey on the rocks with an orange peel. It's exactly what I need after the last hectic week.

I take a long, slow drink of the whiskey, letting it burn my tongue before it goes down my throat. "Thanks, man, I needed this." I put my glass back down with a sigh.

He gives me a charming smile, and half chuckle. "Yeah, I wanted to talk to you about your little cave adventure," he says, accusatory.

"Not you too." I can't help but huff in exasperation.

He laughs with his hands up in front of him. "Hey, I'm just genuinely curious. It's not everyday that your best friend spends the night with a princess." He smirks at me.

"If I had any gossip-worthy stories, I wouldn't be here to tell them, Nik," I say deadpan.

His face crumbles at the mention of what the princess can do. I know we're both thinking of Landric. It's hard to believe that he's gone and even harder to believe that Bellatrix is the reason why. It feels like there's two sides to her; the one you hear about who murders men, and then there's this whole other side that she doesn't show to anybody except for the few glimpses I've seen. A side that is giving, vulnerable, misunderstood and just wants to make everybody happy. I'm finding it more and more difficult convincing myself that those two are the same woman.

Nik sighs heavily. "Well, we're glad to have you back, Ko.

What the hell happened out there?" he asks.

I take another swig of the decadent whiskey. "Where do I start?" I pause, needing another sip before I continue. "Things may be getting very interesting around here soon," I tell him, finishing off my drink and lifting it asking for a refill.

He grabs the bottle and fills my glass. "What do you mean?" he asks, his brows furrowing.

I lower my voice, because I know it's going to sound crazy. "There was a dragon," I confess.

He lifts an eyebrow in hesitation. "A dragon? An actual dragon?" I can see in his face he wants to laugh.

My expression is solid as stone. "Yes. An actual dragon. You can laugh, but they're back. Or they never went away, who the hell knows?" I say, swirling the ice in my drink and trying not to chug this second one.

"Okay," he says slowly. "For argument's sake, let's say I believe you. What the hell does this mean? They're just going to be flying around Tenuma now?"

I shrug as I sip my whiskey. "I have no idea, honestly. All I know is, the princess was being hunted down by some man and tried to take cover in the forest. I found her there, running from a damn dragon. I didn't even realize what my arrow hit until I was right next to it, man." I recount.

He puts up one hand in disbelief. "Wait, what? You're telling me you actually shot your arrow into a dragon?" He's smiling, half in disbelief, and half impressed.

I nod.

"Holy shit!" he says, clapping his hands together. "That's crazy. I can't believe you did that! Did you kill it?"

"No, it was definitely still alive as we ran like hell away from it. After the avalanche trapped us in the cave together, we never saw or heard it again. So, it must still be out there. I don't know if it died somewhere else or just went back from wherever the hell it came from," I tell him, finishing my second whiskey.

"Alright, slow down." He chuckles. "You're drinking those like you've got a death wish." He jokes.

I scoff. "Yeah, I might, actually."

His face gets serious at my remark. "What the hell are you talkin' about?" he asks, refilling the ice and whiskey in my drink, adding a fresh orange peel.

"I can't stop thinking about her," I reluctantly confess, mostly because I need somebody to tell me how stupid I'm being.

"Who?" When I give him an obvious look his jaw drops. "Oooh. The princess. That's uh…" He rubs the back of his neck, not knowing how to finish.

"Stupid. I know, it's stupid and pointless," I finish for him.

One side of his mouth turns up in a weak smile that doesn't reach his eyes. "I wasn't going to say that. You know it can't lead anywhere though. Are you seeing her?" he asks, concerned.

"Aside from that time we got stuck in a cave together, and the fact that I work at her home? No. I'm not seeing her. It's hard to explain, I know it sounds crazy," I tell him, running my fingers through my beard.

He nods. "Yeah, Ko, that does sound crazy. I didn't think that was going to come out of your mouth. All I've ever heard you say is how much you despise her," he reminds me.

"I do! I did!" I say, frustrated with myself. This is new territory for me. I've never had any woman confuse me this way and I've never wanted a woman the way I do her. How can I despise who she is and yet crave her with every bone in my body?

He gives me a wistful smile. "I don't know what to say, Ko. Did something happen between you two in that cave?" he asks, trying to figure out why I'm so clearly messed up over this woman I claim to hate.

"Did my mother send you?" I joke. He shakes his head smiling in confusion. "Nevermind. Yeah, sort of. But we were both asleep at the time. Which makes it that much more intense," I tell him.

A laugh bursts out of him. "Asleep? What the hell happened when you were asleep and how did you even know it happened?" he asks, amused.

"I woke up with her hands... all over me. And my hands were in her pants," I say quietly, sipping my whiskey just to hide my blushing face for a moment.

Nik's eyes go wide. "Holy shit, Ko! Are you crazy? You could have been killed!" he lectures, as if it's something I don't already know.

"Believe me, Nik, I know. It's just not that simple," I tell him.

Nik, who's always so calm and collected, looks frustrated with me. "No, Ko, it's pretty damn simple. She's bad for you, so you need to stay away from her. I'm not losing another one of my best friends. Don't be stupid," he demands.

I flinch at his words. Everything he's saying is true. From every perspective, it's very simple. She would kill me. She's bad for me. But when it comes to how I feel about her, and around her... it's anything but simple. But he's right, I need to be smart.

I comb my hands through my hair in frustration, mostly towards myself. "You're right. I'll be smart. There's just a lot more there. Unexpected things have happened and I've never been drawn to anyone else this way. It feels different, Nik. I can't explain it," I say.

He laughs. "I can, it's the money, the power, the beautiful face, bangin' body, and dangerous pussy. Yeah, you're drawn in the same way all those other schmucks were. Where are they now?" His voice is laced with irritation and impatience.

I feel my blood boil hearing another man talk about her

that way. I bury it down, trying to ignore the possessiveness I already feel for her. "No, man, it's not like that. I don't give a shit about any of that. You know me," I reply defensively.

"Yeah, I thought I did. Now, you're sitting at my bar telling me you have feelings for the *one woman* who can literally put you in the grave. Are you hearing yourself man?" He takes a calming breath. "Look, I know you're a smart man. Just don't let her get in your head. You won't be at the castle much longer, and then you won't have any reason to see her again. Just stay strong, and don't get involved with her anymore than you already are," he begs.

Just then, a rowdy group at the end of the bar flags him down, so he goes over to take care of them while I sit here trying to make myself sip my whiskey versus chugging it all down, letting it burn through me.

"Koen?" I hear a woman call my name from a few feet away.

I look up to see the princess's handmaid in the bar, sipping a drink. I almost don't recognize her without her usual uniform and she's definitely an attractive girl. It's hard to notice under the giant dresses and aprons they make the women staff wear. She's shorter than Bellatrix and curvier. Her short black curls flow freely and she wears a tight black t-shirt and light colored pants with black shoes. It's not the typical outfit you see women wearing in Tenuma, but it suits her. It shows off all her curves, and makes her look more feminine than the uniform the royals make them wear, which makes her look like a little girl.

"Quirina?" I ask, shocked because I've never seen her here. She doesn't strike me as a woman who inhabits bars very often.

She saunters over and stands next to me since there's no seats left at the bar top. "I thought that was you, handyman," she says, giving me a genuine smile.

"Handyman," I repeat, laughing.

She laughs with me. "What? You don't like your nick-name?" she asks, slurring a little bit. She's clearly been here long enough to have had a few drinks.

"Not really, no. Mostly because Bellatrix uses it as a way to insult me," I tell her.

"*Bellatrix*, huh? Are we on a first name basis now? I should have figured when you sent me up with food for her," she says, as her body sways. "You *like* her. You're *sweet* with her."

Even though she's drunk, I don't need her boasting about how I've got a crush on Princess Bellatrix to everybody in the bar. "I'm nice to everyone," I tell her, hoping to derail her thought process.

It works. She pats my back. "You *are* nice. You might be the only nice man left in all of Tenuma." She waves her arm around in front of her from one side to the other dramatically.

I can't help but laugh. "I think you might have hit your limit for this evening, Quirina. Can I walk you home? I should probably get going too. It's late," I offer.

"You see? You're such a gentleman. Unlike my boyfriend, who slept with my best friend," she says, slurring, her voice cracking on the last word.

My teeth clench at the thought of the princess with another man.

"Bellatrix?" I ask, hoping she's referring to another friend.

An emphatic nod confirms my fears.

Fuck.

This explains why Quirina is here tonight. She just lost her boyfriend to the one person she trusted most. I've seen those two girls together and it's easy to see how close they are so I can't imagine how this is tearing her up inside. Although by her alcohol-induced state, I can guess.

"Quirina," I say gently. "Come on, I'll walk you home.

This isn't going to help." I gently set down the drink she was holding and take her arm leading us to the front door. "Nik, we're heading out! I'm going to make sure she gets home safe," I shout across the bar, dropping some money on the bar top to cover my drinks. He never takes my money, but Nik works just as hard as any of us and I don't want to take advantage of his kindness.

He nods his head and throws up his hand as we leave. "Take care, Koen, be safe, man!" he shouts back across the bar, as he slides a few more beers in front of the group of guys at the end of the bar.

Walking through the front door into the brisk night, I can feel the light drops of snow starting to fall from above. The sky is bright, the way a snowstorm always turns the sky before it hits, lighting our way home. Making it easier for me to see the distraught look plastered on Quirina's face.

"It's not her fault, you know," I tell her, even though if there's anybody here who knows that, it's Quirina.

She scoffs, her eyes glistening. "I know that," she says sharply. Clearly, she's not ready for a pep talk.

I'm holding onto her by the elbow, so she doesn't slip and fall, as she wobbles down the road. I'm not sure how much she's had to drink, but something tells me her anger is intensifying it.

"It won't stop, you know. So, I wouldn't waste your time with her. You can never have her," she reveals, slightly lifting her head up to glance at me.

Her remark surprises me, making me unintentionally scowl. "What gave you the impression that I want anything to do with the princess?" I ask, trying to hide my disappointment.

She shoots me an incredulous look, and then shakes her head, focusing on the road ahead. Whatever she wanted to say, she decided against it.

"What?" I ask her, not satisfied with letting her continue with any misconceptions.

"It doesn't matter," she replies.

"You think you have me figured out, but you're wrong," I tell her, unconvincingly.

She laughs quietly. "Okay. Is that why you're defending her? Even though she's been nothing but rude to you?" she asks.

"She hasn't been r…" I start to say, as Quirina looks up at me giving me an 'I told you so' look. "Okay. Let's say, for argument's sake, you're right. Why can't things change?" I ask her.

"Because. Something big is coming. It's not simply about finding a mate anymore," she explains.

My eyebrows furrow and I put my arm out in front of her bringing us both to a stop.

"What do you mean? What is it about?" I ask her.

She pulls her bottom lip in, playing with a few of her curls nervously. "I shouldn't have said anything. Forget about it." She waves me off, trying to keep walking but I snag her elbow keeping us in place.

"No, tell me," I demand and then soften my tone. "Please," I plead.

She nervously looks around, as if we aren't the two people walking down the street at night, and lowers her voice. "There's a war coming. The King of Sperantia is attempting to overthrow Tenuma's monarchy. The princess has taken too long to find a king to rule with, which has left us vulnerable. He has already sent men in an attempt to kill her and they're not going to stop until she's gone," she confesses.

"That's who was trying to kill her that day she ran into the woods," I say with realization. "How do you know all of this?" I ask her.

"I hear things, working at the castle. I'm the princess's handmaiden, so I'm always in close proximity to her and the king and queen. I'm just the help, so they rarely even notice when I'm in the room. I overhear things that could probably get me killed. So, even though I won't be working there anymore, it would be great if you kept this between us, so they don't kill me for revealing their secrets," she requests.

"What do you mean you won't be working there anymore?" I ask in confusion. "You can't really be holding this against her. You know she has no choice!" I tell her, my voice penetrating the quiet of the street we stand on.

She sighs heavily, dropping her head. "I can't stay there. I know it's not entirely her choice to sleep with those men, but he was mine. I thought we were going to get married, and he went off and slept with her anyway," she says sniffling. "She's been my best friend my whole life and I just don't know how to get past this." She starts to shiver.

"If you leave her, she will have nobody. They're forcing her to do this, putting the fate of Tenuma all on her. She can't keep doing this. You see what it's doing to her, this isn't right. She needs you," I tell her, hoping she'll reconsider.

She shakes her head, crossing her arms in front of herself. "I don't think I can keep going back there. It's just too painful."

"You know her better than anyone, how do you think she's taking all of this? Being forced to keep sleeping with asshole men, who are only using her to rise to power as well as losing her best friend." I tell her, but by the look on her face, I can see that she's done talking. I take her elbow again, leading her forward. "Come on, let's get you home. A storm is coming."

25

BELLATRIX

There's a storm coming. I watch from my chamber windows as the snow begins to lightly fall. It's beautiful, but I loathe the cold. I think back to my time in the cave, feeling grateful that I'm in the confines of my chamber walls now, away from the elements. I stand mulling over everything my mother said to me at dinner, and the stupid things that came out of my own mouth. I may have unintentionally put Koen in danger, even though I've been fighting myself to stay away from him. I can't seem to do anything right lately.

I've lost my best friend, and I've put the only man I've ever been connected to in grave danger, despite my best efforts. It doesn't matter what I do, someone is always going to get hurt around me. Nervously twisting the bracelet around on my wrist, I glance down at it.

So much for protecting me, I think, taking it off and throwing it on top of my vanity.

Not only was I wrong about my mother, but she's now insisting that I have sex with multiple men in a day, in order to find a mate quicker. The thought makes me feel queasy.

More men will die.

More families will be hurt.

Because of me.

All of my life, I've been the cause of someone's pain. I'm not the son that my father wanted, I'm not the queen that my mother wants, and I can't even be the friend that I so desperately want to be to Quirina. I've tried to do everything that's been asked of me, and yet I still make the wrong decision.

If I keep having sex with the men that are sent my way, they will die. If I refuse, then my mother will take it out on Koen and his family. I made a big mistake tonight having those materials sent to his house. It seems like the more good I try to do, the worse things end up. I don't want to be known as the queen who brought pain and misery to her land. I want more for the people of Tenuma, and I want more for myself.

I undress and slip into my favorite black silk nightgown. I curl up in bed, because despite the warmth the room now holds due to Koen's work, I still find myself needing warmth and comfort.

I manage to drift off to sleep, in spite of my mind being plagued with worry. I don't usually dream so vividly, excluding that night in the cave with Koen, and I wound up unconsciously acting my dream out with him next to me. Usually, I fall asleep in a heavy whiskey-induced state, thanks to the nightly male visitors I typically have. Whatever dreams I might have, never last long enough for me to process what happens. Tonight, however, I dream vividly.

Koen walks into my room slowly, standing tall and his eyes burning with desire. He is combing his beard with the fingers of one hand, and I can't place why it turns me on so much. The look on his face is absolutely wild, and it makes my entire body tremble.

As he gets closer, my red lips automatically part for him, in anticipation of his mouth on mine. I know I've never kissed another man before, but right here, right now, I can almost feel him on my lips. I can almost taste him. I want to feel his coarse beard on my face, and his tongue force its way into my mouth.

I stand still, transfixed on his handsome face. I'm wearing my black lace nightgown, my hair is down my back in loose curls, landing just above my butt. He hasn't even touched me yet, but I can feel my nipples harden beneath the fabric, trying to push through the material. My breathing quickens as he closes the distance between us, not knowing what he's about to do.

He takes the last step between us and stands before me, looking down slightly to meet my needy gaze, my eyes pleading with him to touch me. He pushes me backwards and I drop to the bed. He towers over me before lowering himself on top of me, each movement slow and intentional. I swear I can feel the weight of his body as he eases himself on top of me.

I want to say his name, but my lips won't form the words. I can't speak, all I can do is lie here, waiting for what's going to happen next, and I want it more than anything. He doesn't speak either, but the look in his eyes says it all. The longing, the desire, the pain of having to stay away from each other building up inside wanting to burst.

He reaches up and cups my cheek with one hand, caressing my face. I can feel my pussy getting wet, making my inner thighs slick and hot. My entire body feels hot from wanting him so badly, I think I might scream if he doesn't touch me.

I grab his hand and start moving it down my body, to place it on my pussy but he stops me. He grips my wrist hard, and shoves my arm above my head pinning it down. My eyes dart to his, as he grabs my other wrist pinning it above my head in the same spot. Suddenly, I feel my hands being tied together with some sort of rope…

Wait. Something isn't right here. This feels too real…

My eyes snap open and a familiar man hoovers over me, but it's not Koen. I see the same man who tried to kill me last week, straddling me in my bed attempting to tie my hands together. He's gripping my wrists so tight, his fingers are leaving indents in my skin. My eyes go wide, and I open my mouth to scream, but he quickly covers my mouth with one hand before I get the chance. I feel his fingers digging into my face, his short uneven nails scraping my skin. His hand smells like sweat and dirt. It makes my stomach turn, and suddenly I'm grateful I didn't eat much at dinner. With his other hand, he brings his index finger to his own lips telling me to be quiet.

What is he doing?

What does he want?

Is he going to kill me, or am I going to kill him?

To be momentarily cooperative so I can think of what to do next, I nod my head and he uncovers my mouth.

"What do you want?" I whisper into the dark room, fighting back tears.

His eyes are wild and menacing. He looks terrified and angry. "You have caused me to bring shame to my family. I can't let that happen again. This could have been so simple, Princess." His voice is taut.

"What are you talking about, who are you?" I ask, slowly reaching with one hand to my side table drawer where I know I keep my jewel-encrusted dagger. I've never had to use it, but my father gave it to me many years ago to keep in my room, should I ever need protection.

"I'm who should be King of Tenuma, and once you're gone, I will be," he replies plainly, as if the thought of killing me doesn't bother him in the slightest.

He brings his free hand and drags it down my body, lifting the hem of my nightgown, exposing my legs and panties. He roughly grabs my thigh, shoving my legs apart. I shiver, and squeeze my eyes shut. He begins tying my hands to my bed. His hands feel rough, and wrong. I don't want him touching me.

This can't be happening.

He's going to kill me. My parents will most likely be next. I can't let this happen. Just as he's finishing the knot on one hand, I lift my leg with enough force to kick him in the balls, forcing him to buckle over and roll off of me.

"Aaagggghhh! You bitch!" he shouts through painful groans.

Quickly, I pull open my drawer and reach for the dagger, feeling thankful that it's just in reach and I grab the handle and turn over and stab wildly into the dark. I know I've hit him when I hear another growl and shout.

"Aggghh, Fuck!" I hear him shout and he rolls off the bed onto the floor with a loud thump.

I take that time to cut my other hand free, kneeling tall on my bed, pointing it in the direction he fell on the floor.

My hand is shaky as I hold it out. "Stand up. Get up, you coward," I demand.

The room is partially lit from the moon outside, though not brightly due to the storm rolling in. I can see the shadow of his body rise slowly, and he puts his hands up in defeat.

"You don't want to do this, Princess," he tells me.

"Since you were about to rape and kill me, I feel very confident that I do actually," I say with a shaky, but harsh voice.

"Please," His tone softens, as he begins to beg for his life. "I didn't want to do this. This wasn't up to me. If you kill me, it will only make him angrier," he reveals.

"Who? It will make *who* angrier?" I demand.

I see him shake his head. "If I tell you, I'm as good as dead," he explains.

"You're running that risk either way. Tell me who sent you," I demand again.

Before I can get anything out of him, he bolts from my room and runs down the hallway. I'm too stunned to chase after him, my body frozen in place. Frozen in fear and disbelief. I eventually get up and slam the door shut to lock myself in. Locking everybody else out.

Placing the knife down on my nightstand that I now realize is covered in blood, dripping down my hand and arm, I rush to the bathroom and vigorously scrub my hands. As soon as I'm done, I lean over the toilet and empty my stomach into it. I rinse my mouth out and dry my face with a nearby towel and stumble on weak legs back to bed. I look over to see the bracelet I took off sitting on my table, taunting me. It's mocking me for taking it off.

Would it have protected me? At the risk of feeling foolish, I quickly place the bracelet back on my wrist.

I can't seem to make my body stop shaking and this time, it's not from the cold. I cover myself up, pulling my legs up to my chest and holding them tightly, forming myself into a human ball. While the fear is still very much present, I feel another swell of emotion rising inside me.

Anger.

Anger is starting to pulse through my veins, causing my body to heat and sweat. I feel an overwhelming urge to run out into the snow and chase that man down, but I don't know how to fight. He was much bigger than I am and easily held me down. I wouldn't know how to defend myself in a face-to-face battle. I was lucky enough to catch him off guard, injuring him enough to chase him out of here. But I can't shake the desire I have to fight. I cringe that I allowed fear to paralyze me .

My entire life, I've done what I've been told to. I've behaved, followed the rules, and never stood up for myself. In doing so, I've been forced to sleep with strange men, lost my best friend, and gave away pieces of myself. I've never fought for what I wanted or stood up for myself to put an end to the non-stop sex.

I want to freely fuck who I want, without the fear of their death hanging over my head. I want to be the one to choose which dick I ride, without it being decided for me. I want my freedom back. The days of letting others dictate what I do with my body is over.

My face feels like it's on fire, and I can still feel his fingers pressed into my cheeks. The scratches and marks he left there will be hard to cover in the morning. I rub my wrist, wincing at the pain and the shame of letting that man mark me. They're tender and I know I'll have bruises there. That asshole came into my chambers and left marks on me. For what? Power. To him, my life was nothing but an obstacle in his way to the power of the crown.

Deciding to sleep with the knife, I grab it off my nightstand, gripping it firmly, holding it close to my body. The adrenaline coursing through me won't let my body relax enough to sleep, but at least if anybody tries to come back, I will be ready for them. I've spent too much time letting things happen to me and it's about damn time I fight back.

26

KOEN

Last night still has my head spinning. Princess Bellatrix is working hard to push me away from her and yet, she keeps performing selfless acts to help my family and I. She's trying to push me away, but it's not what she really wants. It's what we both know is imperative. We both know what would inevitably happen if we pursue one another. It's certain death.

The window supplies she sent over for my home is not what I expected from her in the slightest. After our last conversation, I was certain I would have to fight to get her in the same room with me, until she sent over an olive branch. She's drawn to me the same way I'm drawn to her. We can keep fighting it all we want, but there's something between us. The question is, what do we do about it?

Quirina was a drunk mess last night, but everything she said was true. I can't have Bellatrix. I can never have her the way I really want her. There can never be more than stolen moments, brief conversations and electric brushes of our skin against one another. It's agonizing. Knowing I can never have her is becoming too much to bear, but it's something I'm going to have to deal with. Quirina said there's more going on and the princess will continue having sex with other men, killing them in the process. But why? Why can't her parents just let her choose someone without having to sleep with them? So much of what's going on doesn't make sense, and now that Quirina is leaving the castle, I fear I may never know.

Maybe Quirina had the right idea in leaving. I'm starting to wonder if that may be what's best for me as well. Between my mother, Nikandros, and Quirina, they've all made it quite clear that I'm a fool for even thinking I may have feelings for her. They're right, it's idiotic. It's suicide. There's no purpose in even entertaining it, and I think it might be time for me to just finish my job and get the hell away from her.

As I'm in the shower, I decide to push all romantic thoughts of her aside for good, and stop allowing myself to fantasize about a possible life with her. I will go in today, finish my work and leave. I will stay out of the princess's way and mind my own business. But before I can banish any thoughts of her, my cock twitches in response, begging for one more release from her.

I picture her long black hair wrapped around my hand while my other hand grips her large, firm breasts. I grip my already hard cock in my hand as I imagine her before me, naked and perfect. Her soft skin brushing against my rough skin, my mouth on hers. I can almost taste her tongue in my mouth, imagining how soft her tongue will feel.

I stroke my cock as the warm water falls on my back, and even though I told myself I can't ever have her, picturing having her like this just makes me ache even more for it. I keep stroking until my head bursts with semen. I watch it wash down the tub, wishing I was showering her in it or filling her up with it.

That's it, that's the last time you do this, I tell myself, and I want it to be true. I need to be strong and I need to get away from her. If what Quirina says is true and a war is coming, I need to stay as far away from her as possible, and get my family the hell out of here.

*Y*ou *can do this. Just do your job, and don't approach the princess no matter how badly you want to,* I remind myself over and over during my journey to the castle. Not realizing what a challenge it would be until I walked inside and saw her shiny black hair moving up the stairs away from me. It was a great plan until I saw her in front of me.

I'm fucked.

Already feeling the urge to corner her in her room and ask her what the fuck is going on. To find out if what Quirina said is true, and ask her why she keeps running away from me, just to do something kind for my family afterwards.

No. Keep your ass down here. It doesn't matter why.

Keep your distance.

I hurry over to the windows and realize I still have many more to do, so I need to focus and get started. It's just me in the room except for the staff that is cleaning up the dining table from breakfast. A few staff members come in and out occasionally, but mostly I'm alone. This is a relief. The less temptation the better. I can focus, finish my job and get the hell out of here without doing or saying any other stupid things.

I'm standing on the top rung of the ladder when I hear a voice come from below. "Good Morning, Koen." I hear a female's voice.

For a moment, I panic, hoping it is and isn't Princess Bellatrix all at the same time. I glance below and see Quirina standing under the ladder in her handmaiden uniform. She clearly hasn't left yet, maybe I've changed her mind. Though, I'd be surprised if she remembered any of our conversation last night.

"Good morning, Quirina," I respond, climbing back down the ladder. "How are you feeling?" I ask quietly. I don't know how much freedom the staff has here, but I'm sure they wouldn't be too pleased knowing their staff is out getting drunk and spilling their secrets in town.

She rubs the spot between her eyebrows. "Not great. I feel pretty stupid actually," she confesses. "But I wanted to thank you for making sure I got home safe. I shouldn't have been out last night. And, I shouldn't have said what I did." Her face looks regretful and worried, as if I'd tell anybody what she told me.

"You don't have anything to worry about," I reassure her. I have no reason or desire to tell anybody the things she's told me. Questions I have plenty of, however.

She gives me a weak smile and nods her head as she continues on her way. But my brain is nagging at me to get clarification on some things she said to me.

"Wait," I say, hoping she will tell me more now that she's sober. She slowly turns around, her hands clasped in front of her. "Please, I need to know what you meant," I start, but she looks at me with a confused expression. "About the princess. She's still going to be forced to sleep with men until she finds one that will be her mate? If there are already threats to her life and our land, why keep it going?" I ask.

Quirina shrugs and glances around to make sure nobody else has entered the large room. "I don't really know why, but yes. The queen has arranged for *multiple* men to come through here each day now. They're scared and desperate. For some reason, they still feel that this is the way to keep power in their hands. But that's all I know," she says quickly, as someone enters the saloon style doors that lead back to the kitchen. "I must go now. Be careful, Koen. Don't do anything reckless," she states then scurries off.

If Tenuma is already under attack, why continue to force the princess to have sex with all those men?

And why is the queen now making her do it with multiple men a day all of the sudden? I think to myself.

There's so much about this that doesn't add up. I need to keep my head down and focus on my work, but damn, if it doesn't take all my efforts just to keep my mind off of her. There's no use trying anyway, because as soon as I tell myself to focus, she rounds the corner as if I've summoned her.

The princess looks as beautiful as she always does, but something's wrong. Her face is pale and she has dark circles under her eyes. I could chalk it up to a bad night of rest, except her eyes are darting back and forth like she's on guard, and her wardrobe is completely different from her usual low-dipped corset dress. She looks skittish. Her head is mostly down, her hair is in her face, and she doesn't hold the usual poise and elegance that I'm used to seeing her exude. No, something is wrong. Something is terribly wrong.

Leave her alone, it's not your place. It's none of your business.

I'm frozen at the top of the ladder, unable to divert my gaze from her body moving in my direction. As if she can feel my presence, her head shoots up and her green eyes immediately find mine. She stops in her tracks, our gazes locked onto each other, and I feel my breathing temporarily halt. Just her presence sucks the air from my lungs, and yet, I'd happily never take another breath, just to be near her.

Suddenly she breaks our stare and quickly turns around, heading back up the stairs.

What the hell just happened?

She's hiding something.

Even though I told myself nothing good can come from her, I find my feet automatically moving in her direction anyway. I can't stop myself from gravitating towards her as if another entity is in control of me.

I know I shouldn't, and I know I could get caught and

fired, or even worse–killed, for following the princess up to her chambers, but I can't stop my feet. I follow her up the stairs, and as I reach the top, I see she's already down the hall, about to enter her room.

Why is she clearly running from me?

I reach her room, feeling confused and nervous about what I'm walking into. Is she angry? Is she avoiding me from embarrassment or shame? Any of these possibilities makes my heart lurch in my chest.

When I enter the room, it's only Princess Bellatrix inside, facing the window at the far wall.

"Princess." My voice is deep, but so quiet I'm not sure she hears me. "Princess," I repeat, a little louder.

Without turning around, she responds. "Stop," she commands.

My breathing quickens at her harsh tone, worried I won't get to ask her the questions burning through my mind. "Please. I just want to talk for a moment," I start, hoping she will hear me out. When she makes no effort to move, I gently shut the door behind me, so we have some privacy. The click of the door shutting causes her to turn around.

She backs up against the brick that lay between the windows, eyes fixed on me, but she doesn't speak so I take the opportunity to before she kicks me out for good.

"I'm sorry, I know I shouldn't have said all of those things the other day. It was inappropriate and I'm not the man you want to be hearing that from. I know that now, I'm sorry. I…" I'm so focused on not screwing up my words, and the tension between us that I didn't notice the bruising and scratches on her face until now.

My entire face immediately gets hot, and I can feel my heart racing. My face turns to stone as she stands before me wounded. "Princess, what happened?" I ask her.

She shakes her head, unwilling to talk.

"Princess," I say again, closing the distance between us. I reach up gently and lift her chin with my fingers, and notice that it's worse than it looked from further away. The indents and scratches on her face are clearly from someone's hand, as I can see the outline of fingers. My lip curls back over my teeth, and I swear a growl escapes from my throat. "WHO DID THIS TO YOU?" I demand, my voice unrelenting.

She flinches and shrugs again, making my eyes water. I swear, all I can see is red. Her face has never looked this way. She's scared.

I soften my tone, and ask again. "Bellatrix, who did this to you? Tell me," I beg. I can't move or think of anything else until I know who put their hands on her.

Shaking her head free of my grip, she looks away from me. "It's fine. I'll be okay," she says softly, her voice shaking.

I go to reach for her again, and she lifts her hand to stop me and that's when I see it. More bruising.

I gently grab her wrist, and hold her arm up as I slide her sleeve down further. She has deep purple bruising on her wrists, also from somebody's firm grip. However this happened, it was not done consensually.

My jaw drops and I find her gaze again, my face twisted into a horrified expression. "Bellatrix. Give me a name," I plead. Whoever did this better hope they're already dead because they will be wishing for death after I'm done with them.

She's nervously shifting her weight from one foot to the other, anxiously biting her lower lip and trying to avoid my gaze. I stop her movements, holding her chin so she can look at me. Her eyes are completely filled with tears, they've started to overflow down her pale face. "I'm okay, please just go. You don't need to worry about it," she says softly, her eyes full of worry.

I press my lips to the bruising on her wrist before I let her go. "Princess, this is not okay. You've been brainwashed to think it is. What they have been making you do for their own selfish reasons, is not okay." My voice is quiet, but firm.

Our faces are so close together, I can feel her warm breath on my skin, and it takes everything in me not to pull her closer until we're both breathing the same air. Tears continue to fall down her face, as she contemplates what to say. She's quiet for so long that I don't think she's going to respond at all.

She opens her mouth, and I am immediately drawn to the movement. "Follow the blood trail out of the back of the castle," she says quietly.

My eyebrows cinch together in confusion, and then she nods to the dagger sitting on top of her side table. She injured whoever it was before they left.

I smile weakly, but proudly at her. "Good girl," I say gently, cupping the side of her face, and then backing away slowly. I see her eyes light up for just a moment, before dimming. Knowing she has some fight in her makes me happy and relieved but not satisfied. The man that did this will suffer greatly for leaving marks on my princess.

Just before I reach the door, she stops me. "Wait," she requests, my body turning back to face her. "Promise me you'll return. Promise you'll come back to me," she begs.

I smile affectionately at her knowing that's always been the plan. "With my life."

27

BELLATRIX

I am standing here, covered in bruises, terrified of the future that lay ahead for Tenuma, and yet all I can think about is Koen's lips on my skin. The way my entire body heats up when he's around feels dizzying and intoxicating.

Good girl.

My legs have turned to jelly, and I have no idea how I'm still standing upright. If I wasn't so paralyzed by fear from last night and the fact that Koen is now chasing after the man that tried to rape and murder me, I would collapse.

Koen.

How could I have let him leave? There's no way I can let him put himself in danger. Not for me. That's why I've been trying to stay away from him, fighting every feeling and every urge I have to chase him down and grab his face.

Finally snapping out of the Koen-trance I was trapped in, I run towards the door, determined to follow him out and stop him from doing something stupid. But I'm stopped when I smack right into someone standing on the other side of my door.

"Quirina," I say breathlessly as she turns to face me.

"Trix. I can't let you leave," she says, gently pushing me back in the room shutting the door behind us both.

I don't even know where to begin this conversation.

She's here.

She's talking to me.

She doesn't seem angry.

Why won't she let me leave my chambers?

I shake my head in confusion. "W…what? Why? I have to go after–"

Quirina cuts me off. "Koen made me promise I wouldn't let you chase after him," she states with a heavy sigh.

My hands begin to shake, and my eyes are watering again. "No, I can't let him do this. I can't let anybody else get hurt because of me!" I shout through sobs.

I half expected her to agree, but she surprises me by pulling me in for a comforting hug. An embrace I didn't realize how much I needed. My body collapses against hers and I weep as she holds me up.

I weep for Koen.

I weep for what I've done to her.

And I weep for myself.

We stand there until I finally get control of my breathing and my cries have turned back into soft, controllable sobs. I pull myself off of Quirina's chest and realize I've gotten snot and tears all over her uniform.

Embarrassed, I wipe my eyes, and my nose with the sleeve of my dress. "I'm sorry," I say pathetically.

She takes my hand and walks us to sit down on my bed. "You have nothing to be sorry for. But…" Her head drops and I brace myself for the lashing I know is coming. The lashing I deserve. "I want to know what happened last night," she requests, tracing her thumb over the bruising on my wrist.

"That day that I ended up in the woods with Koen. There was a man that was chasing me down, trying to kill me. He came back. I recognized those hungry, evil eyes. He had the same hooded cloak on. He…" I start, the images replaying back in my mind like a twisted nightmare. "My hands were tied down. One of them was. He was trying to kill me." I sob into my hands again.

Quirina is rubbing my back to soothe me, and when I look up again, she has tears running down her face. "I'm so sorry, Trix. I should have been here. I left. I was angry, and I left, and I… it was stupid. I should have been here."

I shake my head. "You had every right to be angry. And to leave," I tell her.

"No. I know you. We've been best friends forever. I know you never would have done anything to hurt me. You've just been a pawn in this twisted power game. I know you don't have a choice. I should have known then," she confesses.

I pull my bottom lip into my mouth, unsure how to respond. Everything is so clear, all of a sudden. All of the evil my parents have been orchestrating, leaving a path of destruction behind them, never caring to look back. Rina is right and so is Koen. They both see how I've been used and abused. I should have stood up for myself a long time ago.

I wipe my nose on the back of my sleeve again, unable to stop the tears from flowing down my face. "I would never intentionally hurt you. But I've hurt everyone around me by not standing up for myself a long time ago. I should have put a stop to this, no matter what it cost," I profess.

Rina pulls me into another warm embrace, and I don't know if it's more for her benefit or mine. My mind starts wandering to what's going on outside of the castle. I know Koen is supposed to be downstairs working, but instead, he left to seek revenge—possibly getting himself killed.

"He's going to get hurt because of me, Rina," I whine into her shoulder.

She pulls back, gripping both of my shoulders giving me a strained smile. "Koen is tough, Trix, and he cares for you. There's nothing you could have said to stop him. But, please know that whatever happens, is not your fault. You didn't ask for any of this," she insists, her eyes boring into mine.

"I think… I think I really like him, Rina. I've tried to fight it to protect him, and now, none of that will even matter," I confess solemnly. I know that trying to stay away from him isn't working. Somehow, we gravitate back towards each other one way or another. The more I seem to run from him, the harder he tries to catch me.

She gives me a sad smile. "I know you do. It will be okay, Trix." Rina attempts to reassure me, but the look on her face gives her away. She doesn't know any better than I do if Koen is going to come back. That man was determined to kill me, and he got close enough to slide his fingers over my panties. He's clearly trained and stealthy. I don't know much about Koen, but I can't help but wonder if the odds are stacked against him. I feel like I just sent him into the snake pit.

Hours have gone by, and there's still no word from Koen. Quirina and I have been anxiously waiting in my chamber, scared to move or to do anything. We have been sitting on my bed, each taking turns pacing to the windows to see if we can catch a glimpse of him walking back.

A knock at the door startles us both. "Come in," I say as

Quirina jumps up, and pretends to tidy up the room. I don't know how stealth we've been in our friendship, but we still try to keep up appearances to avoid getting her into any trouble. I figure at this point, most of the Royals here have bigger–more secretive–issues they're dealing with, but why risk it?

One of the castle guards enters the room. "My Lady, I was looking for the handyman that's been working on the windows. He hasn't been seen in quite some time, I was wondering if perhaps he was assisting you with an issue on your windows?" he asks nicely, but his tone is laced with accusation. He's trying to catch an employee slacking off.

"N…no, he's…" I start, not sure where I'm going with it when Quirina saves us both.

"Apologies, he went home ill. I meant to report it to the head of staff, but the princess needed assistance and I got side-tracked." Her on the spot lie is impressive, and I have to force myself not to smile.

The man nods once smiling at us, and then ducks out the door, shutting it behind him.

I let out a breath I didn't realize I was holding. "Thank you. That was brilliant," I tell her.

Quirina lets out an anxious sigh. "Yes, but it means he still isn't back. I don't know if that's good news for us, Trix," she declares.

I glance outside and see that the sun is starting to set. He has been gone most of the day, and it's torturing me not knowing what's going on out there.

Did he find the man?

Is he lost?

Are they fighting?

Is he injured out there, alone and bleeding to death?

I have to shake off the last thought, because if that were

the case, surely someone would have found him by now, right? If something bad happened, we would know by now. I hope. Another nagging thought follows, that he won't be returning home to his family once again, because of me. The guilt of that feels like a punch to the stomach, making me want to scream into my pillow.

"Stop," Quirina demands.

I glance back at her. "What?" I ask, because we haven't spoken since the guard was in here.

"Whatever lies you're telling yourself, and guilt trip you're giving yourself internally… just stop." I'd think she was a mind reader if she weren't my best friend.

I smile at her, but it's weak. It portrays exactly the way I feel.

She gives me a worried look.

"What is it?" I ask.

"I know this isn't what you want to hear, but your mother set up two meetings for this evening. Back-to-back. It's getting later in the day, and one of them should be arriving shortly in time for dinner. What do you want to do?" she asks me.

What do I want to do?

It's a loaded question. What I really want to do is take Koen back to that cave and finish what we started. I want to escape anywhere with him and know that it won't kill him. What I want is to have a normal sex life with someone I'm actually attracted to, both mentally and physically. I want to go back a few days and take back the hurt I caused my best friend. What I want is to feel safe and there's only one way I'm going to accomplish that.

"I'm going to shower up and get ready. Tell my mother I will be down for dinner on time. If she wants to keep sending men my way, I'll show her exactly how strong of a queen I can be,"

I tell her.

While I don't have an exact plan formulated just yet, I know one thing for sure. I'm done fucking any man that's sent my way.

28

KOEN

Small blood droplets trail along the floor outside of the princess's room. The wood flooring is dark and you wouldn't notice it if you weren't looking for it. But I was. I lose the trail in the castle, but see it reappear outside of the back door of the castle, leading into the forest.

Good. Blood trail means he's injured enough to have continuously lost blood and with any luck, it will lead me directly to that sick fuck.

The day is freezing cold as the storm rolls in. There was a light dusting last night, but stopped in the morning and feels like it could hit anytime now. The cold doesn't bother me, but the forest is still not an ideal place to be before a storm hits. I need to find this asshole fast, and then get back. I don't need to be stranded out in the forest without all my gear and supplies.

What am I going to do when I find him? I didn't bring any weapons.

Allowing the anger to take hold, I left the castle without grabbing so much as a tool that I could have used as a weapon. I was completely focused on finding the asshole who put hands on the princess, *my princess,* that I wasn't thinking clearly. Even now, the thought doesn't worry me. My anger is so intense, I feel like I could set the entire forest on fire to find him, to punish him. If he is still here, I will find him.

I'm getting further and further into the forest, and starting to lose hope, because if he's gotten this far, maybe he's made it out alive. Maybe he had someone waiting on the outside for him to help him escape.

The thought sends a shudder down my back.

The blood trail is getting thinner and harder to see. The footsteps start to get messy, as if whoever left them realized someone might follow and started purposefully messing them all up.

Fucker.

I stop to formulate a plan because it suddenly feels like I'm at a dead end. I won't go back to the castle with this asshole still roaming free out here. Just as I'm about to give up hope, I hear a sound.

It's so quiet, that at first, I'm not sure it's real. I think I may have imagined it. Wishful thinking.

There it is again. Oh, it's real.

It's a quiet groan of a wounded animal or man. After all my years of hunting, I'd recognize that sound anywhere. The sound of defeat and suffering.

It's him.

I take slow, intentional footsteps toward the sound so I can keep the element of surprise. I want to scare this asshole like he scared her. I want him to suffer like she's suffering, and I want him to hurt like she's hurting.

I walk closer, *closer, closer* until I see him. A black bundle curled up on the ground behind a tree, in a pool of blood. It's a wonder an animal hasn't come and finished him off yet. His back is to me, so I'm easily able to come up behind him, without him knowing. I see he's got a knife laid out next to him lying in the snow, and I know it's my only shot at getting a weapon and having the upper hand. Not that he looks like he's got much fight in him, but an animal backed into a corner will show you a side you didn't expect.

Anger still pulsing in my veins, I take my boot and give him a sharp kick in the back, sending him sliding forward on the snow away from the knife, allowing me to easily grab it.

I point it straight at him, as I circle around to face him. He's groaning louder now, but not making any effort to move. "Get up, asshole. Let me see your pitiful face," I command.

He makes a groaning or gurgling noise. "What for? You're just going to kill me, anyway," he forces out through groans.

"You're a coward," I declare.

His face lifts from the snow and he attempts to sit up against the tree. I can see his thigh has a giant stab wound in it and he's bleeding through the man-made tourniquet he made from his clothing.

"You don't know anything about me," he scowls at me. His eyes are dark and yet somehow familiar. I don't know the man but he has a familiarity about him that's unsettling.

"I know you tried to rape and murder Princess Bellatrix. That makes you a coward by anyone's standards," I remind him.

He chuckles humorlessly. "You're out of your depths here. Go back to your day job. Whatever you think you feel for her isn't real. She's a whore that fucks men before she murders them. She's no better than I am," he taunts.

My eyes narrow and my jaw clenches so hard I think I might break my teeth. "You're not in a position to be speaking this way. I'd be careful with your words, lest they be your last," I threaten.

His droopy eyes and heavy breathing let me know that

he's all but given up already. "It doesn't matter. I'm as good as dead when father realizes that I didn't do the job he sent me to do, for a second time," he confesses.

"Who is your father? He sent you to harm her? Why?" I demand to know.

He laughs menacingly. "You can't stop it. He will send another and another until it's done, and power is his."

I point the tip of the knife directly at his chest. "Who is your father? Before you answer, you should know that I don't plan on killing you. I plan on torturing you. Doing just enough damage to make it as painful as I can, while making it last as long as I can. It's too bad I didn't bring any supplies, so I could heal your leg and keep you alive, while causing some new injuries. I could make this misery last for days or I can end it quickly. You might want to cooperate," I disclose.

The man takes a deep breath and hangs his head for a moment before raising it again. "Lothar. My father is Lothar. The King of Sperantia," he reveals.

My eyes narrow at him. "What does the king want from her?"

"Power. He wants the princess dead so he can overthrow the monarchy and take over Tenuma for himself. This land has been weak for some time now. He wants to expand and he doesn't care who gets in his way. He's determined. You can't stop him. Soon, all of Tenuma will be under his power," he confesses.

I shake my head, trying to make sense of it all. "Why the fuck does the princess need to be dead for him to take over? Can't he just come in and force everybody out?"

Because surely Lothar isn't planning on killing every person on our land just to take it over, is he?

"Ask her mother," he says, giving me a sinister grin.

"I'm asking you." I remind him of the situation he's in by

shoving the knife in his chest.

He winces as he tries to shift on the ground. "I don't know. What I told you is everything I know. Her mother is involved somehow. There's something she knows. Ask her," he pleads.

While I don't know if I believe him, I'm fairly certain that this conversation is over. The light is fading from his eyes and I would be more than happy to see an asshole like this no longer walking our lands.

I'm used to killing during a hunt, but am I willing to end a man's life right now for a woman? A woman that isn't and can never be mine?

Why does she feel like she's mine then?

I'm toeing the line between good and evil in the name of love and once I cross this barrier there will be no going back. I'm about to give up a piece of my humanity for her, but is it worth it?

The man groans and shifts on the ground. "You're fighting for a whore. There's no way you don't know what she's done. You will mean nothing to her. Just another body to add to the pile." His words slice through me as he taunts me further, making the answer to my question even easier. This asshole doesn't deserve a second chance.

My jaw clenches and I bend down so I'm level to where he sits with my knife at his throat. "Don't ever call my princess a whore," I demand, and then pull the knife across, slitting his throat. I watch the blood spill out and the life fade from his eyes with a stone expression.

I should feel something. I should feel sickened, sad or devastated that I just took a man's life. But I don't. I don't feel anything other than gratification that the man who hurt my princess is now gone.

One of the men.

Lothar is known to be a ruthless, selfish, and cruel ruler.

I've never seen him myself before, because I've had no need. He doesn't visit our lands and I've never left ours. Even though kings don't bother themselves with the commoners, it sounds like we may be getting an introduction soon, if what his son said is accurate.

He may have been just a pawn in a bigger picture here, but at the very least, this will be a message to Lothar. A message that we will not be fucked with and the princess will not be collateral damage in his game plan.

I watch the man finish bleeding out so I can be sure that he's no longer a threat, and then I make my way back through the forest towards the castle. It's late now, and I'm not sure how I'm going to explain my absence or my late return to the castle, but I can't go home without seeing her. I need to know she's okay, and she needs to know I am too. I forced Quirina to stay with her, because I knew she'd be too stubborn to not run after me. I didn't want her in any more dangerous situations, but I need to go back so she knows I'm okay, and that that asshole won't be back. Although, from the sounds of it, there will certainly be others. But at least for tonight, there's one less threat we need to worry about.

29

BELLATRIX

My breasts are held up high in my red corset dress that Quirina helped me into. It has a high slit on one side, thin straps on my shoulders, and red sheer fabric that falls off the shoulder, adding a touch of delicacy. On the outside, I'm perfectly put together and seductive, but inside I'm seething. Just like this evening; it will be alluring, yet dangerous.

My mother decided to increase the number of men I sleep with in a day, knowing I had an issue with the one man per evening already. There are no words I can say to change her mind and I am done begging. I am done asking for the rights to my own body. If my mother wants to play games, then I am ready to play.

There are black strappy stilettos on my feet, my shiny black hair is curled and hangs loosely around my shoulders, and my lips have their signature red stain. As far as my mother knows, I will be cooperative and ready to fuck the next victim. Little does she know, this will be the last night a man comes to my chambers.

"Are you ready, Trix?" Quirina asks softly coming into my room as I'm fastening the last strap on my shoe.

I lift my head to meet her gaze. She looks worried, while I know my eyes are filled with fire and determination. "I am more than ready. It's time I end this shit," I tell her, my voice resolute.

She gives me an encouraging smile and a nod. "I'll tell your mother you will be right down then."

Once my shoe is secured, I stand and lean over my vanity mirror taking one last glance at myself, making sure I look the part. My usual seductress glam is on point with dark eye makeup and my red lips. The red silk of my corset dress hugs my body, accentuating all of my curves tight against my soft skin. If I want this to work, I need to look as if I'm trying to get this man into bed—not that it takes a fraction of the work I've done.

This look is wasted on these men.

I only want to look this way for HIM.

I gather up the rest of my courage with a deep breath and make my way downstairs, which takes longer in these tall stilettos. Once the dining room is in sight, I can see my mother standing there with a tall man, awaiting my arrival.

"Darling," my mother announces lovingly, as if we are closer than ever. "This is your date for the evening, and dinner should be out shortly. Here, have a drink," she says as she hands me a glass of wine before I can even shake the man's hand or receive a hug. These meetings are always awkward, so I never know if it's going to be a handshake or a hug.

I scowl at the wine glass. Remembering I have a plan for this evening, I soften my face and plant a fake smile on my face. "Actually, I think I would prefer a whiskey tonight," I tell her.

My mother snaps her fingers at one of the waiters standing nearby, and he quickly scurries off and returns with a short glass of whiskey on ice for me and one for my gentleman friend.

"Shall we sit?" I ask, gesturing to the table.

The man, clearly feeling awkward, follows my lead. "Of

course, let me get your chair," he responds, and stumbles over to pull my chair out for me.

I almost roll my eyes, but manage to keep my face in check. "What a gentleman," I respond, my voice laced with honey.

"I will leave you two to it then," my mother says cheerfully, not realizing what is about to unfold starting with tonight.

The man sits uncomfortably in the chair next to mine and turns towards me. "You look incredible."

"Well, if our evening is to end in my chambers, I want to do my part and make sure you enjoy every part of tonight," I entice, slowly crossing my legs.

He smiles as his gaze travels from my bare leg–thanks to the very high slit on one side–all the way up to my breasts that are mostly on display–thanks to the deep neckline of my dress. "I don't think I'll have any trouble enjoying myself," he says, smirking.

It makes me want to vomit. I don't want his eyes on me, thinking of all the possibilities tonight will bring. Thinking of all the ways he can have my body. This poor fool is a slave to his dick and has no idea what's coming.

I smile back, deviously. "That's what I was hoping for. In that case, what do you say we finish these drinks and head upstairs. I'm not very hungry for dinner…" I start, rubbing my shoe up the inside of his leg up to his dick. "But I could go for something else," I suggest seductively.

A flash of worry passes through his face quickly, as it usually does with these setups, and instead of responding right away, he tosses back his drink.

"Another?" he asks the waiter standing close by. The waiter nods and goes off to fill his glass.

I look at him with a pouty face. "What? Don't you want to fuck me?" I ask sweetly.

His eyes light up at my vulgarity, and it's right then that I know I have him. He nods, and once his drink is brought back, he stands and reaches out his hand for mine. I stick my hand in his and he follows me upstairs.

Quirina has made the room quite cozy with the fireplace lit and multiple candles burning around the room, casting a dim, warm lighting.

We walk in, and I close the door behind us, slowly making my way over to the man who's looking around my chambers curiously, no doubt imagining what his life would be like here. He stands by my bed, and it's exactly where I need him.

"Finish your drink so we can play," I command.

He smirks, and does as I say, finishing off his glass and setting it down on the floor. Standing back upright, he attempts to take mine, but I shove him backwards on the bed and he lands softly on my plush bedding. I stand over him, taking my time finishing my drink.

"Why are you here tonight…" I start, realizing I don't even know the poor schmuck's name.

"David," he finishes for me.

"David. Yes, what is it that made you decide to take your chance with the Soul Snatching Princess?" I ask facetiously.

He leans up on his elbows, and his voice cracks. "Your mother summoned me. The queen… she…she's been sending, requiring men to come and spend the night with you," he tells me, shakily.

Pausing mid-sip, I lower my hand and my face jerks down to meet his gaze. "She *WHAT?*" I ask, my eyes burning with fire.

He gives me a confused expression. "She's been requesting men all over Tenuma to come and spend the night with you. Isn't that how this works?" he asks.

No. This is not how this works. I've always understood that the men have come under their own pretenses, never being forced.

This is new.

Why would my mother be now forcing men to come and spend the night with me now?

What is she up to?

I relax my face, realizing that I'm scaring him off much too soon. "Yes, I-I misheard you." I give a fake smile and finish my drink in one gulp. The whiskey burning its way down my throat is a nice reprieve from the burning in my ears.

I will deal with my mother tomorrow.

Flicking my finger at him, indicating I want him to move back on my bed, he scoots back towards the headboard. I hike my dress up, and climb on top of the bed so I can straddle him.

His eyes light up with both surprise and anticipation of getting to fuck the princess, as his hands grip my thighs.

I lean far over him with one hand on each side of his head and my breasts over his face, just inches away. "Now, what else did my mother say about me?" I ask, because I doubt I will get the full story out of my mother.

"I was told that you are still searching for your king, but are no longer dangerous. We were told that you would choose your king in a few weeks after meeting more men," he explains.

That manipulative bitch.

These men are being led to their deaths under the guise that they aren't in any danger with me, and giving the illusion that I have final say in who will be king. My blood boils at his confession, and I feel dumber for not seeing this sooner.

How could I have been so blind?

This man—David—grabs my face to pull my lips to his, but I slap his hand away, dramatically pulling my face away.

Kissing is off limits.

Instead, I slide one of my dress straps down my shoulder, and then the other slowly, before I fold over the top part of my dress revealing both breasts. My nipples react to the sudden exposure and anger racing through me, though I'm sure he sees it as excitement. What I'm really doing is distracting him, so he doesn't realize I'm reaching for one of my daggers.

If my mother won't listen and stop setting up these 'meetings', then I will make sure nobody ever agrees to them again.

Just as his mouth is hovering under one of my nipples, I grab the handle of my dagger, and place the cold steel at his throat.

He shoves his head back into the bed as far as it will go, to create space between his neck and my blade.

"What are you doing? I... I'm not into this sort of thing," he stammers.

Poor thing, another reason we would never work out.

"You are going to leave and relay a message to all the men of Tenuma," I demand.

His eyes show horror, as he realizes that this isn't some sort of kink or a joke. He nods his head in agreement.

"Good. You are going to tell them that they're not welcome here anymore. My body is not for sale. There is no promise of the title of king. Whoever disobeys and comes here, under the set up of my mother or father, won't be killed. No. They will be tortured. I will torture them until they beg for death. Don't forget, I will be your ruling queen very soon, and I can make their families' lives miserable as well. It's not the queen I wish to be, but I'll do it if I have to. Tell them that nobody else will have access to Princess Bellatrix's body," I elucidate.

Just as I see the words sink into his brain, I hear the door fling open. I'm still straddling the man, topless with my knife at his throat, and as I swing my head around, I see Koen standing there, fuming. His jaw is clenched, and his hands are in fists at his sides, I swear I see them shaking.

"Koen," I say weakly. Through his eyes, I imagine this looks pretty fucking bad, and it's not something I would ever want him to see.

Before the room erupts, and all hell breaks loose, the last thing I see is the fire raging in Koen's eyes.

30

KOEN

There are moments that even when you're experiencing them, you know are going to change the trajectory of your life. You can't pinpoint exactly what or how, but you can feel it. I've had two of those moments tonight.

It all happened so fast. One minute I'm looking at the princess straddling some asshole, topless, and the next I feel my body explode and I'm holding the man by his neck ten feet in the air with one hand. Only, it doesn't look like my hand. It's much larger. Not only that, but I'm taller, and the ground underneath feels different.

The fury of seeing her with another man while I was out there killing for her, is too much to bear. This anger I feel is more intense than anything I've felt before. I know this is what she's done since before we knew each other, but how could this be going on now? How could she do this after what she just went through? I thought she was done with this shit. I thought maybe I was somebody she really wanted.

Gurgling and groaning pulls me from the swirling thoughts. I'm holding the man off the ground, his feet dangling, and he's gasping for air. He's clawing at me, trying to break free. Suddenly, I hear yelling as the ringing in my ears dies down. My head is dizzy and I'm trying to find my bearings.

Bellatrix's voice comes into focus. "Koen! Please, put him down! Stop! Please!" I see the princess on her bed, still topless, holding a dagger.

Why is she holding a dagger?

I drop the man and he falls with a heavy thud. I don't even take a second glance at the man as he scurries out of the room without another word. My eyes are fixed on…my body.

The princess is staring at me, horror filling her eyes. The shock of her face prompts me to glance over and catch a glimpse of myself in the princess's large oval vanity mirror. I don't understand what I'm seeing. I can't make sense of it. I'm still me, but I've changed. My body is completely different.

Part animal, part human.

My clothes are gone. I now stand on four tall legs instead of two, and they're hoofed and covered in short fur. Behind my legs, I see a long…tail. I have four legs and a tail. But from my torso up, I still look like me.

Why am I looking at the reflection of a centaur? I think to myself. This can't be my own reflection, but somehow, I know it is.

My hands have stopped shaking, and I feel my heartbeat slowing back down. By the time I'm starting to put together what's happening, I've turned back into my human form. Trembling on unsteady feet, I grab the clothes on the floor and quickly dress. Once I'm dressed, the princess is throwing herself into my arms.

I tighten my grip on her, even though I'm struggling with how I'm feeling. I look down at her, and she's already gazing up at me. "You came back," she whispers, her voice cracked.

I give her a puzzled look, while holding her in my arms.

The confusion evident on my face as she steps back, and pulls her dress back up, suddenly realizing how this all must look. Throughout all of the commotion, she didn't realize she was still half naked.

She shakes her head. "Koen. This wasn't…" she starts, waving her hand around, choosing her words carefully. "It was a set up. I wasn't going to have sex with him," she insists.

"A set up? Isn't it always a set-up, Princess?" I ask through clenched teeth. The remark is uncalled for, but I just can't stop my wounded heart from forming the insult. My mind is buzzing and I don't know which way is up.

The expression on her face shows hurt, but she lets it slide. "It's a really long story. Can we talk about what just happened?" she asks.

Her avoidance feels like an admission to guilt. It somehow feels like a betrayal after what I did for her, although she never asked me to. Maybe this is what she does. She gets into your head, clouding your judgment, making you do her dirty work, only to betray you in the end. "Yes, Princess, that's exactly what I'm trying to do. Why did I walk in on you topless and straddling that asshole, while I was out hunting down a man that tried to hurt you last night?" My voice comes out throaty.

"I never meant for you to see that. My mother set it up, but nothing was going to happen, Koen. You know…you know what I feel for you. I know you can feel it," she pleads, placing her hand flat on my chest.

Rubbing my temples, I feel my head pounding from the events of the entire evening. I don't know what to make of this, unsure if I can trust her. Right now, I feel too overwhelmed to figure it out.

I lean in towards her, and gently grab her face between my hands, my bracelet still buzzing the flesh underneath.

It would be nice to know why the fuck this always happens.

She stares at me with teary eyes, pleading with me. "That man won't be back to hurt you again. That's all I came here to tell you. I shouldn't have come, but I had to see you. I know what I feel for you, but I don't know where you stand. Seeing this was… it was an eye opener," I explain, softly.

Her head shakes in between my hands, her lips parting. Even now, a part of me thirsts for her lips, for her tongue. It takes massive willpower not to bring her face to mine and take what I want. The heat between our bodies is electric as we stand this close. I can smell the whiskey floating off her breath, the floral scent of her hair, and it's pulling me in. I can feel it making me dizzier than I was a moment ago. Whatever pull she has over me, it's strong.

Attempting to break the trance, I try to drop my hands and back away, but her hands grab my wrists before I can break away. Her grip is firm, holding me in place. "Please, don't go. Just stay with me," she begs, her eyes flicker with sadness.

Fuck me, if I don't want to forget everything and take her back to bed. But even as the thought bubbles to the surface, I remember seeing her there just moments ago with another man. I shake my head, and break our hands apart. "No. I need to go. I can't be here right now. You were just with another man, you're drunk, I murdered a man tonight, and I just saw myself turn into a fucking animal!" I shout, frantically. "None of this is okay, and I need to go home to my family."

Princess Bellatrix stares at me in shock, and defeat, her face crumpling. We stand in silence for a few moments; me not wanting to leave, and her not wanting me to go. My words tell her I'm leaving, but my body stands still. I should go. I need to be smart, and strong, but as soon as my body finally moves towards the door, her voice stops me.

Her voice trembles as she speaks softly. "Koen, please…"

In three strides, I make my way back to her.

I'll be smart tomorrow.

Grabbing her face, I pull her towards me, and our lips crash together frantically. Her lips are soft and plump and everything I knew they would be. She parts her lips for me, so I push my tongue into her mouth, desperate for her taste. I've never felt a need quite like my need for her. As my tongue pushes inside her mouth, she lets out a soft needy moan, and her hands move to my back, gripping me tighter to her. Her mouth is warm and inviting, and her tongue drips with sweetness. Her mouth is like honey with a hint of spice, and it makes me love whiskey even more than I already do.

Her hands trail under my shirt as mine travel down her shoulders, her back, and I plant my hands on her ass. I grip it hard, wanting nothing more than to lift her up and throw her back onto that bed.

No. Be a little smarter. She's still a threat to you.

I find myself getting lost in thought again, as my intellect tries to force its way back in. Kissing her can only lead to misery on my part. She has nothing to lose, but I have *everything* to lose. Knowing the risk should be enough to send me running from this room, but the truth is, I would die for her. I would gladly let her take my soul, just to have her once.

Our frantic kisses continue, and it doesn't feel as if either of us have any intentions of ever stopping. Now that I've tasted her, I know it will never be enough. I smile against her lips, because I know without a shadow of a doubt now, how she feels. There's no way she can fake the way she's kissing me right now, the way she's moaning into my mouth, the way her body is pressed into mine with aching desire.

My cock is rock hard and pressed into her body, as our hands travel one another's body, exploring places we've been fantasizing about in private. I feel her press tightly against me, as my cock grows and pulses against her body, needing more. The clothing that separates us feels like we're miles apart, though for the best, it's torturing.

My hands move to her breasts, and I feel her nipples are hard against the thin fabric of her dress, making me want to pull them into my mouth and feel her against my tongue. The thought passes in a flash as she grabs my cock in her hand, making me want to remove my clothes again and feel her mouth wrapped around me. She's gripping me firmly, but her body is trembling against me. I don't know if it's because she's cold or nervous.

Abruptly, she pulls her mouth off of mine and takes a step back, leaving us both gasping for air. She brings her hand to her mouth, her fingers pressed against her lips where my mouth was a second ago.

She shakes her head. "I want this. I want you, but I can't do this to you," she says softly.

"Princess, you're not making me do anything. We aren't doing anything wrong," I reassure her.

Taking a few more steps back, putting even more space between us, her face shifts from passion to worry. "I'm no good for you! Can't you see that?" she asks, her eyebrows pulled together, her lips pulling downward.

Every time I'm with Princess Bellatrix, she surprises me. She's nothing like I thought she would be. Instead of the self-absorbed, ruthless princess, I see a compassionate, selfless woman before me.

"Princess," I start softly, moving back towards her. Touching her is electric, and I need to feel her under my fingertips again. I place my hand on her cheek, gently stroking her with my thumb. "You're exactly what's good for me. Can't *you* see that?" My voice is so low, it's practically a whisper.

She leans into my hand, letting me cradle her face, and her mouth pulls up into a soft sweet grin. She opens her mouth to say something, but we're interrupted by a knock at the door.

"Trix," Quirina says softly, the door opens and her head peeks inside, while we break apart. "I'm sorry, I don't want to interrupt but the guards are wondering what's taking Koen so long to gather his things. Is everything okay up here?" she asks, eyeing how close together we're standing, our faces inches apart.

The princess clears her throat. "Yes, everything is fine," she responds, her voice raspy.

Quirina shoots us a polite smile.

"I'm leaving right now," I assure her.

Quirina nods her head, and then backs out of the room.

I pull Bellatrix back into me with both hands on her hips. "No more men, Princess. I'm the only man that gets to touch you from now on," I order.

Biting her bottom lip, restricting a smile, she nods her head. "Just you," she confirms.

I'd be lying if I said it didn't make my chest swell hearing her say it. I don't know what compels me to demand anything from her, all I know is that it feels right. She feels like mine, and I feel like I'm hers.

I kiss her softly once more on the lips, and force myself to pull away before I leave. Whatever we just started has more questions than answers and more problems than solutions, but fuck it, I am ready to figure it all out with her by my side.

Downstairs, the guards are all glare at me with suspicion as I come down without any of my tools or supplies.

"Did you find what you needed?" one of them asks me in a

curt tone.

I make my way over to the hallway leading to the dining area as I respond. "Sure did," I answer.

It's not lost on me that there are guards in every part of this castle. They stand at all entrances–except the back staff door–one at the bottom of the stairs, and one outside the king and queen's room. They most likely know exactly what's been going on for weeks now between the princess and I, even if we didn't quite understand it ourselves.

Folding up the ladder, and picking up the tools and supplies that I left abruptly earlier in the day to go hunt down that man, I try to tidy the work area.

Was that really just earlier today?

I feel like a completely different man than the one that walked into the castle this morning.

"Koen!" I hear my name called from behind me.

It's Bellatrix's mother, the queen.

Shock etches my face at the realization that her mother knows me by name. My eyebrows pull together in confusion, and I slightly bow my head in respect. "Your Majesty, what can I do for you?" I ask. I'm not sure I've ever really spoken to her aside from passing greetings in the halls. From what I know of her, I don't have any desire to be near this snake. If she's willing to throw her daughter to the wolves for her own benefit, then there's no saying what she'd do to the rest of us.

"Ask her mother."

"There's something she knows."

As I stare into the green eyes of the queen that remind me of my princess, I hear the voice of the man I killed in the woods. His words echoing back in my mind, like a warning.

The queen is staring at me with curiosity, amusement and something I can't quite put my finger on, but it feels dangerous.

"My apologies for being here so late. I had an emergency to attend to, but I wanted to make sure I came back and took care of this. I didn't want to leave your home a mess." I think of an excuse quickly, trying to force any façade of respect.

I see her hands fold in front of her, and a wicked smile dances on her lips. "Oh, Koen, you're just as wonderful as I've heard," she muses.

What the hell is she talking about?

What has she heard about me, and from whom? Surely not the princess.

"Thank you, Your Highness," I force my most sincere gratitude.

"I'm glad I found you, surely you aren't leaving. Have you looked outside? A blizzard is coming through, and there's no way you will make it home," she informs me.

Just as she described, I gaze out the window and sure enough there's nothing but white blanketing the world outside.

Fuck.

Unfortunately, she's right, and I won't make it back to my cottage in this weather. I wouldn't be able to see two feet in front of my face with the wind whipping the snow around like it is right now. I'd freeze long before I found my way back to my mother and sister.

Mellani.

I can't help but feel guilty for the fact that this will be the second time now that I won't be making it home to her, no doubt making her worry until I return. The thought makes my skin crawl. I don't like the feeling of letting her down or making her feel sad or worried. She had enough of that shit from the father that walked out on her.

The queen comes up and loops her arm through mine. "Leave this and come with me. You will stay in one of our guest rooms for the night, and when the storm dies down you can return home tomorrow. I can't have my best handyman wandering about in a storm in the middle of the night to freeze to death. What kind of queen would I be?" She chuckles, but it makes the hair on my neck stand on end.

"Oh, thank you kindly, Your Majesty, but I must decline. I couldn't impose. I must…" I start to decline her offer, because as much of a risk as it is to try and make my way home, it's impossible to stay here.

She waves her hand, brushing off my words. "Nonsense, I won't hear of it. You will stay tonight. You're much safer here." She gives me a smirk, and her eyes twinkle with delight.

She's up to something. Don't let your guard down.

I suddenly feel anything but safe here.

The queen leads me back up the stairs, down the hallway in the direction of the princess's room. I don't know what the queen has on her mind, but something tells me that I need to be very careful with whatever happens next.

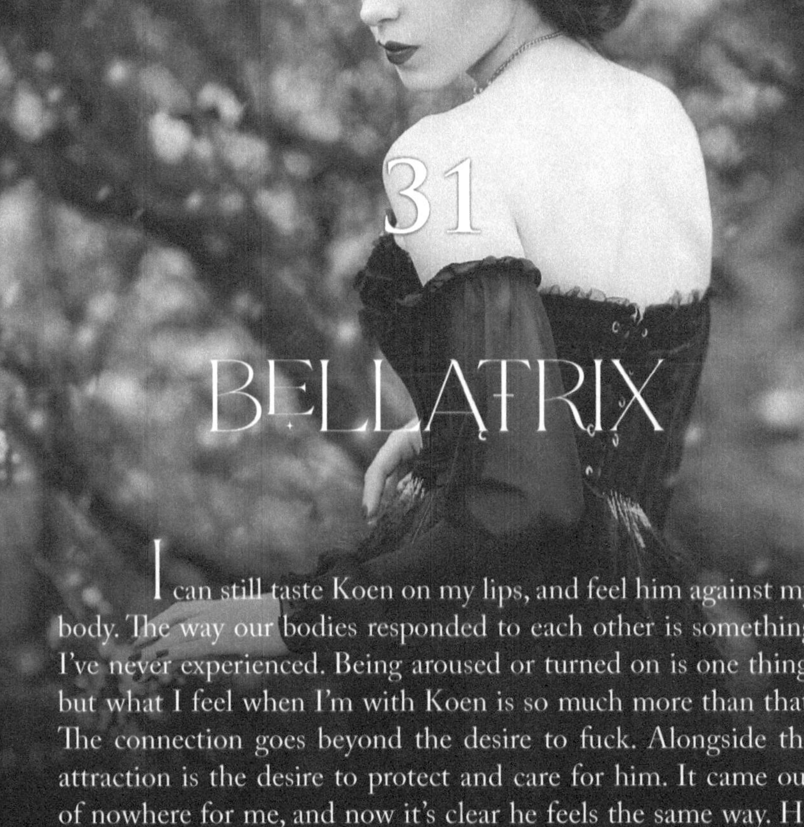

31

BELLATRIX

I can still taste Koen on my lips, and feel him against my body. The way our bodies responded to each other is something I've never experienced. Being aroused or turned on is one thing, but what I feel when I'm with Koen is so much more than that. The connection goes beyond the desire to fuck. Alongside the attraction is the desire to protect and care for him. It came out of nowhere for me, and now it's clear he feels the same way. He has killed for me. He killed to protect me. The protection and passion I saw from him today shattered everything I thought I knew about love. When his lips met mine, I knew that things were going to change. I've never kissed a man before. Koen was the first, and I can't help but wonder if he could feel the way my body shook with pure lust and desire. Sure, I've had sex with a lot of men, but this is new territory for me.

Having genuine feelings for a man, and wanting—no, needing him to want me back is new and terrifying. It feels so fucking good, but at the same time is achingly torturous. The control he has over my body is something I've never experienced before. The electricity that freely flows between us is intoxicating and I can't get enough.

I smile, thinking of the way he made me feel both weak and strong at the same time. The control he took had me wanting to give myself to him but finding the power to stop us before I could harm him.

My body is still trembling and vibrating with my need for him. If this is what it feels like just to kiss him, I can't help but wonder what it would feel like to give myself completely to him.

You can't ever have him like that, I think to myself.

Reality sets in and I feel myself slump over sitting on my bed. I won't ever have him, but maybe that's enough. I think it could be enough for me, if all I ever get is to kiss him. But how could it ever be enough for him?

Somehow my life has gone from finding *a man,* to now needing just *one man,* and I have a curse on me that prevents me ever truly having him. There's more standing in our way, than allowing us to be together, and yet what scares me most is not being with him.

My mother.

My father.

Lothar.

War.

The curse.

Everything feels stacked against me, and there's so much to figure out, and I don't know how all of this has landed on my shoulders. I'm not the queen yet so I don't know why the fate of Tenuma has fallen on me. I want to be a good queen, but it feels like I'm already set up to fail.

Tenuma is on the brink of war, because I can't find a man who can survive sleeping with me, even though one is needed for me to become queen. In retrospect, the curse wasn't my mother's smartest move. If her goal was to help me find a king, the curse wasn't needed. Now we are here and there's no denying that it's all my fault. Yet, all I can think about is Koen. The tall, brooding man who came in and uprooted everything I have ever wanted. He made me want more for myself, for my life. Being queen isn't something I had a strong desire to be, but my bloodline demands it. Now that I know there's more to life, I want it desperately. I want it more than I've ever wanted anything. I have to find a way to end this curse once and for all, and there's only one person who would know how to reverse it.

The hot water of the shower hits me in the face and it's exactly the comfort I was looking for. I feel like I'm washing the strain and shock off of my skin. I'm washing the fear out of my hair, and watching it all wash down the drain. The steam from the water thickens, clouding the room, making it hard to see and I can't escape the irony that it's how my mind feels. The last few days have revealed things that have made me both excited and terrified.

Koen is a centaur.

Koen has killed for me.

My mother might be a murderer, having blackmailed me to protect Koen.

Dragons are on the loose.

Tenuma is on the brink of war.

Koen wants me.

Koen wants *me.*

I don't know if it's that thought or the hot water comforting me more at this moment. As I rinse the day off of me, washing off the last random man to ever touch me, I feel relief. Even though everything is at stake and I could lose it all, I feel stronger and more capable than ever before.

The raw desire and affection I've developed for Koen has awoken something new within me. If it's been there all along, I'm unsure, but suddenly, I am ready to take back control of my life. My mother is showing her true colors, and now, looking at things from a different lens, her 'protection' looks a lot like manipulation.

Hopping out of the shower, I'm drying off when I hear muffled talking next door.

That doesn't make sense, the room next to mine is always empty, I think.

I towel-dry my hair quickly and dress, quietly padding over to my door and opening it a crack so I can hear better.

I hear my mother's cheerfully-honeyed voice in the doorway of the room next to mine.

What is she up to now? I think to myself.

"Alright, Koen, make yourself at home and please do not hesitate to let the staff know if there's anything you need. Princess Bellatrix is right next door to you, as you know, so I'm sure she could be of help if you have any…needs."

What the hell is she doing?

Why is she talking to Koen? I thought he left.

Koen's voice is what I hear next in response. "Thank you, Your Highness. This is much too kind, and I hope I can repay you for your kindness. I will be out of here as soon as the storm lets up."

Storm? I think as my head swivels back towards my windows.

All I see is a white world of snow blowing around rapidly. The snowstorm has hit. It's been blowing towards us all day and in the midst of everything going on, I completely forgot about it. Which means Koen can't get home and will be staying here tonight. He will be right next door to me all night.

I quietly close my door, biting my lip. Clearly my mother is up to something. She threatened me with his life not that long ago, and now she's turned on the 'nice queen' act. Something isn't right here. There are tons of rooms she could have put him up in but she chose the one next to my room, and was talking loud enough so I would know he was here. If she's hoping I don't have enough restraint to keep my body to myself, and keep him safe, she's vastly underestimated me.

My entire life, she's only seen my submissive, cooperative side. I've never shown that I can stand up for myself or make decisions on my own. Somehow, in allowing my mother to put that curse on me, I gave up my voice. It's hard to know you even have a voice when you're that young. Trusting my mother has cost me everything and I won't make that mistake again.

I finish my nighttime routine, brushing my teeth and applying my moisturizer, and climb into bed. If my mother wants to try and entice me with the man she knows I want by housing him next to my room, then so be it. Not only will I prove her wrong, but I will show her that I am not a puppet to be controlled.

Not by her, anyway.

As I lay here, I realize that my own impulses are driving me mad with the desire to go next door and lay with Koen. I would never put him in a position to get hurt. I know he's not foolish enough to give in to our impulses either, but the need to be next to him is overpowering. The need to feel his skin, touch his face, and feel his lips is almost maddening.

The skin under my bracelet is tingling, as if it's beckoning me to move. I don't know whether this bracelet is actual protection or can just sense when I'm getting worked up about Koen. Either way, I know every time it starts to tingle, it's because of him.

I'm trying my best to ignore the urge to go next door, but it seems like the harder I try to ignore it, the stronger it gets. I've been tossing and turning, and there's no way to shut my mind off. The rest of the whiskey is downstairs, and I'd have to pass Koen's room in order to get it. Let's face it, if I go out there, I'm not walking past his room, I'm going straight in.

Leave him alone.

Let him sleep.

Don't put him in a dangerous situation, the man has already killed for you.

Go to sleep.

If he wants to be with you, he would have come in here by now.

It's the last thought that calms me, making me realize I need to leave him alone. He may have kissed me, but he's probably regretting it by now. I'm sure that once he left the room, he realized what a colossal mistake it was, and how this couldn't possibly lead anywhere good. While our chemistry is undeniable, I wouldn't be surprised if he had his reservations and regrets kissing me. I just hope he knows that I would never let things go that far. Even if he decides he wants to risk it, I would never let him risk giving up his life for me. He has that sweet little sister to take care of, and I couldn't live with myself if I took him away from her.

My mind is made up, and I finally quiet the voices beckoning me to jump into his bed. I close my eyes and just as I'm dozing off, I hear my door slowly creak open.

Panic rises in my chest, and my body goes ice cold thinking of the last time that someone entered my room at night. I reach for the dagger I now keep under my pillow, holding it firmly by the handle. Whoever just entered my room made a big mistake. I wait until I hear the footsteps get closer, and then I spring up and lunge forward with my knife.

32

KOEN

The kindness I received from the queen is unsettling, to say the least. The royal family isn't known for their generosity, so the fact that she welcomed me like a family member into her home leaves a sour feeling in my stomach. I've had my guard up anytime it considers this family for a reason. It simply doesn't feel right. I'm lying in this enormous, comfortable bed–which is way better than my thin cot on the ground–trying to sleep, which should be easy, considering the luxurious feeling of the linens, but find I am unable to. Scenes from the day keep flashing in my head.

Watching a man bleed out from an injury I caused.

Turning into a centaur.

Seeing the princess with another man.

Kissing the princess, *my* princess.

Telling her I'm the only one that can touch her.

Everything is playing on a loop in my mind, and I don't know how I got here. This was supposed to be just another job and somehow, it's gotten to the point where I'm killing men for the princess, and I think I might be falling for her. There's no other way to describe this feeling. The possessiveness and the way I want to protect her when she can kill me with her body, can only be described as love. It's the only thing that can explain why I've been acting so incredibly stupid and irresponsible. I've never been the type of man who thinks with his dick, so this has to be something more.

I have to stop acting like a love-sick teenager.

Even as I think it, I don't want to. I want to keep feeling this way. There's no way I'd voluntarily give up the intensity of what I feel for her. The electricity that forms between us when we're together doesn't just happen, so it seems worth exploring.

You're playing with fire. Stop being stupid.

I'm being stupid, I know that. But it feels too good to stop it. Princess Bellatrix has unleashed a whole new man within me. *Literally.* I turned into half a beast in front of her. I've never done that and didn't even know I could do that. Is the princess responsible for it or is this something I've always possessed?

Lying here, I have so many unanswered questions.

How is it possible I can turn into an animal?

What does the queen have to do with Lothar trying to kill her daughter?

Then it occurs to me that I never had the chance to even tell the princess that her mother is most likely an internal threat, which makes me grateful that I'm staying in the castle tonight. If I'm here, I can protect her. The entire evening has been such a whirlwind that I briefly forgot that the queen could very well be leading her own daughter to slaughter.

Before I can talk myself out of it, I'm out of my bed and heading for the princess's room. Slowly opening my door, because I know guards post up at just about every point in the castle, I'm careful not to alert anyone.

I see she's already in bed and I feel a pang of embarrassment at my intrusive entry. I hesitate for a second, thinking I should just let her rest, but then I see her body shift more than a little. Thinking I've woken her up, I proceed, really wanting the chance to talk to her.

I'm almost at the end of her bed when she suddenly springs up and I see her lunging towards me with her dagger.

Barely dodging a lethal slice to my abdomen, I involuntarily shout. "Princess! What the fuck?!" I yell as I jump out of the way, watching as she lands on her hands and knees on the ground in front of her bed with a loud thud.

"Aaaagh," she groans and rubs her elbows, as she turns to lay on her back, trying to soothe her now reddened skin.

Bellatrix is laying on the ground, soothing herself as I go to help her up. "Princess, are you okay? I shouldn't have snuck in here like this. I'm so sorry." I feel like a total asshole. She had an intruder try to kill her last night, and I decided to come in unannounced right now, as if there's nothing wrong with it.

She should have stabbed me, I think. Because at this point, I deserve it.

The princess covers her face for a moment of embarrassment, and then takes my hand so I can help her up. "Yes, I'm fine. I'm sorry I almost stabbed you," she tells me.

I chuckle. "It–" I start, but I am cut off by a pounding on her door.

"Princess! Is everything okay in there?" a booming male voice from the other side shouts. A guard, I presume. The commotion we just made was sure to stir up attention.

I should have just stayed in my own damn room.

"Shit," she grumbles as she runs to the door, opening it just a crack. "Yes, I was having a nightmare and fell out of bed. Everything is fine here, thank you." She dismisses the guard quickly, shutting and locking the door behind her, and then walks back over to me. I can't help but smile at her excuse to the guard.

As she comes towards me, I pull her into my arms. "I'm so sorry. I wasn't thinking when I came in here like that. I didn't mean to scare you," I tell her, holding the back of her head, caressing her hair with my thumb.

"It's… I'm okay. What are you doing here?" she asks curiously, and to my surprise she doesn't seem upset at all with me.

I smile at her. "For starters, I really needed to see my princess." She holds my gaze, giving me a flirtatious smile. "But I also need to talk to you about something," I tell her, causing her face to fall. Whatever I'm about to tell her, she must sense it's nothing good.

She takes my hand, guiding me to the bed so we can both sit down. She sits in the center of the bed, crossing her legs. The nightgown she's wearing isn't very long, so it rides up just enough that I can see her red lacy panties. I sit in front of her, trying to stay focused.

Taking a deep breath, I brace myself for what I'm about to tell her. I don't know the dynamic of her relationship with her mother. All I know is that she's been forced to have sex with strange men, and that Bellatrix hasn't been completely on board with it. There is more to the story, I'm sure but I don't really want to be the person to break the news to her that her mom could be trying to kill her.

Princess Bellatrix takes my hand in hers, and I notice two things. One, I see the bracelet she wears that mirrors my own, and two, I see the bruising on her arm from that asshole last night. I can feel the anger starting to rise inside of me again and it's a good thing he's dead, because I'd kill him all over again. Taking his life is not something I'll ever regret. An animal like that doesn't deserve the chance to hurt more women. This new version of me isn't one I've ever seen or known I had inside of me, but it's one I'll choose every single time to protect those I care about.

Morality and ethics mean nothing when somebody you love gets hurt. It's easy to justify almost any act when it's to protect those you love. Seeing those marks on her from another man, just ingrains in me the fact that I'd do it time and time again, and not feel an ounce of remorse for it.

My thumb rubs over her bruising. "I have something to tell you, and I don't know how you're going to take it," I confess.

Her opposite hand rests on my leg that's bent on the bed in front of her. "Okay, so just tell me. I'm a big girl." Her reply makes me smile against my own somber mood.

"The man that tried to kill you last night. He… he told me some things. You're still in danger, Princess… and your mother might be involved," I reveal.

She bites the corners of her mouth, her face revealing nothing. Not shock, anger, or sadness. "What did he tell you?" she asks.

"He told me that his father is the King of Sperantia and his goal is to kill you. His ultimate desire is to gain power over Tenuma. With you next in line, you're standing in the way, so he plans to kill you." As I tell her what the man told me, her face stays neutral, just listening intently.

"I don't get it. I'm not even queen yet. Can't he just come in and overthrow my parents? Why do I need to die?" she asks, confused.

I shrug. "Maybe that's where your mother comes in," I say plainly. As much as none of this makes sense, it would make sense that her mother is involved. There are missing pieces, and if Tenuma and Bellatrix are under attack, there's no reason the queen should be as calm and collected as she has been unless there's something she's hiding. Every part of my being tells me she cannot be trusted, but I need to allow Bellatrix to come to her own conclusion with the information I have.

Bellatrix pulls her hand back, and rubs her forehead as

she thinks. "Wow. That's…not much of a surprise, I guess. But, disappointing. She never really was trying to protect me," she says with a huff, but it's more to herself than to me.

"I'm sorry, Princess," I tell her. "I didn't want to be the one to tell you, but I thought you should know, so you could be on guard around her."

Her gaze comes back to me, and her lips lift in a weak smile. "Thank you. I'm glad you did."

"I will do whatever I can to protect you, Princess. I hope you know that. There's nothing I will allow to harm you." I try to sound as confident as I can in these uncertain times, hoping it's offering some comfort.

"This is all just…I never wanted to be queen that bad. I didn't ask for any of this. The curse, finding a mate, now making sure all of Tenuma doesn't fall into the hands of Lothar. How is this happening?" Her voice is soft and she sounds defeated, as she runs her hands through her hair in frustration.

Her head falls and I pull her into my chest, wrapping my arms around her. She opens her legs, shifting so I can come between them, pressing our bodies together. I can feel her heartbeat against my chest. It feels so fucking good. It feels right.

She begins rubbing my back with one of her hands. "Koen?" she says against my chest, her voice muffled.

"Yes, Princess?" I respond, my chin resting on top of her head.

"Why do you call me Princess?" With everything going on, it's not the question I thought she was going to ask me. It's not even in the top five questions I thought she might ask.

I feel myself smile. "What do you mean?" I ask back.

"Princess is not my name. You're the only one who has ever refused to address me formally, or use my actual name. I know you're not using Princess as a formality. I am just curious."

I feel her shrug lightly underneath me.

It takes me a moment to figure out how I want to respond. I never thought about the reason why I call her Princess. I think it started out as a sarcastic way to greet her without getting fired, but now I know it's more.

Taking a big breath, I tighten my hold on her. "I think I rejected the idea of you as Tenuma's princess for so long before I knew you, but now that I do…" I pause.

"Now that you do, what?" she asks curiously.

"Now that I know you, I can call you Princess and know it's true. You're not just Tenuma's princess, you're mine." My honesty shocks even myself.

I feel her arms squeeze around me for just a moment, causing the bracelet on my wrist to tingle. Her affectionate gesture lets me know that what I said makes her feel good. She has enough people in her life, forcing her to do things and telling her who to be, so she deserves someone to make her feel good about herself. I don't have much to offer her, but I will always make sure she knows how fucking amazing she is, even if she doesn't see it herself.

"Princess, can I ask you a question?"

"I call you Koen, because it's your name," she says playfully, giggling.

I gently poke her ribs. "No, smart mouth. I was going to ask…" I pull us apart, holding up her wrist. "Where did you get this bracelet?"

Looking down at it, she twists it once around her wrist. "From one of the merchants in town. I passed by her one day when I was going to give money to the children and she stopped me," she explains.

Could it be? No. But how many merchants would be selling the exact same type of hand-woven bracelets?

"The lady stopped you?" I ask, confused.

"Yeah, the whole thing was sort of strange. She insisted I wear it for protection and wouldn't leave without me taking it. I'd say she was a heck of a saleswoman, but she wasn't even trying to take my money. I had to leave it on her table just so she would take it." The way Bellatrix describes the encounter is lighthearted and innocent, but I can't ignore the ominous feel of it.

My eyebrows pinch together. "Hmm. That's weird," I say, more to myself.

"What is?" She asks.

I hold my wrist up, sporting the exact same bracelet. "My mother is the one that makes and sells these," I say factually.

The princess's head jerks back in surprise. "Does yours… does yours ever feel weird?" Her question surprises me. It never occurred to me that she may be feeling the same sensation with hers that I do.

I nod. "Only when I'm with you," I confess, rubbing her wrist.

She smiles at me sweetly, before the corners of her mouth tilt down in worry. "Do you think she saw me coming? Your mom?" she asks me.

One of my eyebrows raises and I scratch the thick hair on my chin, contemplating her question. While my mother has said on many occasions that she has powers, I'm not sure which powers she exactly possesses or possessed. I don't know if she can sense danger coming, or people coming into our lives. If she could, wouldn't she have known about the dragon? Wouldn't she have warned me that morning? "I don't know. It's possible, I suppose. Before today, I wouldn't have thought I had any sort of… powers, but I saw myself turn into a centaur. So, yeah, it's possible she saw you coming." As I'm talking, I realize I believe it. It is possible, and now I have some questions for my mother.

"That explains why you run so hot all the time," she says,

giggling.

A chuckle escapes my lungs too. I guess she's right. It makes me realize that this power must have been within me all along, but the overwhelming anger I felt seeing her with another man set it off. The thought is unsettling. Will this happen every time I'm angry or will this be something I can control?

As if reading my mind, the princess interrupts my thoughts. "It's okay that it made you angry. I would have felt the same way. I think it might kill me to see you with somebody else," she confesses.

My eyes darken as I meet her deep emerald eyes focused on my lips. I want to lean in so fucking bad, but now that we're in her bed alone, I don't know if I'll be able to stop myself.

"Kiss me," she begs, her eyes flickering with desire, her lips parting.

"Princess…" I pause, grabbing the back of her head. "I've spent days trying to control myself around you. If I let loose now, I don't know how I'll stop myself," I tell her.

She grabs my muscular arms with both hands, her face serious now. "I would never hurt you. I will never let things go that far. I just…" She pauses, looking away, embarrassed or ashamed, I'm not sure which. "I don't know how this could ever be enough for you. How I could ever be enough for you. This is all we will ever have," she explains.

"Princess, kissing you is more than enough. Having you in my life is enough. If this is all we can have, I'll take it because *you* are who I want. I can't honestly say I'm even living if you're not in my life," I confess.

"But, what about all the things I've done? I can't change what I've done or who I've…hurt. The men in town, your friends…" Her voice is fragile, looking for reassurance. It's clear to me now that she's spent a long time hating herself for what she's capable of. Hell, I've hated her for it.

With my hand still cradling her head, I pull her closer to me. "I don't care what you've done. It's not who you are. I see you, all of you and I'm going to be by your side. I want you. I've tried to convince myself to hate you, to fight it, but I want you more than anything and that's not going to change, Princess." I give her just a moment to absorb what I've said and then I pull her face to mine, fusing our lips together. It was only hours ago that I felt her on my mouth, but it feels like it's been an eternity. Much too long. Too much time has passed since I felt her soft lips, her warm sweet tongue swirling in my mouth.

She's not someone you have once just to get out of your system. She's the woman that if you're lucky enough to get, she embeds herself in your DNA, always leaving you aching for more of her. The need is forever growing, never able to sate the hunger.

That's what Princess Bellatrix has done to me. While she might be deadly, like voluntarily ingesting poison ivy, I'm willing to risk it all for her, because life isn't worth living without her in it. Whatever she can give me, however big or small, is exactly what I want. Any piece of her is better than not having her at all.

Our kisses are passionate and frantic, intense and deep. She's moaning into my mouth and I'm releasing low growls back into hers. I feel her hands move from my arms and chest, exploring my body. I'm still holding her in place, scared to let go in case she realizes what a mistake this could be. The way her lips feel on mine, I'm happy to give up breathing forever if this is what takes its place.

Suddenly, she pulls me against her as she lies back on the bed with me on top of her. Her black hair fans out around her on the bed and she opens her legs, inviting me in between them. Positioning myself between her legs, I take my knee and push her legs wider.

"I want you spread out on the sheets, Princess. Let me see you." My voice is low and husky.

Her breathing accelerates as she opens her legs wider for me. Her lacy panties shift, now revealing part of her pussy to me, causing me to suck in a breath. She's perfect and her damp panties reveal she wants me as badly as I want her.

"You're perfect, Princess. Can I touch you? What are the limits?" I ask.

"Yes, touch me. Touch me, please," she requests desperately, her hips already bucking up towards my hand hovering over her.

Slowly, my fingers graze the side of her panties, gently moving them completely to one side so her bare pussy is on full display for me. I can feel her wetness on my fingers, tempting me to taste her. She's fully shaven and perfectly soft. I take my fingers and open her up, so I can see more of her. I want to see every fold and crevice of her body. I want to memorize every inch of her.

"Princess, you're so wet." My voice turns guttural.

My praise makes her moan with need. "Mmm…"

"Is all this for me, Princess?" I ask her, rubbing her bundle of nerves, causing her to squirm underneath me. Suddenly, I can't imagine a better view than Bellatrix's naked body squirming underneath me until the end of time.

"Yes," she responds in a silken voice. "Please," she begs.

"What do you want, Princess?" I ask, tauntingly.

"More. I need more." Leaning up, she pulls my head down and presses our lips together, her kisses frantic and messy. Her tongue is in my mouth, around my lips, and it feels like she's going to eat me alive.

No, that's what I'm going to do to her, I think, causing a cunning grin to spread on my face when our faces pull apart.

"You have to tell me what I can and can't do, Princess." I say to her, not wanting to meet my maker in the middle of pleasuring her.

As if someone just came in and caught us, she stops cold and sits up pushing me off of her, pulling her nightgown back down.

"What's wrong?" I ask, my eyebrows pinched with concern.

"I-I can't lose control with you. I don't know what the limits are," she confesses, crushing the mood, and my arousal.

"Oh." I sit back on the bed, putting space between us.

She's shaking her head. "It's not something I'm willing to risk with you. I… I think I have a plan to fix it, but until then… we can't." Her voice is low and fragile.

I reach forward and tuck her hair behind her ear, as she's looking down at the bed. "Hey," I say, forcing her to look up at me. "It's okay, Princess."

She shakes her head. "No, it's not. None of this is okay." Taking my hand in hers, she pulls us both until we're laying down, side by side. "Will you lay with me?"

Pulling myself closer to her body for comfort, I whisper in her ear. "Always, Princess."

33

BELLATRIX

I've never been much of a fighter. My parents have always told me what I can and cannot do, and I've followed without any questioning. I've followed them blindly, even when I know what they're doing is wrong.

Forcing men into my bed is wrong.

Taking more and more dues from the people of Tenuma until they can barely feed and clothe themselves is wrong.

All of it is wrong, which is why I swore I'd be a better queen. I'd rule with peace and love. I'd be powerful, but loved. I don't want to cause more suffering, I want to ease it. Thinking I'd be queen soon enough, I figured I just had to wait a little while and then I could change things.

I was wrong.

Things are worse than ever, with a dragon on the loose, Tenuma on the brink of war, and my future as queen uncertain.

But one thing I'm certain of is, I'm finally ready to fight. Lying in Koen's arms makes my heart ache in a way that forces me to open my eyes. I've been so cavalier with my time, thinking there's time to waste while there are families starving and fighting to survive. His family is one of them. I want to fight for him, and the rest of Tenuma. I want to fight for myself.

Koen shifts next to me, spreading out on his back and stretching his long limbs. We fell asleep in each other's arms, and I don't think I've ever felt that kind of calm. The sunlight is starting to come through the large windows in my bed chambers, and I'm feeling grateful that we managed to keep our hands to ourselves last night–for the most part.

His eyes flutter open, as he takes in the unfamiliar surroundings. I see the second his memory pieces it all back together, and he smiles when our eyes meet. "Good morning, Princess." The rasp and huskiness of his morning voice sends a chill through my lower half, and I swear my nipples harden at just the sound.

Smiling back at him, I pull myself back into his body heat. That's another great thing about sleeping in Koen's arms, we could be outside in the snow, and I'd still be perfectly content with his heat. "Good morning. I like seeing you in my bed," I tell him.

The smile he gives me is pure and sweet, and I can't resist caressing his face, gently scratching at his thick facial hair. But, before he can respond, we're interrupted by a quiet, but frantic knock at the door.

I pad over to the door quickly, opening it just enough to see who's on the other side. "Rina? What is it?" I ask.

"Your mother is awake, and you need to get Koen out of your bed before she sees," she says.

Looking back at Koen sitting up in my bed, and then back to Quirina confused. "W-what–how did you know he's here?" I ask.

She gives me an incredulous look. "For starters, the sun is barely up, and the door to his room is wide open and his bed is empty." Her face is fighting a smile.

"Shit," I respond.

"The storm has passed, and he will be able to head home now. I think it's wise if he doesn't stick around, even for work today. Something is going on," Quirina confesses.

The tension in the castle is palpable, so it's impossible for anybody inside to miss. It's as if we're all tip toeing around grenades, just waiting for one to go off.

"Thank you for the warning, Rina. He'll leave right now," I tell her, feeling grateful that I can continue to call her my friend after everything.

Closing the door, I make my way back over to Koen who's dressed and ready to head out. The moments we have together aren't enough, but I suppose it's for the best. He doesn't need to spend more time with a woman who could easily kill him.

"Thank you for staying with me," I tell him softly, meaning every word.

"Happy to. Thank you for allowing me," Koen says back, moving the hair out of my face, caressing my cheek.

"I know I've brought danger into your life, and I–" I start, but he stops me by putting his fingers against my lips.

He shakes his head. "Stop. You're not getting rid of me that easily, Princess. I told you, you're what I want. Even if this curse never goes away, whatever we *can* have is what I want." His morning voice is gone and has been replaced with confidence and intensity.

The way he can read me so easily surprises me. He's right, I was going to tell him that maybe he's better off without me, but it's not what either of us want. There's no use kidding ourselves. While we know better, there's a pull that neither one of us can ignore any longer.

I smile, and nod my head. "Kiss me," I demand sweetly.

His hand curves around the back of my head, his fingers threading through my hair, pulling me towards his mouth and I swear I could melt just from feeling his lips, his tongue, his facial hair against me. It lights my body on fire, and I'm going to need to extinguish it soon or I might explode.

When we pull apart, I don't know why but it feels like we're saying goodbye. I hold onto him for an extra second not wanting to let go just yet but knowing I need to.

"Will you come back?" I ask, the desperation in my voice, impossible to hide.

He smiles at me. "Always, Princess."

"Promise?" My heart speaks for me now.

"With my life." Koen kisses my forehead, and quietly leaves the room, leaving an even larger aching in my chest.

My day continues its usual course of breakfast, pampering, and meetings with the king's armed forces top leaders to discuss who hasn't paid their dues, and what's to be done about it. To my surprise, not one word is spoken of the dragon, or an impending war upon Tenuma. No discussion of the attack on myself, or the fact that the castle wasn't properly guarded the night of my attack.

Something is definitely wrong here.

Once I've gotten all of the day's formalities out of the way, despite my best efforts to avoid her, the queen has found me.

"There you are, dear." Her voice is smooth as honey, which is unsettling, knowing what I do now.

I look up from my vanity mirror, to see her standing in my doorway in one of her floor length elegant dresses. She wears similar corset dresses with low cut necklines as I do, but hers has much more material around the base of the dress making it much wider and heavier than it needs to be. This dark red dress looks gorgeous on her, but it makes me even more guarded. She's used her beauty and fake sweetness to get her way for far too long.

"Here I am," I say dryly.

"How did you sleep?" she asks, making her way further into my room.

I feel my spine stiffen, and my cat-like eyes narrow in suspicion. She's up to something, and I'm not falling into her traps. "Good, why?"

Her Cheshire cat grin sends a chill down my spine, as she shrugs. "Oh, I thought you might have," she replies coolly.

"Is there something you want to say, Mother?" I ask in a clipped tone, already exhausted from whatever game she's playing.

"I noticed that your handyman decided to forgo his own bed chambers last night, and I figured he ended up in yours." The tone of her voice tells me that she already knows, because she was up checking on us last night.

Pulling my lips together in frustration, I stand up, turning in her direction. "What are you trying to do?" I ask her, anger rising quickly inside of me.

Her face is still relaxed and amused. "I was going to ask what *you* did. Did you two enjoy your time together?" She's asking if I had sex with him. Something tells me she wanted me to. This entire night was a set up.

I lift one eyebrow, sucking my cheeks in, unable to hide the anger and disgust any longer. "If you're asking if we had sex. I hate to disappoint you, but there was no sex involved. I am able to control myself, you know," I snap back.

"What?" The cool exterior of the queen has vanished, and

in its wake lies an angry ruler who was disobeyed. "You two were supposed to fuck, so he would stop getting in your head and in my damn way!" she shouts at me.

The sting of her confession and anger feels like a slap to the face. I take a step back, needing space between me and whoever is standing in front of me. I don't recognize this person. "You set me up to kill him? What is wrong with you? You've been lying to me my whole life, haven't you? This has never been about my *'safety,'* has it?" Now I'm shouting back at her.

She steps closer, her green eyes like pistols aimed for me, pointing a finger in my face. "You are a senseless child, Bella! You have no idea what's coming. You've let this *handyman* put foolish ideas in your head, and he's going to ruin everything!" The intensity of her anger scares me, but for once I refuse to back down.

"What could he possibly be ruining, Mother? He's been the only one to look at me like a human being—not like a tool, not like a murderer, and not like a pawn in a power struggle like you and Father have done my whole life. I'd never do anything to hurt him. So whatever games you're trying to play, you can stop. You won't win," I bark back.

"You are our only chance at survival. The only way we will survive this coming war. If you do not continue letting those men into your bed, we will lose." Her confession rocks me, confusing and terrifying me at the same time.

"Why would killing more men help us win a fucking war, Mother?" I shout, my exasperation evident.

The words that come out of my mother's mouth next are enough to make my entire body shake, and my mind cloud over.

"Bella, none of those men ever died." These are the last words I hear before everything goes black.

34

KOEN

While Mellani is delighted to see me, my mother is quite vexed that I was missing all night.

"You could have been dead! With the storm, and you spending all that time with that princess, you don't even want to know what was going through my head. What were you thinking?" My mother's angry voice isn't as scary as it is scared and frustrated. Her anger always comes from fear and in this case, fear of losing me.

"I'm sorry, Mother. I was working late, and I…" *I killed a man, and then I slept with the princess in her bed to protect her, because her mother might be trying to kill her. Also, I think I'm falling in love with her.* I have no idea what to tell her, without lying. I'm not much of a liar, and I don't strive to be one either.

"What? Tell me. It's her, isn't it?" she asks, and I should have known that she already knows.

I nod.

"Koen. You cannot be serious. She's not good for you. She's the only woman on Tenuma you cannot have. What are you setting yourself up for, baby?" she asks, her voice now soft and even more terrified if possible.

"She's not what you think. Hell, she isn't even what I thought she was." I try to defend. "There's more to it than what I feel for her though, Mother. Something bad is coming, and they're setting her up to be killed," I confess.

"Who? Who's setting her up to be killed?" My mother's eyes are wild, realizing that I have been in more danger than she even thought.

"The king and queen," I reveal.

My mother paces our living room, mulling over what I just said. I feel awful for making her worry and leaving her and Mellani here alone during a storm, but I didn't have a choice.

"I'm sorry I worried you," I finally say when it's been silent too long. "I would have come home if it weren't for the storm, but we have bigger things to worry about now, Mother. Something big is coming, and we need to go somewhere safe." I can't tell if she believes a word I'm saying, or if she's simply stewing in her anger.

"What do you mean, what's coming?" she asks me with concern in her voice.

"I'm not sure. A war, eventually. A fight is coming, and we need to be prepared. I think we should pack up and head for the castle." It's a crazy idea, but it's the only place I can think of that I know we'll be safe. I know the princess would allow us to hide out there.

Laughter bursts out of my mother, as she goes to sit down on the couch. "The castle? Sure, let me go pack my jewels first," she responds sarcastically. I can't blame her for that response, because even to me, it sounds insane.

"Mother, I know this sounds crazy. Bellatrix will allow us to stay there. The castle will be safe." Even saying it out loud sounds crazy, and a few weeks ago I would have laughed at the words myself, but it's our only option if something bad is coming.

The caves are another option, but will be overrun with townspeople if it's as bad as I think it will be.

"Bellatrix," she echoes, with a huff. Clearly recognizing the familiar way I'm referring to her all of a sudden. Letting out a heavy sigh, she continues. "If they're trying to kill the princess, wouldn't that make the castle the most dangerous place for us to be?" she asks, and I can tell that she's starting to take me seriously.

I shake my head. "No, it's not just her. The King of Sperantia is coming to take over the entire land and she's just in his way. He plans on taking complete power, so I don't think any of us are safe." My revelation settles as her face crumples. Her face stricken with worry, frustration, and something else resembling guilt.

At least at the castle, there are guards and armed forces, dungeons, and a wide protected perimeter. Our flimsy little cottage wouldn't withstand a strong breeze from an attack.

"Are you… with the princess?" she asks the question I don't want to answer, the question I don't know how to answer. I don't want to disappoint her.

I shrug. "I don't know how to answer that. There's something between us. It's strong. You know me, I never do anything risky or dangerous. That's not me. But with her… she makes me want to light the world on fire to keep her safe," I admit. Even this conversation I couldn't imagine having had with my mother a few weeks ago. Overnight, I've turned into a different man with different priorities and aspirations. I feel both stronger and weaker at the same time.

Staring at me in silence, she considers what I've said. I see her eyes drift to my wrist, at the bracelet I'm wearing.

I spin it around once, glancing back up at my mother. "You saw her coming, didn't you?" I ask.

She nods.

"That's why you forced her to take one of your bracelets

that day you saw her in town, isn't it?" My voice is getting shaky, at the thought of my mother knowing this was going to happen all along. I don't understand why she wouldn't say anything to me.

Again, she nods.

Goosebumps go up my arms and legs. "You knew that even from the first day I went to work at the castle. You saw her coming. Why didn't you just tell me?" I ask. Would it have changed things? Would it have prevented me from going, knowing how much I hated her then?

"I couldn't," my mother answers softly.

"Of course you could have. You could have warned me," I respond.

Her face twists into both rage and defeat. "I did warn you! I told you repeatedly to stay away from her. Why did you have to take that job at the castle? I asked you not to!" The words come pouring out of her quickly, in one breath.

I put my hand over hers as I sit next to her on the couch for comfort. "You could have told me *why*." My voice is low, and soft.

My mother shakes her head. "No, my son. There are things you don't understand. Things I cannot discuss."

My eyes narrow at her statement. "Mother, why are you being so cryptic? You can tell me anything," I tell her, feeling sad that she feels like she can't talk to me.

I squeeze her hand and she looks up at me with worry in her eyes. I can see that she has so much to say, but she's holding back. I just wish I knew why.

We never get the chance to get that far, because just then a knock sounds at the front door.

"I'll get it!" Mellani shouts in her sweet, small voice.

I rush over to stop her. "No, sweet girl. You don't answer the door to strangers, remember?" I tell her firmly.

"But you do!" she replies, giving me her best pouty face. It always makes me smile.

"And when you're a grown-up, you can too." I kiss the top of her head, and nudge her to go sit by our mother on the couch.

Swinging the door open, I see Nik standing in front of me panting, with a wild look in his eyes.

"Nik? Wh–" I start, but he cuts me off when he shoves me, both of us stumbling into the cottage.

"They're everywhere. Pack a bag and get the hell out of here, right now!" His voice is panicked and erratic.

"What? What is everywhere?" I ask calmly.

He stops moving, and stares me straight in the face. "Dragons."

My blood goes ice cold, and my ears start to ring. The dragons are back, and they're in town. "Where? How many?" I ask, finally grasping the seriousness of the situation.

Nikandros runs his hands through his hair. "I don't know, man. A few? They're burning down the town. My bar–it's… it's gone man. We need to go, now."

Fuck.

I turn back towards my mother. "Mother, it's time. We need to go. We're going to the castle," I tell her, and she gives me a worried, hesitant look. "I know, I'm sorry. But you have to trust me." We don't have the luxury of panicking right now, we need to move.

Quickly, we each pack one small bag of our necessities, making sure to collect all the coins that the princess has been giving to Mellani over the last year. I don't know what's going to happen from here, but we need something to ensure our safety and that we won't go hungry.

Mellani insists on bringing her drawings, my mother brings all of her bracelets, and I mostly bring weapons. Throwing everything over my back, I guide us towards the edge of the forest, and we start our hike to the castle. Nik seemed certain that the dragons were targeting the populated areas specifically, so we're traveling on the border of town, trying to stay out of sight. I convinced him to come with us, since it would be the safest place for us to be. As my best friend, there's no way I was leaving him behind. It didn't take nearly as much convincing on his part, as it did with my mother. Mellani was happy to go on an 'adventure' as she calls it, to the castle, not realizing the severity of the situation.

As we begin to pass town, the smell of burning buildings invades our nostrils and stings our eyes. We can see the flames from where we are walking high up through the trees. Smoke and ash are floating through all of Tenuma like snow.

A loud gasp comes from my mother. "Heaven, save Tenuma," she says softly, gazing at the flames flickering in the distance with tears in her eyes.

I put an arm around my mother and squeeze her for reassurance. "Come on, Mother. We will be okay. Let's keep moving," I tell her, urging her to move on. I don't know how much time we have left and I'm just hoping it's enough to make it safely to the castle grounds.

We just need to get to Bellatrix, and then we will be okay, I tell myself over and over again. Maybe if I say it enough times, I will convince myself. But it's hard to believe that when I'm watching the only place I've called home go up in flames.

35

BELLATRIX

Flames surround me and I can feel the heat licking my flesh from my toes all the way up to the crown of my head. I don't move as I stand in awe, watching the way the flames dance around me, wrapping me up in a warm embrace. Red and orange flames dance angrily around me, but two outstretched flames reach for me, bringing me closer and making me feel something I've never felt before. Loved. I blink and the flames are no more. I stand before Koen, his arms wrapped around me tightly, smiling warmly at me, his gray eyes intense and ready to consume my soul. For just a moment, I see a flicker in his eyes, a flicker of worry. Just before I can ask him what's wrong, his mouth opens and forms a word I cannot hear.

What did he say? I think to myself.

"Run." His mouth forms the word, but again, I cannot hear it.

When my eyes meet his again, they're full of panic and I can see sweat forming on his brow. His gaze moves behind me, and as I turn to see what he's looking at, everything erupts in a bright light.

I open my eyes to realize I'm in my own bed. Koen isn't here. The bright light streams through my windows making it harder to open my eyes through the pounding in my head. I try to sort my thoughts.

Why am I in bed?

I was just talking with my mother…

Oh. My. God.

As everything comes flooding back, I crash back hard into reality, intensifying the pounding in my head. I sit up straight, hoping there's a glass of water nearby, because it feels as if I drank an entire bottle of my favorite whiskey last night.

I glance at my nightstand and notice an enticing glass of water—still with ice, meaning it hasn't been here long—and drink greedily from it. I can feel the cool liquid slide down my throat and down to my stomach, filling me back with life. It's refreshing, and instantly I feel the pain in my head ease.

My mother is nowhere in sight, and I'm in bed alone. The last thing I remember is that we were having a conversation, and she told me something that just can't be true.

"None of those men died." Those men never made it home to their families. I know it, the townspeople know it. That's the truth I've always known. I'm a murderer. That's the other truth I've always known. To tell me that now, and give me the slightest bit of hope that I may not be the monster they led me to believe my whole life is…unfathomable.

If what she says is true, it will change everything.

Koen. My train of thought immediately derails and heads straight for the bearded handyman that I can't seem to get enough of. The one I can't have. But maybe, just maybe, I can.

Pulling myself out of bed, I change into a long sleeve purple velvet dress that has a scoop neckline, and high slit up the side. It's not as tight as most of my corset dresses, so it fits more comfortably. I'd rather stay in bed naked and fight off this migraine, but something is compelling me to figure everything out right now. Time feels like it's slipping away, and I need to know the truth.

$\mathcal{B}$efore I swing the door to my bedchambers open, I can hear the sounds of chaos on the other side. Sounds of shouting, footsteps running up and down the halls, panicked voices.

Something big is happening.

I open my door, and there's a guard standing out in front of my door catching me off guard.

"Oh." I clear my throat. "Excuse me, I'm going to look for my mother," I tell the man, hoping he will move the hell out of my way.

He turns as I speak, his face stern and shoulders rigid. "Apologies, Princess, but I cannot allow that," he replies.

I furrow my eyebrows at him. "Excuse me?" I ask in confusion. There's no way in hell that I'm about to become a prisoner in my own home as well. Even though I'm not permitted to wander about the town for safety reasons, I've never been confined to my room for any particular reason.

"Your Majesty, the king and queen requested I stay posted at your door and not permit you to leave under any circumstances," he explains.

Popping my hip out, and resting one hand on it, growing impatient I snap back. "Is there a particular reason I'm not allowed to leave my bedchambers?"

His facial expression stays neutral, and voice is monotone. "The city is under attack. We will need to move shortly, but for now the order is to stay here." With that, he turns around, his back facing me now.

I step back and close the door. Clearly, I'm not getting through this guard unless I stab him—which I don't plan on doing.

Under attack. What the hell is going on? It has to be Lothar and his men. But now? It seemed like we had more time. I thought I had more time.

I run back over to the window to see what I can make out of the chaos ensuing. My hand reflexively covers my mouth at what my eyes witness.

In the distance all through the land, are smokestacks rising high into the sky. I can count seven of them from my window. There are fires everywhere, and though most of them seem to be closer to town, it fills me with dread.

Koen and his family.

My stomach twists as I realize that I am the cause of everything happening right now. I'm the reason Lothar gained the courage to take over Tenuma. I failed in finding a mate, and leaving our throne unattended has left us weak and vulnerable. Bringing Koen into my life just endangered him in ways I never imagined. Everything boils down to me.

The fires in the distance are growing rapidly, and overhead, I can see what I was dreading since the day I was rescued from the cave.

Dragons.

I can see not only one, but multiple dragons flying overhead, breathing fire down onto our beloved land, scorching it to ash.

Dragons are ravishing our town and I'm stuck inside my bedchambers like a child. My parents want me to become a strong queen, and yet they treat me like I'm useless. I could be doing *something, anything* to help instead of sitting in here hiding out. There are people out there losing their homes and dying but

I'm trapped inside this enormous room, because what? Because I'm too important to get hurt? Too fragile to help win a war?

My parents knew a war was coming and instead of preparing me, all they did was stick man after man in front of me. I was only useful when it came to how good my body could make someone feel–which is ironic, because all it does is harm.

Years have been wasted from me sleeping with shallow men in hopes of becoming king, when I could have been training in combat. I could be out there helping to fight off Lothar and his armies. This is as much my fight as it is anyone else's, and in many ways, it's more my fight. I should be the one out there risking my life, not the innocent townspeople.

I may have done some horrible things in my life, but none of it was because I wanted to. All I've ever done is try to please everyone around me. Those days are done. Sitting here while the town turns to ash is not what a strong queen would do. That's not what I'm going to do.

Walking to my bedside table, I grab my dagger and place it on my bed. I reach underneath my bed, pulling out a long skinny rectangular wooden box. I lift the lid off of it, revealing the sword presented to me when I turned fifteen. This is the sword I will be ruling with. I slide my finger up one of the long, sharp smooth edges, and it scrapes a small slice of flesh, blood rising to the surface of my finger. Pulling it into my mouth, I can't help but grin wickedly.

This is a queen's sword. This is how I'm going to get my power back.

Pulling it out of the box entirely, I hold it up to the light, its weight a reminder of the damage it can cause. The handle of the sword contains a blue howlite gem in the center of it, around beautiful iron intricacies. The craftsmanship of this sword is worth the money it costs, but I don't give a shit about any of that. Right now, all I'm concerned with is fighting back and saving Tenuma.

This is *my* home, and I'll be damned if I sit back and watch it be taken away.

36

KOEN

We can't just let them take everything away!" I shout as my mother tries to drag me back into the trees of the forest.

"My son, you have to stop! You have a death wish!" she shouts back frantically, tugging on my arm. Despite her short build, she's surprisingly strong.

On our way to the castle after Nik's warning, we see the devastation of the dragons' wrath. Our land is crumbling before our eyes. Family and friends are perishing and we are running away. It's never been my strong suit to run from a threat. I don't go looking for danger, no—but I will protect what's mine.

This town.

This land.

My family.

My friends.

My princess.

Cowards take the easy way out, and that's not a trait I ever want to have. My father was a coward. He wasn't man enough to love our mother or to take care of his children. Leaving was his final performance in the cowardly saga of his life. That is never going to be me.

"I can't just run and hide. I have to do something. I can…I can help," I say as I remember the beast I transformed into in the princess's chambers. Except figuring out how to transform back into it is something I haven't had the time to figure out yet.

My mother eyes me suspiciously at my comment in silence. The fact that she's not saying anything tells me everything.

She already knows.

I pull my arm out from under her grasp. "You knew, didn't you?" I ask her, taking a step back. "You knew what I was capable of this whole time."

Her eyes fill with tears at the realization that I've discovered my gift, or curse, or whatever the hell is happening to me. Right now, it doesn't even matter. We don't have the luxury of arguing on the edge of town right now. Time isn't on our side, and we have people to save.

"Aaahhh, Koen! Mama!" Mellani calls out, as a fireball hurls towards the forest, landing not far behind us, setting the trees ablaze.

I glance back to the destruction, the sight making my heart twist. This forest has provided our land with wood, and food, and now it's all being destroyed. "It's getting closer. We don't have time. Take Mellani and get her to the castle. Ask for Bellatrix or find her. By any means, mother. Do you hear me? You have to find her. She will ensure your safety. Both of you will be safe until I can get there," I say to my mother, then turn to Nikandros. "Nik, please make sure they get there," I say firmly, begging and pleading for him to get my family to safety.

Nik gazes out ahead of us where the town is burning to the ground, where we can hear screaming and chaos. He pulls his shoulders back and puffs his chest out. He shakes his head. "I'm coming with you." I open my mouth to protest, but he stops me.

"This is my town, too. These are my people, too," he says firmly. And I know I won't be talking him out of this, because I know nobody could talk *me* out of it.

I nod, offering him a tight smile. One that soldiers might share before they run into battle together, knowing it could be the last time they see each other.

Pulling my mother and Mellani into a tight hug, I squeeze them before pushing them in the direction of the castle. "I love you both. I'll see you soon."

Mellani looks up at me with fear and tears in her eyes. "Promise?"

I give her the most genuine smile I can muster, hiding the pain and fear beneath the surface. "With my life. Go," I say softly, my voice cracking on the last word.

I watch them disappear in the distance as they rush through the trees to safety. The pit in my stomach is getting bigger and bigger, as my family gets further away from me. The idea of leaving them doesn't sit well with me, but abandoning everyone in town feels even worse. My family will be safe where they're going, and I know I can do some good here. I know that whatever *gift* I have can do some good.

"So… do you have a plan here?" Nik asks me, pulling me from my train of thought.

As my eyes meet his, I can see that he's having some serious second thoughts about this, realizing that I don't actually have a plan. While the fear might be settling into our bones now, I know neither one of us wants to run and hide either. "You should have gone with them to the castle, Nik," I tell him. There's so much he doesn't know, and I don't know if I can protect him.

He scoffs. "And let you have all the fun and glory for saving the town? I don't think so." He elbows me in the side, attempting to lighten the mood.

"There's something I can do… something I can become,"

I confess.

His eyebrows pull together in confusion, and his lips form a lopsided grin. "What do you mean? Become what?" Curiosity taking over his expression.

"A centaur," I say, not believing my own words. It sounds ridiculous.

"You're gifted?? How long have you known?" he asks, excitedly. It's not the response I expect, but I'm pleased he's not horrified that his best friend just admitted to being a monster.

"I don't know if it's a 'gift.' I just found out. My mother has known for some time apparently. I don't even know how it works." As I say this, I wonder if my mother knows how it works, and I'm wishing I had asked a few questions before I sent her off.

According to legend, centaurs once roamed freely and abundantly on the land of Tenuma. They were known for their impressive size, strength, and speed. They could outrun any animal in nature, and bend steel beneath their feet/hooves. Man did not fear them because they were unpredictable or brutish, but one did not go out of their way to anger a centaur. Attempting to harm one or his family, would prove fatal on their part, so it wasn't wise to risk doing so. Centaurs didn't need weapons to protect themselves and they were known to be quite clever.

I wish I felt any of this right now.

"Well, can you summon it or something?" he asks.

I shrug. "I don't think it works like that."

"How did you find out about it to begin with? What was going on when it first happened?" he asks, and it takes me back to the princess's room.

Anger. Blind rage sent me exploding into centaur form.

"It's anger. Anger and protection, I think." I contemplate what I'll need to see or do in order to transform back into it.

"Well, I guess we're in the right place for that then," he

deadpans, his gaze panning to the destruction ahead.

I close my eyes channeling every shard of anger from my entire life that I can muster into this moment so I can transform into the beast and hopefully save some of the town.

My father leaving me.

My father leaving Mellani.

The king's never-ending taxes crippling the town.

Landric volunteering for his death.

Seeing the princess upset.

Seeing the princess with bruises on her body.

Finding the man who hurt her.

Seeing the princess with another man.

As I run through some of the most infuriating moments I can recall, I feel my fingertips begin to tingle and my blood begins to boil. The heat in my body is rising quickly, as my heart begins to beat faster. My head is pulsing, cloudy, and feeling heavy with both the memories, and tension of the situation ahead of us.

This time, I feel it when it happens. The world explodes around me, and I know I've transformed. From man to beast. My clothes fall to the ground, and I know when I open my eyes, Nik will be looking at the body of a beast.

"Holy shit, Ko!" Nik shouts up at me, impressed and shocked.

My eyes meet Nik's and he doesn't fear me like I suspected. He looks excited and intrigued. "Let's go save our people," I tell him, feeling the anger coursing through my veins like a good whiskey working its way through my blood. I feel strong and solid and fucking livid.

"I can't do that..." he says, gesturing to my large figure. "I'll need weapons." He gestures to the bag next to me full of my daggers, and my bow and arrow sitting on the ground.

Taking one dagger out of the bag for myself, I toss the bag to him along with the bow and arrow. "Are you ready?" I ask, picturing the last time I was face-to-face with one of those beasts. Their sharp, disgusting teeth, those razor talons, and the large wings. Wings wider than the trees are tall. I have no idea how the dragon wedged itself inside the forest to begin with. Its grand size should have made it impossible, but it seemed determined.

Determined to find the princess.

Fuck.

"Nik!" I shout, having an epiphany. "You saw the dragons up close?" I ask.

"Yeah, right before they burned down my bar. Why?" he asks, confused by my sudden need for conversation.

"Did you see anybody with the dragons? Were there soldiers…" I hate to even say the word out loud. "Controlling them?"

His eyes go wide. "I did see men on top of the dragons actually. I didn't even think about it with everything going on," he says, shocked.

Shit, I think, realizing that the dragons didn't suddenly come out of the blue. They rode in with an army. The King of Sperantia must have been training them and using them as weapons. He is here with his army and an arsenal of trained dragons to take over our entire land.

"We have to go. We need to take down as many of those things as we can," I tell him, also realizing that if they need weapons of that magnitude, it tells me that their army cannot withstand ours alone. So, if we can separate them from the dragons or kill them, we can defeat them.

Nikandros nods and grasps one of the larger daggers in his hand. "I've got your back, Ko," he says to me, and we race towards the fire.

37

BELLATRIX

The shouting and chaos continues outside my door, and I brace myself before I swing the door open, knowing that I might have to threaten the guard at my door in order to get free of my chambers. I don't want to, but I will if I have to. I feel the fear building inside of me like a fire, but instead of letting it consume me, I breathe deep and extinguish it. Fear will not take hold of me, not this time. I'll have to just feel everything later, but right now I'm pushing it all down and facing the dangers head on.

You are the Queen of Tenuma, you can do this. These are your people, and you must find a way to protect them.

You are not a coward like your parents. You will fight to protect, not to harm.

I think of the way Koen protected me and fought for me, even though I could kill him. Even though he's had a hatred for me as long as he's known about me. His selflessness and loyalty are giving me the strength to be brave. With everything I've put our people through, I want to be better. I want to do good. *Be* good.

Koen is the first person to look at me as more than a

prize, or something to be bought. He doesn't want anything from me. Not once has he taken from me, but instead, he's been the one giving and giving since we met. It's my turn to give back. I need to do it.

Whipping open my door, my sword held out in front of me, ready to threaten or strike, but the doorway is empty. I stick my head out of the doorway, looking down the long hall to the right, realizing that I don't see anybody on the entire floor. I'm unsure whether this is a good sign or not.

Quiet as a cat, I run down the hall to my parent's room to see if I can find the king or queen there. The door opens to reveal an empty room. I move further into the room determined to hunt them down, but I come up empty handed. I check the bathroom, it's also empty.

Closet. Empty.

Except it's not entirely empty. On a shoulder-high pillar topped with a small cushion sits my mother's crown gleaming in all of its beauty and power. I don't know what compels me to do it, but I pluck the heavy crown off of where it rests, and set it atop my head.

The gold and black colors make the jewels pop even more so. A thousand tiny diamonds make up the length of the crown, making it sparkle in any room and any lighting. The large jewel set in front is what drew me to pick it up, as if it were a calling, beckoning me straight to it. The pear-shaped diamond is so perfect, I can nearly see straight through it. Held up by two swords intertwined in iron underneath it like a cradle, it evokes both beauty and power.

I feel electricity flow through the crown of my head and through my fingertips. The electrical charge I only feel in Koen's presence is suddenly tangible. I can see the electrical currents buzzing off of my fingertips. The hand that grasps the sword is hot and buzzing with power.

My hearing goes temporarily mute as the ringing in my ears takes over while the current flows through my body, and when it comes back it's as though somebody turned the volume back up in the room around me. It happens just in time to hear footsteps approaching from behind.

I spin around holding my sword outward, assessing the danger.

Standing before me is a soldier from Sperantia. The serpent insignia on their green uniforms gives him away immediately.

His cold, empty eyes and sinister grin makes my hair stand on end. In one hand he holds an impressive dagger that appears to be covered in a dark liquid. All it takes is one twitch of his hand before I'm hurling my sword towards him, plunging it through his chest. With one swift movement, it pierces straight through his flesh, and I pull it back out as he crumbles to the floor.

I stand before him, as the blood pools at my feet, stunned. I didn't know I had it in me. My breathing picks up, my hands are shaking and I'm worried I might come apart.

Instead, I take a deep breath, narrowing my eyes at the asshole who came into my home, to harm my family. To harm me.

I will not have guilt over this.

A queen protects.

I am a queen, and I will never back down from a threat again.

I am taking back control of Tenuma.

I am taking back control of my body.

I am taking back control of my life.

I adjust the crown that sits atop my head, and make my way downstairs where commotion is still taking place. I hear running, panicked screaming, and loud orders being shouted over everything.

"Nobody comes in or leaves the castle! They could be in disguise, and we cannot let the men get near the princess!" one of our armed forces shouts to another.

"Sir, the king has already been taken and the queen is missing. How will we protect the princess?" another man asks back.

My parents are missing? I think as my concern doubles, and I can't help but wonder if Quirina is somewhere safe.

The man doesn't answer his question, which sends a chill down my spine. "Make sure there's protection at every entrance. Now, go!" he demands once more, and I hear the man run off.

I make my way downstairs, and the man I presume was just giving the orders, takes in my appearance.

Sword in hand, crown atop my head, blood covering the bottom of my dress and shoes.

His eyes go wide. "Princess… are you wounded?" he asks, assessing the situation.

I shake my head, looking around at the chaos of my home. "No. How can I help?"

The man bites his lip, contemplating what he should tell me. It's clear he isn't going to send me into battle. "Princess, you should be up in your chambers, away from all of this." He comes towards me, gently offering me his hand to lead me back upstairs.

I step backwards out of his reach. "There's a man dead upstairs in the king's room. I'm covered in his blood. Clearly, my bedroom is not the safest place to be." My tone is clear and firm, as if the crown is giving me the confidence of a queen. But it's true, upstairs isn't safe, hell, the lower levels below the castle would be safer. Only one entry, and is impenetrable. I don't know why we all weren't ushered down there to begin with.

"With all due respect, Your Majesty, you cannot be here

with the fight. Harm cannot come to you. You must… please," he begs, lost for words, and clearly unsure what to do.

Part of me sympathizes with the man who just wants to fulfill his duty and protect me. Afterall, that was me not too long ago; following orders blindly, unable to decide on my own. But a bigger part of me is filled with anger. Anger from years of being told what to do by men, by my father, my mother. The anger lives deep in my core, and is finally being set free. I don't want to be angry, I want to be free. The freedom to decide my own fate. If I fight, I may die, but it will be my choice. I'm happy to fight for my freedom. Unlike the men who were sent to my chambers, I want the choice. I will no longer succumb to anyone else's pawn.

"With all due respect, I will be your queen. I will no longer be taking orders from you or my parents. This is my land, and these are my people. I am here to fight *for* and *with* my people. Tell me how I can help." The thunder in my voice intimidates the man into submission as he finally backs up a step and bows his head to me.

"We need more men…" he starts, and then corrects himself. "We need more forces to take the horses to town. The dragons have set fire to most of the town, and the townspeople are fleeing their homes, with nowhere to go," he explains.

"Direct them here," I suggest.

"Your Majesty, I don't think–" I stop him before he can decline my order.

"I'm not asking. Direct the people here. They need shelter and safety. We have the manpower to protect them here. I will go to town," I tell the man, and then dart off towards the back of the castle to find my horse.

Footsteps follow quickly after me, and I know the man is hot on my heels. "If you insist, let me help you," he offers, getting my saddle set up for my mare.

Once I'm all set to go, I mount the horse, my sword in one

hand and reins in the other. Before I can take off, I hear my name being called from behind me.

"Bellatrix. Lady Bellatrix! Wait!" A woman's voice shouts desperately in the distance, coming up the side of the castle.

I force a double take, as I see a short stocky older woman with warm brown shoulder length hair, and familiar eyes I'd recognize anywhere. Koen's mother and younger sister are racing towards me. Koen isn't with them, and my insides twist at all the possibilities why he would be away from his family right now. The town is under attack. He would never abandon them, unless he's hurt or worse.

I hop off the horse and embrace the little girl in my arms once she reaches me.

"Tattoo lady!" Mellani greets me as sweetly as she always does, though clearly distraught and exhausted from their travels.

"Sweet girl! Are you okay?" I ask, bent down to her level so we are eye to eye. I glance up at her mother, my eyes asking her the same question.

She nods at me. "My son told us to come here and assured me that you would provide safety for us." Her voice is soft, but hurried.

"Of course…" I pause, realizing I don't know how to address her.

"Fira," she says firmly, her gaze cold upon me.

"Of course, Fira. You are both more than welcome here. Please, follow the courtier here, and he will see to it that you two will be hidden and safe." I gesture to the man who was helping me with my horse. He bows his head, and I think I see the corners of his mouth twitch up just for a second.

Fira and Mellani follow the man as he leads them towards the castle, but I need to ask one nagging question. "Wait." All three turn around, and wait for me to continue. "Where…

is he okay?" My once strong voice cracks, and she knows I mean Koen.

Fira's eyes soften just a little at my question, though she still looks guarded. She nods. "He's in town. Says he didn't want to hide like a coward. He wanted to fight for his people."

My eyes well up at the pride and fear I'm now simultaneously feeling. Of course, he offered to stay back and fight off dragons burning down the town. It's just who he is. I can't help but feel the desire to strangle him for the dangers he voluntarily puts himself in though. I remember the size of the dragon we encountered together, and the ugliness of its claws and teeth. They're designed to kill, and I don't know how he is going to survive this.

One tear escapes the barrier of my lower lash, and descends down my cheek. I swipe it away quickly. "Thank you. I will see to it that he makes it back," I say, trying my best to reassure us both.

Fira approaches me and takes my hand in hers caressing the top softly. "My son was right about you, My Lady. Bring him back to me, and I will make a way for you two to end up together, if that's what you wish."

What does she mean? How could she do that?

Not needing to know the details, I nod my head yes. A few more tears roll down my cheeks, and I clear my throat, trying to will them to stop.

She pulls her hand back and rejoins her daughter as they quickly make their way inside, away from the war I brought into Tenuma.

Mounting my horse with my sword in hand, I now have two missions at hand.

1. Stop the dragons.
2. Bring Koen back alive.

38

KOEN

Staying in my beast-like form proved easier than I expected it to be. Clearly, seeing my entire world burning around me made it simpler. Nik and I rush towards the center of the chaos, pulling people from burning buildings and telling them to run towards the forest for shelter. I'm receiving terrified stares at first, but they quickly understand that I'm here to help.

The damage is devastating. Nik's bar is gone, completely burned to the ground. Only a mound of rubble and ash remains. The town fountain where the local kids gather and hang out is smashed to pieces and most, if not all of the homes lay in ruin.

How someone could do this unprovoked to an entire land of hardworking people is beyond comprehension, and I won't stand for it.

My centaur form stands around ten feet tall which gives me a great viewpoint of the larger buildings, and I am able to help the people that Nik can't reach. We are in the middle of a neighborhood that we followed two dragons into and are trying to formulate a sneak attack. Although, it's difficult with my heavy feet and large stature not exactly blending in.

"We don't have time for a plan, man, just shoot the fucking thing!" Nik shouts. His anger has risen since we made it back to town the same way mine has. There's really no way to put into words what watching your entire town go up in flames and watching people scramble for their lives does to you.

"I'm going for the soldier riding and controlling it, but I need you to have my back. Once that dragon realizes it's under fire, it's going to come for us," I explain.

He nods.

The dragons are ripping through the neighborhood, their giant clawed feet crushing everything in their path, and the fire from their mouths burning anything that is left. My eyes are immediately drawn to the real monster, the man on the dragon's backs. He's my target. Using an inherently peaceful animal to wield as their personal weapon makes my pulse race and blood boil. It represents exactly the kind of ruler Lothar is: preying on the innocent and using them for his personal gain.

I pull back my arrow and shoot, hitting the man right in the back, watching him fall to the ground. Me and Nik both rush forward, Nik going for the man, me heading for the dragon.

As much as I don't want to, I'll have to take the dragon's life in order to protect Tenuma and its people. They've been trained and turned into weapons that have ravished our land. The cowards couldn't fight us on their own, therefore leaving us no choice but to eliminate them.

Nik slices the man's neck with one of his daggers, to be sure he won't recoup and come back after us, and I shoot another arrow, this time at the dragon's chest.

My arrow hits its target, causing it to release an ear-splitting snarling noise that sounds like a mixture of pain and anger. As it turns towards me, I can see its red bloodshot eyes, narrow and zero in on where I'm standing.

The dragon is pissed.

The giant beast with its scaly black iridescent flesh, and long razor-sharp claws at the end of its feet moves nimbly towards me as I wield another arrow. I was hoping that wounding the giant beast would simply scare it off, but they seem to be set on killing. I don't like the idea of killing an animal I won't use for food or fur, but in this case, I'll make an exception.

I nock the arrow into place, draw back and release it. Blood sprays from the dragon's neck where the arrow landed. Quickly, I race to get behind the dragon, mounting it and using my dagger to perform a final blow. Whispering a quiet prayer and apology, I pull the dagger across its neck, causing the dragon to forfeit any fight it had left, crumpling to the ground in a mound of flesh.

Jumping off the large animal as it falls the long distance to the ground, I look down and see a monster of myself. My arms and fur are covered in blood and dirt. The smoke from the air sticks to my flesh like molasses, making me look like a combat warrior.

Nik and I stand in a moment of silence as we catch our breath and our adrenaline slows down. Both of our eyes filled with terror and sadness. The other dragons have flown off in the struggle with their lost brother, and I have to say I'm relieved. Killing one of those animals was hard enough, I'm not sure I could continue.

People are still scurrying in every direction, looking for their loved ones and helping others to safety. The streets are completely gone, so they're forced to climb over the mounds of debris to get anywhere.

Sirens from the castle are wailing in the distance; warning and directing them to the safety of the castle. In my twenty-five years of life, I've never heard those sirens sound. It's deafening even from far away, and it makes my blood boil that it's even happening.

Glancing around in shock, I can't make my feet move any longer as the adrenaline wears off and exhaustion starts to set in. My mind is racing in a thousand directions as I worry about my family, the town, Bellatrix, and how I'm going to get my friend Nik out of this mess.

Seeing the strain of worry on my face, Nik comes over to put a hand on my shoulder turning me back to face him. "Are you okay, Ko?" he asks, but his voice sounds like it's underwater.

I nod.

"Koen," he starts again. "Are you sure, man? You don't look so good." His gaze takes in my horrific state.

Am I okay?

I've never killed an animal for anything other than hunting. For survival.

I suppose this was also for survival.

I've spent the last two days covered in blood.

No, I'm definitely not okay.

I hear my name being called again but I don't see Nik's mouth move. I tilt my head in confusion, wondering if I imagined it, but I hear it again. This time, Nik turns around at the call.

We see Quirina racing towards us in a once-green dress that's now mostly black and tattered at the ends, covered in smoke and debris. Her face is covered in soot and there's tear lines streaking through it down her face.

She reaches us and thrusts herself into my arms for a hug. A heavy sigh against me tells me she's relieved to have found somebody she knows. Somebody who's still alive.

My shock wears off at seeing a friendly face, and my focus shifts to her well-being. "Are you okay? What are you doing here?" I ask, pulling back to check her for any injuries.

Quirina nods and wipes the fresh tears falling down her face, smearing the dirt around her cheeks. "Yes." Her voice cracks.

"I was–I was coming to check on my parents, but…" she stops and becomes hysterical.

"Quirina, did you find them?" I ask her, my eyebrows pinched together.

She shakes her head. "The house was gone by the time I got here. There's nothing left, Koen." She loses what remains of her composure, as she gives in to the emotions of the situation, letting them pour out of her like a fountain.

I pull her back into my embrace again–now that I'm in my human form again–and hold her tightly, comforting her. "Maybe they got out before it was hit. Don't lose hope yet, okay?" My voice sounds more sure than I feel. There's no sense in all of us losing hope and giving up right now.

Shaking her head against me, she takes a deep breath and pulls back, pulling herself back together. "Where's Bellatrix?" she asks, looking around expecting to find her.

"Back at the castle, being protected, I hope. I sent my family there to be with her." Even as I say it out loud, I'm not so sure I believe they're all safe there. The princess was attacked in the middle of the night just a few nights ago, after all. How safe is it really?

Quirina gives me a sad smile, which tells me she's not sure she believes they are either.

"You guys, we need to get out of here," Nik chimes in, and I forgot momentarily that he was standing there. He runs his hands through his dark hair, getting it out of his eyes and reaching a hand out to Quirina. "Come with us. We'll be safer together."

She takes his hand in hers, returning the greeting. "I remember you, you own the main bar in town," she states, matter of factly.

He nods as sadness fills his eyes. *"I did."*

I can't help but have empathy for him. Knowing how hard he worked to build that bar into what it was took years and more hard work than anybody can imagine. It wasn't just work for him, it was his livelihood and his pride. In an instant, everything was taken from him and I can see the anguish in his face. The defeat in his eyes. He worked his ass off despite the circumstances created by the king. We have fought for every single scrap we've gotten, just to watch it all crumble before our eyes.

Quirina's expression mirrors Nik's as she comes to understand the significance of his statement. "I'm sorry," she says, giving his hand a squeeze and then letting go.

He shrugs as if to say, "What can you do?" But in reality, I know it's killing him.

"We need to get back to the castle. It looks like the dragons all took off, at least for now," I cut in, taking us back to our current state.

Both Quirina and Nik nod, although they're still locked onto each other's eyes.

That's interesting, I think to myself, and for a brief moment, my mind forgets that our land is at war and that we could all perish at any moment. For one short minute, my mind wanders to the simplicity of life. A man, a woman, a spark of attraction. Life can be so painfully ugly and so blissfully beautiful at the same time that it makes me wonder if one can exist without the other.

My mind drifts back to Bellatrix. Although there's things about her I really hated before I knew her, she's also full of so much beauty. I'm realizing that there's both good and bad in us all, and I just hope there's more good than bad in both of us to make a future worth fighting for.

A few weeks ago, I never thought I would be capable of killing a man I didn't know—especially over a woman—and now that I have, I can't help but wonder if there's more dark inside of me than I knew.

"Koen!" Nik says my name loudly, snapping me out of my thoughts.

I shake my head, like it can clear my mind. "Sorry, man, let's go."

We begin the journey back to the castle from the place we called home. Where debris and rubble stand in place of our favorite bars, most cherished memories and our homes. Walking away with trepidation of what's to come, knowing that whatever lies ahead, we are all forever changed.

39

BELLATRIX

When I was a little girl, my mother and father told me stories of the war that ravaged our land once upon a time. They described tales of catastrophic fighting and the streets overflowing with blood and bodies. The picture they painted was one of horror and sorrow. Growing up with such tales, I never questioned the way my parents ruled Tenuma. As far as I knew, the lands were at peace, and it was my understanding that my father and mother were the basis of that.

Standing on top of this hill as I overlook our beautiful city, I see now just how erroneous my assumptions were.

Smoke and fire rise high above the city, creating an angry black cloud blanketing our once peaceful land. Where a beautiful, quiet city once stood, now sits debris and ash.

No, I think to myself, as my hands begin to tremble with my sword in hand. I stand next to the horse I rode here on, in shock and horror watching the people below fleeing and dragons circling above, taunting their prey.

This is all because of me. This is all my fault.

My inner monologue is tangled up in guilt and shame.

for a situation I feel could have been prevented. Why did this devastation need to happen? I would have gladly handed over the reins had it saved even one of our people.

Before I can even finish the thought, my blood begins to boil, and I realize that's not the answer. We were unprovoked. These families didn't ask for this. Hell, I didn't ask for this. I can't go back in time and there's no way I will roll over and let Sperantia overthrow my family. Handing over the kingdom to somebody so wicked is something I could never do.

Inhaling deeply, mustering up any ounce of courage I can, I mount my horse again, charging down the hill. I don't know what I plan to do, but I'm hoping instincts will kick in and I will know what to do.

As we get closer to the destruction, my heartbeat only increases, causing my hands to tremble and my eyes to water. The town knows me as the Soul Snatcher, but I want to be more to them. Death and pain are not things I wish to be associated with. This has never been the path I chose for myself. It would never be a path I'd choose for myself, unless in defense.

Like right now.

I pull back on the reins when I see a group of Sperantia soldiers standing guard up ahead, hoping they didn't hear me approaching. They're at the edge of the city, clearly preventing people from getting out of the city. But they weren't anticipating people trying to get back in.

We are close enough that I am able to make a sneak attack. My horse speeds towards the group of men and without a word, I stick out my sword, making a clean slice of each of their necks. One by one, every skull drops to the ground with a loud thud, and I keep surging forward.

Twice more, I find groups of Sperantia soldiers standing guard, and I'm successful in eliminating the threat with my trusty sword, the crown still safely sits atop my head.

Above, the dragons have been dipping in and out of the sky into the city, engulfing it in flames, and suddenly they all rip into the sky and take off in the same direction.

That was odd.

Maybe they're finally retreating.

It would seem odd that their army would be giving up so soon, as ours hasn't even left the castle grounds yet. That's the royal code; ensure the grounds are secure, hide and protect the king and queen and don't send soldiers in right away.

It always struck me as strange, and during one of my many royal meetings I even asked why we don't immediately respond. The response I got made me want to puke.

"We don't send our men in right away, because that's when the army is at its strongest, and we don't want to kill off all of our men. We let them think they're winning, and then we intervene and take them down."

Basically, it's their nice way of saying, "We let intruders kill our people, until some of them die off and we can go in and look heroic." Which is why our army hasn't come in to defend the city yet; they're waiting for some of the Sperantia soldiers to be picked off.

For some reason though, the dragons seem to be backing off or got scared off. I don't know what could have caused that.

"Trix!" I hear my name called in a relieved, frantic tone.

My eyes dart to the side of me down what used to be a street, where I see my best friend Quirina and two men follow her up to me.

Not just any men, one of them is Koen.

"Oh my god, Rina!" I shout back, hopping off the stallion once again, so I can embrace my friend. She looks like she's been through hell. She's covered in soot and her near blackened face is streaked with tears. Thinking about what they've endured down here in the middle of the fight makes my stomach lurch.

I pull back from Quirina and she's wiping more tears that are free-falling down her cheeks. Her short black curls are matted and covered in dirt. My eyes move from her to Koen, who is standing a short distance behind with another male ally.

The look in his eyes shows both relief, intrigue and fear. In that moment, I know he's feeling the same thing I am; relieved to have found each other, but terrified of what's to come.

What's the look of intrigue?

I see his eyes wander up to the crown I forgot I was wearing, atop my head. His eyes glisten with pride.

I manage a weak smile at him. "Are you all okay?" I ask them.

Koen and his friend nod, while Quirina is the one who answers. "We're okay, are you? What are you doing here?" It's a valid question. The royal family isn't usually seen on the front line, they're the ones behind the scenes, pulling strings of the puppet army, while they cower in safety–under the guise of importance. As if their lives matter more than anybody else's.

Seeing the people I'm closest to like this is painful, but somehow it gives me the strength I need. "This is my land, my people. It's my job to protect it. When I'm queen, I won't be ruling the way my parents did. I will be here. With you all. I won't let others do my fighting and I will never sit back and let anybody take our land from us." I say, my voice is strong and unshakable.

Quirina's bottom lip quivers, and her eyes continue to swell with tears as she gives me an approving nod, and hand squeeze.

The man I don't know addresses me. "Your Majesty, I'm Nik. I own..ed Nik's bar. Is…is the army here with you?" he asks, looking around, his eyes wide and hopeful. Nik and Koen are both covered in blood, and I cringe to think about the things they've had to endure.

My eyebrows come together in confusion, and I purse my lips. "No, they're not. They're still back at the castle trying to locate my parents in the chaos."

The three look back and forth at each other then back to me. "What?" I ask when nobody speaks.

It's Koen who speaks first. "The dragons…they randomly took off. Like something spooked them. We have been down here, trying to fight back as I'm sure others are. But there can't be enough of us fighting back that it scared those giant monsters away. It doesn't make sense. Could they be giving up and going home?" he asks.

His question takes me by surprise, because from everything I've been told about Lothar, there's no way he would ever retreat or pull back unless he already accomplished what he wanted. But I'm still standing here alive, so why else would his troops be leaving?

I shake my head, and narrow my eyes as my mind works through the possibilities when I hear Koen speak my name sharply. His gaze is focused behind me towards the top of the hill I just came down, and I cannot even wrap my mind around what we're looking at.

My eyes immediately fill with water, and my head begins to spin as I process the unimaginable sight before us. "What? What is that? I'm not seeing that right…no." My voice shakes and my hand grips my sword so hard my knuckles turn white.

Quirina and Nik gasp. Wordlessly, Koen slips his hand into my open palm and gives me a squeeze as he too takes in the scene unfolding ahead of us. It doesn't make any sense, but I know we're all seeing the same thing.

And they're all heading our way.

40

KOEN

It feels like snow has just been shoved down the back of my shirt, or I've been slapped awake from a long slumber. Looking ahead at the top of the hill has all four of us frozen. Nothing but questions bursting from each of our mouths.

"What? What is that? I'm not seeing that right…no," the princess says, alarmed.

My hand squeezes hers to let her know that I'm right here and that I'm witnessing the same thing.

"Landric?" Nik's voice is soft and uncertain, unsure if what he's seeing is real or a dream. On some level, I wonder if we're all having the same thought–'I must be dead.'

"Edwin," I hear Quirina whisper to herself. I glance over at her and her face reveals shock and confusion, mirroring the rest of our expressions.

We watch as the enormous group of men robotically move in formation, each one equipped with a weapon.

"She used them to build an army." I hear the princess mutter as realization hits. "That monster used me to build a fuck-ing army." Her hand shakes in mine, and I find myself wanting to pull her into an embrace and shield her from all of this.

"Princess, who?" I ask softly, approaching her with the same caution I would a bomb. With extreme caution. I have no idea where her head is right now, but it's definitely not in a good place.

"The queen. My mother. She used me... used those men to build an army. All of them. They never died, not really," the princess reveals.

Suddenly, I have a flash of a memory of my mother telling me a tale when I was a child of a monstrosity that used to walk our lands. Mostly, they're used as ghost stories as scare tactics by parents to get their children to listen, but what stands before us is anything but a made-up tale.

"They're daemons," I explain.

"What the hell does that mean?" Nik suddenly chimes in, impatiently.

I let go of the princess's hand to face him.

"It means they're not alive. Not really. They're stuck between the supernatural and human world. They're stuck in this form and bound to their creator," I say, looking at Bellatrix on the last word.

Her eyebrows raise in shock, as if to say "Me?" She manages a sarcastic laugh. "I didn't orchestrate this army. This was my mother's doing, she all but told me herself just before the attack," she reveals.

I nod my head at her, offering a weak smile to let her know that I believe her.

As we try to piece together how this is possible, the men uniformly march down the hill towards us. Since we are unsure of their intentions, I decide that the how and why aspects of our current situation can wait. "We need to get out of here. We can figure out the rest later. If the sight of this daemon army was enough to send Lothar's army running, we surely don't want to be here right now," I suggest, and everyone nods and we run off in a new direction.

Using the forest as our hide-out until the army has passed us and moved on through what used to be our town, we huddle undetected in pained silence, processing what we just witnessed. The cold nipping at our skin, with the fresh snow still on the ground, and a bite in the air. The only sounds were our footsteps as we entered and nothing since. I haven't heard as much as an animal scurrying about or a bird in a tree.

Nobody says a word, and yet, I can feel the energy coming off of every person here.

Quirina from seeing her boyfriend that decided to betray her and sleep with Bellatrix.

Nik from seeing our best friend Landric who decided to gamble with his fate as well, only to become lost to the spell.

The princess having to see every man she's ever slept with—I have to admit it's more than I thought, obviously enough for an army—standing before her, and not dead as she was made to believe.

There's not a single emotion I can settle on for myself. The feeling of relief that washed over me when my eyes first saw Landric was incredible. Quickly, I realized that it wasn't quite right. Fear settled in shortly after I realized what they were, and now I just feel sympathy for everything my friends are going through. Thinking you lost somebody you loved, only to watch them return in another form isn't something you're taught to cope with.

"I think it's clear," Nik's voice startles me from my thoughts, sounding abrasive in the silent forest.

My thoughts shift back to the present and I take in our surroundings as we rise, slowly making our way back out of the trees.

Seeing the defeated look on Bellatrix's face as we exit the woods has me pulling her back for a moment. As she turns back towards me, her somber expression barely holds my gaze before she's looking back down.

I take my fingers and lift her chin, forcing her to look at me again. "Princess," I say as softly as I can. "Are you alright?" I ask her, knowing it's a stupid question, but unable to stop myself.

Her shoulders lift and then drop in a heavy shrug and the corners of her mouth tilt downward.

"Everything is going to be okay. I'm not going to let anything happen to you." My hand slides from her chin up to her cheek, and she leans into my hand letting her head rest there briefly.

She lifts her head and tears fill her eyes. "I guess I really am the Soul Snatcher. They might not be dead, but they're not themselves either. I don't know which is worse." The guilt thickly coats her words as she says each one. For a circumstance she had no control over, she's spending a lot of time blaming herself. I can't help but realize that people like me are probably why.

"Princess. I didn't know…people don't know that you don't have a choice. There's so much Tenuma doesn't know about you. What I do know is that you are not to blame for this. Any of this," I say, gesturing my arms to the devastation around us. "But you're definitely the Soul Snatcher. You stole my heart and my soul the first time I met you. I never stood a chance," I say, smiling genuinely at her. Despite everything going on, my heart beats a little faster thinking about the way she makes me feel. The draw I feel to her is uncontrollable and I wouldn't have it any other way.

This earns a sweet smile from her back, and God help me, I can't resist those beautiful lips. My hands grip the sides of her face and gently pull her towards me, fusing our lips together. She tastes as sweet as she usually does, but now she's salty from all of the tears.

"Let's go, we have a town to save," I tell her, pulling us both out of the forest and into a reality that none of us are quite ready to face.

41

BELLATRIX

Back at the castle, I stand before the queen, no longer able to feel any semblance of compassion for the woman I used to call my mother. We haven't spoken since before the attack when I passed out at her confession. There are so many things I want to say, that I want to ask and now standing in front of her, I don't know where to start.

"Darling, I'm a little busy, did you have anything to say, or may I leave now?" My mother's voice is dripping with condescension. It's exactly the fuel I needed to push through this conversation.

I may be covered in blood and sweat and exhausted beyond belief, but I feel the power surging through me whether it be from the crown that still sits atop my head, or finally being fed up with all the lies and manipulation. "I haven't even begun, Mother. Were you ever planning on telling me?" I ask.

A heavy, bored sigh leaves her body in a huff. "Telling you *what* exactly?" she asks.

My eyes narrow at her. "That you've been using me to create a damn army! Those men were never dead, not fully anyway.

Why have you been building an army with those men? We have an army already!" Even as I ask her now, it doesn't make sense.

Her eyes drift up to the crown on my head. "That look suits you, Bella. You're going to make a lovely queen." She ignores my question.

"Enough!" I shout, my patience has worn out, and I refuse to let her leave without answers. "Tell me the truth. Tell me everything."

We stand in the middle of her chambers where my father usually rests, but per my mother's request, was moved to a 'safer' location in the castle. While the rest of the land fought to keep control, our leader was hiding. I can't help the shame that creeps up my spine.

The giant blood stain in the middle of the usually sparkling pearl-white tile stares back at me mockingly, a reminder of the killer that I am.

My mother stares at me for a few moments, considering what to tell me, if anything at all. It's clear she's not interested in giving up any information, but my feet are ground into the floor and she knows I'm not relenting or letting her leave without answers.

I'm attempting to summon whatever strength I have left to the surface as I feel my eyes begin to sting and swell at my mothers betrayal. "All this time." My voice cracks. "All this time, you said it was for *my* protection. You made me believe I was a monster, a murderer." A tear slips down my cheek and I quickly wipe it away, furious at the weakness breaking through the cracks of my soul.

"My dear daughter, there are so many things you do not know. It was for your protection, for all of our protection." Her face doesn't show any emotion and it makes me feel worse.

"You don't even care, do you? I need to know why you did this," I demand.

She takes a deep breath, and confesses everything. "Yes, I used you to build an undead army. They were not originally part of the plan. I was really trying to protect you, but after we realized that the men weren't actually dying, we had to keep them here. We couldn't let them wander Tenuma the way they were. But we could…direct them in a sense. They obeyed us and with the looming threat of Lothar over our heads, it all came together." Her confession hits me like a ton of bricks. All along, she knew and kept me in the dark.

My jaw is clenched so tight I think my teeth might crack. I'm not sure I'd care at this point. "You didn't think I was privy to that information? I was the one creating this army. Me! How dare you use me as a weapon." I shake my head, my palm rubbing across my forehead in disbelief.

"Bella, what you did served to protect all of Tenuma, that's what a queen does. She protects her people, no matter the cost." Her justification is only being used to cause me guilt, and in turn, letting herself off the hook.

Lifting the crown from my head, I hand it back to my mother. "No, that's not the kind of queen I will be. I will protect my people, all of *my* people. Not just the ones I don't choose to sacrifice. Those men didn't have a choice!" Forcing myself to stop to collect myself, I take a deep breath realizing I'm not getting anywhere with her. Getting worked up is wasted effort.

The look on my mother's face has barely shifted. She glances at the crown that's now in her hands, then back up at me and I think I see a flash of remorse, before it's gone again. "Those men choose their fate when they get into bed with you. If you choose to be ignorant and overlook everything I've done for you, so be it. But I will not feel guilty for saving your life, and our land." Her voice is becoming more and more strained.

"What do you mean 'save my life'? You condemned me! You ruined my life, never leaving me a choice in the matter," I shout, feeling frustrated that she's refusing to see the part she's played in all of this.

She takes a step towards me, lowering her voice but making it even more stern. "You're an ignorant girl. Who do you think Lothar was here for?" Her expression shifts into one of condescension. When I don't respond to the obvious question she continues. "*You* are who he's been after for a very long time."

Something twists in my gut at the thought of having been so blind to my obviously dangerous life. Not only were all those men on borrowed time, but so was I. Everything is starting to come together.

The restrictions for leaving the castle.

The multiple attacks.

The attack. It was Lothar's son. I recall the conversation I had with Koen after he killed the man who was in my bedchambers.

I am Lothar's main target. He wants me dead and he wants power over Tenuma.

My mother's voice interrupts my thoughts. "You created an army that saved what's left of Tenuma. Think of how bad it would be if those men weren't out there right now. Those dragons would be here destroying the castle with us inside." She stands directly in front of me and lays her hands on my shoulders. "You saved Tenuma. Sometimes, we have to do things we don't want to as the ruling queen. Just because you don't like how it was done, doesn't mean it was the wrong choice. It was a necessary evil."

I shrug her hands off of me, holding my head high. "No. If you never had this damn curse put on me in the first place, Lothar would never be after me. You caused all of this and now are leaving me to clean up your mess." I pause, feeling defeated. "I need to go see Koen and his family to make sure they're okay," I say walking past her to the doorway.

"That boy," she calls over her shoulder at me. I turn back and she's turning towards me as well. "You can never have anything real with him. Both of you know that. You will get him killed. You're playing with fire, young lady."

I scoff at her. "What Koen and I have is already more real than anything I've ever felt from anybody else in my entire life. Sex doesn't make something real or not." My tone is clipped. Not waiting for her to respond, I leave the room in search of the one person I can trust.

42

KOEN

Bodies flood the castle in every room. Luckily, this place is massive and can handle the crowd. The princess went straight to find her mother and father, while Nik and I searched for my family amongst the crowd that had already found their way here.

Under Princess Bellatrix's command, the guards allowed the townspeople entry to the castle until Tenuma was no longer under attack.

From what we saw, the daemons had chased off the majority, if not all, of the dragons and remaining soldiers that we left, so I'm sure our welcome here will be cut short very soon.

My body is still covered in dirt, sweat, and blood, but I press my mother and Mellani to my chest. I'm sure I smell even worse than I look, but I can't help but think how close I was to losing them today. I can't make myself let go. So many people were lost, and we were the lucky ones that managed to make it out alive.

"You're crushing me, Koen!" Mellani squeaks from underneath my arm.

A small laugh bubbles out of me. "Sorry, sweet girl. It's because I love you so much. I just missed you like crazy," I tell her, as if it justifies how hard I know I'm squeezing her tiny body.

I pull back and smile down at my mother, who's looking around with a worried expression on her face.

"It's okay, Mother, we're safe now. We're in the best place we can be while Tenuma is under attack," I tell her, trying to ease her worry.

Instead of looking at me when I talk, she continues gazing around the room.

My eyebrows pinch together in confusion. "Mother, did you hear me? It's okay now. What's wrong?" I ask her.

She starts wringing her hands together. "We shouldn't be here, my son. We need to leave." Her voice is quiet, yet frantic.

I grab her hands in mine. "We can't leave," I tell her, unsure why she thinks there's anywhere else we can go right now.

"Koen!" I hear my name shouted in the sweetest voice.

Princess. My princess.

I turn my head to the right and see Princess Bellatrix racing down the stairs, holding her dress with one hand so she doesn't step on it.

"Princess," I say, walking over and meeting her halfway.

Once we're in front of each other, it occurs to us that we're in a room surrounded by other people; both royals and commoners alike. We can't embrace the way we want to without causing both attention and probably a few issues.

She offers me a sweet smile, and I smile back at her even though what I really want to do is pull her into my chest and never let her go.

The bracelet on my wrist starts to tingle, and where it used to make me anxious, now it makes me smile. It tingles for her. Only for her.

"How did it go?" I ask, referring to the talk with her parents.

Her smile fades, and she shrugs. "My father is in another part of the castle, basically hidden away for safety, and my mother was no help. I don't even know what to think. All this time..." Her voice fades off.

My lips form a thin line, and I already know where her mind is headed. "All of this lands on her. All of this was her doing, Princess," I tell her, not able to stand seeing her upset for one second without it causing me pain.

She nods her head. "Yes, but even if that's true, it doesn't mean that I didn't contribute. Now, here we are and it's my job to fix things." She pauses to wipe her hand across her forehead in frustration. "I don't even know where to begin. I need to secure our land borders, deal with the daemons, find a mate..."

As she's listing off her to-do list, I stop her before she can continue thinking further about the last one.

"No." I tell her firmly.

Her head snaps up at me when I interrupt. "No? No, what?" she asks.

"Your search for a mate is over, Princess. We already discussed this," I say softly, caressing her cheek with the back of my hand, suddenly not caring who's watching. When I'm with her, it feels like there's nobody else around. "You're mine, Princess and I'm yours. We will figure this out together. I cannot live thinking about anybody else having their hands on you." My confession shocks even myself. There's something about this woman that tears down all of my shields and makes it easy to pour my heart out to her. She makes me feel brave and stupid at the same time.

"That's not what I meant. I..." She pauses looking for the right words. "I'm supposed to find a king to rule with, one I can produce an heir with. That's the only way I will be queen," she explains.

"According to who?" I ask.

"The king and queen," she states bluntly.

"Exactly. Look at the choices they've already made. Their choices have thrust Tenuma into a war, sacrificed your body to countless men, and then turned all of those men into daemons. Fuck what they say." My voice is still quiet, because we're surrounded by royal courtiers, guards, armed forces, etc. We don't need to draw any more attention to ourselves by openly offending the king and queen, but I have had enough of her thinking she needs to listen to any more of their rules or guidelines.

Her lips turn up into a genuine smile and I know she's considering what I'm saying. It makes my chest warm.

"Tattoo lady!" Mellani shouts as she scoots from my mothers arms and shoots into the Princess's arms like a little fireball.

The princess giggles and then embraces Mellani in a genuine embrace that makes my heart squeeze. "Hi, sweet girl. I'm so glad you and your mother came here. I would have worried about you so much." Mellani hears her words and glances up at her with those big brown eyes smiling.

I laugh at the nickname. "Tattoo lady, money lady. Mellani, her name is Bellatrix. Princess Bellatrix," I inform her.

Her eyes go wide. "You're a real-life princess?" The excitement in her voice is hard to miss.

"I am a real-life princess, sweet girl. But you can call me Bellatrix if you like," she tells Mellani sweetly, like they're old friends.

Mellani nods her head excitedly. "Can I call you Bella?" she asks.

The princess bends down so she's level with Mellani and whispers to her. "You know what? My mother calls me that and I've always hated it... but I don't think I'd mind if you called me

Bella," she tells her, taking her pointer finger and tapping Mellani's nose once, making her giggle. "And this must be your dad, right?" Bellatrix asks her accusingly.

Mellani giggles nervously knowing she's been caught and just shrugs. I can't help but shake my head at her for the white lie she told. It makes me proud that Mellani sees me as a father figure.

As we stand there, a loud commanding voice cuts through all the conversation and commotion, drawing all attention to him.

"Attention! We will be moving everybody to the back rooms of the castle, until we ensure that the perimeter is safe. Until then, nobody leaves the castle. Your safety is our number one concern and will get you all home as soon as we can." The man in tall black combat boots, wearing the official Tenuma soldier attire with the sword insignia on the front stands before us, ushering everybody to the back of the castle.

I can't help but scoff and make a disgusted face at his announcement.

Our safety. Pfft. They don't give a shit about our safety.

My mother hesitantly comes over to us, as we are all being ushered to the back, and I can tell she doesn't want to be near the princess. She has had the same distaste for Bellatrix I once had, only hers hasn't gone away.

Bellatrix grabs my arm. "Koen, I'm going to the roof. I need to see what's going on. It won't be very safe up there, so please stay down here. I will be right back."

As much as I don't want to let her go by herself, I don't really have a choice. We're in the middle of a crowd and I can't exactly be sneaking off with the princess right now.

I nod. "Okay. Please hurry back, and be safe. I'll go find you if you're not back soon," I say with a smirk.

She offers me a sweet smile, squeezes Mellani's shoulder,

and offers my mother a nod and a kind smile before taking off up the stairs again, and she disappears down the right side of the hall.

It's been too long. The princess should have been back by now, and as much as I'm trying not to worry, I'm becoming more and more agitated, unable to stifle the nagging feeling that something bad has happened.

My mother and Mellani are sitting against a wall in one of the back rooms and I'm tapping my foot and thrumming my fingers on my knees pulled up to my chest.

This doesn't feel right. Why doesn't anybody seem to be concerned that she's not around?

"Are you going to go find her?" my mother asks, interrupting my thoughts.

I lift my head and meet her gaze, thrown off that I'm so easily read. Looking down, I realize my body language is an obvious tell. I gaze towards the entrance of the room, out to where the stairs are. "I want to. I'm worried…something doesn't feel right." As I finish saying the words, the bracelet on my wrist tingles, sending a shiver up my arm.

It only does that when the Princess is nearby.

Quickly standing, I turn my head in every direction in search of her.

She's not here.

I look down at my bracelet, and then at my mother who's also staring at my wrist. "You know, don't you?" I ask her.

Without answering me, she offers me a tight smile and grabs my hand. "Let's go find your girl," she suggests.

"I'm not bringing you both up there with me, it might not be safe," I tell her.

She taps her foot. "We are not separating again. Now, let's go," she demands, and grabs Mellani as we make our way out of the room and up the stairs while the guards are busy with other groups.

The wind nips at us once we get to the top, whipping around Mellani and my mother's hair. Looking around at the massive rooftop, we don't see anybody. It's empty.

"Princess! Princess Bellatrix!" I shout into the open air.

"Bella!" Mellani shouts.

She's gone. Where did she go?

"You! What are you doing here? Why are you looking for my daughter?" The queen's frantic voice suddenly appears behind us, causing all three of us to turn in unison to face her. But she's not looking at me and she's not talking to me.

My gaze darts to my mother, who's expression is wide-eyed and cautious.

"Mother? How do you know the queen?" I ask.

She ignores my question, instead addressing the queen. "My son and your daughter have bonded. The princess is missing and we're looking for her. Which is what you should already be doing." My mother's words come out like venom, though I'm not sure why.

The queen moves towards us with determination and anger in her eyes. Just as she reaches us, a huge gust of wind picks up, causing us all to shield our eyes from the debris floating around, threatening to blind us.

There's a loud noise, like the flapping of wings and as we all turn, we see a dragon coming up over the side of the castle with two passengers on its back.

Instinctively, I grab Mellani's arm and quickly shove her behind me as I try to process what I'm looking at.

Princess Bellatrix sits atop the dragon, blindfolded, hands bound and held onto by the man behind her.

They took her. They have her.

The man holding onto her grimaces at me and I feel a snarl rip out of me. I'm trying to hold myself together because I can feel my body about to transform into its other form, but I can't let myself do that in front of Mellani.

The dragon hovers in front of us and over the loud flapping of wings, I hear the man speak. "Hello, Koen." His disgusting voice nearly makes me leap off of the roof.

The queen chimes in. "You two know each other?" she asks me.

"Yes. That's my father," I reply.

To be continued….

ACKNOWLEDGMENTS

First and foremost I want to thank my incredible fiance for giving me the support and encouragement to put my stories down on paper in the first place. The confidence you gave me allowed a childhood dream to become a reality, and for that I am forever grateful. Thank you for being my soulmate in this crazy life, and being my inspiration for Soul Snatcher.

Thank you to my best friends, and beta readers who gave my wild story a chance, and for being so receptive to such a crazy idea. I love you all! The way you guys hyped me up until release day has been incredible.

To all of my new friends in the bookstagram community, I could not have done this without you. Thank you for always being willing to give feedback, answering any and all (there was a lot!) of my questions through this process. I'm so appreciative and taken aback of all the support I've found in this amazing community. We are all in this together!

To my readers, I'm just a girl with a lifelong dream of putting words to paper and hoping to elicit buried emotions from my readers. I hope that whether you enjoy this book, or if it's not for you, that it brings emotions to the surface and makes you feel something you didn't expect to. Hopefully it inspires you, and gives you the courage to follow through with your own edgy story.

Thank you to everyone who made this beautiful novel come together: My editor, my cover artist, my formatter, you guys are the real magic behind books.